TERRY VENABLES
AND GORDON WILLIAMS

———

THEY USED TO
PLAY ON GRASS

PENGUIN BOOKS

These are players; men who play with their
heads and their hearts – Ferenc Puskas

We dedicate this book to the great game of football.
May the magic never be lost.

PENGUIN BOOKS

Published by the Penguin Group
Penguin Books Ltd, 27 Wrights Lane, London W8 5TZ, England
Penguin Books USA Inc., 375 Hudson Street, New York, New York 10014, USA
Penguin Books Australia Ltd, Ringwood, Victoria, Australia
Penguin Books Canada Ltd, 10 Alcorn Avenue, Toronto, Ontario, Canada M4V 3B2
Penguin Books (NZ) Ltd, 182–190 Wairau Road, Auckland 10, New Zealand

Penguin Books Ltd, Registered Offices: Harmondsworth, Middlesex, England

First published by Hodder and Stoughton 1971
Published in Penguin Books 1995
1 3 5 7 9 10 8 6 4 2

Printed in England by Clays Ltd, St Ives plc

1

THE following article is reprinted here by courtesy of the editor of *Winner*, the weekly soccer magazine.

HAMPDEN SEATS AND CASH SET
FOR ALL-TIME BRITISH RECORD

With a week to go before the game they're calling the greatest club clash in British soccer history, cash takings for Saturday's British Cup semi-final at Hampden Park, Glasgow, are certain to smash all existing records (writes *Steve Egan*).

When Glasgow Rangers and London's dark-horse heroes, Commoners, trot out on Hampden's new plastic pitch it will be to the roar of 105,000 spectators, the largest all-seated crowd this country has ever seen.

Cheapest seats in Hampden's new stands are £1.50, dearest £15. This week London ticket spivs were asking £50 for the dear seats and £10 for the cheapest. A Camberwell man who showed his ticket in a pub was afterwards beaten and robbed by two men—who ignored his money but took the ticket!

At least 20,000 Commoners fans are expected to pay up to 50p to watch the game live on giant T.V. screens at Oaks Common Stadium back in London.

Queues two miles long stretched round Ibrox Stadium, home ground of Glasgow Rangers, on Sunday, when Rangers say they could have sold double their allocation of 50,000 tickets. Commoners originally asked for 25,000 but these were sold in a day and when an extra 15,000 tickets went on sale at Oaks Common police had to quell a near-riot. British Rail are putting on twenty extra football specials from London to Glasgow. All London–Glasgow flights have been fully booked for two weeks.

Rangers and Commoners will each take home around £80,000 from the match, whose money-spinning magic got a big boost when the luck of the cup draw meant that Rangers would play their semi-final at Hampden—only a mile or two from their own ground.

For the Hampden Stadium itself this will be its debut as glamour showpiece for Scotland's biggest matches. Since they took it over, Glasgow's other football giant, Celtic, have spent more than £2 million in providing seating and cover for all spectators.

In its first season as replacement for the English, Scottish, and Irish cup tournaments, the British Cup has more than justified itself. When Manchester United and Leeds meet next week at Villa Park, Birmingham, the takings will be around £170,000.

The winners of the two semis meet in the New Wembley final on April 21. Gate receipts there will exceed £250,000.

"The money is indeed fantastic," said Commoners chairman George Jackson, the millionaire hotel tycoon, this week, "but to all of us at Oaks Common the real satisfaction will be in beating Rangers and proving that we are now firmly re-established as one of the top clubs in Britain—and Europe.

"More than forty years ago I was one of the small lads who climbed through holes in the corrugated iron to see great Commoners teams of the past. It really gives me pride to think I've had some hand in saving the club from ruin.

"At the beginning of the season they were calling us Gallagher's Hasbeens. I think we'll bury that nickname at Hampden."

2

IT was still only twenty minutes to nine in the morning, a sunny Wednesday in March, and Oaks Common Stadium was apparently deserted when Bill Peterson paid off the taxi that had brought him south of the Thames.

"Tell you what, squire," said the driver, holding up Peterson's five-pound note, "I'll settle for a spare ticket for Saturday's game."

"You must be joking," said Peterson.

"Fifty quid the touts is asking for the dear seats—to see Commoners! Coupla year ago they couldn't give their season tickets away! Changed days for this mob—I'm an Arsenal man meself—think you'll win on Saturday?"

"Indubitably."

"That mean yes or no, Prof?"

"Take fifty pence for yourself and buy a dictionary."

"Cheeky!"

A faint smile on his thin, grey-cheeked face, Peterson picked up his heavy leather holdall and portable typewriter case and went through the open stadium gates onto the asphalt slope of the official car park. The holdall was expensive and so was his dark mohair suit, yet there was about him a general air of dishevelment and carelessness; he had stooped shoulders and straggly dark hair; even the way he walked seemed unrehearsed.

Heading towards the massive concrete wall which formed the outer face of the North Stand, he looked for John Gallagher's white Mercedes but the manager's parking space was unoccupied. A puzzled frown crossed his face. Even on ordinary training days John Gallagher made almost a fetish of arriving at the ground before his players.

He tried the handle of a blue door over which hung a sign, white

7

lettering on green board, PLAYERS AND OFFICIALS ONLY. It was locked. Whoever had opened the outside gates was lost somewhere in the great spaces and dark tunnels of the huge stadium. Feeling too tense to hang about waiting for the first arrivals, he walked slowly to the end of the North Stand, coming to the foot of a steep bank of wide, concrete steps. Right hand gripping the centre crush-rail, left hand holding the typewriter case and holdall, which bumped against his knee, he climbed the seventy-two steps to the summit of the East End terracing, reaching the top uncomfortably breathless, thigh muscles stiff with a dragging ache. As a boy he had always sprinted up this slope, on the golden Saturdays of the past, heart racing at the blinding prospect of seeing the heroes of his youth.

Now the heart races for more toxic reasons, he thought. He put down the bag and the typewriter case and looked out over the great rectangular arena. Automatically he felt for his cigarettes. Apart from a few pigeons, he was entirely alone. The pigeons swooped down across the green pitch from their unseen nests under the roofs of the stands. He wondered if a particular tribe had territorial rights on the arena. He hoped so—perhaps he was seeing the distant descendants of the pigeons who had flown about the ground when he was a boy thirty years ago. He felt slightly sad as he watched them, for little else reminded him of Commoners' stadium as he remembered it then.

The old architecture of soccer, the grim shabbiness of the corrugated iron age, had gone now. Where once there had been one upright stand and three sides of uncovered, weed-threatened terraces, there were now massive cantilever stands on three sides of the arena, their apparently unsupported roofs jutting dramatically into the blue sky like the dark dorsal fins of monstrous sharks. Only the open East End terracing, with its concrete steps and red crush hurdles, was left to remind older fans of days when a seat was a rich man's indulgence and a good rain-soaking part of the manly enjoyment. And plans had been announced by the board to replace this last enclave of old-time soccer with a double-decker stand incorporating bars and restaurants.

Today even the grass had gone. Commoners had been one of the last clubs in the First Division to install the new plastic turf. In the summer close-season they had dug up the old grass pitch and replaced it with the new man-made wonder stuff, bright green and totally dead. They had sold off the old pitch at twenty shillings a square foot. People had formed queues to buy a slice of sentimental sod. Today, all over south London, people were tending these precious roots of grass, in gardens and tiny backyards, keeping alive some golden memory of the past when the studs of the great had skimmed over these very blades, growing remnants of a pitch which had once been sacred, tended by groundsmen acolytes, re-sown and fertilised and trimmed and rolled and guarded with religious devotion. On the new stuff you could do anything without fear of damage. Commoners were currently running Sunday afternoon pop concerts, with fifty thousand teenagers stamping all over the very ground where once Stanley Matthews had dribbled and swayed and glided. It was progress, the new indestructible pitch, but it felt a little bit like death.

He shuddered. There had been no wind behind him, down there in the shabby streets of South London, but up here a breeze ruffled his hair and flapped his jacket and through the gently rustling gusts he began to imagine he heard familiar noises. He frowned and shook his head, but when he listened again his ears caught the faint roars of long-vanished crowds, tiny echoes of bygone tumults playing hauntingly in the wind.

He seemed to catch glimpses of packed, swaying masses, pale oceans of blob faces, and there on the pitch he began to see players from his past, still doing the things that gave the game its magic . . . he saw the salmon leap of Denis Law, the Viking Scot . . . he saw Jimmy Greaves, the little man, gliding past slicing boots and scything legs on a deadly run to goal, protected by invisible rays . . . he saw the silky poetry of Alec Young, the man they called the Golden Vision . . . he saw the flowing black hair of George Best, the little boy genius who had it all . . . he saw Bobby Charlton, pride of England, one blond lock flapping off a bald head as he gracefully veered this way and that before letting go the cannon-ball shot . . . he saw little Tommy Harmer, who could make the ball talk but who didn't look big or strong enough to cross the road, until they tried to take the ball away from him . . . he saw the doughty, indomitable Dave Mackay and the slim, cultured Danny Blanchflower, one driving the other prodding on the great Spurs team that won the league and cup double, especially Mackay who came back from two broken legs and showed that it

9

was heart that counted, not age ... he saw Big Bill Foulkes and Tiny Bobby Collins ... he saw stocky Ian St John, most relentless of a truly relentless Liverpool front line ... he saw Peter Broadbent, who had such instinctive command he could stand with his back to the ball and still beat the charging defender ... he saw little Ernie Taylor with midget legs and giant's brain ... he saw Joe Mercer ploughing the straight furrow on bowed legs ... he saw John White the Pale Ghost of White Hart Lane ... he saw Johnny Haynes, the original Brylcreem Boy, spraying reverse passes with radar precision ... Jimmy McIlroy was still out there, treating the crude muscle-men with the disdain of a matador ... there was blond Bobby Moore, cool, impeccable, the captain who never lost command, the first Englishman to lift the World Cup ... there was needle-sharp Bryan Douglas, ball skill beyond belief, a tormenting little devil ... and the mythical Duncan Edwards, who died so young ... and all the others who had flown away, like the pigeons ... but who would always be remembered, at least by one man, who hoped somewhere they were all doing well ... *you'll ne—ve—er wa—aa—lk alone* hymned the invisible armies and he blinked, for the chanting, roaring crowds were always on the edge of his vision, always disappearing faster than his eyes could move to trap them.

With brisk movements he took out another cigarette and lit it from the end of the one he had been smoking. He threw away the butt and blew out smoke in a sharp sigh. A middle-aged romantic alone in the stadium of dreams, with the pigeons and the ghosts of his youth! You sentimental sod! We all believe in progress now, not the hazy magic of the past. Soon they will be shutting out the sky altogether and your boyhood will be truly dead. Nobody will ever get wet and no game will ever again be cancelled through snow or ice. No man will remember the sky or the feel of a breeze on the cheek.

He looked up, seeing a few white clouds racing each other from east to west over the great stretch of South London, chasing and overlapping at speed—even up there second place wasn't good enough. He frowned. The more he looked up the more certain he was that one cloud was travelling in the opposite direction.

Feeling actorish impulses induced by the emptiness of the mighty auditorium, he began to talk out loud.

"Your eyes must be in a worse condition than your lungs, oh noble Caesar," he declaimed, barely resisting an urge to raise a clenched fist in gladiatorial salute.

"You always speak to yourself then?"

Startled by the sudden voice, Peterson turned quickly, face going red, to confront a small, white-haired man who was glaring at him aggressively, shoulders hunched, hands jammed so tightly on hips they might have been permanently fixed there. He wore a blue serge suit, very new and very smart except that it was at least twenty years out of date, so much white handkerchief hanging out of the top pocket Peterson wondered how there could be any handkerchief left inside the pocket, unless the hankie was a white tablecloth.

"Oh, it's you," he said, realising who was behind the smart disguise. "You gave me a fright."

Albert Stone's face registered a slight movement that could have been meant as an apologetic smile.

"I thought for a moment you was a trespasser. Get a lot of them we do, bleedin' nuisances."

"Sorry to disappoint you."

Stone was official odd-job man at Oaks Common Stadium, a sixty-two-year-old errand 'boy' whose job, as far as Peterson had ever seen, consisted mainly of dragging the team 'skips' in and out of trains and coaches and dressing-rooms. These heavy basket skips held the team gear, jerseys and pants and socks and track suits and medical equipment. They were Albert's responsibility. He did other things, like driving the club mini-bus to and from the training ground at Epsom, or washing a player's car for a pound, but Peterson found it hard to picture him in any other position than bending down, panting wheezily, over a hamper.

"When I first started coming here as a boy Harry Mason and Dick Duffy were the stars," Peterson said, as if this would explain the fanciful soliloquy which Albert had interrupted, at the same time offering the little man a cigarette, which Albert took almost suspiciously, examining it closely, perhaps to discover whether chain-smokers used some secret brand of their own. Heavy cigarette smoking was as rare now as chewing tobacco had been when Peterson was a boy; successive governments had pressured public opinion into regarding tobacco as the new black death, although none so far had done more than dither over the legalisation of marijuana, the public smoking of which was still, technically, a crime.

"Mason and Duffy weren't bad," Albert said, grudgingly. "But they used to have real stars in this game—Stan Matthews and Tom Finney and Wilf Mannion—and Peter Doherty—and Tommy Lawton and Raich Carter and Len Shackleton. They had real players in them days. They don't know half of it nowadays—it's all technical and plans and that."

"I often wondered what happened to Mason and Duffy in the end," said Peterson, blowing a lungful of lethal smoke into the breeze, wondering idly if cancer had already established a tiny foothold in his lungs.

"I dunno about Duffy but Mason chucked all his money away—he got partners in a bettin' shop business and lost the lot—his sister lives near us in Balham—he went to South Africa and did himself in—cut his throat."

Peterson looked away, tightening his lips. To think of the great Harry Mason, *his* hero, so reduced by life that it was not worth living. . . .

"Wouldn't the club have helped him out with money?"

"It's a business, innit, they can't go on payin' out for memories, can they?"

Peterson stared at the pigeons zooming down over the plastic pitch. Did anybody know or care when one particular pigeon disappeared from the stadium?

"You going to Glasgow?" he asked, just to break the silence, hardly thinking of what he was saying.

"Course I am!" Albert was instantly resentful. "I go everywhere with the team, don't I? Anybody knows that! This is the lucky suit I'm wearin', innit? The lads would go spare if I wasn't there with the lucky mascot suit. I've wore it every round of the cup, ain't I? Course I'm goin' to Glasgow." He subsided into bitter silence. "Course you wouldn't know that, you not havin' travelled with the team before."

There was something almost touching about the neat way the little man had reminded him which of them was more of an outsider than the other. Albert had been on the staff for fourteen or fifteen years. He, on the other hand, had only three years connection with Oaks Common—and that was only as part-time editor of the match programme, which was a fancy way to describe the dogsbody work he had done on a pathetic little advertising sheet for an honorarium of fifteen pounds a week and a free seat in the stands. The fifteen quid a week had come in handy, especially after he'd become a freelance journalist, another fancy way of describing the fact that he'd drunk himself out of enough Fleet Street staff jobs to create a reputation which made it difficult for him to get another.

He had been slightly surprised when the new management had not immediately sacked him as programme dogsbody. He felt sure Jackson would have ambitious plans for a glossy new programme as part of his campaign to bring the glamour back to Oaks Common. He owed his retention to John Gallagher. They had known each other years before when John was still a player and Peterson had ghosted a book for him, but it hadn't been sentiment that had saved him from the sack.

"I'm giving everyone the same chance, Bill," John Gallagher had said. "This club almost went to the wall because of the people at the very top. I want to give everyone the opportunity to prove they can do better under proper management. If you can't—well, I'll sack you then."

He'd been almost inclined to give up the job anyway, for these days he had little stomach for such Boy Scout concepts as proving himself anew. He had proved himself often enough in the past, disastrously. However, perhaps through sheer indecisiveness, he had gone on doing the programme and then the cup run started and things began to look up and they'd increased the size of the programme and then, just after the quarter-final game when Commoners beat Hibs, Alec Hood had come to him from the team and asked him to organise the business side of the players' pool — should they beat Rangers and reach the New Wembley final and find themselves able to earn a lot of side money from advertising and marketing souvenirs.

And that was why he was here this morning with his packed bag and his portable typewriter, still a bit of a hanger-on but perhaps nearer the inside edge of the fringe than previously. He didn't really think Commoners had much chance of beating Rangers but even if they didn't make any money it was a nice little trip, all expenses paid, and for a few days he would escape the complicated mess of his so-called private life.

"I've got the lads a beer contract for T.V. commercials," he said to Albert. "Fifteen thousand pounds." He immediately regretted the childish impulse to impress the little man. What the hell did it matter what Albert thought?

"Cor!" Albert looked at him with new interest. "Bleedin' footballers today—get money at every turn they do."

They heard a car. Peterson reached the top of the terracing first. A bright red Jaguar seemed to be driving straight for the wall of the North Stand. Just when a crash seemed inevitable it slewed round and stopped with a screech of soft tyres on asphalt. Two men in light grey suits got out, laughing loudly.

"Sammy Small and Danny Peck," said Albert, sniffing. "Mad Cockney prats! That Small will get himself killed, mad bastard, serve him right an' all, no skin off my nose."

"You sound as if you hate him."

"They're all as bad. Cruel lot they are. You know what they call me—to my face? Limpalong Leslie! They don't think I might be hurt, oh no."

"I wouldn't take it seriously, they're only pulling your leg."

"Don't you start as well!"

Peterson did not think it worth apologising for the unintended pun. Albert had a slightly deformed right foot, which required an oddly-shaped shoe with a platform sole. This gave him a rolling limp, hardly noticeable. More cars began to pull into the ground. Albert knew at first glance which player would be driving each car and to which other players he would have given a lift. He referred to them in a tone that was a mixture of sneers and self-pity. They had real players in them days, he would always say about the past, not like today's professionals, them pampered, overpaid bigheads. Peterson remembered how his own father had said the same things about the players of his day—how they didn't do a Friday night shift at the coal-face and then come up and have a few pints and go on to play like demons. It was always the same when men talked about football, only the stars of the past had the true magic. Today's players might be fitter and faster and brainier —but they could never compare to the heroes you worshipped as a boy.

He picked up his bag and typewriter and began down the concrete steps. The funny thing about Albert was that for all his sneers it was obvious from his attitude to the players in person that he idolised them. Maybe the sneers helped him keep his self-respect. Football brought out some funny things in men.

"You knew John Gallagher pretty well—in the old days, didn't you?" Albert said, touching his arm.

"Quite well," said Peterson.

"I heard somethin' John Gallagher ought to know about," said Albert, standing on the top step, beckoning to Peterson to stay close. "Maybe you're the one that wants to tell him."

"Tell him what?"

"Well, it's me hearin' things I shouldn't and John Gallagher don't stand for no gossipin'—but I overheard two of the directors talkin' after last week's board meetin'—you know the board is approachin' other people for John Gallagher's job?"

"Nonsense!"

"It's what they said. I was fixin' a flat on Dave Spencer's car, they didn't see me behind it, they was sayin' they thought Frank Smith of Brighton would jump at the job."

"Commoners have never had such a successful manager as John Gallagher. Jackson wouldn't sack him, not in a million years."

"Why did they fall out then?"

"Who?"

"Jackson and J.G."

"Fallen out? Who told you that?"

Albert looked surprised.

"You don't know about that? I thought you bein' a friend of his you'd have heard."

"What do you mean, they've fallen out?"

"Oh well it ain't my business to tell you if J.G. ain't told you."

Peterson sucked air noisily through his front teeth, an irritating mannerism which he was unable to suppress at times of uncertainty. If John Gallagher and the chairman had fallen out they had kept it very secret. Albert Stone's mind was probably fogged by fantasy. Yet there was a doubt in his mind. Professional football had strange, seemingly illogical undercurrents which outsiders could not fully understand, even if they knew of their existence. When John Gallagher had been appointed manager one of his first steps had been to issue a rule barring all directors, including the chairman, from going near the dressing-room, or having anything to do with the players unless he was present.

"John Gallagher is the professional," the chairman had said to the press. "We directors are the businessmen, our job is to give him the conditions and the money he needs to make this a successful club. He is in complete charge of everything to do with the playing side."

Had Jackson really meant this? Everybody knew the Jackson story, the street urchin who had climbed over the wall to see the Commoners of his boyhood and who years later as a tycoon had taken over the club. Had he really bargained for the fact that he would be denied the chance to play with his expensive toy?

Whatever the truth, Peterson decided to have no part of it. The last thing John Gallagher would appreciate was a hanger-on spreading tittle-tattle. That would count as meddling. In the high-pressured tension of big-time football any irrelevant irritation could only lead to a blow-up. And Peterson had more at stake now than fifteen quid a week for scratching together a programme. If he managed to make a success of the players' pool . . . well, he had long ago realised that his time for seeing dreams come true was over but there was a faint chance the directors might appoint a full-time public relations man and marketing manager. Say—six thousand a year? For a forty-three-year-old hack who had to scrabble for bread doing freelance rubbish for impoverished magazines that was a heady prospect. He didn't even want to hear about trouble behind the scenes.

"Look—there's Roy Christmas—the Aston Martin," said Albert. "The big star and don't he know it, flash bastard."

Peterson started down the steps again, Albert a few paces behind him, breathing heavily. As they reached the bottom Roy Christmas was getting out of his long, low sports car, his face extremely pale and his hair cut short and parted in the old-fashioned style of by-gone days when men asked barbers for short back and sides. As always there was a preoccupied look on his thin face. At this range he did not look like a great star for whom one football club had paid another one hundred and forty thousand pounds. Only on the field did he suddenly acquire the electric aura of the true star, the magnetic presence that attracted all eyes, as if he moved in a personal spotlight. He nodded to Peterson and Albert but made no effort at conversation. Somebody shouted. Peterson saw Alec Hood coming towards them through the parked cars.

"Morning, Bill, you look well—been ill?"

Hood, the centre-back and club captain was wearing the official club suit, light grey with the club's initials scrawled in green thread on the breast pocket. He, too, had shorter hair than was currently fashionable among players, but it had been styled to suit his heavy, rectangular face, black hair cut short and brushed forward. He stood six foot two, a big, lean man who weighed a hundred and ninety-six pounds stripped. He had been with Commoners since the age of sixteen and fifteen years in London had given him a suave, cosmopolitan veneer which still did not hide the craggy, foundry-moulded Scot. To most of the team he was a genuine hero. On the field he was indomitable—for season after season only his rock-like presence had stood between Commoners and relegation to football's nether regions. Although he was as hard as nails they always said about him that he had never done a dirty or underhand trick in four hundred and nineteen top-class games for Commoners, a club playing record that would probably never be equalled, not now when soccer had become faster and more competitive than anyone had ever believed possible. Off the field he was a different kind of hero, for his motto was to work hard and play hard and he could out-drink and out-wench any one of them and still be there for ten o'clock training, red-eyed but ready to run players ten years younger than himself into the ground.

"I'll tell you what's ruining my health," Peterson said, "the strain of trying to make you muscle-bound morons rich."

The imagined state of Peterson's health had become a general joke among the players. There was nothing wrong with him, apart from smoker's lungs, but the team had seized on his air of thin, crumpled dissipation and nicknamed him Poor Old Bill. On the one occasion he had made the mistake of thinking he could hold his own in a practice kickaround—had he not played the game brilliantly as a schoolboy?—he had given them a laugh by pretending to collapse, anticipating a genuine flake-out by about thirty seconds. It all helped towards being accepted in the tight little world of the professionals. They were very physical people and their humour was robust and aggressive and if you didn't give them something safe to laugh at they would soon find the thing that could hurt.

"He went to the doctor yesterday, Poor Old Bill," said Sammy Small, the little Cockney left-wing man. "You know what the doc says? I won't say it's serious, me old son, but don't risk your money orderin' four-course dinners."

Even Roy Christmas managed a faint smile. Peterson raised an eyebrow and said nothing.

"Poor Old Bill is the man who never laughs," said Steve Randall, the first-team goalkeeper, a big blond boy with a Sussex burr. "He don't think his body can stand the strain."

"Ha ha," said somebody, sarcastically. Randall always tried too hard with jokes; he wanted to be a character, goalkeepers having a reputation for being slightly crazy, but his witticisms had an irritating quality which made the teeth grate. The others called him Randy, ironically, implying that his much-publicised success with women was all talk. Peterson looked him in the eye.

"Did you hear about the butter-fingered goalkeeper who couldn't even play with himself?" he asked, voice very casual. "He kept dropping it all the time."

The others laughed, pointing jeeringly at Randall, who sniffed disdainfully. The public image of players was mostly based on newspaper and television interviews, which normally took place in connection with some important match when they would, by the very nature of things, be at their most tense and uncommunicative. Here, with the big game three long days away, they were different people altogether, friendly and relaxed and able to think of other things than their own inner fears and insecurities. Peterson was about to mention this to Alec Hood when Sammy Small tossed a tenpenny piece into the air. Peterson watched it fall. It was inches from the ground when Sammy caught it on the top of his shoe. He stood there, balanced on his left foot, the silver coin lying flat on black shiny leather.

"Impressed?" he said, winking, when he saw Peterson's face.

"Very. What do you do for an encore?"

"I used to know a fella who was able to toss the coin from his foot—somethin' like this—and catch it in his top pocket—oops! There's a lucky thing." Peterson laughed involuntarily. Danny Peck did not look impressed. He took a handful of change from his pocket and picked out a tenpenny piece.

"That's nothing," he said. "I knew a fella who could throw up a coin—" he flicked the tenpenny piece into the air—"catch it on his foot—" the coin landed on the flat upper of his right shoe while he balanced effortlessly on his left leg—"then flick it up and catch it on the back of his neck—" he arched his body, head bent forward, eyes looking at the ground—"then let the coin slide off his neck—" he made little twisting motions of his neck and back—"and catch it on his foot again and walk away." He finished by flicking the coin up from his shoe in a high, narrow arc, catching it in his right hand.

"That's nothin', you should see Jimmy Riddle," said Sammy, "he can do the same trick only he can catch a pound's worth of pennies on his nose."

Dave Spencer, one of the midfield linkmen, known as Debonair Dave, pulled out his tenpenny piece.

"I suppose you know a fella as well," said Peterson.

"You're joking—I am the fella."

Spencer threw up the silver coin and caught it on his forehead, head craned forward and up, using outstretched hands to maintain perfect balance. He began twitching his face until the coin started to slip sideways off the flat of the brow into the hollow of his right eye. He kept twitching and then suddenly straightened up, the coin fixed in his eye-socket like a monocle.

Within seconds all the players were tossing up coins and catching them on shoes or foreheads or necks, a mad little ballet of one-legged men calling desperately for applause at some new manifestation of skill, dropped coins being chased among the cars, others trying tricks with Yale keys. Peterson fought a strong temptation to see if he could catch a coin on his foot. If you didn't have the skill the best thing you could do was stand and admire those who had it.

"Here's bleedin' Cinderella—walkin'," said Sammy, who had rapidly tired of coin tricks. Johnny Parkinson, the reserve goalkeeper, came walking hurriedly over the asphalt. Peterson started laughing.

"Why do we call him Cinderella?" Danny said. "Because he always misses the ball!"

"Where's yer chauffeur then, Cinders?" Sammy shouted.

Parkinson raised his hands for silence.

"Mister Ingrams has sent me on ahead to get you ready for his arrival," he said. They all looked at the gates. Into the ground rolled a long, white American convertible, the roof down, driven by a young boy in dark glasses.

"It's Wiggy!" Sammy exclaimed. "Cor—even the new car's got to have a false roof." He put his hand to his mouth and shouted. "Wot, no syrup today, Wiggy? You look quite bleedin' normal."

They gathered round the car, one of the longest Peterson had ever seen, while Wiggy—Bobby Ingrams, the star teenage winger—sat in state, proudly explaining that his new model was only four years old and had cost him two grand.

"She does eight miles to the gallon," said Wiggy, with some pride.

"The king of syrup does it again," said Sammy, admiringly. In his rhyming slang, a syrup was a wig, from syrup of figs, and Wiggy's business made him king of syrup. He was only a boy—his nineteenth birthday was on Saturday, the day of the big match, which seemed typical of his flair for publicity—yet he was one of the most outrageous personalities in the game. When he first signed for Commoners there was an argument about the length of his hair, which he solved by having a skinhead crop and then turning up at the ground wearing a wig. This blossomed into a business—fashion headpieces for men. At the moment, because John Gallagher had been adamant that he did not wear one of his hair gimmicks on official club trips, he looked like any normal London teenager, if you discounted the white suede ankle boots.

"Everybody's here except the two kids and John Gallagher," said Hood when they tired of inspecting Wiggy's new car. "Hey, George, you any idea where the boss is?"

"No, why, you want to borrow a fiver?" said George Westbury, the club physiotherapist, a dapper little man of fifty-one who was standing beside Dave Peacock, the dark-haired striker. "Right then, Dave," he said, "let's have a look at it."

Peacock lifted his left leg and rested his foot on the front bumper of Wiggy's car. He rolled up his trouser leg and revealed a pinkish scar running for about four inches diagonally across the shinbone.

"That looks a lot better," said Westbury, prodding into the wound with his index finger.

"Better?" said Peterson. "I would like to have seen it when it was bad."

"It's the worst I've ever had," said Peacock, scratching round the drying edges of the scar.

"When did you do it—last week?"

"Last week!" said Westbury. "Five weeks ago. When he did it

20

you could see the bone. It looked pretty horrific then, I can tell you."

Peterson shuddered. Peacock began to roll his trouser leg down over a shin that looked like an old battle-field, with white patches where the hair had not grown again over old wounds, here and there patches of yellow and purple bruising, drying scab tissue over minor cuts. As the front runner of the team's strikers Dave got more of a hammering than most from defenders. He didn't seem to mind. As he stamped his foot to shake down the trouser leg he grinned at Peterson's horrified face.

"You wouldn't win the Miss World contest with legs like that, eh Bill?"

An unusually rough-sounding engine noise made them look towards the gates, through which came an old van, painted yellow.

"Look at the smoke from that exhaust!" said George Westbury. "You'd think the Apaches were on the warpath."

From the van jumped the two young reserves, Barry Ross and Ian Rowland, both teenagers, both embarrassed at being so conspicuously late. Ross showed his embarrassment by his red face. Rowland, being black, showed it by looking at the ground.

"Sorry we're late," Ross blurted out to Alec Hood. "The van broke down."

"It's amazing," said Hood, face serious, sounding like a junior edition of John Gallagher, "when I was your age if I'd got into the first team squad I'd have been here since daybreak. You lads are getting it too easy. Better tell the Boss to fine them fifty quid apiece, eh George?"

The boys looked sick. Then they realised Hood was joking. Peterson stood back, listening and watching. If the fans could see their heroes now they might be surprised, he thought, for the sixteen youngish men joking in the car park sounded just like boys in a school playground. Yet they were grown men and they owned expensive cars and houses and earned big money, very big indeed—probably as high as two hundred a week in one or two cases, and that wasn't counting bonuses. Collectively they were probably worth more than a million pounds. Yet here they were, just a bunch of laughing lads, none of the individual sense of presence that you found in even the humblest actor, if there was such a thing as a humble actor. These guys were in the entertainment business—but only as hardened pros who happened to do something that millions of people wanted to watch. They didn't go out on the field to entertain. They went out to win.

It was peculiar, he thought, he had followed this game all his life and read the sports pages and known a player or two—yet every day he spent at Oaks Common Stadium brought home to him just how little he and the outside world knew about what went on behind the scenes of a football club. He was even beginning to think of soccer as a secret conspiracy which took place in full view of a million, unseeing eyes.

Sammy Small started banging in bongo time on the side of the big red and blue coach, chanting the words of some pop song, a real little London live-wire, eyes as sharp and quick as a hawk's, cheek written all over him, just a raucous little tearaway—you might think, if you had not seen him play.

"John Gallagher would have told us if he was going to meet us at Euston," said George Westbury, coming round from the rear of the coach, where Albert Stone and Henry the driver were lifting in the skips.

"Harry Barnes isn't here either," said Alec Hood. "I'm beginning to feel neglected and unloved."

"Harry's meeting us at Euston," said Westbury.

"There's the boss now," said Alan Shackle, one of the midfield men, a Welshman with a broken nose.

A white Mercedes saloon rolled smoothly over the car park asphalt and came silently to a halt between the white lines of the space marked MANAGER J. P. GALLAGHER. Out climbed a dark, swarthy man in a light brown tweed suit. He leaned back into the car and lifted out a bright yellow travelling case and a raincoat. Peterson watched him lock the car door and swing the raincoat over his shoulder. His black hair was styled very short and combed forward. Peterson suddenly realised that Alec Hood had changed his hair to the same style since John Gallagher had been appointed manager. That was a manly kind of hero-worship for you. The whole impression John Gallagher gave off was of athletic efficiency. He was not particularly big, perhaps about five foot ten, but there was a bigness about him, an aggressive need for more space than his actual measurements required. Only the simplest of intelligences would have failed to realise instinctively that here was The Boss.

"Hullo, John, we're all here," George Westbury said.

The players seemed to gather towards the manager, wanting to be near him, to find out what he had in store for them.

"I bloody well hope you're all here," said John Gallagher, quite curtly. "Come on then, get into the coach, we're late enough as it is."

He sounded bad-tempered. Peterson caught a quick exchange of momentary frowns between Hood and Westbury.

"Hullo, Bill," said John Gallagher, nodding briskly, still not smiling.

"Morning, J.G.," he replied, conscious of being glad at his special mention. As they began to climb into the coach he stood back, not wanting to interfere with the players' own seating preferences. Perhaps it was his imagination but he sensed a definite tension. It was John Gallagher's fault that they were late, yet his snappy words had made them all feel that they, in some way, were to blame. Then he looked at the players and realised he was being over-sensitive. They seemed cheerier than ever. He took an empty seat second from front on the left, throwing his bag up on the rack, keeping the typewriter on his knees. John Gallagher stood beside Henry the driver, ticking them off on a mental list. Albert pulled the door and John Gallagher sat down and the driver started the engine. John Gallagher did not sit beside Peterson, as he had hoped, but in the front seat, his raincoat still over his shoulder, a very Scottish habit which Peterson associated with wet golf courses. Peterson leaned forward.

"Well, we're off on the big trip, John," he said. "How do you feel about the game?"

"I'll let you know how I feel on Saturday at twenty to five when the final whistle goes," the manager said, not looking round. Peterson sat back, feeling that he had been rebuked. He decided not to mention the T.V. beer commercials until the tension had died down. Behind him the players were having their usual good fun.

"My trophy cabinet at home is pretty full already," Sammy Small was saying. "I dunno if I should put my British Cup medal on the left or the right or bang in the middle. Anybody know what it looks like?"

"Let's win this bloody semi-final first," growled Shackle, his face intense with what Peterson assumed to be genuine anger. Sammy

23

started laughing, pointing a scornful finger at the Welshman.

"I was just testin', you stupid taffy nit—you're so superstitious it ain't bloody true."

The coach pulled out of the gate and turned right to head north.

"Hey—stop a minute," came a shout. Peterson looked round. Tommy Riddle, the right-wing forward, known as Jimmy, a big, sad-faced man with a particularly large nose, was coming down the gangway. "I've left my bag in the car! Hey, Henry, stop here a minute, I'll run back for it. Sorry, Boss, I won't be two shakes."

"Ain't that bloody typical?" shouted Sammy Small.

"Keep driving, Henry," John Gallagher snapped. He looked up at Riddle, face explosively tight. "Don't you give the driver orders, Riddle. I'll be damned if we're losing any more time over your stupidity."

"But my gear's in the bag, Boss, my razor and everything!"

"Buy a new bloody razor then! We pay you enough."

In the face of the manager's ferocious gaze Riddle blushed heavily and went back up the coach. The whole party went silent. Peterson stared out of the window. He had never heard of John Gallagher behaving like this. Was there some truth in what Albert Stone had overheard? Did John Gallagher know the directors might be trying to replace him?

On the pavement some fans recognised the team coach and stopped to wave and shout at their heroes, a hunger for excitement and glamour on their faces. Among them was a small boy, jumping up and down, face alight with ecstasy. In thirty years this would be one of the magic moments of his boyhood existence. He would tell his own children about Roy Christmas and Sammy Small and Dave Peacock and say, ah, we had real players in them days.

And meanwhile, the mythical idols of his future adult nostalgia were sitting in a state of uneasy tension caused by one of them stupidly forgetting his travelling bag. They stared at each other through walls of glass, hap-happy fans and tight-faced players, knowing less about each other than goldfish in a bowl.

"You don't need a razor anyway, Jimmy me old son," came the voice of Sammy Small. "A beard would go great with that fireman's of yours."

Sniggers now, instead of open laughter. Peterson watched John Gallagher's dark head. The manager gave no sign of having heard the joke.

3

REPRINT of this article is by kind permission of *Winner*, the weekly soccer magazine.

HOW GENTLEMAN JOHN GAVE THE HASBEENS BACK THEIR LONG LOST PRIDE
by Steve Egan

Eighteen months ago this week John Gallagher, the ex-Burnley, Arsenal and Scotland star, walked into Oaks Common Stadium on his first day as manager of the once-proud South London club. After only a year as player-coach of the Arsenal reserve team, he had landed the job that most of the experts said was impossible.

Ten years ago Commoners were the pride of south London — two F.A. semi-finals in two years, winners of the Inter-Cities Fairs Cup over mighty Internazionale of Milan. Their average gate then was 51,000. Who could have foreseen the slump?

But it came — inexplicably, as these things often are in soccer. Two or three stars grew old at the same time, the chairman died, near neighbours Chelsea ran into a period of phenomenal success climaxed by two successive League championships and victory in the European Cup. Crystal Palace were also doing well — and Fulham were back in the First Division. Competition for success was pretty ferocious.

Commoners were rich in money but impoverished of policy. Vast sums were spent on new stands and ground improvements — when fans knew it was players the club needed.

Four seasons ago the club reached the F.A. semi-final but the revival was a flash in the pan. Crowds dropped to last season's average gate of 23,000—barely enough for first division survival in London.

It's now part of soccer history—how millionaire hotel tycoon George Jackson bought the club with £250,000 of his own money and another quarter of a million floated by a city syndicate. Most experts said they might as well have bonfired the money but Jackson wasted no time. Veteran manager Vernon Jones was sacked. The experts sniffed when John Gallagher got the managerial hot-seat. A great player—28 times capped for Scotland—possibly a good coach—but he was absolutely untried as a manager.

John Gallagher—known throughout the game as Gentleman John—couldn't help a club that was going down as surely as the *Titanic*, they said.

So there he was, that first sombre morning, faced with the impossible. What was his first action?

HE CALLED IN TOP INTERIOR DECORATOR AND DESIGNER ROBERT FRANCE TO REDESIGN THE DRESSING-ROOMS! FASHION CONSULTANT EMILE WAS ASKED TO CREATE A BRAND NEW IMAGE FOR THE TEAM, FROM STRIPS TO CLUB SUITS AND TIES.

You could hear them laughing from Home Park, Plymouth, to Pittodrie Park, Aberdeen!

"Yes, the ridicule was nationwide," John Gallagher told me last week. He was smiling. "We hadn't won a game for two months but here we were rebuilding the dressing-rooms, giving each player a fitted wardrobe, laying out a split-level lounge, papering the whole place in dove-grey and green!

"Of course it was all a gimmick—but it had a serious purpose. Nobody was to be in any doubt—things had changed.

"My real job was to convince the players they were not doomed to failure. They had lost all confidence in themselves and in the club.

26

"While the headlines were all about the gimmicks, coach Harry Barnes and I were overhauling the training system and evaluating the playing staff. I won't mention names—but I sold every player who didn't share our enthusiasm—even if they were better players than the ones I kept. Every man got his chance—and most, I'm proud to say, took it."

At the same time George Jackson and his board were busy finding money for the club. They created the idea of associate membership, open to the public at £30 a year, giving fans a chance to use the club's new amenities, the gym and the squash courts and the restaurants and so on. Seven thousand people took the offer. Now other clubs are rushing to follow Commoners' example.

"We escaped relegation by three points last year," John Gallagher went on, "a considerable achievement considering we had only thirteen experienced professionals and a lot of untried reserves.

"All the credit goes to them—and to Harry Barnes and George Westbury, the physiotherapist—they all worked very hard. And the board backed us a hundred per cent.

"What did I do? Let's face it, good players can exist without a brilliant manager but the greatest manager in the world can do nothing without good players. Let's say I convinced the lads that they were good players."

That's typical of Gentleman John. Yet despite the confidence and ability he hides behind his modesty, even he could hardly have prophesied the run of cup success Commoners have enjoyed this season. When the three football associations, England and Wales, Scotland, and United Federal Ireland, decided to scrap their domestic cup tournaments in favour of a truly British Isles cup, bookies listed Commoners among the 500–1 also-rans.

Bookies, fans, writers—they all plumped for the big battalions of Manchester United, Everton, Newcastle, Chelsea, Arsenal, and Glasgow's Celtic and Rangers.

In the first round proper, Commoners were drawn away to humble Exeter. They were lucky to win. Big money buy Roy Christmas — John Gallagher's only major transfer venture — scored two goals in the last ten minutes, after Exeter had been on top for the whole game.

Then came a home tie against Swansea and another lucky win — the only goal being scored by Dave Peacock from a hotly-disputed penalty.

In the third round Commoners were drawn away to Dundee United and again were thought lucky when they got a draw at Tannadice Park, Commoners only goal coming from link-man Dave Spencer. In the replay, however, Christmas got two and the other went to the new Oaks Common star, Bobby 'Wiggy' Ingrams, giving the Londoners a fairly convincing 3-0 victory.

Ingrams — the 18-year-old boutique owner and fashion leader — scored the goal that beat Sunderland in the fourth round. This was Commoners' best performance so far, the revitalised Sunderland being nobody's walkovers. The crowd was 62,000, the largest at Oaks Common for seven years.

Then followed a devastating display against first division Luton at home. Peacock scored two, and Riddle two to make it 4-0. The sixth round draw brought a home tie with the mighty Liverpool! That's the end of *them*, the experts said.

None of the 65,000 fans who saw that game will ever forget it. Liverpool came looking for quick goals. They ran up against what is now, belatedly, regarded as the tightest defence in the league. Veteran Scottish international Alec Hood played the game of his career. Fullbacks Gurr and Williamson, unknown reserves before John Gallagher's arrival, completely dominated the fearsome Liverpool wingers. Danny the Destroyer Peck, much-travelled veteran never thought of as much more than a stopgap blocker, not only stopped everything in sight but found time and space to link up with the suave Spencer in brilliantly constructive attacking play.

With the score level at 1-1 and six minutes to go Roy Christmas went down in the Liverpool penalty box. Was he tripped or did he take a dive? My answer is that Christmas is too goal hungry to take a dive when there's even a ten per cent chance of a shot.

The arguments will rage as long as men talk football but Sammy Small, the dynamic little Cockney with the fastest brain (some say tongue) in the game, isn't a man to worry about terracing arguments. He rammed the penalty home and Commoners were in the quarter-finals against Hibernian, pride of Edinburgh.

Another home draw. Luck? There was certainly nothing flukey about the game. Commoners devastated the Scottish champions, Peacock, Christmas, Peck scoring one each, Ingrams giving one of the finest displays of wing play seen on an English pitch since the heyday of George Best.

Now the whole soccer world waits to see if Commoners luck holds out at Hampden Park. It's neutral ground in name only — I doubt if 40,000 London throats will make much impression against the fervent Scottish hordes.

The Gers have had a tremendous season or two, almost eclipsing their traditional rivals, Celtic. And Scottish football in general has improved by leaps and bounds since that inspirational performance in the 1978 World Cup.

Whatever the result one thing is certain. The British Cup has been a fantastic success. It's kept a lot of money in the game that otherwise would have gone into Europe. The games themselves have been conspicuously lacking in bitterness and wrangling and mayhem so often associated with European matches.

My own tip for Hampden? Sorry, all you great guys at Oaks Common. It has to be Rangers. They have power in every department. Few defences have found an answer to their world-class superstar Jackie Caskie. Derby County are reckoned one of England's top six clubs — yet Rangers obliterated them in the quarter-finals. And this time they'll have the bulk of the crowd behind them.

But never mind who wins — any man who takes part in this St. Crispin's Day of soccer will carry his pride down the years. In the words of John Gallagher:

"This won't be an occasion I'd recommend to anyone suffering from a weak heart."

And to think that for Commoners it all began the day a man from Mayfair brought his colour-chart into the Oaks Common dressing-room!

4

"HE'S taking it worse than I expected," Roy Christmas murmured to Alec Hood.

"I suppose he's got more at stake on Saturday than the rest of us," Hood replied, voice too low for the others to hear. "Anyway, Jimmy asked for it, he's always leaving things behind."

They were sitting together near the back of the coach, Roy Christmas young and pale and intense, Alec Hood dark and hard-shouldered and relaxed, both slightly aloof from the sniggers and the muffled laughs around them.

"I haven't felt it all this morning," Roy said, rubbing his palm over the inside of his left thigh.

"There you are then, what did I tell you, you'll be okay by Saturday."

"I bloody well have to be okay for Saturday!"

Hood had known yesterday there was something wrong, the moment he stepped into the manager's office and John Gallagher asked him to close the door behind him. That door was always left open, a piece of John Gallagher psychology, a sign that he was always available to his players, visible proof that no dirty work was going on here.

"Roy's just told me he felt it worse than ever this morning," John Gallagher said. He was sitting behind his desk. Roy was standing by the window. He grimaced. No need to say what 'it' was. Two weeks before, Roy had strained a thigh muscle, against Spurs at White Hart Lane. He had missed the league game at Liverpool and the home game with Wolves, making his come-back in Wednesday's floodlit evening match against Hull City, who were going great guns at the top of the First Division. Hull had won and taken away the four points for a win, but Commoners were safe from relegation and were thinking now solely of the

British Cup. Roy had come through without aggravating the muscle trouble, that was the main thing.

Now the boy was staring at his feet, looking pretty sick.

"How bad is it?" Hood asked.

"I got through training but it got worse as the morning went on — I was frightened I would pull it."

"Alec, I've told Roy to go straight home after treatment," John Gallagher had said. "We're travelling tomorrow so there won't be any training and he can also miss training on Thursday in Scotland. That'll give it a good long rest. George can give him treatment — massage, ultrasonics, deep heat, the lot. We'll give him a fitness test on Friday morning."

"It's not all that bad," said Roy, trying to put some confidence into his flat Lancashire voice. "I'm just worried if I start the game and then break down — I don't want to put the team right in trouble."

"We'd just have to bring on a substitute," Hood said abruptly. He could have known something like this would happen, this week of all bloody weeks.

"We might have already used the two outfield subs," John Gallagher said. He did not look unduly worried. He had a deserved reputation for never panicking. "The main thing is, I don't want this to get in the papers. Rangers will be organising their defence to cope with Roy. If he's not playing and they don't hear till Friday it won't give them much time to reorganise their defensive formation."

"So what do we tell the reporters when they see Roy isn't training?"

"They won't know, will they? I won't let them watch us training." John Gallagher and Hood stared at each other and for a long moment Roy might not have been in the room. They could both have cursed their rotten luck but they were the two old hands and they knew what things were best left unsaid. When Roy left, John Gallagher produced a solid block of cream-coloured tickets, the players' allocation of complimentaries for Hampden, half a dozen a man.

"Some of the lads have a lot of friends who'll want to see the game," said Hood. "Can they buy extra tickets from the club?"

"They'll have a lot of new friends now we're getting a bit of success," said John Gallagher, smiling wryly. "I've made arrangements with Harrison, they can buy up to ten each. But these are for their friends. The chairman hates touts and anything to do with ticket rackets. If he caught anybody flogging them to spivs he'd come down like a ton of bricks."

"They're good lads, they won't do anything silly."

"I know they're good lads—but some spiv gets at them and offers them eight times the face value, especially the young ones—they might just fall for it and then some newspaper starts a campaign against black market tickets and they trace the serial numbers back to the club—the chairman would do his nut. He's a fanatic about playing fair with the fans. I had an argument about getting you the chance to buy the extra ten."

"We can't stop touts making approaches," Hood said.

"You put the fear of death up them. They all look up to you. My God, I wish I was coming into the game now. They don't know they're born, half these lads. Wiggy's going round telling everybody he'll make his first million by the time he's twenty-five! Christ, I remember big stars, internationals, who ended up labouring in gasworks and selling newspapers."

Hood nodded. John Gallagher suddenly laughed.

"I know what you're thinking—all us of the older generation are always telling you lads that you're overpaid and money-mad."

"Maybe."

"It's envy, Alec. You make as much as you can while it's going and good luck to you."

Sitting now in the coach, which was slowly approaching Kennington Oval in a dreary jumble of rush-hour traffic, Hood could see the top of John Gallagher's head, a pale gleam on top where the dark hair was thinning out. He smiled, thinking of Sammy Small's retort to a remark that John Gallagher was going thin on top.

"Who wants fat hair?" Sammy had said. A joke for every occasion, that was Sammy. Out of the corner of his eye he saw Roy's hand moving up and down the injured thigh. It was typical of football, you were just on the point of achieving something really important when you found you were tied in with other men in a way you couldn't escape. You were never in full control of your own life. John Gallagher liked to say that you made your own luck, but Hood didn't believe that. Roy would be desperately trying

33

to convince himself the injury was not too bad but all the time there would be a sinking sensation in his guts, the hopeless feeling that every injured player knew, the sickening realisation that events were out of your hands.

Hood felt a slight sinking in his own stomach. John Gallagher's edginess must be spreading. He clenched his fists and drew in a sharp breath. Winning this game on Saturday was more important to him than to anyone else in the club, that was a certainty. The others would all swear blind that it meant more to them—every man thought his own ambitions or troubles more crucial than anyone else's—but Hood knew that he was in a special position. He was thirty-one and slowing down and he would be finished in another two seasons at most, already a veteran by today's standards. Peterson had asked him why he had such a burning desire to beat Rangers in the semi-final and then win the British Cup, and he'd given the usual answers that players gave to outsiders, players are very competitive by nature, winning makes us happy, losing makes us sick, success and winning are what the game is all about.

"I suppose the medal is visible proof of success," Peterson had said. "And there's the money, of course."

Hood hadn't said anything at the time, you could lose a lot of energy explaining what you felt about football to people who had never played the game professionally, but he had reacted to the insult in Peterson's comment. Why did everyone automatically assume players thought only in terms of money?

This is my living, he could have said, I came into the game because I had the ability and the determination to be a footballer—but the ambition was to play the game, not to make money. That came afterwards, it's what we pick up because we're good at the game. Of course we're out for as much money as we can make—so are dockers and miners and doctors and financiers and stockbrokers—maybe we do have to look a bit sharp about it, in most jobs a man is just beginning to earn good wages at the age of thirty but that is when our earning days are coming to an end. So in ten or twelve years we have to grab what's going. But it's still just a fact of life, the stuff they give us for being good at the game. A medal is different.

I've been in this game for fifteen years, he could have said to Peterson, I never got a medal and I want this one so badly it hurts. It means so many things to me I could make a list; it means I won't feel so sick when I have to give up playing; it means I'll have something to show my kids and their kids, apart from the battlefield scars on my legs; it's not just a pretty bit of gold in a nice box; you'd have to know what it's like to play football for a living, it's not the same as an ordinary job—ordinary people don't have to worry all the time about winning or losing or keeping their place in the team; when I'm finished playing I'll be thinking back over all the games and all the seasons and asking myself—what was it all about? Did it mean anything at all? One pound note is exactly the same as another but you can't pick up a medal from the gutter. Two years after you've given up playing you're still a young man but already the fans are cheering somebody else. A medal is proof that they once cheered for you and that you counted for something, once. A boxer who won a world title never had to justify himself—he had been one of the best and the record books did the talking for him. The medal said the same thing—I was there and I was one of the best.

Out of the window he saw the blank faces of the men driving to city offices and again he felt a slight edginess in his guts, for he had no idea of what their kind of life was all about. He had come down from Scotland to join Commoners as an apprentice, the day after he left school, and since then he had not done a single day's work outside of football. For years he had ignored the future, like all young players half-believing it was all going to go on for ever. But he wasn't young any more and the future was beginning to hang over him like a dirty big cloud.

Behind him the team jokers were jumping about like schoolboys on an outing. Hood suddenly wanted to turn round and knock their heads together and shout at them—you're going to get old as well, you dopes, think about it now, while you've still got the time.

Roy caught his eye and he made a little grimace, turning his head to look out at the crawling lines of cars. I couldn't live outside the game, he told himself. Not like those men out there. To stay in the game—that was the player's dream, but only one in a hundred achieved it. And only one per cent of those who were lucky enough to get jobs as coaches or physiotherapists or managers made a success of them. Luck? Was that what it all boiled down to? Every player swore blind that if he became a manager he would do it properly, avoiding all the mistakes and tricks managers had pulled on him. They all said it, yet the funny thing was that they changed as soon as they became managers. Was it so different, playing and managing? Were the pressures so much greater? He continually studied John Gallagher, not just as the manager who might win or lose him his last chance of a medal but also as a yardstick, wondering if he also had what it took to run a team. It would have cost them only a minute for Jimmy to run back to the car park. John Gallagher's outburst was the silly sort of thing he expected from bad managers, the insecure and the incompetent, the ones who could not communicate with men, let alone lead and inspire them. But would he have done any better, with the tension beginning to show itself? He looked again at John Gallagher's dark head. Most of his hopes centred on that man. Nothing had been said but he had a shrewd idea that when he stopped playing John Gallagher would offer him a coaching job. Then, maybe, he would begin to learn what it was all about.

The coach was past the Oval now and heading by a backstreet route for Waterloo Bridge. Sammy asked Danny Peck if he had remembered to bring the two packs of cards for the rummy school. *Think about it now, you dopes, while you've still got time.* His lips tightened. He had been only nineteen when Commoners — still a successful team then — reached their first semi-final. Manchester City beat them at Villa Park. They were back again in the semi-final the following season. Chelsea beat them at Old Trafford. Even then he had not been too upset for he was only twenty and he had a vague idea Commoners would be reaching the semi-final every year. But then had come the seasons of mediocrity. Bad luck, that was all he could say, he had improved as a player but the club went downhill and his chances of success went down with it. Then had come the temporary revival, four years ago. He still cursed to himself when he thought of that semi-final against Newcastle at Old Trafford, Manchester. It was like an old film, continually rewinding itself and playing over and over again in his head.

There were ten minutes to go and the score was two each and we knew we had the game won, all we needed was that one goal to clinch it.

We got a corner kick at the Stretford Road end. We went forward, leaving only Johnny Godfrey in goal and Brian Seymour behind me as the spare defender. I was marking Hinney in the centre circle. Everybody else was packed round the Newcastle area.

Pat Stewart took the corner. He hit it too near their goal-keeper, who caught it and kicked it upfield in one clean sequence, knowing where Hinney was. He hadn't given me much trouble, I knew I had the beating of him in the air. The ball went so high I thought it would come down with snow on it. I had to run back-wards nine or ten yards as it came dipping towards me. Hinney was backing into me but I knew it was my ball.

I timed my jump perfectly. Crash! Somebody crunched me full in the back, a tremendous thump. Instead of powering it away with my forehead I was pushed under the ball. It skidded off the back of my head. Bloody Brian Seymour, the idiot! He had been ball-watching, the stupid bastard, instead of covering. He should have seen it was my ball and got round behind me in case Hinney won the jump. But he had panicked and decided he could outjump both of us. He didn't even give me a call, which is one of the first basics a professional ever learns.

The ball went out to the left. Their right-winger, Farquhar, had started running from a deep position as soon as their goalie kicked it upfield. He sprinted onto the ball twenty yards inside our half. Seymour took the shortish route to goal to try and cut off Farquhar's run but he was yards behind. Johnny Godfrey came racing out to narrow the angle and make Farquhar go away from goal.

Hinney was sprinting towards the goal, me three yards behind him. Johnny dived and Farquhar toed the ball forward under his body. He leapt over Johnny. I thought the ball would go out of play but he caught it at the line—at least the linesman didn't say it was out, although a lot of other people did. Farquhar crossed it before Seymour could get to him, a firm, head-high ball. The ball was between me and the goal. My only chance was to head it over the bar. I flung myself headlong but as soon as my feet left the ground I knew I wasn't going to get it. All Hinney had to do was nod it into the net, simple.

I smashed my forehead down onto the ground and beat my head with my hands. I can still see that hard, dusty dirt. I can still see myself dragging to my feet. We kicked off but the whistle seemed to blow almost immediately. We had been *ten minutes* from Wembley.

I can still see me turning and sprinting for the tunnel, the first to get into the dressing-room. Without thinking I knew where I was heading. I locked myself in the lavatory and put my face against the wall and cried.

I'd lost my chance. It wouldn't come again.

He looked down the coach to where Brian Seymour was sitting with George Westbury. Seymour was thirty-five now, still on the playing staff but only as a last-choice reserve. He was only seeing this season out before he went on the coaching staff. They were the only two left from that semi-final against Newcastle. It didn't make them great friends. He cost me a cup medal, that creep, Hood thought, but at least I'm getting another chance. Seymour doesn't care, he's worked bloody hard to achieve *his* ambition. A safe number, that's what he always wanted and he's got it now, his reward for loyalty, as they call it. He never cried when he lost his medal, that creep, he always knew what he was after . . . you don't need luck to be a bloody arse-crawler.

John Gallagher suddenly got to his feet and came along the gangway handing out train tickets. The players looked at him cautiously, not too sure what his mood might be now. He didn't smile. Hood remembered standing on the terraces of Hampden as a boy when John Gallagher was Scotland's right half, he was dark and slim then, now he was solid and full-faced but still black-dark.

As John Gallagher turned to go back down the coach Steve Randall stood up.

"Oy, driver, switch on the radio then, I think that's still allowed."

Hood gave him an angry glare.

"That was nice and discreet," said Danny Peck.

They all watched John Gallagher's back but he gave no sign of having heard. Sammy Small shut his eyes and winced dramatically. Randall was blushing.

"Don't you ever think before opening your big mouth?" Hood snapped.

"Well, what's he carrying on like that for?" the goalkeeper said, huffily. "He should be trying to settle us down, not upset everybody. Wev'e got a game coming up on Saturday—or do you think he's forgotten?"

Hood gave him another glare and then turned to face the front. What Randy had said was true but it didn't make it any more welcome coming from him. They were going over Waterloo Bridge at a crawl when another bunch of people spotted the team and started waving and cheering at the coach. Most of the players waved back. Roy stared emptily over the heads of the fans.

"You're allowed to wave, Roy," said Sammy. "You ain't got cramp or anythin', have you?"

Roy ignored this.

"Have you been to the barber's again then, Roy?" asked Shack the Welshman. Roy half-turned and nodded.

"What did you ask for then—plenty on the floor?"

The mickey-taking was a good sign. John Gallagher's strange mood was not seriously upsetting them, not so far. He could hardly believe his ears, however, when Randall got to his feet again and shouted down the coach.

"Oy, Henry, how about that radio then?"

Hood cringed slightly. He saw the driver lean forward. A noisy pop number came blaring out of the speaker under the rear window. He saw John Gallagher say something to Henry. The radio went off again. Randall cursed.

"The miserable bleeder!"

"I can't get over that Peterson," said Danny Peck, shaking his head in wonder. Peterson seemed to be doing nothing. They all looked at Danny. Randall, red-faced and angry, postponed his next outburst to hear what the hell Peterson had to do with the radio.

"Wot do you mean about Peterson?" Sammy Small demanded.

"How thin he is," said Danny. "Haven't you noticed."

The others began to laugh and Randall's moment for an explosion had passed.

"You're always on about Peterson," said Sammy. "I'm beginnin' to think you fancies him."

"He smells nice, you got to admit that. Here, did I ever tell you, a friend of mine once shared a room with Peterson in Manchester. Peterson was sleeping and my friend come in and threw him over his shoulders—thought he was a pair of braces!"

"You twit," said Sammy, "I thought you was serious for once."

39

"And did I never tell you about the time my friend went swimming with Poor Old Bill?"

"Go on, I'll buy it."

"Peterson was in the pool and an alsatian dived in and got him out between its teeth, thought he was a stick."

Hood felt himself relaxing. The continual double-act could be exasperating when you felt they ought to be serious, but their clowning had changed the atmosphere in the coach. Roy asked him which team he thought would win the other semi-final, Leeds or Manchester United.

"United—if they keep up the form they showed against Celtic in the quarter-final," said Hood. "Mind you, Leeds are always a hard team to beat. I suppose it boils down to whether the Leeds defence can hold Shane."

"You think he's that good?"

"Eighteen-year-old, he beats people as if they weren't there. We used to think George Best was phenomenal—but he was playing when the game was a lot easier than it is now."

"You've been in three semi-finals and lost them all," said Roy. "Is it right what they say—the real pressure is on you in the semi-final game? I mean, you wouldn't feel so bad losing in the final at Wembley—at least you would have had the experience?"

"Dead right," said Hood. He didn't really agree but he was glad of the chance to pep Roy up a bit. "With a semi-final you're so near to Wembley—and then you lose and you've got nothing to show for it."

"And once you get to Wembley you do get something out of it, win or lose. The glory—and the money, of course."

"Too true. With the official bonus and what Peterson's organised for the pool we can make about five thousand pounds each if we get to Wembley. Just win this one on Saturday, kid, and you'll be rich!"

"You think John Gallagher's beginning to panic?"

"Nah, of course not. John Gallagher doesn't panic over small things like semi-finals."

"You would say that. You and him are getting as thick as thieves."

"He's number one, kid, don't forget it. I've been under seven managers since I first came to Oaks Common and compared to J.G. none of them could manage to put the cat out."

Roy seemed to sit happier. Hood felt quite pleased with himself. Funny how a little bit of spiel at the right moment could jolly people along. Maybe that was the secret of being a good manager.

"Come on, lads, let's have a song," he shouted.

As they came into the main concourse of Euston Station they were recognised by a group of lounging porters.

"All the best Saturday ... we'll be rootin' for yer ... give us four goals against them Scotch twits ... how yer goin', Roy? ... Up the Commoners ..."

On and on went the raucous voices. People who knew nothing about football turned to see what the shouting was about. Men leaned out to touch their arms and pat their backs. A crowd of young kids waving green and black Commoners' scarves followed them through the station, singing and chanting. Hood had never found out where these kids got their information but they were always there when the team travelled, dancing and cheering and swamping the players with autograph books.

The players spent half their lives in situations like this. In the coach or dressing-room they horsed around like a lot of teenagers themselves but as soon as they stepped out into the public gaze they immediately changed, becoming calm-faced heroes who walked modestly, self-contained, through the fun and games of the fans.

"The atmosphere here is exciting enough," said Roy above the racket. "What'll it be like at Hampden?"

"You don't know what atmosphere means till you've faced the Hampden crowd," said Hood.

Some of the players stopped at the bookstall. Hood bought the *Mirror* and the *Express*, quickly looking at the sports pages before shoving them under his arm. He saw the chairman and his party standing in the open space before the ticket barrier. He saw Wally Scott, the *Mirror* photographer, moving about in the crowd, getting shots of players and cheering teenagers, coaxing some of the team to pose with girl fans. Wally was beaming as always, everybody's friend, Fleet Street's star football photographer. When players saw him in the vicinity they knew the smell of success was in the air.

The ticket barrier had been hung over with green and black

cloth. On a big sheet of white cardboard was a hand-lettered message: GOOD LUCK THE COMMONERS!

Hood saw Mr. Jackson, the chairman, standing head and shoulders above the others, six foot two with a fine head of grey hair and a rich man's suntan, the kind that lasted the whole year round. With him was his wife, Jemima Jackson, not at all what you would have expected, a tall, sad woman in a heavy green coat that might have been fashionable when England won the World Cup back in sixty-six. With them was the chairman's brother, Norman Jackson, the vice-chairman, thirty-four, young enough to be mistaken for a player, a mistake which always gave him great pleasure. Norman had a new girl with him. Hood did not recognise the long black hair or the black and white coat. Norman usually had a good-looking richard in tow. They never lasted long, which wasn't surprising, Norman's richards tending to be pretty-pretty dolly birds with artificial faces and artificial conversations. They suited this circus atmosphere of success, all this surface glamour of crowds and photographers. They looked good at first and then you began to see how empty they were. Over the years Hood had travelled every way known to football and he knew how superficial this glamour circus really was, an old, old story, the team going places, the crowds suddenly bigger, everybody wanting to know you, everybody proving he was your buddy, every hand wanting to shake yours and to touch you, every face smiling. This was fame and it made young players feel like gods, but after a while the clutching hands and the beaming faces meant nothing to you. Of course all players would tell you it was better to be liked by the crowds than disliked, but the older pros knew just how quickly the circus would evaporate if the team lost.

"Come on, Wally," John Gallagher shouted, "we want to get on board."

"No panic, J.G.," said Wally, "the train's going to be late—somebody's trying to blow you up."

"It's just a hoax," the station master said reassuringly. John Gallagher stared at him heavily. "We're searching every inch of the train just to make sure—but there's nothing to worry about. Anonymous phone call, the usual thing. You'll be about fifteen minutes late leaving."

As soon as they heard about the delay Danny Peck and Sammy Small began to sidle away from the main party.

"Where are you two off to?" John Gallagher barked.

"Just for a cup of tea, Boss," Danny called back through the mêlée. "That all right?"

"Be back here in ten minutes—not a second later."

Peterson came towards Hood, followed by a younger man in a white raincoat, a rolled umbrella hooked over his arm.

"Alec, this is Gerald Sims of the *Guardian*," Peterson said. "He's the one who's travelling with us to Largs, you remember the arrangement?"

"Oh aye," said Hood, shaking the bloke's hand. "You're the one who's paying us a hundred pounds just to hear our small-talk, eh?"

Sims didn't look too sure of himself.

"You got the jake with you?" Hood asked.

"I beg your pardon."

Peterson laughed. Hood looked round the crowds, idly wondering about journalists in general, when he saw the fat, round face and dumpy figure of Harry the Hat pushing towards them through the crush.

"Let's go for a stroll," he said, moving Peterson and Sims in the opposite direction. He didn't want the reporter to hear the tout's cheery brand of villainy, especially on the subject of black market tickets, which was the only conversation Harry the Hat had, apart from anti-Jewish jokes, usually about himself. At the confectionery kiosk he bought some chewing gum. Peterson seemed a little bit nervous about explaining things to the *Guardian* reporter. He was probably worrying about the reception his fancy friend might get from the team—with good reason. Sammy and Danny would go a bundle on a grown man who carried an umbrella.

"I've had an approach from Whitbreads the brewers," Peterson told Hood. "They're interested in using the whole team for T.V. commercials—if we win on Saturday. They're talking about fifteen thousand quid. You think the management would have any objection?"

"I don't see why."

"I didn't think soccer players were allowed to drink," said Sims. Hood started to laugh but then he got a glimpse of John Gallagher pushing through the crowd, face very grim. He followed the manager's progress through the busy hall and saw him walking up and down the line of hooded telephone cubicles. They were all engaged. John Gallagher stood impatiently, looking at his watch and then at a station clock. Nobody moved away from the phones. John Gallagher looked at his watch again, muttered something and then started back for the platform.

"Here, Boss," Hood said, stepping in front of the manager, "Bill's got some good news. Whitbreads want to use the team for a few T.V. commercials if we get to the final. Fifteen grand they're offering. You think that's fair?"

"It wouldn't be for the players to decide," John Gallagher snapped. "That's a decision for the board to make. I don't think the chairman would approve."

They walked back to the platform in silence, John Gallagher a pace or two ahead. Hood looked at Peterson and shrugged. Peterson frowned. Crash right in—that was how players dealt with matters of delicacy. He hoped Alec's bluntness hadn't cost them fifteen thousand pounds. The train had been searched and found free of bombs. They began to pick up their bags. John Gallagher stood to one side, watching his players file through the barrier. Danny and Sammy came pushing through the bands of raving teenagers.

"Where the hell have you two been?" he demanded angrily.

"We was just finishin' our cuppa—"

"I told you ten minutes!"

"It is ten minutes, Boss, exactly," said Danny.

John Gallagher looked at his watch, breathing deeply as if making a deliberate attempt to control his anger.

"You cut it very bloody fine," he said. "Let's get on the bloody train or we'll all miss it."

Danny and Sammy made little faces at each other. They reached the barrier at the same time as Norman and his new girl. They bowed and gestured her through. Norman had excelled himself this time, Hood thought. She had extremely light blue eyes that made an unusual contrast with her black hair and fair skin. A cracker. Very tasty.

At the carriage door Wally Scott and the other photographers wanted shots of the lads climbing into the train, the usual send-off shots for the London editions, six faces grinning round a carriage door, thumbs raised from an open window. Four Scotsmen wearing tartan tammies and blue Rangers scarves came running up the platform. As they passed they yelled at the Commoners party.

"Ye won't be smilin' on Saturday night!"

"Up the Gers!"

"We are the people!"

"There's your bleedin' jocks for yer," said Sammy, digging Hood with his elbow. "Only Wednesday but they're gettin' up home for the game."

"They live in London and take our bleeding wimmin and our bleeding money but they still want Rangers to beat us," said Danny. "They think football's a holy war."

Hood threw his bag up on the rack. Just before he slumped down beside Roy he saw the top of John Gallagher's head. Roy noticed his frown.

"Something up?" he asked.

"No. Wish we were flying, that's all."

"It makes Shack and Gerry sick."

"A few vodkas and they'd have been all right."

"Gerry doesn't drink, you know that."

"I don't know what he's doing in this team then."

He shoved a stick of gum into his mouth. SCOTS C.I.D. PROBE HAMPDEN TICKET FORGERY RACKET was one of the *Mirror* headlines. He reminded himself to speak to all the lads before Harry the Hat got near them. Success brought its own complications. The more he thought about it the more he was certain Roy's strained muscle couldn't be the reason for John Gallagher's strange behaviour. It would take a lot more than that to put John Gallagher off his stride.

He thought back to the first morning John Gallagher had appeared at Oaks Common. They'd all been expecting the usual bollocks about you helping me and me helping you, but instead John Gallagher gave them a short chat about team spirit.

"When you're in a tight situation, with a pal on the floor, I want you all to get in there and help him out," was the thing Hood remembered best. It didn't take them long to regard him as the ideal boss. He treated each man as an individual, he was fair and consistent and honest. He explained to a player why he was being dropped and he filled the whole team with enthusiasm. He made them all want to win games for the club, because he was the club, as far as they were concerned. Danny Peck had summed it up.

"I want to win this bloody cup for John Gallagher more than for myself. John Gallagher knows my bloody face! He can recognise me in a pair of long trousers. Some managers I've been with, if they met me now they'd ask to take off my shoes to see if my feet were vaguely familiar."

Hood chewed hard on his gum and thought of all the stupid things that might lose him his chance of a medal. Suddenly he felt very violent.

Roy blinked with amazement as the captain smashed his big fist down on the low coffee table.

"Hampden here we bloody come," he roared down the carriage, a big, mad Scots bastard who at that moment looked fit to be caged. Other voices took up the shout. Hood jumped to his feet and banged his hands together, bawling out the Commoners chant.

"Cheer up you mournful twit," he roared down at Roy. "We're going to murder the bastards!"

5

THE following news item appeared in the *Sun*, London edition, Wednesday, March 15.

RANGERS STAR CASKIE GIVES
WARNING TO COMMONERS

Nineteen-year-old Jackie Caskie, boy wonder of Scottish football, came back to form with a bang in Glasgow Rangers 3–0 win over St. Mirren at Ibrox last night.

Caskie scored an amazing solo goal and made another, tearing open a packed St. Mirren defence with devastating speed and ball control which had the 64,000 crowd roaring their heads off. After his recent indifferent form Caskie showed why he is the man Commoners must fear in Saturday's British Cup semi-final.

Says Rangers captain Davie Lindsay: "This game was an ideal try-out for Saturday. We're all very confident we'll give Scottish football something to be proud of."

6

"COR, it's just like royalty," said Sammy Small as they milled about finding seats in the de luxe lounge carriage reserved for the Commoners party. "Prince Charles himself wouldn't be ashamed to travel with us."

"He'd be ashamed to travel with you," said Danny Peck.

"Why me in particular?" Sammy demanded, glaring indignantly.

"Well he ain't got your class of money, has he? He'd be ashamed he's so poor."

Instead of the upholstered benches of the old rough and ready days of railway travel each man had a swivel armchair in black leather, set in groups of fours and twos round low-level coffee tables. Flush into the wall under each window was a T.V. screen and if you didn't fancy television you could listen to piped music on miniaturised headphones. At the top end of the carriage was a bar where a white-jacketed attendant was checking his refrigerated supplies.

Before he fell into his seat Danny was already pulling his tie away from his neck with a desperate twisting of his chin, as though the knot was choking him. Farther up the coach Steve Randall was still shouting *Hampden here we come*, going on too long, as usual. Sammy was trying to find space on the rack for his bag. Danny suddenly snapped his fingers.

"Blast it!"

"Okay," said Sammy, looking down, "come out with it, what've you forgot?"

"My glasses," said Danny, horror all over his face. Sammy frowned.

"But you don't wear glasses," he said.

"Oh." Danny's wide-eyed face took on a daft clown's grin. "It doesn't matter then."

48

"You berk! I wish you'd stop makin' feeble jokes and do something about this bag of yours. It's too big for this bleedin' rack. I can't get mine in."

"Why not—it's small enough! I've never seen such a small bag. I s'pose you've only brought one bleeding shirt. I daresay you think you'll borrow all my lovely gear, eh?"

"I've got two shirts," Sammy said. "You can stick your lovely gear up your lovely khyber."

With an aggressive shoving movement, standing on tiptoe, shins pressed hard against the edge of the low table, the little man jammed his bag into a narrow space. Even as he eased past Danny into the window seat his forefinger was pulling his tie-knot loose and his left hand was unbuttoning his jacket. Shack, already slumped in the other window seat, gave them both a look of suspicious appraisal, rolled his eyes towards the roof and settled back in apparent slumber.

"I haven't got you two for four bloody hours, have I?" he groaned, eyes closed. "Why couldn't it be some little darling who sits with me, for once? Oh no, what do I get—Sammy Small, Britain's ugliest footballer!"

Sammy started a long spiel about how he was, in fact, one of the best-looking players in the First Division. The real test, he said, would be to shave the heads of all the players in the game. With no hair to hide behind you would soon find out who were the really handsome blokes. Hair, he reckoned, was saving the bacon of a lot of really repulsive geezers. Then he wanted to know where the bleeding cards were. Danny looked down the gangway of the carriage, seeing all the familiar faces doing all the familiar things, pushing bags onto racks, pulling off jackets, patting hairstyles into place, bending low to stare at a girl on the opposite platform, shouting diabolical insults at each other, whistling and whooping at the girl. It was one of the best parts of being a professional, travelling with the team, all mates together, all doing and saying the same things. You never felt alone, never had a chance to be alone.

"Hey, Shack, look out," Sammy said, "there's a lovely little richard comin' to sit beside you."

"Where?" Shack jerked himself upright, craning his neck to look back along the carriage.

"Is anyone sitting here?" Peterson asked.

49

"Even if there was there would still be enough room for you, Bill," Sammy said.

Peterson raised an indolent eyebrow and sat down next to Shack, who folded back into his sleeping position, moaning with disappointment. A whistle blew and the train began to slide along the platform.

In the four seats at the end of the carriage nearest the dining-car sat the chairman's party, George Jackson and his wife in the window seats, Norman Jackson sitting opposite the new girl on the outside. As the train moved out of the station the chairman found himself looking first at the girl Carole and then at his wife. Norman didn't have many talents but the ability to enjoy himself was one of them.

"Well we're on our way," he said. "I'm going to have a brandy and soda."

"It's too early for me," said Jemima Jackson, grimacing at Carole, as if to enlist her support.

"I had no idea football was like this," said Carole, looking round the carriage. "You travel in real luxury."

"They were losing so much business to the airlines they came up with the idea of these club lounges to win back our custom," said the chairman. "Most of the top teams use them for long journeys. A lot of players hate flying—something to do with the ear balance mechanism, I suppose."

"I think they're just cowards about flying," said Norman. He was hoping that he and George would be able to change seats, possibly when lunch was served. The prospect of a long train journey in close proximity to his sister-in-law did not appeal to him.

"Let's call the waiter, shall we?" said George Jackson. Norman turned in his seat and held up his hand to catch the attendant's attention. George Jackson offered cigarettes bearing the club crest from a gold dispenser case also engraved with the Commoners crest. Jemima did not smoke. Norman preferred one of his own ninety-shilling cigars. Across the gangway Paul Franks, the club doctor, was sitting opposite George Westbury, the physiotherapist. George Jackson had been annoyed when Norman said he was bringing the girl, for the doctor normally sat with the chairman's party and George Jackson much preferred his company to

50

that of Norman's girls, who were generally very dreary, pretty little nonentities of the kind players called one-night stands, no doubt because no sensible man could stand them longer than one night. But this Carole was certainly in a different class. She had approached them on a business basis and he had left Norman to deal with her. Now he wished he had handled it himself. He looked quickly at his wife but on this occasion she had not been reading his thoughts.

"Did I hear Norman saying that you were a model, my dear?" Jemima asked.

"I've given it up," Carole said. "I'm in the cosmetics business now. I'm hoping to interest your husband's company into giving me the franchise for cosmetic boutiques in the Jackson hotels."

"That sounds very interesting, my dear," said Jemima, who knew exactly why the girl was with them but preferred, as always, to hide behind an outward pose of simple ignorance. "You're quite young to be a businesswoman."

Carole smiled.

"Tell me, Mr. Jackson—" she began.

"George, please, we're all one big happy family here."

"There's one thing I've always wanted to know about footballers—why do they hug and kiss each other so much when they score a goal on television? They're not exactly effeminate, are they?"

"On the contrary," said George Jackson. "I can vouch for that." She was a most attractive girl but he wished she wouldn't speak so loudly. Her voice was carrying over the low shelf that separated them from the next table. This was his club but he was very conscious of the gulf between the professionals and himself and he did not want to be made look silly, even by association. No amount of money could buy membership of the freemasonry of those who played the game for a living. To keep the respect of the professionals required a very delicate touch.

Paul Franks had been listening. He leaned over towards them from the other side of the gangway, a smile on his fat, ruddy face.

"I think if you were playing, my dear, they'd go a lot further than hugging and kissing."

"Go away, you old lecher," said Norman.

The doctor made ogling motions with his bushy white eyebrows. George Westbury laughed with the rest but said nothing.

He knew how to tread lightly in this kind of company. He didn't have any inferiority feelings towards the chairman but he'd been in this game when they counted the money in shillings and over the years he'd seen them come and go—the great and the famous, forgotten heroes who were now anonymous men at factory benches—and always he had been determined to survive in the game. He'd held the job of physiotherapist through ten years and seven managers and three boardroom bust-ups and he intended to go on holding it through the fat years ahead. When he caught the chairman's eye he smiled politely. The chairman barely nodded. In business, George Jackson found, relationships were always clear-cut, master and servant, superior and inferior. In football the divisions were less well defined. At the club his employees were highly-skilled specialists who knew more about the game than he did. Even the youngest sixteen-year-old apprentice had more access to the inner mysteries of football, what actually happened out there on the pitch. He had a vague impression that, behind his back, men like Westbury did not give him their full respect. No doubt they took their line from John Gallagher.

At the very thought of the manager's name he felt a swift twinge of resentment. He could see John Gallagher's dark head diagonally across the gangway, talking to Harry Barnes the coach. He frowned, telling himself that he must try to relax. There must be no unnecessary tensions over the next few days. Winning the game on Saturday meant everything. He took a long sip of brandy. It helped, a little. He called out to the doctor.

"I say, Paul, tell Carole about that cut Dave Peacock got in the West Ham game," he said. "That should convince her there's nothing sissy about our lads."

He smiled benignly. The small boy who had climbed the wall to see Commoners forty and more years ago still got a very distinct thrill at finding himself on the inside of the game.

Harry Barnes had several sheets of paper on the low table between himself and John Gallagher, giving the manager his ideas on various midfield plans to counter the menace of Jackie Caskie.

The manager did not appear interested. He stared emptily at the sheets of scribbled diagrams. Harry Barnes went on.

"If they're going to come at us we could bring Shack and Sammy back for the first half-hour, leave Roy and Dave up front and

Wiggy operating deep." He thought for a second, then leaned forward. "You think it's serious with Roy—the injury?"

John Gallagher shook his head.

"No, he'll be all right."

"I'll bet the chairman wasn't too pleased when he heard."

John Gallagher frowned. It had all been such a shock on Tuesday afternoon when the clinic phoned that he'd forgotten to telephone the chairman that night about Roy's strained muscle. If Jackson thought he had been kept in the dark there was bound to be another row. The chairman of a club was supposed to be informed immediately of all serious developments.

"Don't mention Roy's trouble to anyone else," he said to Harry Barnes. "I want to cut out as much tension as possible."

"Tension?" Harry Barnes frowned. He was young and redhaired and freckled and he made John Gallagher feel quite old, although, in fact, at thirty-nine he was two years older than the manager. "Look, J.G., it may be none of my business—" he suddenly appeared unsure of himself.

"What isn't?"

"That business about Riddle's bag, they're all talking about it—"

"The clown forgot it, that's all."

"Is something else bothering you, J.G.?"

"No, why, what makes you think that?"

"Nothing, I just wondered."

Yes, John Gallagher thought, you just wondered but you're scared to come out and say it. You know something's wrong with me but you're a bloody yes-man and you haven't the guts to make an issue out of it.

Harry Barnes had already been chief coach when John Gallagher arrived at Oaks Common. He'd been with Commoners under three managers and had never applied for the job himself. He was a competent chief coach. Perhaps he had decided that he was safer as number two when things were going wrong. Now things were changing. Harry was bright enough to know that in football the real rewards for success went to number one. He was beginning to wonder if he was ready to take the top job. Travelling to Euston station with the chairman, instead of reporting to the ground, that could be a sign he was pushing himself forward for bigger things.

Yet none of it seemed very important now, not after the phone call from the clinic and the unbelievable things they'd told him after the third X-ray this morning . . . why me, he kept thinking. Why *me*?

"Look, Harry," he said wearily when the coach began to show him more diagrams, "I can never concentrate properly on trains. Let's leave it till we get to Scotland, eh, we can have a proper go at it then."

"Sure," said Harry Barnes.

John Gallagher sat back, lifting the *Daily Telegraph*, seeing words that meant nothing. He could try to phone the clinic again at Crewe. Surely they would know something by then? If he had to wait much longer he would go out of his mind.

Alec Hood had been keeping an eye on John Gallagher and he was growing more certain that something serious was bothering the boss. He could *smell* it. Beside him Roy was reading a detective story. Opposite him sat Tommy Riddle looking morose, no doubt bothering himself sick over the bollocking he'd got in the bus, staring out of the window, mouth slack with gloom.

"You'd better get into the card school, Jimmy," said Hood. "You look like death warmed up."

"Stuff the cards," said Riddle.

Hood knew there was more to Jimmy's depression that the slagging he'd got from the boss over the missing bag. Vernon Jones, the last Commoners manager, had bought Jimmy from Walsall for seven thousand pounds. He was big for a winger but exceptionally fast and in four seasons at Oaks Common he'd scored sixty-two goals, which would have established him in the first team beyond all doubt but for the advent of Wiggy. Jimmy had gone through a bad spell at the beginning of this season, giving Wiggy his chance to become a first team regular. Until now Jimmy had been lucky. For most of the season there had always been one forward or another out through injury and he'd missed very few first team games. The crunch was coming now. If Roy was fit John Gallagher was going to have to drop somebody for Hampden. Jimmy would be thinking the bollocking was John Gallagher's way of letting him know he was out of favour. Some managers warned you in advance by being especially nice to you, others prepared you for the chop by going the other way. John Gallagher would be feeling guilty at the prospect of dishing out the biggest single disappointment of Jimmy's career. Bad feeling between them would make it easier to tell Jimmy he was out of the team. This was how Jimmy would be reasoning it all out. Like a lot of players his self-confidence rested on a knife edge. When things were going well he could take a little shouting match in his stride, for success meant total happiness.

Beside him Roy was kneading down on the injured thigh with the heel of his palm. A lot of people, even in the team, thought Roy was a cold-blooded guy who cared only about money and his own personal success, but he knew Roy put up this cold, withdrawn front as a protection. Roy was a shy, sensitive lad who had suddenly found himself up to his neck in the hysterical pressures of big-time London football, fantastic pressures, the relentless publicity that surrounded anybody who'd been bought for one hundred and forty thousand pounds. Smooth-talking men chased Roy night and day, some to get his views for newspapers and magazines, some to offer him big money for the use of his face and his name. He'd tried to help Roy through this early stage but even after all his years in the game he'd had no real idea of what the pressures were, for a headline star ... th y pestered him relentlessly, a hundred quid a week for a ghosted newspaper column, Roy, you won't even have to read the stuff we write for you, Roy, let me be your advertising agent, Roy, let me handle your literary career, Roy, come on T.V., Roy, open our new supermarket, Roy, this one's for a good charity, Roy, put your name to our new wonder health food, Roy, our new wonder hair-lotions and plastic footballs and breakfast cereals and shoes and toothpaste and petrol ... make the money while you can, Roy, you're a big star now, Roy, the millions are interested in you, Roy, never mind that you don't eat our cornflakes or use our hair-cream, Roy, it's the endorsement business, Roy, nobody cares whether it's true, Roy, don't be naïve, Roy, you won't be a big name for ever, Roy, grab it while it's going, Roy. . .

Success, they called it, when they wouldn't leave you alone.

"Is this cup run doing much good for the sweet shop?" he asked Riddle, hoping to turn Jimmy's thoughts from imminent despair onto his ambitions to become a confectionery tycoon.

"Yeah, it helps a bit," said the big winger, looking even more sorrowful. "But it also means I haven't the bloody time to spend behind the counter."

"God, Jimmy, you find a dull lining in every cloud. Cheer up for Christ's sake. I'll get you a coffee."

Dave Peacock and Dave Spencer had been doing the *Telegraph* crossword together, the paper on the table between them, their necks screwed round so that both could read the clues at the same time. Danny Peck was just going to ask them why they didn't lash out on two copies of the paper and have a race, with money on it, when Dave Peacock slammed down his ballpoint pen.

"Are you doing this crossword or looking at that bird?" he demanded. "If you've lost bloody interest I'll do it myself, save my neck getting stiff."

Spencer, known as Debonair Dave, said nothing. Danny Peck craned his neck, leaning out into the gangway to see what Debonair was looking at. Norman's new girl was laughing at something the doctor was saying. Danny could understand why Dave was clocking her so keenly. She was very tasty and classy with it. Just right for Dave, beautiful and smart and glossy. Danny had liked the look of her face when they'd almost bumped into her at the ticket barrier. She looked as though she had a sense of humour. Far too good for Norman. Far too good for himself, was something else he had thought. He had never had a bird like her, always found that type too high-powdered and brainy. He knew how he operated best. Bump it into 'em and then wonder what all the fuss had been about, find a subtle way of saying a quick goodbye, like looking at the time and saying, "Here, I'm late—ta ta, mush!"

"Save your energy, big boy," he said, hitting Debonair Dave's elbow with his hand. "She's out of your class, not one of them run-of-the-mill scrubbers you're used to."

"You must be joking," said Debonair Dave, his dark, film star's face going all haughty. "Birds are two a penny. She's no different. They're all easy meat, to an expert."

"She's different."

"Meaning what?"

"Meaning you couldn't pull her."

"No? Hmmph. I could get a date with her before we get off this train."

"How much?"

"Tenner?"

"Only a cockle? Not confident?"

"Twenties then?"

"A score? You're on."

News of the bet travelled round the team. Danny was craning sideways to look down the carriage when she looked up. She must have seen all the faces having a butcher's at her but she gave no sign of noticing. Class there, she wouldn't have anything to do with Debonair. She was travelling where the real money was. Pity, really, when a girl like her let money and that sort of thing dominate her life. She looked as though she could be really nice, too.

"I'll run a book on it," Sammy was saying. "You want odds?"

"Shut up," said Danny. "Ain't you got no respect for nothing?"

"Hark at Preacher bleedin' Peck! Who laid the bet in the first place, eh?"

"I only bet Debonair cos he thinks he's jack the lad," Danny said to Peterson, just a slight touch of guilt in his voice. He looked across at Debonair. "Look at him, the flash twit, thinks he's Mister Wonderful. I'll tell you about him, Bill—"

Debonair pretended to find this conversation beneath his contempt but Peterson could see him barely controlling a desire to smirk with pleasure.

"—it's in our last game with Crystal Palace," Danny went on, "Debonair gets in a mix-up in their goal mouth—next we see he's flat on the deck, blood gushing down his face. I run over—he's groaning and twisting about in agony. 'Is it bad, Dan?' he gasps, sounding like he's due to snuff it any minute. 'You got a kick in the head,' I says. 'Where?' he moans. 'Just above the hairline,' I says. He opens his eyes. 'Can't you see it?' he asks. 'No, it's above the hairline.' He sighs with relief. 'Thank Christ for that,' he says, 'I'm going dancing tonight.' "

Only Peterson had not heard this before but they all seemed to find it brilliantly amusing, including Debonair Dave himself.

"Oh yeah, Dave knows wot's important and wot ain't," said Sammy. "You know wot he always says to the trainer when he gets a kick in the niagaras?"

"Niagaras?" said Peterson.

"Niagara Falls, balls! Maybe you know 'em better as your orchestras or generals? Orchestra stalls—General de Gaulles. Anyway when Dave gets a boot in the balls and George Westbury runs out to give him treatment, he always says, 'Don't feel 'em, count 'em!' "

57

Peterson found it hard to reconcile this Danny with Danny the Destroyer Peck of the sports page, the ruthless defensive player whose career had been punctuated by fights and fines and suspensions. He had calmed down a lot since John Gallagher had brought him to Oaks Common, but Mercy was still not his middle name.

"I'm glad to see you weren't upset by John Gallagher's little outburst back there."

"Upset, Bill? Why should we be upset? Most managers don't think they are managers unless they're shouting at somebody."

"I can't think of many other jobs where highly-paid grown men would get bawled at in public by the boss," said Peterson. "A shop steward would have called the whole factory out. I wouldn't have taken it myself, I don't think."

"Well, Bill, it's as well you're not in this line of work," said Danny. "People blow up now and again, it's just part of the game —just tension, I s'pose. Anyway, John Gallagher would have to go a lot stronger than that before we'd get bothered. The only thing that bothered me was wondering what was bothering him."

"You have any idea what it could be?" Peterson asked.

"He'll be all right on the night," said Sammy, shrugging the question aside.

"Right then," said Peterson, "let's get down to this stuff for the brochure."

With help from Sammy, who had a phenomenal memory for anything connected with football, even to being able to recite whole teams from cup finals played years before he was born, Danny went through the facts of his playing life. He'd been born in Plaistow, father a docker, and left school at fifteen, the day it was legal, to join West Ham as an apprentice. He failed to make the grade. West Ham discarded him at eighteen, just one of hundreds of boy hasbeens whose dream had ended before it began. However, he was lucky to be picked up by Orient, where he did a little better. After a couple of seasons Fulham bought him as the make-weight in a part-exchange deal. At Craven Cottage he had finally found his feet as a professional, not as the constructive, attacking midfield man he had started out to be, but as a purely defensive player. Peterson remembered seeing him about then, a short, stocky man whose relentless aggression was channelled into grim destruction.

Danny was quite happy at Craven Cottage but Ipswich had

offered forty thousand for him, they were in trouble and half-way through the season they needed an out-and-out destroyer to bolster their defence. He had been a little surprised that Fulham were willing to let him go but as he hadn't asked for a transfer he was entitled to a few thousand out of the deal.

"You didn't really want to go to Ipswich?" Peterson asked.

"Not really—I don't like anywhere outside London much."

"But you were willing to move, just for the money?"

"If the club wanted to sell me I obviously wasn't included in their plans for the future, was I? I mean, I'm a professional, I've got to go where there's a job for me, don't I?"

"Have boots will travel?"

"Yeah, a bit like that."

"That's always interested me. How can a player be with a club one day, giving all he's got—then next day he's transferred to another club—can you really switch loyalties over night, just like that?"

"When a club buys me they show they think something of me, I give 'em all I've got."

"But can you change your emotions overnight? I mean, just suppose Sammy was transferred to Rangers in time for Saturday's match? Would you really be able to treat him just like any other player—your closest mate?"

"Course I would. I'd go into Sammy just as hard as anyone else. And he'd whack me just the same. The moment the whistle blows you ain't got no old friends—not on the other side you ain't! But we'd know it wasn't personal—just the game. And afterwards I'd buy him a drink and—"

"That's a bit strong," Sammy interrupted. "I'd have to buy you a drink cos you never buy a drink."

"Can a club really buy your hundred per cent loyalty and enthusiasm and effort?" Peterson went on. "Surely after moving about as much as you have you must become a bit—well, in-different? Not really heart-broken if your current club wins or loses?"

"Nah, winning is everything, Bill. That's what the game is all about. Maybe your first club is your real love, of course—specially if you signed for a team you worshipped as a boy, like I did. It comes as a bit of a shock when they don't want you. Your second club suffers a bit—for a while you begin to think this is just a job,

59

take the money and that's that. Now a manager will tell you the club is bigger than the player—but suddenly it dawned on me—the game is bigger than the club. I was playing the game long before any club came for me. My first loyalty is to football. I love the game for itself. We all do, you'll find—ninety-nine per cent of us anyway. When I go out it don't matter what strip I'm wearing—I go out to play football and to win. It's the only way I know. And if you think a wandering twit like me has a soft spot for his old clubs you can forget it. I want to win every game but when I'm playing against an old club I want to win really badly. Just to show 'em. You didn't think I was good enough for you, eh? Right then, you twits, I'll bloody well prove you were wrong. I love it when we beat West Ham, *love* it." He looked quite vicious for a moment. Then he added, almost sadly, "though I don't s'pose they even remember me at Upton Park today."

Peterson looked at Danny for a moment, realising how little he had ever guessed of what went on in the minds of players. He asked Danny about his reputation for being dirty.

"I was never once sent off or had my name taken for dirty fouls," Danny said. "You know what an over the top was?"

He demonstrated in the space between Peterson and himself at the end of the low table, still sitting down, shoving the sole of his right shoe against Peterson's shin, twelve inches off the ground, above an imaginary ball. 'Showing six' was a phrase he used, meaning the six studs on the sole of a football boot, a type of foul difficult to detect, consisting of a kick or stabbing downward boot over the top of the ball, almost impossible for the inexpert eye to detect from a genuine miss, the scientific way to maim or injure an opponent.

"I always got done for retaliating against cloggers who did that to me," said Danny. "If I'd been the kind of bloke who could check his temper I reckon I might never even had my name taken."

"Oh yeah?" Sammy winked at Peterson. "But why did all them other geezers have a go at you in the first place, eh? Cos they didn't like your underarm perspiration?"

"Forwards get fed up being tackled, that's all."

"And you're no shrinking violet when it comes to the tackle, are you?" Peterson said. "Sometimes when you go in I feel myself wincing with pity for the poor bloke you're going to hit.

Dave Spencer, for instance, he doesn't crunch them the way you do."

"It's different for him, he's operating more in midfield. He's still got to go in hard and get the ball but he has to think one move ahead because he's in midfield—not just get the ball away from the other guy but what to do with it next. So he'll try to intercept the ball or whip it away from the other man's toes, rather than crash in feet first. He doesn't want to leave himself on the ground because his job is to be constructive. At the back it's stop 'em first and foremost, so your tackles can be pretty crunching —you really only care about stopping the bloke with the ball. They shall not pass. Another point, you find most defenders will try to give the opposition forward a bit of a thump at the start of a game—just to get across the message who's going to be boss. That needles a few of them!"

"I saw you that time you thumped Vic Thomas of Charlton. You crunched into him all right!"

"Yeah—me and Vic was only talking about that the other night."

"You're still friends then—after the fight you had?"

"Oh yeah. Matter of fact we were out together the same Saturday night as the fight. Most pros cool off in the dressing-room, I never heard of anybody going on with it outside the ground or anything like that. Crikey—look at Sammy and his cousin, Brian Sparks of Queens Park Rangers! I've seen things going on between them in a game that made me wince! Yet they're thick as thieves off the field."

"You know why that is?" Sammy said. "Cos we are thieves! Least most of the family is. Brian and me reckon if we hadn't got into the professional game we'd have become villains. Bound to."

"Soccer saved him from a life of crime," Danny said, looking ironically at his little pal. Sammy grinned.

"Unlike you, me old son, the way you play it is a life of bleedin' crime."

Sitting with their backs to Danny and Sammy in the next group were Andy Gurr and Gerry Williamson, the two fullbacks, both trying to read through a verbal battle between Wiggy Ingrams and Brian Seymour, the old man of the squad. Gurr and Williamson were a quiet, domesticated pair who always roomed together.

They were both twenty-three and had both joined Commoners as apprentices in the same season, Gurr from school in Maidstone, Kent, Williamson from school in Chelmsford, Essex. They had married sisters from Pinner, Middlesex, and lived within walking distance of each other on a new residential estate at Chertsey, Surrey. Gurr, who was reading a gardener's digest, did not look up when Wiggy got to his feet and dragged his briefcase out of the rack, a most extraordinary briefcase made not of leather but of velvet and orange velvet at that, the most vivid orange Wiggy had found in any shop in London, looking deliberately for something to outrage reactionaries like Seymour.

"An orange velvet briefcase," Seymour sneered, hoping to catch the interest of the two fullbacks and enlist their support in badgering Wiggy. "I'm surprised you don't wear an orange wig, you horrible little poof."

"Now then, Brian," said Wiggy patiently. "I've explained about the wigs a hundred times. They're fashion headpieces for men, not wigs. The idea isn't to look ludicrous—an orange wig, indeed! The idea is a different hairstyle for whatever mood you're in, a different look for different occasions. Women have had them for years—why not men?"

"Men? Get lost."

"We think six different hair changes would do the average man—I'm sure we've something to suit you, Brian. Why don't you drop by the salon some time for a colour-matching session? I could fit you up at trade rates."

"Piss off!"

Wiggy shook his head gently and took a sketching pad out of his briefcase. Men of Seymour's generation called anyone a poof who did not go in for prison haircuts and bitten fingernails. Men of Seymour's generation still thought of themselves as loyal club servants, happy to be in the game at all and grateful to their masters for being paid wages to use the only talent they had.

For Wiggy it was all different. To begin with he did not come from the traditional working-class reservoirs of London football talent—Shepherd's Bush, East and West Ham, Dagenham, Paddington, Barking, Hackney, Edmonton, but from Hampstead, where his father was a carpenter. They lived in a working-class council block and he'd gone to a state comprehensive school, like most of the team, but all around him he had seen wealth and arrogance and phoniness and some of it had rubbed off. He could have gone in for commercial art but he had a natural flair for football and he found this impressed his classmates more than the artistic stuff. He signed for Commoners at sixteen. After a year of cleaning the boots of the senior players, sweeping out dressing-rooms, rolling the pitch and all the usual apprentice players' chores he would have chucked the game in, but his phenomenal ball skill and self-confidence brought him into the first team at seventeen. Then Riddle's bad spell had been his chance to become a first team regular. Having been born without what they called the embarrassment factor, he soon found ways to make himself not only a soccer star but a soccer celebrity.

He scored one goal against West Bromwich Albion that made him a national football figure—by a happy coincidence television was covering the game. Shack chipped a long ball into the West Brom penalty area. It came to Wiggy's head. Any other forward would have headed for goal, or back-flicked it to give one of the other forwards a scoring chance. Not Wiggy. He took it on his forehead, killing the bounce, nodding it up a few feet, then lay on his back in mid-air and hammered an overhead bicycle shot into the net. It was that week's T.V. goal of the season.

Established as a young star he became a front-page celebrity with the argument over the length of his hair. Business offers flowed in. He became a partner in a trendy Chelsea boutique for young males about town. Women's magazines seized on him as the new glamour male. He recorded an L.P. He designed clothes. He went on T.V. talkshows and said audacious things. He openly announced that he was living, without benefit of marriage, with a well-known model. A bishop denounced him. A life-size colour poster of him in a floral-patterned blouse outsold all other posters of pop and film stars.

Through all this he kept a straight face, for to him the joke depended on seeing how peculiar people could be. His first dabbles in eccentricity only proved to him that the world was run like a circus. Cynical wasn't quite the right word for how he reacted to his lucrative notoriety. It was more an amused kind of curiosity.

"You think this will catch on, Brian?" He held out his sketching pad, with the rough of a new idea for men's suits, Bermuda trousers with knee-length socks and a flared smock jacket.

"Bloody awful! God almighty, if I'd behaved like you when I was your age—you know what the senior pros would have done?"

"Something uncouth, no doubt."

"They'd have cuffed my ear that's what they'd have done, no two ways about it."

"That sounds sexy, Brian, give it a try."

"Jesus wept!"

Seymour went off to the bar without asking what the others wanted. Andy Gurr put his gardening book on his lap.

"Brian will go berserk in a minute. Why do you always stir it up with him? You know you don't mean half the nonsense you tell him?"

"I know it, you know it—why the hell doesn't he know it?"

"I like Brian," said Gerry Williamson, not looking up from his book. "He's a good pro. Backbone of the game."

"How bloody dreary," said Wiggy. "That the kind of crap they give you in that computer jargon?"

Gerry smiled condescendingly and went back to his beginner's textbook on computer languages, part of a course he was taking through the Professional Footballers' Association vocational training scheme. All players were encouraged to study some trade or profession but not many had the patience. Randy had started to learn photography but had chucked the course. Andy Gurr was supposed to be starting a retail management course in the summer. Only Dave Peacock, Barry Ross and himself were actually taking vocational training seriously. Dave was learning hotel management, Barry Ross was studying life insurance—which always made Sammy annoyed.

"Studying for your old age?" he usually snorted, looking disdainfully at young Barry. "You ain't even learned how to play football yet, you teenage twit!"

Sammy, like many others, said the pressure of the game was enough to contend with in your playing days. Andy thought it was all right for Sammy to take that attitude—he would always fall on his feet—but he felt sorry for those players who would one day find themselves walking away from the ground for the last time with nothing to do and nowhere to go and no other skill but the ability to play a game for which their bodies were no longer fit. The very thought made him shiver. He looked at Wiggy, who was doodling on his sketching pad. He wondered what really went on in Wiggy's head. Wiggy was a natural and like all naturals he took the game for granted, as if it was the easiest thing in the world to play top-class soccer. All parts of the game were easy to a natural, except the hard work. Naturals never wanted to work. Yet there was more to Wiggy than inborn talent. In the last issue of *Winner* it had said that Wiggy actually did the books for his five boutiques and spent two evenings a week at book-keeping classes.

"A lot of players have lost their money in business ventures in which they left everything to someone else to look after," Wiggy had said. "Well, no con-man is going to skin me."

This just proved to Andy that you could spend two or three years in the same team as another bloke and never see beyond the fooling.

"I suppose we're all a bit square to you, Wiggy," he said.

"I dunno—okay, you are. Why are you all so happy to jog along doing the same old things, grateful for what they hand you? Anybody can be a millionaire, if they work at it. You could do it, Andy, make a name for yourself overnight, become a celebrity—just like that."

"Oh yeah? How?"

"Always wear one of your own roses in your buttonhole when you're coming to the ground—Saturdays and weekdays. Become the player who wears the rose. George Best grew his hair long, Derek Dougan shaved it off, Danny Blanchflower walked out of *This is Your Life*, I got my wigs. Remember that American footballer, Namath—he said on the telly he always had a few whiskies and a good screw the night before the game. They played to capacity crowds from then on. It's just a case of drawing attention to yourself so that you get off the sports pages onto the front pages. It's easier to make money than not make it."

"I wouldn't fancy all the bullshit," said Andy. "Money isn't that important."

"It will be when you have to give up the game."

"What'll you do when you hang up your boots, Wiggy?" Gerry asked, eyes still on a page of his weird computer language. "Join a youth club?"

Brian Seymour came back and picked up his football magazine. He sipped his tea and ignored Wiggy. There was an interesting article in *Winner* by old Vic Morecambe on the changes in football. He would have liked to discuss it but Wiggy would only take the mickey. The thing that got the acid rising in him was the awful feeling that Wiggy could be right. He'd strained and sweated and worried his guts out all these years and now it was almost over and what the hell could he say he'd achieved as a footballer? One mistake had cost him the friendship of the man he admired most in the whole of football. Alec Hood had never forgiven him for that stupid collision in the Newcastle semi-final. He'd gone on hoping somehow the chance would come to make it up to Alec, but it would never come now. That was all he had achieved — to be known as the guy who had cost his team their big chance of playing at Wembley.

7

THE following article is reprinted by permission of *Winner*, the football magazine.

THE REVOLUTION HAS GONE FAR
ENOUGH, SAYS VIC MORECAMBE

Soccer's longest-serving manager, celebrates his 30th year in the hotseat this month. Here he gives his opinions about the dramatic changes soccer has seen in the last decade—and what is still to come.

When I first became a manager, players earned a maximum of £20 a week. Heavy shinguards were still the rule and greasy dubbin was rubbed on high ankle boots. The ball was leather and had a heavy lace. Teams still lined up in the classic pyramid shape, goalkeeper, two fullbacks, three halfbacks, five forwards. Players went third-class on trains, directors first. Nobody had ever beaten England on English soil. And it *was* soil in those days—for they used to play on grass.

Then came the abolition of the maximum wage and the invasion of Europe. For the first time British teams became defence-minded. Rewards for success were so great, especially for clubs who got into the big European competitions, that the game changed its character.

Violence was common, on and off the field. Mounted police had to control gang warfare between rival factions of 'skinheads', teenage louts who wore big 'bovver' boots and even, at one stage, carried crowbars and meathooks!

The terrible tragedy at Ibrox Park, Glasgow, when 66 people were killed, really gave the whole of football the impetus to look at itself afresh.

The soccer revolution that followed is almost ten years old this month. Has it been a success?

Definitely! First of all, nobody can deny the success of having almost all our referees drawn from the ranks of ex-players. At £60 a week and compulsory retirement not till 50, many older players have found refereeing a worthwhile second career.

At the same time the scoring system was overhauled, to discourage grim, negative play. With four points for a win, one for a draw and none for a non-scoring draw, there was no longer any profit in travelling to an away game with the sole intention of stopping the other team from scoring. Forwards came back into their own. The new, fulltime referees stamped out the various 'professional' and tactical fouls that had given the game a bad name. At the same time the disciplinary bodies not only suspended dirty players for long periods, but began to fine clubs for fielding players convicted of dirty play. Managers soon found it wiser to stamp out deliberate fouling. The 'clogger' became a liability to his own club.

The first two-year gaol sentences for terracing troublemakers very quickly achieved peace in our grounds—something all the police riot squads, dogs, mounties, two-way radios, surveillance by binoculars had been unable to do.

We were then at stage two of the revolution. Most clubs were operating at a loss. The top dozen or so were making disproportionate fortunes.

Under the Farson Plan the Third and Fourth Divisions of the League were abolished in favour of area football, our present North, Midlands and Southern leagues. Players with these clubs had the option of going part-time. Many clubs that were almost bankrupt under the old system were saved by the cutback in travelling and staff expenses.

There was a lot of opposition to the Farson Plan — and to the complete abolition of the player retention system. In the old days a player signed for a club and was then its property for as long as it wanted to retain him. Discontented players were usually transferred to a new club — but they had no right to change their employers.

Nowadays a player signs a contract for as many years as he and his club mutually agree. At the end of his one, two, or three-year contract period the player is a completely free agent, able to sign for any club that wants him, without any transfer fee to his old club.

Many said this would make football into a game of musical chairs, with players drifting in droves from club to club. We know now this wasn't true. Most players don't want to move — they have houses and children at school and friends and roots just like everyone else.

Players will tell you today they are treated with more consideration. And the richer clubs get no more of the game's stars than they did before. As the players' union always maintained, the richest club in the country can only field one centre-forward — and stars don't join a club which can't promise to give them regular football.

There were other, minor changes. We now have two outfield substitutes and a goalkeeper substitute allowed during any part of a match. Injured players, as a result, are taken off the field earlier, no longer asked to play on and possibly aggravate their injuries.

My young players laugh when I tell them we used to settle drawn cup matches by tossing a coin — or having a ten-kick penalty competition. A real circus, that was those ten penalty fiascos. Today we settle these games by giving the result to the team which has conceded fewer corner kicks. A corner isn't a goal but it's some indication of the way the game actually went.

I'm convinced soccer is a lot healthier and cleaner and more enjoyable now. I see no need for more changes. I'm totally behind the F.A. and the League and in banning all forms of sideline coaching.

Soccer is an art form. It can never be played by robots directed from a control box. Older readers will remember great names like Dave Mackay, Johnny Haynes, Danny Blanchflower, Len Shackleton, Jackie Milburn, Nat Lofthouse. I can well imagine where they would have told the electronic manager to stuff his earhole transistors!

8

"THAT Frankie Stewart," Parkinson the reserve goalkeeper was telling the young reserves, "he was the most suspicious guy in the world. He used to hide in cupboards so he could hear what we were saying about him. Listen, I was sitting in the carsi once and sensed this movement and looked up and there he was, staring down at me over the partition!"

"What the hell for?" said Randall, the first team goalkeeper.

"Just general suspicion, I suppose. I said to him, you always reckon you've modelled yourself as a manager on Matt Busby. I can just imagine Sir Matt peering down at his players in the bogs!"

"Any guy did that to me I'd give him a bunch of fives in the mush," said Rowland, the black reserve. Randy sniffed contemptuously.

"That Vernon Jones, he was a bit of a nutcase, wasn't he?" said Parkinson amiably, looking at Randy.

"Cor, wasn't he just," said Randy eagerly, forgetting instantly his urge to tell Rowland the facts of life. "The meanest man in football. D'you ever hear about the time Brian Seymour got his ankle done and they had to carry him off on a stretcher in case it was broken? Brian's lying in the dressing-room in agony and the doc's looking at his ankle and he says, it's so swollen I'll have to cut the laces to get the boot off. Vernon Jones looks at George Westbury. 'How are we off for laces, George?' he asks."

Parkinson could easily top that story. He had a million of them. He'd been around a long time and he had only one ambition left—to go on drawing seventy pounds a week as Randy's understudy. He had no chance of playing at Hampden, unless Randy got injured, and Randy had played two hundred and eighty-five consecutive games without even breaking a fingernail. Parkinson could afford to see the funny side of football because he was not still involved in the tense battle for success.

Young Barry Ross listened to all the stories with eager eyes. Football was all he had ever dreamed of, and here he was, eighteen and actually travelling with Commoners, a full professional, a member of the first-team squad. He thought he was the luckiest individual in the whole world.

"You thought up yet how you're actually going to get near enough to that bird to chat her up?" Dave Peacock, the twin striker, asked Dave Spencer, the midfield linkman.

"Just watch me, sonny boy," said Spencer. "Take a lesson from the master."

"Confident bastard, aren't you?"

"That's what it's all about."

"That's what it's all about? You're always saying that. What the hell does it actually mean?"

"If you have to ask you wouldn't understand."

"I wish my old man had been rich. Don't you ever feel you're slumming with us common buggers—you didn't need to play football for a living, did you?"

"It's good money."

"Yeah—that's what it's all about."

"Too true, sonny boy."

Sammy took Peacock's two quid and made a little note on the back of an envelope. Danny gave him a heavy look.

"Don't worry, me old son," he said, "it's money in the bank. Debonair won't make her. Not a class darlin' like her. Cor—wouldn't mind a bit of it meself."

"You're bloody sex mad," said Danny.

"Yeah, well, I'm married, ain't I? Time you got married, Dan me old son. You take women too seriously."

"Why have you never got married, Danny?" Peterson asked.

"Never met Miss Right, Bill, that's all."

"Nah, only Missus Right," said Sammy. "You ain't met one of Danny's steady pieces, have you, Bill? She's a real darlin'. Know her nickname? Everybody's Wife!"

"Shut up!"

"Most players seem to get married in their teens," said Peterson.

"Well," said Sammy, "you gotta have somebody to look after the kids, donchya?"

"Ignore him, Bill," said Danny, "he's all talk. He's scared to death of his missus. I'll tell you, I've been near getting hitched but I always managed to get transferred in time."

Sammy threw up his arms and suddenly began to sing.

"Rangers in the night," he warbled. He stopped singing and said, quite seriously, "Them's my two all-time favourites, Sinatra and Nina Simone."

"Well, you've done your Nina Simone imitation—now give us Sinatra," said Shack, his voice very high-pitched and Welsh.

"Get stuffed," said Sammy, going into a huff.

"May I join you?" Gerald Sims asked, standing in the gangway, looking slightly nervous.

"Don't tell him any lies," said Peterson, getting up, "he'll immortalise them in fine prose."

Sims sat in Peterson's chair and looked at them expectantly. Sammy leaned towards him, face very knowing.

"Here, you had yer minces on that richard down there wiv Norman? What's the score, you reckon?"

"I beg your pardon," said Sims.

"Have you had yer minces on Norman's richard?" Sammy looked puzzled. So did Sims. "Yer mince pies—eyes! The richard the third—bird! Wot part of the country do you come from then?"

"London," said Sims, defensively.

"And you don't know minces and richards? Dint they teach you nuffink at all at school?"

Dave Spencer got to his feet and started down the carriage.

"Hall, hallo—Debonair's off," said Sammy. "Goin' to the ben for a song then, Dave?"

Spencer ignored him. He had disappeared round behind the bar, into the toilet section, when Norman's new girlfriend came past, heading for the same place. Sammy was twisting round in his seat to get a good look at her legs. Sims asked what going to the ben for a song meant.

"Benghazi—carsi, of course," said Sammy, genuinely surprised.

"Is song rhyming slang as well?"

"Nah. Spencer likes singing in the carsi, the echo improves his voice. I'm always tellin' him he's good enough to go on the stage—long as they let him appear sitting on a carsi! Here, you play rummy much, me old son?"

They tried to explain the rules of ten-card runmy to Sims but he did not look promising. Danny kept thinking how lucky he was to have bright mates like Sammy and all the others. They knew what it was all about.

As soon as he had seen the girl moving to rise from her chair, Dave Spencer had got to his feet and headed for the toilets. To the others it must have looked as though she was following him. Following her from the front! He liked that. He locked himself in the first cubicle and stood, listening. He heard the other door shutting and the sound of a bolt being pushed home. He ran the hot tap and gave his hands a rinse. He touched at his dark hair with a small comb. He didn't really need to smarten himself up for he was always pretty smart, inside and out, a lot smarter than the rest of the team, that was for sure. To the others this train journey to Scotland represented excitement, the very fact of coming through a crowded station and playing cards in the club's private carriage and telling old football stories. To him it was all a drag. He had jumped at the chance of a bet on whether he could date Norman's new chick right under Norman's nose. It was something to do.

Right from the start Dave's father, whose money came from a chain of hairdressing salons, had decided that his boy Dave would be a star. Of what he was not too fussy. By the time Dave was twelve he was being coached professionally in tennis, golf and boxing. By the time he was thirteen several first division clubs had made approaches to his father. Soccer didn't offer the huge fortunes of golf or tennis, but a competent first division professional could, given ten years at the top, earn about a hundred thousand pounds from the game alone.

At first it worked out exactly as planned. He signed for Commoners as an apprentice at sixteen, seven years ago when Oaks Common still lived on the backwash of recent glory. He made the first team by nineteen, the England team by twenty-one, a smooth, intelligent midfield man with an instinctive ability to read the state of the game at any moment, never having to hang on to the ball while he looked up to find his forwards, able to see

74

through rucks of players and place the ball at the point where it would do most damage, killer passes that tore defences apart.

Although he was dropped from the England team after only two caps, and despite the long Commoners slump, a certain glamour had attached itself to his public image and the money had come in as expected. They marketed Dave Spencer hair lotions and Dave Spencer deodorants for men, and he had endorsement contracts with a shirt manufacturer, a firm of multiple tailors, an electric razor manufacturer and a football boot manufacturer, all of it worth around twenty-five thousand a year.

So why did none of it mean much to him any longer? Why was he bored to the back teeth?

It might have been different if he had signed for Spurs or Chelsea—apathy and mediocrity had been the keynote at Oaks Common. The general slump had probably cost him his England place. Without any hope of real success, the game had become a grind. Dreary journeys to Middlesbrough and Newcastle and Hull, slogging days of repetitive training under managers whose idea of success was to get through another week without the sack, nothing to look forward to but bitterly defensive league games and boringly available women—it all left him cold. Most players thought it was fantastic, just to make a living playing football, but the alternative for most of them was the factory.

This season, under John Gallagher, some of the old excitement had returned with the cup ties, but between the cup games there was still a lot of boredom.

When she came out of the toilet he was standing in the doorway to the main part of the carriage, pretending to check his pockets for something he couldn't find.

"What have you lost?" she asked.

"My wallet," he said, frowning, looking around at the floor. Then he tried his pockets again and grinned with relief. He brought it out, a smart crocodile-skin job brought back from a summer tour of Australia. "It's got great sentimental value," he said. "I'm very sentimental about money. How are you enjoying the trip. By the way, my name's Dave Spencer."

"I know," she said. "My name's Carole."

"Enjoying yourself, Carole?"

"It's very interesting."

She had very distinctive eyes, light blue and very clear. They were an unusual colour for someone with her very black hair. He liked the contrast.

"You know much about football?" he asked.

"I've only seen it on television."

"You'll see it in the raw, pulsating flesh on Saturday."

"I think I saw you on television—didn't you score a goal against somebody? I remember seeing them all jump on you. Quite passionate, I thought."

"That was the Liverpool game—one of my best he said, modestly."

"I'm curious about that—why do you hug and kiss each other so much?"

He grinned.

"They were doing it to me. I don't do it to them. I'm very particular about the kind of people I kiss and hug."

"I bet you are," she said. Her accent was not exactly high class, but very pleasant. "Can we go back to our seats now?"

He stood aside, making a courtly sweep with his right arm.

"You'll find the game becomes more interesting when you know somebody who's playing," he said, following her closely.

"Yes, I'll know who's kissing who," she said.

"See you later then," he said to her back. She looked round and smiled and walked on. He sat down opposite Dave Peacock and yawned. Looking round he saw all their faces, eager and curious.

"Got any more clues then?" he said to Peacock.

"Come on—what happened?"

"Nothing happened. You think I grabbed her in the carsi and had my evil will with her on the floor?"

"Did you get a bloody date or not?"

"Don't be naive. You don't barge in with a class item like that."

"Garn, she turned him down," Sammy exclaimed.

"Wiggy's right," Debonair said, "some of you can be very uncouth at times." He smiled condescendingly at Danny and touched his hair with splayed fingers, a Wiggy mannerism. Danny did not look too pleased.

Debonair Dave waited until lunch before he made his next move.

As she came up the gangway of the dining-car he got to his feet and stood in front of her, smiling casually. Norman Jackson was still at the chairman's table.

"I've been asking the lads why they kiss and hug each other after a goal," Dave said.

He liked the cool way she looked up at him. Her eyes were an extraordinary shade of light blue. She looked as though she knew what time of day it was.

"And what did they say?"

"Sammy Small says he doesn't kiss them, it's more like heavy petting."

She laughed. When she walked on he fell in step behind her, all very casual, doing nothing that would alert Norman Jackson, not responding to the various winks and nods and leers he was getting from the other players.

"There's a big game next Wednesday," he said as she reached the connecting door. "Chelsea are playing Spartak in the European Cup." He had to lean over her shoulder to push open the slide door. He sensed people coming behind them. "Would you like to come along to the game? Be quite exciting."

"I'm sure it would," she said, moving quickly through the dark connecting passageway, very cool, not needing to balance herself against the wall. He opened the next slide door, careful not to touch her. She sat down in her armchair. He stood over her.

"I'll give you a ring," he said.

"Do that," she said, looking steadily up at his face.

"Okay then," he said. "I'll take your number later."

"Will you?" She smiled sweetly at Norman Jackson, who patted Dave on the back and sat down.

The others were again waiting desperately for news.

"I told you, it doesn't do to rush some women," he said. He knew now it might not be as easy as he'd thought. She might be the kind of girl who got her kicks by making it difficult. She was pretty cool — almost as cool as himself. He liked that. She was worth a bit of effort.

"Nah, she turned him down flat," said Sammy to Danny. Dave leaned across the gangway and touched Danny's elbow.

"Tell you what, Dan," he said, "if you extend the time limit till lunchtime tomorrow I'll double the stakes."

"I'll take forty quid off you with pleasure, mate," said Danny. Dave winked and sat back in his chair.

"You're too bloody cool for words you are," said Dave Peacock. Debonair picked up the paper.

"Oh yeah?" he said, patting a stagey yawn.

"I know you better than most," Peacock said, "but even I didn't think you'd keep your so-called bloody cool when we're only three days away from the biggest game we've ever played in. Doesn't it excite you—just a little bit?"

"Oh well, I suppose so, it's better than a league game at Leicester or Birmingham on a lousy wet Tuesday night. I think I could even get quite excited again about football—if we were playing in a cup final every week."

"You still thinking of going to America? What the hell would you do there, screw starlets and run your own T.V. show and become President?"

"Soccer's getting pretty big in the States."

"Go on—it's pretty ropey compared to England."

"Yeah?" He dug into his hip pocket for his wallet, a snakeskin job which matched the billfold. He took out a carefully folded newspaper cutting. "That's from the *Sunday Times*," he said. Peacock opened it out.

U.S. SOCCER HITS THE BIG TIME

A crowd of 80,000 watched New York Generals beat Santos of Brazil at Yankee Stadium last Sunday—and American soccer could at last claim to have established itself on the North American continent.

"This is the realisation of all our efforts," said America's Soccer League commissioner, Phil Woosnam, former West Ham, Aston Villa and Welsh international. "Some people said we'd never see the day when an American team could compete with the world's best. That's just what we have seen."

For long the poor relation among America's sports, soccer really began to get a grip across the Atlantic after the reorganisation of the league system and the appointment of a national coach —Dettmar Cramer—back in 1970.

The league had only five teams then. It has now grown to a twenty-strong major cities league stretching from San Diego to New York, with average attendances of thirty-one thousand.

American soccer can claim to have led the world in some respects, innovating plastic pitches, building some of the finest stadiums in the world.

"Our big target now is to qualify for the World Cup finals," says Woosnam. "We're developing our own players through the college leagues and I'm sure we'll soon have a national team of native-born Americans who can give Brazil and England and Germany a run for their money."

As the train began to slow down outside Crewe Station Alec Hood wiped his mouth and let the napkin fall on his plate. Briskly brushing down his trousers he walked to the toilets at the other end of the dining-car. Both were engaged. The platform slid slowly by the window and then the train stopped with a jolt, as if it and the driver didn't quite understand each other. Hood overbalanced slightly.

"His brakes are good anyway," he remarked to John Gallagher, who was coming out of the dining-car. The manager barely nodded at Hood as he opened the carriage door and then ran quickly across the platform, disappearing round a corner.

Hood was suddenly curious. Trains generally stopped for five minutes at Crewe to load mail-bags—you didn't have to run if you wanted to buy a paper or stretch your legs.

Opening the carriage door he stepped down onto the platform and walked towards the bookstall, a big, craggy man in shirtsleeves, walking in the same direction as John Gallagher. He felt a little guilty at spying but he wanted to know once and for all what the hell was wrong with the man.

Leaning on the bookstall counter he glanced to his right. He saw John Gallagher standing by a telephone box, glaring impatiently at a fat, red-faced lady who stared right through him, talking nineteen to the dozen. Hood bought the new issue of *Winner* and stood with it raised to his face, sneaking quick looks at the telephone box. What was John Gallagher so mad to phone about? Could it be Roy's injury? No, he'd still been in good spirits after that session in the office yesterday. Was it just big match tension— no, he was too cool for that. Trouble at home—no, even if his house was burning down and his kids caught smoking pot and his wife having it off with the milkman John Gallagher wouldn't let such small details come between him and his job.

Hood felt himself getting frustrated to the point of anger. None of this was doing him any good. Without thinking he replaced the magazine he had just bought and ambled back to the train. For a moment he held the door-handle without turning it. He couldn't get the blasted man's strange behaviour out of his head.

"I hope you're a bit livelier on Saturday," John Gallagher snapped behind him. "We haven't got all day, you know."

Hood felt his face colour up with embarrassment, as if John Gallagher could know what he had been thinking about him. In momentary confusion he spoke without thinking:

"It might be none of my business but what the hell is wrong with you, Boss? You're not yourself at all." It was a mistake but having started he couldn't stop. "It must be something important for you to be upsetting everybody at a time like this."

The manager stared at him. The guard raised his green flag. John Gallagher stretched across in front of Hood and turned the handle, holding the door open.

"In you go, Alec," he said, the snap gone from his voice.

A whistle blew and the train gave a tiny lurch and the platform began to move past the window. Hood turned to go back to the club lounge, hoping the manager had forgotten his question.

"Just a minute, Alec," said John Gallagher.

Hood stopped. They stood facing each other in the narrow space by the window, Hood's white shirt reflected in the dark shine of the mahogany panelling. For some reason Hood felt slightly guilty at being bigger than John Gallagher. It should be the other way round, he thought. The train picked up speed. John Gallagher leaned heavily against the dark brown wall. He drew his hand down his cheeks, pulling hard on his jawbones.

"I suppose I'd better tell somebody," he said at last.

Peterson stretched his legs, accidentally kicking Sammy on the shin.

"It's more dangerous sittin' opposite you than playin' in a game," Sammy moaned, rubbing his shin with the calf of the other leg.

"It's your own fault," Danny said, annoyed at being interrupted, "I'm always telling you to wear shinpads. Anyway as I was saying, I think on balance Jimmy Vallins was the weirdest guy I ever met in football. We'd just escaped relegation from the Second Division into the Third Division South, beat the big chop, a win at Bolton did it. So on the Monday we're just finished training and Vallins says, 'Lads, we've escaped relegation an' I'm proud of yer

—soon as you've dressed come into my office, I got a special bonus for all of yer.' Well, you never saw players getting in and out of the bath so quick, shoving on our clothes—cor, we thought, he's going to hand us fifty quid each—no, maybe a hundred! So we all file into his office and he points to the corner and says, 'There you are, lads, help yerselves.' It was a crate of bleeding apples! Vallins says, 'There's enough for three a man.' Then he looks at me and says, 'I'm watching you, Peck, I know you, you'll take more than your share!' "

"So what did you say?"

"I couldn't say much, my mouth was full of apples. Our big pay-off for the season's efforts, nine months of gruelling endeavour —three bloody apples!"

"Give you the pip, did it?" said Sammy.

"He was a one that Vallins," Danny said, shaking his head. "He was a big greyhound man. One Monday I go into the treatment room and there's Vallins with one of his dogs on the couch—he's only giving the brute deep heat treatment under the lamp! 'He's got a bad hock,' he says to me all serious like. 'Sure he ain't just putting it on to miss training?' I says. He goes all serious again. 'I never thought of that,' he says."

"I've played in teams with dogs like that—mystery injuries keep them off training till Friday and then they declare themselves fit," said Sammy. "When I first come to Oaks Common and got to train with the first team squad I'm desperate to do well, show I'm willin'—I'm startin' off round the cinder track when Vic Mullins— he was the club captain—growls at me, all bitter like, 'You tryin' to show us up, are you? Get to the back and don't run faster than me or I'll smash yer chest in!' Remember Jock Toms the goalie? He was a quick-change artist—he'd leave his shirt and tie on under his tracksuit so's he could get away from the ground quicker'n anybody else after trainin'. He used to boast he could leave the dressin'-room and do his laps and be back in before the door stopped bangin'. After a game that Toms could be washed and changed and in the pub across the road havin' his first pint before any of the fans got through the pub door."

"Funny case Toms was," said Shack. "You know his wife never ever saw him playing? He wouldn't let her near the ground."

"Lot of Scots players like that," said Danny. "It's all that religion, they don't think a football ground's a fit and proper place for a respectable woman, all that swearing and everything."

"Alec says it's because they don't like their wives gossipin' wiv the other players' wives," said Sammy. "Alec's wife was at Wembley watchin' Alec playin' for Scotland and all the Scotch wives are sittin' together and one of them says to another, 'Your Archie's playin' a stinker.' 'Oh yeah,' says Archie's wife, 'tell me, is your hair naturally blonde or do you just dye the roots black?' "

They discussed players' wives, deciding on balance that they tended to be a bit prim and proper, not perhaps the kind of flashy girls one might have expected rough, tough pros to pick.

"Mine was bein' all prim and bleedin' proper this mornin'," Sammy said, pulling a wry face. "Off on your travels then, she says, flash hotels and fancy little scrubbers, eh?"

"She resents you being away from home?" said Peterson.

"It's difficult, bein' a player's wife, innit? We're away from home so much. Oh, she understands that's wot it's all about — we gotta get away to a hotel 'fore a big game to get a proper night's sleep. Any married player will tell you — one of his saucepans wakes up in the night and starts bawlin' his perishin' head off — that's your sleep ruined. A player's gotta have his kip — eight hours kip a night, me old son. Lose your sleep and you can't play football."

Shack got to his feet, moving in his usual off-the-field manner, slowly and deliberately as though sleep was about to take him by force. As he passed the two goalkeepers Randy called out:

"Hey, Shack, get us a bottle of Double Diamond from the bar, eh?"

"It's a bit early for beer, isn't it? You want to end up on a charge of drunken diving?"

They jeered after him. He ignored them. By tonight Randy would be claiming the pun as his own. He had bought the soft drinks and was coming back to his seat when he met Alec Hood. The captain's big-boned face had gone almost grey.

"Crikey, Alec, you all right, boyo?"

Hood looked Shack in the eye but sat down without speaking. He knew now why the manager had been losing his temper so easily. He felt quite sick. To think he'd been getting worried about a medal!

Peterson leaned over the low partition and touched his shoulder.

82

"About that beer contract, Alec, you think we could have another chat with John Gallagher —"

"No, leave him alone," Hood snapped.

Peterson sat back with a frown. Hood stared out of the window. The train was going through flat countryside, fields and trees and cottages. He was numb.

"When they told me what it might be I felt just the same as getting a boot in the balls," John Gallagher had said in the passageway. "For a few seconds there's no pain but you know it's going to come. And then it starts and you want to curl up in a ball and just *die*."

He had phoned the clinic from the Crewe platform but the specialist had gone for the rest of the day. He was now going to have to sweat it out till tomorrow morning. Hood didn't understand how the man could just sit there. If it was me, he thought, I'd be going *mad*.

9

THE following news item appeared in *The Times* on March 15.

SCOTTISH DOLE QUEUES KEEP GROWING

Unemployment figures released yesterday for February show that Scotland is Britain's black spot, with $12\frac{1}{2}$ per cent of the work force on the dole.

Ministry of Employment officials blame bad weather and normal seasonal variations for the increase in numbers of Scottish jobless, but a political storm is bound to blow up in both the Edinburgh and Westminster parliaments, with Opposition M.P.s making all-out attacks on the Government's economic policy for Scotland.

Yesterday 15,000 trade union demonstrators marched through Glasgow demanding a five-hour day so that available work would be shared out more widely. Police made fifteen arrests outside Glasgow City Chambers.

10

WHEN camera angles and colour balances and a rough timing of the interviews had been finally worked out to the director's satisfaction, Peterson left the squad in the coach and walked across gravel to the big B.B.C. outside broadcast unit parked on the edge of the Strannoch Hydro Hotel car park.

They had arrived an hour earlier, leaving the train at Kilmarnock and coming by hired coach to the Hydro Hotel, a few miles north of Largs on the Firth of Clyde coast, where they would stay until it was time to board the coach again on Saturday morning and head for Hampden Park.

After the train journey the players were hard to keep together in the coach during the seemingly interminable preparation for the T.V. filming, one of two sessions for which the B.B.C. were paying six hundred pounds into the players' pool. The pool committee had thought it very clever of Peterson to get them this money before they played the semi-final, especially as it was not an exclusive contract, leaving the I.T.V. companies free to make a separate offer, but when it came to rehearsing the coach arrival the players had quickly become bored, tending to behave like a rabble of schoolchildren. At one point Peterson had barely stopped himself from bawling at Randy and Wiggy to stop mucking about. John Gallagher had not been much help. His bad temper had given way to a kind of absent-minded indecisiveness. In the end it had been Alec Hood who had jollied and cursed them into order; they liked the idea of bunce money but the game was the solid, all-demanding truth in their lives and all fringe activities, however lucrative, were a chance for a giggle.

"I'm beginning to realise what it takes to be a football manager," he said to the O.B. director, who was sitting in the gloom of the big wagon watching three monitor screens.

"Not to worry, old man, we're all set now," said the director, adding that he had plenty of experience with footballers. He said something to his girl assistant. He spoke into a desk-mike, getting a wave on one monitor from the interviewer, who had a button-sized receiver concealed in his right ear. Peterson saw the coach roll into the car park, for the third time.

"And here we are on the Clyde coast watching the Commoners from London arrive at Strannoch Hydro, where they will spend the next two days preparing for Hampden on Saturday when they meet Glasgow Rangers in what many people are calling the glamour game of the decade. . . "

The commentator was a stocky Scotsman with briskly-curled red hair, a youngish man, slightly naive and very earnest, like most Scots taking football as a deadly serious business. He came into shot as the coach rolled up to the side entrance of the hotel, where a wide flight of stone steps were flanked by a pair of stylish stone lions, relics of the hotel's previous existence as a duke's country seat.

"There's a million pounds worth of football talent in the coach you see behind me," the red-haired interviewer said into camera. Behind him, at the top of the picture, Peterson could see the leaden-grey waters of the Clyde and the dark purple of islands and low mountains. For a quick moment he felt a strange sense of panic. In that coach were sixteen crack professionals who were looking to him to make them the big money. He found himself keenly desirous of a large drink.

John Gallagher was the first to step down out of the coach, very dark round the chin.

"Welcome to Scotland," the interviewer said, making it sound like a great honour. The players said they were always amazed at the almost vicious enthusiasm the Scots showed when it came to games against English teams. Some said the Scots had gigantic chips on their shoulders, others said it was only a sign of their fantastic devotion to football. Peterson thought it probably had something to do with national identity. The English had it and didn't know they had it, and didn't care either way. The Scots didn't have it and looked for it desperately, seeing direct echoes of national issues in club matches played between pros who didn't give a monkey's for politics and who would probably define Home Rule as a biased referee.

"It's always nice to be back in Scotland," John Gallagher was saying, pleasantly enough without smiling.

"Well, special training isn't exactly correct," he said to the next question, "we'll be going through much the same routine as we have at home—it's a kind of superstition not to change your usual training routine—I mean, we won't be doing any hard training on soft sand to build up muscle or anything like that—one of the real advantages is to free the lads from the pressures you get before a game like this, the incessant phone calls, the friends who want tickets, the reporters—we can clear their minds of everything but the game . . . no, I won't prophesy the result but it will be very close."

"Thank you, John Gallagher. And here's another leading Scot in the Commoners' party—Alec Hood, captain and centre-back, five times capped for Scotland. You left Scotland as a boy, Alec, how does it feel to be coming back home to play at Hampden in a big game like this?"

"Oh it's a big thrill," said Hood, nodding emphatically. "I'll tell you next month if it's as big a thrill as actually winning the British Cup."

"Oh—you're confident you'll beat the Rangers then?"

"Very confident—this is a great team we've got, the lads have been playing some great stuff."

"How about Jackie Caskie, you made any special plans to contain him?"

"Aye, we have a plan—but you won't tell anybody else, will you?"

In the darkness of the O.B. wagon the technicians laughed. Then came Roy Christmas, pale and quiet.

"You scored for England at Hampden on your international debut a season or two ago," the interviewer said. "You think you'll get among the goals on Saturday?"

"I hope so."

"Roy, a hundred and forty thousand pounds is a lot of money—when Commoners paid that much for you did it affect your game? Did it worry you in any way?"

"Not really."

"Do you know much about the Rangers defence, who'll be marking you?"

"No."

"Have you seen Rangers playing?"

"Only on the telly."

"Were you impressed?"

"You can't tell from the telly."

"But you have played against Dave Lindsay—or Killer as he's called. Would you say he is one of the strongest centre-backs you've ever come up against?"

"Mmm. Probably."

Peterson snorted mirthlessly. To get a decent interview out of Roy you'd need blinding lights and rubber truncheons. Andy Gurr came next, thick-set, darkish hair fairly short, a very young face above a body that might soon become quite portly. The interviewer didn't waste much time on him, or on Gerry Williamson, whose red hair covered his ears in little bangs. Peterson noticed with a slight wince, as he did every time he saw Gerry close-up, how bad his teeth were, discoloured and uneven, 'dodgy railings' as Sammy called them. Gerry had said he wanted to have them done properly but it would take three clear weeks of daily attendance at a dental clinic and what with summer tours and family holidays and pre-season training trips he had not had three clear weeks at home for four years.

Danny Peck was next, looking like a South American revolutionary, heavy set and dark and slightly ominous.

"I believe your nickname is Danny the Destroyer," said the interviewer. "Tell me, Danny, you think you'll be able to destroy the Rangers attack? Jackie Caskie came back to form last night, scored a truly great goal. You worried about him?"

"Oh yeah, I'm worried." He frowned. "Every time I come to Scotland I get worried."

The interviewer was genuinely puzzled. Peterson knew something peculiar was coming.

"Why do you get worried about coming to Scotland?"

"I'm worried in case I can't get out again."

"I see." He smiled weakly. Danny put his hand to his forehead and gave a big, slow American army salute at the camera. As he walked away he said, quite audibly, "Och aye the noo, Jock."

Then came Dave Spencer. Devilishly handsome and doesn't he know it, the big-headed English swine, they would be saying in a million Scottish homes tonight.

"We know most of the crowd will be cheering Rangers," he said, "but a big crowd brings out something extra—even if they're all against you. It's the atmosphere—gets the adrenalin going."

Next came, as Sammy would say, Riddle's big nose followed by Riddle. The interviewer got little out of him but unenthusiastic grunts. Peterson made a note to bring this up at the committee. Surly grunts were no way to exploit the mass media. Shack had little to say either. Dave Peacock, looking like a moustachioed gunfighter from Wyatt Earp days, said he thought the game might be decided in the air, himself and Roy Christmas trying to out-jump the tall Rangers defence.

Wiggy, playing it cool, described his wig business quite sensibly. Yes, he was looking forward to meeting his Scottish counterpart, Jackie Caskie.

"You could discuss your mutual interests in the boutique business," said the interviewer archly.

"Oh, they have boutiques in Scotland?" Wiggy looked genuinely impressed. Then he ran his splayed fingers back over his hair, the poofy mannerism that usually made Brian Seymour froth at the mouth. "I thought it was only us English nancy boys who went in for boutiques."

Peterson thought of the Hampden hordes and the hard men of the Rangers defence and he hoped Wiggy knew what he was doing. It would be just Wiggy's style to decide deliberately to needle the Scots. He seemed to thrive on general contempt. The more the crowds jeered him the more likely he was to put on the kind of display that would rub his skill in their faces.

Three and a half minutes running time were left when Sammy jumped out of the coach and ran towards the clearly surprised interviewer.

"Cor, never thought I'd get here in time," said Sammy, panting heavily.

"Sammy Small, left-wing forward," said the interviewer. "Small by name and small by nature, eh?"

"That's abaht it, me old son." He had obviously decided to lay the Cockney accent on thickly for the benefit of what he normally described as 'them bleedin' haggis-bashers'.

"Looking forward to the game?"

"Yeah, not arf."

"Rangers are the third Scottish team you've met in the British Cup. How did you find Dundee United and Hibs?"

"Ah well, I didn't actually find 'em, did I? It's the coach-driver wot deserves the credit, innit?"

The interviewer glanced at his clip-board.

"Tell me, Sammy, what does a London footballer do in his spare time? Up here players seem to be keener on golf than anything else. What are your hobbies?"

"Me hobbies? Oh well, nuffink extraordinary—just a lager and a gamble."

"A lager and a gamble."

"That's abaht it, me old son, a lager and a gamble. I'm not one for grumble."

Sammy gave the thumbs-up sign to the camera and walked off. The rest were barely named as they came past the camera. The interviewer wound up. In the gloom of the O.B. wagon somebody was still laughing over Sammy's lager and a gamble. Peterson felt quite breathless. It was to be devoutly hoped nobody in Scotland understood rhyming slang.

When he got into the hotel most of them had gone to their rooms. It was a quarter to six. He went up in the lift to the third floor, where he was sharing a room for one night with Gerald Sims. For a moment he wondered who he would have been given as a room-mate if Sims had not been in the party.

"Well, old boy," he said, taking off his jacket. "I trust you enjoyed the trip."

"Most illuminating," said Sims, who was sitting at the writing-table, legs neatly crossed, writing on copy paper with a small, neat hand. Peterson went into the bathroom and rolled up his shirtsleeves. He washed his face and hands and pulled at his hair with wet fingers till it was all going in roughly the same direction. He stood in the doorway, drying himself. Sims looked away. Peterson had a quick realisation of how much he would like to be a player, to travel in a team of friends, to share a room with a real pal. Comradeship, he thought, that's what the Sims and the Petersons of this world have lost.

"I find it difficult to know what I think of these football people," Sims said. Peterson sat on his bed. Through the gauze curtains he could see darkening island shapes to the west. All day in the train he had been moving about and talking and making plans and now he felt gloomy and indecisive. That first large drink was sending advance vibrations through his mouth and down his throat but he made no move. There were times, for a man like him, when sitting still was an act of heroism.

"You couldn't hope to get to know them in so short a time," he said. "They don't communicate their real thoughts readily to outsiders. Every day I realise I know less and less about what makes players tick."

"The whole ethos of the game itself interests me. Is it big business—a game—a sport—entertainment industry—opiate of the masses?"

"Probably all of them. That's why it's so big. It's got something for everybody." He lay back on the bed and closed his eyes, hand feeling for the ashtray on the bedside table. "It was all I ever dreamed of as a boy, to become a football player. I wasn't very good and I wasn't very fast and I wasn't very strong—but every game I played for the school or the youth club I literally ached for the man to tap me on the shoulder and say, 'Not bad, son, how'd you like a trial at Oaks Common?' I'd stare at every man on the council pitches, wondering if he was a scout—Commoners, Arsenal, Spurs, Chelsea, West Ham, Fulham, Queens Park Rangers, Millwall, Charlton, Orient, Brentford—I wasn't fussy, any London club could have had me!"

"So you've always been interested in the game."

"Interested? You know, I'm forty-three now and I've been a Fleet Street journalist for years and I've interviewed celebrities of every description—Hollywood stars, politicians, multi-millionaires, sex symbols, great men of literature, Arctic explorers, you name it—and none of them has ever moved me one iota compared to the magic of football. Put a teenage dunderhead with spots into a football strip and immediately I have a terrible urge to ask for his autograph."

Sims seemed ready to listen and he went on in the deepening gloom and chill of the room, lighting new cigarettes, speaking with a tired passion.

"I used to think of it as pure magic," he said. "Then I got to know a little bit of what went on behind the scenes and I began to think of it as a nasty little rat-race. They're all in it only for money, I thought. You see Sammy Small and Danny Peck? Before Danny came to Oaks Common Sammy's best friend was a bloke called Chris Grady. They shared a room together, they went everywhere together, they lived near each other, they went on holiday together. Before lunchtime on a Sunday morning Chris Grady would be round at Sammy's house, they both had wives and families but they couldn't keep away from each other. You ever been in the house of a big soccer star? It's some atmosphere, believe me. The phone never stops ringing, the kids cycle up and down the road outside, peering at the windows. That Sammy, he was the first player I ever saw at home—talk about men of action! He came into the living-room and the fire wasn't lit. He buzzed about like a dynamo, sticks and coal, then he got the packet of fire-lighters and bunged every one into the coal, a whole packet. Two would do it, I said. Oh fakk it, he says, bung the lot on, mate, get the bleedin' thing goin'. I'd never known anyone use a whole packet of fire-lighters every time he lit a fire. Anyway, last season Chris Grady was dropped and John Gallagher bought Danny to take his place. Chris Grady was transferred to Torquay. Two weeks later Danny was Sammy's bosom pal, exactly the same as Grady had been, I mean *exactly*, sharing a room, going for a drink, slipping off to a nightclub, planning a holiday in Majorca together! I couldn't understand it. A lot of people thought John Gallagher had treated Grady unfairly by making him the scapegoat for a bad defence. Sammy said he thought John Gallagher had been a bit hard on Grady. I was a bit naive then, more naive I mean, I asked him if he'd never thought of standing up for his best pal— solidarity and all that. He looked at me as if I was mad! That's the way the game goes, he said. You just accept these things. Players play and managers manage."

"Sound like very shallow people."

"What else could Sammy do? His best friend had gone to Torquay, no chance of keeping up the old relationship. Danny was just his type—so why not make friends with him? It's a short life, so they just get on with it. None of them go about with long faces thinking deep thoughts about capitalism and the law of the jungle— but deep down they know it is a jungle—no feather-beds, no safety-nets—you might even say the last bastion of naked capital-ism left in Britain. And they're not going to be in the jungle for very long, either. Their lives are castles built on wet sand. No matter how good they are, or how fit or how dedicated—come thirty and they're getting old. Most of them, the good ones certainly, live for football and nothing else. It rules their lives the way no ordinary job rules a man's every waking moment. Yet inexorably, relentlessly, the years are eating into them."

"Into us all."

"Ah, but you and I can go on working and earning till we're in our sixties. Sir Stanley Matthews went on playing till he was over fifty but we won't see his like again. They only have half-lives — don't you see that? By normal standards they're young when they give it up but by their own standards the moment they give it up they're really *dead men*."

"Like sex, I suppose. Do old men torture themselves with desires they are physically incapable of realising?"

"I can't help you there, I'm glad to say."

"But even if what you say is true — does it matter? It's just a sport at which a few lucky men get paid very good money, isn't it? What would they be doing otherwise — fairly mundane jobs, I imagine."

"Just a sport? If you weren't brought up in it you wouldn't begin to grasp what this game means to all of us. Football is our magic. It's our culture and our history, our theatre — it's even our version of nationality. Sometimes I do think it's just a drug for the masses, a sop to keep us from wanting decent houses and good food and proper education. Maybe it is — but social injustice isn't the fault of football. It's the one thing we do all by ourselves, all the ordinary people, for once without the bosses and the establishment and the Eton élite on our backs. We organise it ourselves and play it ourselves and watch it ourselves. I'm always hearing condescending intellectuals saying what a tragedy it is that Britain is no longer a real world power, only a football world power. Well — maybe if this bloody class-ridden country gave the ordinary man a go he'd make us into a real power, but all we've got is football. Geoff Hurst's hat-trick against Germany in the 1966 World Cup — was that just a sports page achievement? Was it hell! That was us, mate, the ordinary common bloke in the street. When did our bloody Foreign Secretaries and Prime Ministers last score any hat-tricks? I see the great men of football — true leaders like Sir Matt Busby of Manchester United or Sir Alf Ramsey who made us world champions or Jock Stein who made Celtic the best team in Europe, Don Revie of Leeds, Billy Nicholson of Spurs — only football gave them the chance to show they were great men.

Society didn't — not our wonderful cosy élitist British society — not our masters of the Eton Mafia. Left to politicians and bankers and industrialists where would those men have been — down the mines or doing robot jobs on production lines — or dead in trenches? Oh yes, football might be escapist entertainment for the masses — but we know what we're escaping from. It's our game, run by us and not by our overlords. When we get in a big crowd we're cheering on our own kind, our own heroes. What we're really cheering for is our own very existence."

He was breathless and embarrassed. Sims said nothing. Peterson swung his legs off the bed.

"Sorry, old boy," he said. "I must have an attack of something coming on. Fancy a quick drink."

"No, I'll finish this and phone my wife. I'll join you later."

In the corridor Peterson shivered. Imagine spouting all that to Sims, of all people. In the bar he found Paul Franks and Norman Jackson and Carole.

"Large scotch," he said to the waiter, still trembling with the force of his outburst. He smiled at Carole. "I'm so brainwashed being part of the players' pool I have to keep reminding myself I'm entitled to drink all I want."

She laughed. Norman smirked.

"It'll be a strange day when you need to remind yourself to have a drink, Bill," he said. Peterson shrugged.

"I'm a self-made failure," he said. Norman was too full of himself to notice the insult. Carole had changed out of her travelling clothes into a woollen dress, dark blue and tight-fitting, showing a fair bit of tasty leg. Peterson felt the old urge.

"I must say, Carole," he said, raising his glass, "I'd find it a lot easier to market this team if they all looked like you."

"Ah," said Paul Franks, eyes opening wide with a degree of undisguised lasciviousness permissible only in old, jolly men, "what joy the treatment room would be, my dear, if you were a player. For such cartilages an old quack would give his all!"

After dinner most of the party had coffee in the lounge. John Gallagher let it be known through Harry Barnes that he wanted the team in bed by eleven o'clock. By now they had changed out of their club suits into various types of casual clothes. Shack and Riddle said there was something they wanted to see on television.

94

Sammy winked at Danny and Danny said he and Sammy were going to play snooker with Johnny Parkinson. They disappeared. John Gallagher and Harry Barnes and several players went off in hired cars to a Scottish League match at Cappielow Park, where Greenock Morton had a floodlight game with Heart of Midlothian. Several Scottish journalists were sitting in a group with Wiggy and Alec Hood and Dave Spencer. Peterson came over and spoke to Hood.

"Sorry, Bill, I got talking here and forgot the time," said the captain. By seven-forty they had a committee of sorts, Hood and Seymour and Peterson. Danny Peck was nowhere to be found, although he had been told of the meeting.

"Right then, Danny's off the committee," said Hood. He stood up and looked round the lounge. "Dave Spencer, he'll do, he knows a bit about business." He walked off through the tables. Debonair Dave had only a minute earlier found a good excuse to join the chairman's group, going up to the doctor to ask for a sleeping pill. The jolly old doc had, as always, offered him a drink. He had taken his first sip of lager when Hood tapped him on the shoulder.

"Dave, we want you in the corner, committee meeting."

"I'm not on the committee."

"You are now."

"Everything all right, Alec?" said the chairman.

"Oh yes, Mr. Jackson, we're all in good nick. We need Dave here for a committee meeting. I suppose he's been trying to get racing tips from you."

Dave cursed under his breath. He could hardly make an issue out of it with the chairman looking on.

"I'll see you in a few minutes," he said as he got up, looking at Carole. As they went across the lounge he took hold of Hood's arm. "Here you twit, what's all this cobblers? Don't you know I've got to get a date with that chick before lunchtime or I'll lose forty quid?"

"Peterson's done a lot of work and Danny has just pissed off— I don't want him to think we don't appreciate what he's doing— he might chuck the whole thing in."

"Course he bloody won't," said Dave, trying to hold Hood back. "He's broke and he's supporting one wife and keeping another bloody woman—he won't walk out. God's sake, Alec, I *want* to date that girl!"

Hood turned round.

"I always thought education raised the level of the mind. You ever think of anything else but grumble?"

Opening his red folder Peterson began to outline the various contracts he had ready to be signed as soon as they had won Saturday's game.

"The *Sun* has offered three hundred pounds an article for a series of a dozen, one on each player ghosted," he began. "The *Evening News* wants the same but they're only offering two hundred and fifty."

"Take the *Sun*," said Seymour.

"But the *News* will also give us a thousand for certain picture rights—snaps of you all as babies, a group of wives, that sort of thing."

"Take the *News* then," said Seymour.

"Give Bill a chance to finish for God's sake."

"My inclination is to split these things up among as many papers as possible, they all give you yards of free publicity throughout the season. I'd give the *News* the ghosted series on each player—it's a London paper, they support you all the year round. By the way, remind everybody to dig out a snap of themselves as a baby. I'll sell the idea to somebody for a Cup Final day quiz, match the baby to the star."

"Good idea, Bill."

"We can also have a shot of each player standing by the front of his car in a long row outside the ground. Then a big group photo of all the wives and children—what did we reckon, eleven wives, thirty-one babies? Should make a good picture."

"Should make a good rabble."

"Now then, the T.V. contracts. Oh—before that, Wiggy's been offered his own series in the *News of the World* if we win on Saturday. They'll run it in the weeks up to Cup Final day. They've offered his business agent ten thousand. Is that pool money? What does Wiggy say?"

"He's all right, Wiggy," said Hood. "He can put a percentage of it in the pool—a couple of grand would be fine, eh?"

"Yeah but—" Seymour looked bitter—"that little berk is getting eight grand to do T.V. commercials for Top Ten Tailors—he won't put any of that in the pool. I asked him."

"He told me about that," said Hood. "They won't be showing

the commercials for three months at least—it isn't anything to do with the British Cup."

"Look, this is all very fine but you don't need me," said Spencer, attempting to rise. "I've got to get a date with that Carole person or I'm forty smackers down."

"Look, Dave," said Hood, holding Debonair down by the shoulder, "we're talking about thousands and you're all bothered about forty bloody pounds! Act your age."

"It isn't just the money!"

"Sit down and belt up. I'll have a word with Wiggy, Bill, let's see what he thinks is fair."

Peterson outlined the T.V. contracts they had been offered if they reached the final. The I.T.V. companies were suggesting a flat ten thousand pounds for exclusive coverage of training sessions, personal profiles, home backgrounds, pre-match and dressing-room interviews. The B.B.C. were offering eight thousand down for the same facilities plus another four thousand if Commoners actually won the Cup.

"That's a gamble if you like," said Hood. "What do you think, Dave?"

"Will we win the Cup, do you mean?"

"That's about it. We'd be betting four thousand on ourselves."

Seymour twitched his nose and upper lip. Peterson didn't like the man. There was a lack of generosity about him, a mean-spiritedness lacking in all the others.

"Football's a funny business," Seymour said. "We could lose this semi-final or the final itself for some stupid reason—something we had no control over. No, I'd take the ten grand, the certain money."

"I'd take the gamble," said Spencer.

"Yeah—the big gambler," said Seymour, "look at you, twitching like a neurotic over a forty quid bet! You gamble with your own money, mate, I want mine in my hand."

"Brian's right," said Hood, to Peterson's surprise. "If we lose we'll have ten grand to soften the blow. If we win we'll have ten instead of twelve—but we'll have a lot of glory to make up for it, two grand's worth of glory! I vote we accept the I.T.V. offer."

"And me," said Seymour, holding up his right hand, which Peterson thought was a pretty stupid gesture considering there were only four of them round a coffee table.

"Whatever you say," said Dave, "now can I piss off?"

"No."

While they were talking a man came up to the table and plonked a hotel menu in front of Hood.

"Sign that will you?" he said abruptly.

Hood looked up at him.

"Want a ticket as well?" he asked.

"You got any?" said the man.

"Only for people who say please," said Hood, handing him back the menu, unsigned, staring steadily into his face. The man went red and walked away.

"As you were saying, Bill."

Peterson picked up another sheet of paper. He could get ten thousand Commoners ties printed with a gold cup motif for five thousand pounds. They could sell them at one pound fifty each, making a profit of ten thousand pounds. They would also market fifteen thousand lapel badges. Selling ten thousand souvenir brochures at twenty-five pence, with advertising at a hundred and fifty pounds a page, meant another profit of three thousand pounds. As the club had been careful not to allow anyone to photograph a proper team group in full strips they would have the only colour photograph for sale—ten thousand on thick, glossy paper at twenty-five pence a time, profit two thousand four hundred pounds. Individual postcard-size colour photographs of each player, overprinted with an autograph, would be sold in packets at twenty-five pence a time.

"Now then, what about this idea of making a record of the team singing?" Peterson asked. He put down the papers. By now he knew the figures by heart. "We can have them done for about two hundred and fifty quid a thousand—quite a good profit if we sell them at seventy-five pence a throw—"

"Let's do it then," said Seymour.

"But?" Hood asked, looking at Peterson.

"It would take at least a full day to record it. Can you imagine the likelihood of us getting every man together on the Monday after you'd won the British Cup?"

"We could record it in advance," said Seymour.

"Oh yeah?" Hood shook his head slowly. "Make a record of us celebrating victory before the game is played! So we lose—and we're stuck with five thousand stupid L.P.s of us talking about how we won, singing and leaping about? A collector's item that would be!"

"I didn't think of that," said Seymour, nodding wisely.

They decided to forget the record. They discussed the percentage they should ask from the T.V. companies of the profits from the film cassettes sold of the Cup Final. It was agreed to accept the Milk Board's offer of five thousand pounds for the players to carry bottles of milk on the victory lap of honour at New Wembley. Spencer said he was bored by shots of cup final players drinking milk. Why couldn't they approach a champagne firm, he wanted to know, especially as that was what they would really be filling themselves up with, but the point was lost as they got on to the subject of the beer commercials. It was here that Seymour changed his line. Desperate so far, it appeared, to grab at every pound available, he seemed to become very apprehensive about the possibility of a row with the management. It was eventually agreed that Hood should have another word with John Gallagher before deciding what their next move should be.

Hood stretched up his arms and yawned. They sat and watched as Dave tried to rush suavely back into the chairman's party. He succeeded. Seymour went to watch T.V. Hood and Peterson went through to the Lochinvar Lounge, where a waiter brought Hood a lager and lime, and Peterson a large scotch on the rocks.

"Imagine all that money at stake on the result of one game of football," Peterson said, wonderingly.

"Aye—and just imagine if you were a player, Bill—you know what the club's giving us in bonuses?"

"No. I never like to ask about that side of it."

"Twelve hundred a man if we beat Rangers and get to New Wembley—and another three thousand a man if we win the cup!"

"I suppose that's fairly generous. I would have thought it would be more. Here, Brian was a bit peculiar, wasn't he, one minute he wants every penny we can screw out of anybody, the next he's got cold feet about the beer ads."

"He's scared if we had a row with the board—it might jeopardise his coaching job."

"Funny bloke," said Peterson. "I would have thought that at his age he would have been—well, what's the word—independent?"

A middle-aged man, Scottish, probably a businessman of some kind, came up to their table and put down a small notebook.

"Here, lads, ye think I could have your autographs, please?" he said, wheezing a little. "It's not for me, mind, it's for my boy, he's football daft."

Hood signed quickly, more of a wavy scrawl than a true signature. The man pushed the notebook towards Peterson.

"I'm not a player," he said, embarrassed for no logical reason.

"Ye're for a hammering on Saturday," the man said cheerily, patting Hood on the shoulder. "Rangers will eat ye alive." He went away.

"You get used to it," Hood said casually. "They always say the autograph's for their son—just letting you know they're above such things."

A waiter came over and asked, very politely, if Hood would mind signing his son's autograph book.

"I hope ye win on Saturday," he said, thanking Hood profusely.

"Don't let them hear you saying that," Hood said, "they'll hang you for a traitor."

"Ach, I'm a Celtic man myself, I hope ye slaughter them blue-nosed gets."

Peterson didn't understand this. Hood explained that the waiter was a Catholic. The old religious bitterness was still red-hot in Scotland, at a time when the English seemed to have forgotten what the inside of a church looked like. Rangers represented Protestantism, the true blues, and Celtic were Catholic and Irish and green. Over the years they had shared an almost total dominance over Scottish football. Coachloads of their supporters—the brake clubs—left Scottish towns and cities every Saturday to follow Rangers or Celtic, ignoring local teams which did not have the commercial advantage of a religious connection. Celtic, it was always said in pub arguments, had always been willing to field Protestant players and the great Jock Stein, the manager who made Celtic champions of all Europe, was not a Catholic. It was Stein who had given Scottish football its proudest moment, the day Celtic devastated the Italian champions Internazionale-Milan in Lisbon, the first British club to win the European Cup. ("As far as the London papers are concerned," said Stein, ironically, "we're British when we win in Europe, but Scottish when we lose.") But Rangers were true blue almost to the end; in the old days they would not hire a Catholic to sell programmes let alone wear the famous blue strip. It all boiled down to the colours, Protestant blue or Catholic green. In Scotland there were men made so hysterical by Irish green they would not have grass in their gardens, or have their window frames painted green. The hardcore of Rangers fanatics sang about the sash of the Orange Lodges and regarded the Roman Catholic Church and its adherents, Irish or Scottish born, as Fenians best rewarded by boot or bottle. Yet Stein made it possible for all Scotsmen to hold their heads high in the world of football—and the Rangers management had joined the twentieth century by signing Catholic boys—yet there were still those Scots whose ancient religious prejudices were so deep they would cheer any team that beat the Celtic—Communists or Germans. To the genuine bigot Celtic were the true enemy.

"What's the fastest thing on two legs in Britain?"

"I don't know," said Peterson.

"The Pope doing a lap of honour of Ibrox Park."

The Old Firm of Rangers and Celtic had ruled the divided city of Glasgow in a way that transcended mere sporting rivalry. In the mythology, or demonology, of the blue-green war death was a grim reality. Johnny Thompson, the Celtic goalkeeper, died on the pitch at Ibrox Park when he dived at the feet of Rangers centre-forward Sam English and the Rangers man's knee caught him accidentally on the forehead, snapping his neck. In Catholic households in Glasgow there used to be two hallowed pictures on the mantelpiece, Johnny Thompson and Benny Lynch the boxer, great martyrs and heroes, one to football and one to booze. Only the old men remembered them now, for others had died in more recent times, sixty-six men and boys suffocated in the struggling hell of a jammed stairway at Ibrox Park on New Year's Day, nineteen-seventy-one, sixty-six out of the eighty thousand who had come to see the Old Firm do battle, more martyrs to the old drama. Yet their deaths had made bigoted men think again—or think, perhaps, for the first time.

"John Gallagher reckons he couldn't get a trial for Rangers because of his name," Hood said. "Gallagher? You'd assume that was a Pape—or a left-footer as they call them up here. His father was a bhoyo but he gave it up to marry John's mother—and they didn't have many mixed marriages up here, I can tell you. And you couldn't have a Gallagher playing for the true blues, not in those days. A mick playing for the Gers—even a lapsed mick?

The big red stand at Ibrox would have fallen to the ground! Still as John always says, if you can't join 'em, beat 'em."

"How quaint. Sounds like a great deal of nonsense to me."

"You're right. Me, I'd play a homosexual Hindu hunchback if I thought he could win games for me."

Peterson finished his whisky. He signalled the waiter.

"Alec, there's something I want to ask you about," he said tentatively, wondering how far he could trust Hood.

"What's that?"

"John Gallagher—I heard something this morning—it might be only stupid gossip—probably it's nonsense . . ."

"No, come on, tell me."

"I don't want to look as though I'm meddling, you understand that? I wouldn't mention this to anyone but you. Maybe I shouldn't even tell you."

"I won't drop you in it," Hood said, smiling. Another resident, a portly man in tweeds, put another piece of paper in front of Hood.

"Sign it for my nephew, will you?" he said, his voice suggesting years of whisky pickling. Hood just looked at him "I saw you when you played for Scotland against West Germany," the man rasped. "You know something, Alec, I think it's a crying shame you never got more caps. Lindsay's had twenty or more and you only got four. A bloody disgrace to the name of Scottish football."

"Flattery will get you everywhere," said Hood, signing the paper.

"You don't have any spare tickets, I don't suppose," the man said. "They're scarcer than virgins up here. I'm willing to pay well over the odds, too . . ."

Hood shook his head. The man sighed.

"Oh well, all the best for Saturday," said the man. "May the best Rangers team win!" He went off, laughter changing to a coughing fit. Hood said he'd long ago got used to the fact that strangers called him by his Christian name and patted his shoulders and interrupted his conversations and demanded autographs for their sons and nephews.

"I don't mind, as long as they're civil about it," he said. "Which isn't always the case, believe me."

Peterson told him what Albert Stone had told him on the terracing at Oaks Common that morning, how the chairman and

John Gallagher were not on speaking terms and that the club was looking for another manager.

"Of course it's all fantasy," he said. "Yet J.G.'s been behaving very strangely today, hasn't he?"

"Aye, he has," said Hood, taking a slow sip of his lager. "Did you mention this to anyone else?"

"Of course not. Do you think John Gallagher ought to be told?"

"Don't bother him with it now, Bill, take my advice."

"Bother him? I should think it would bother him! He's taken this club to the greatest level of success it's had in ten years and they might be doing the dirty on him! Behind his back! Maybe he knows already, maybe he's heard a whisper and that's why he's been so grouchy. What do you think?"

The waiter returned with the drinks. Peterson asked him to charge it to his room number but Hood said briskly that it should be charged to the club.

"Look, Bill," Hood said when the waiter had gone, "I know what's bothering J.G. It isn't what you think."

"Oh?"

"Believe me, the last thing he wants now is to be told some fairy tale by Limpalong Leslie."

"Can you swear blind it is a fairy tale?"

Hood made a little grimace.

"To be honest, no. The word is about that J.G. and the chairman are not exactly horny about each other."

"Well then—he's got a right to know, hasn't he? Yes, I've decided, I'm going to tell him when he gets back from Greenock."

Hood put down his glass and stared at Peterson. Then he came to a decision.

"Bill, I'm going to break a confidence," he said. "I wouldn't do this in any other circumstances—and if you breathe a dickybird to anyone else about what I'm going to tell you, I'll—"

"Look, Alec, you can trust me, you know that."

"No matter how much you drink, Bill, you utter one hint that you know anything and I will break your neck, so help me."

Peterson blushed and said nothing, feeling he had been slapped in the face. Hood didn't seem to notice.

"The fact is we went for a mass X-ray on Monday—you remember, they wanted the whole team to take publicity pictures?"

"Yes, I saw them in the *Evening Standard* on Tuesday."

"Anyway, Tuesday afternoon they phoned John Gallagher and said he'd need another X-ray, the plate was smudged or something."

Hood stopped talking. He bit the knuckle of his right thumb, unsure whether to go on. Peterson said nothing.

"So they did him again yesterday afternoon. Just a formality, they said. They made him wait till the plate was developed." He rubbed his hand down his face. "It wasn't a smudged plate this time. They didn't tell him anything definite, just that he would have to have *another* bloody X-ray. That's why he was late this morning, he was at the clinic."

"What happened?"

"They wanted him to wait till a specialist saw the three plates but he had to catch the train with the team. They wouldn't tell him anything definite but he kept on asking them what it could be. They said there might be a shadow on the lung, just might be, they wouldn't commit themselves till the specialist examined the plates. When he phoned they said the specialist had gone. He's got to phone again tomorrow morning."

"Oh my God!"

"Yeah."

They stared at each other.

"Nah, it could be smudged plates," said Peterson.

"It could be. That's what J.G. is trying to tell himself. But you know what a fanatic he is about fitness and health and all that. He's never been ill in his life!"

"They can cure T.B. in a month nowadays," Peterson said.

"Yeah. If it was T.B."

"What else could it be? Not—no, it couldn't be *that*!"

"Don't even say it, Bill."

"Christ Almighty!"

Debonair Dave filled his fourth cup of tea from the white pot on the silver tray in the centre of the big table. The doctor and Norman Jackson were sitting between him and Carole. The chairman had been outlining his plan for using the success of the British Cup as a basis for amalgamating the Scottish First Division with the English First and Second Divisions. Jemima Jackson looked as bored as Dave felt. Around half-past nine she said she was going to bed. Dave watched her leave, wondering how a successful man like George Jackson could have married a dreary old mount like her in the first place, let alone put up with her for twenty-eight years. Some said she had the money.

"I don't see the Scottish clubs being willing to let Rangers and Celtic and four others leave their league," Dave said, not at all interested in how the hell they organised the league but wanting to catch Carole's attention. "Most of the smaller Scottish clubs would be totally bankrupt, wouldn't they, but for the four big gates they get each season against Celtic and Rangers?"

"They'd find their league would be more competitive without the big battalions," George Jackson said. "My experience is that fans will turn up to see a winning team—it doesn't matter what league it is they're winning. It worked in England, didn't it? By taking out the big, dominating clubs you make the lower leagues much more competitive—the rewards for success are much greater—new interest is created."

Debonair Dave wondered how he could reorganise the current seating positions on a better geographical basis. He was genuinely interested in Carole, not just because of the bet. Tasty was the word for her, very tasty. A class richard. What could she possibly see in a twit like Norman, compared to himself? Norman was a nonentity. The players liked him well enough but they didn't take him too seriously, except perhaps as a spy for Big Brother. In the days before George Jackson took over Commoners had become so poor they used to say it was the only club in England whose players were richer than the directors. This still applied to Norman, for everyone knew he had nothing his brother had not given him.

When George Jackson stood up to leave it was only ten minutes to ten. Jackson was one of those rich eccentrics who didn't use his money to sport around nightclubs but went to bed early, generally before ten, rising again at six a.m., reversing what the players thought was the natural order of things for any guy who had made his readies and didn't have to train in the morning.

In the general shake-up caused by Jackson's departure—the doctor going to the lavatory and not making it too clear if he was coming back—Dave saw his chance to move at least one seat nearer Carole. His hands were on the chair-arms to lift himself up when Peterson appeared from behind and slipped into the doctor's chair.

"Can I get anybody a drink?" Peterson said, raising his hand for the waiter. "Norman? Carole? Dave?"

Drinks were ordered and Debonair Dave sat with a stony face, hoping the whisky would choke Peterson.

Sammy had a nose like radar for the best places for a good-time and here they were in a Scottish discotheque, supposed to be having a good time. Danny had never done any socialising in Scotland. In London he had a whole circuit of clubs and pubs and beer-cellars and discotheques where he went to toy with the odd light ale or twenty after a match, but the atmosphere was different up here. Even though they had changed from the club suits into their own gear they had still been recognised. In London a first division player would often be recognised but most London geezers didn't go to discotheques or night spots to stare at footballers, they'd recognise you and point you out to their mates and then carry on with the search for grumble. Up here the blokes seemed to find three footballers more interesting than richards.

"They are bleedin' football crazy," Sammy said as they sat at a corner table. "The way they keep clockin', you'd think they fancied us."

"They think we're English pigs," said Danny. "Tell you what, Sam, I don't fancy pulling no bird in here, these geezers are all Rangers fanatics. Let's try somewhere else, eh?"

"Nah, let's sit tight. How about that little darlin' in the white blouse? I could give her one."

"I fancy her mate," said Johnny Parkinson.

Danny went up to the bar and asked for three more half-pints of lager and lime. This being Wednesday they allowed themselves about four half-pints. John Gallagher had no set rules about drinking. He assumed they were all experienced professionals who knew how much they could take without hurting themselves. Danny made it a rule never to have a drink at all on a Thursday or Friday night, and to take it very easily on Tuesdays and Wednesdays. Saturday night was the players' break-out time. Then he would sink a few pints, or vodkas and lemonade, or rums and coke, or whatever else he fancied. The drink he looked forward to most all week was that first pint of bitter on Saturday. After all the sweat of the match that first big pint seemed to drink itself by a process of instant evaporation. On Saturday it would be champagne! He was thinking about the game, waiting for the barman to fill the glasses, when a man bumped into him, a young-ish man with the over-bright eyes of the quarter-drunk.

"Ye'll need a drink, pal," the young man said, face taking on a squinty sort of smile. "Drown your sorrows in advance—the Gers will blast yese off the face of the earth."

"Will they beat us though?" Danny said, nodding in friendly fashion.

"Aye, they'll beat yese, pal. They are the greatest team on earth. They'll bloody well show yese what this game is a' about. Here, huv a drink with me. Don't want yese saying we Scots are no' hospitable. Give the man a glass a whisky, John," he said to the barman.

"No thanks," said Danny. "The boss doesn't like us on the hard stuff."

"Is that John Gallagher? By Christ, there *was* a player! Aye, there's no' many like him nowadays."

A friend joined the young man. Danny picked up the three glasses and went back to the table. He saw a few girls who were not bad-looking but he didn't feel in the mood. He wished now he hadn't made the bet with Debonair Dave. It would sound very silly if Norman's girl friend got to hear about it. She'd think they were a right crowd of yobs.

They came back into the lounge at twenty past ten, the party that had seen the Morton game, John Gallagher, Harry Barnes, George Westbury, Randall, Gurr, Williamson, Shackle, Riddle and the two boys, Ross and Rowland. The players had cups of tea or coffee and sandwiches, then drifted off to their rooms. Peterson was surprised to find that Christmas and Peacock had not gone to Greenock but had spent the evening in the T.V. lounge. John Gallagher joined them and said he would have a small whisky. He said it had been a fairly dull game at Cappielow Park. He didn't seem to be interested in making conversation. Every time Peterson looked at him he felt sick. Harry Barnes and George Westbury said they were going to bed. It was exactly three minutes to eleven when Danny, Sammy and Johnny Parkin-son came through the front entrance, glanced into the lounge, shouted their good nights and hurried to the lift. It occurred to Peterson that he had not seen Albert Stone. Only Norman and

Carole and the doctor and himself were left now, Sims having gone to bed around ten-thirty. Peterson did not feel drunk, but he was sober enough to tell himself that drunks never do feel drunk. He decided to keep a close watch on his tongue. Tread warily on thin ice, was a phrase he kept repeating to himself. He couldn't keep his eyes off John Gallagher, trying to think himself into the manager's mind. John Gallagher took a long time over his small whisky, being content to listen to the conversation of the others, which at that time meant the doctor. While Carole laughed merrily at the jolly old doc's cheery tales of wrongful amputations and fatally erroneous diagnoses, Norman Jackson sat smirking dutifully but looking tense. With drunken clarity, Peterson realised what the situation was between Norman and Carole. Norman had not yet made her bed but was hoping that tonight was the night. Somebody started talking about great players of the past. Peterson hadn't heard the opening of the subject but he blurted out that in his opinion as a soccer fan for thirty-five years man and boy the greatest single player he had ever seen was John Charles, the gentle giant who could play equally brilliantly at centre-half or centre-forward. It seemed important for him to tell Carole, in great detail, that John Charles had been one of the few British players who made a success in Italy.

"A lot went to Italy because we had a twenty pound a week maximum wage and the Eyties were paying big money. Greaves went from Chelsea and Law from Manchester City and Joe Baker from Hibs. Baker threw a photographer into the Grand Canal in Venice! Only John Charles stuck it out—I don't think the others learned the lingo."

"Gerry Hitchens stuck it out quite well," said John Gallagher.

"Ah yes," said Peterson, "that's true." He began to tell Carole all about Hitchens, the miner's son who went to Italy in search of fame and fortune. He was going to tell her in great detail about the transfer situation and the Italian points bonus system and how Italian players didn't break legs but spat in your eyes or nipped your skin while pretending to help you off the ground, it all seemed vital for her to know, but he changed his mind and asked John Gallagher who he thought were the greatest players he had ever seen. It was the sort of thing he was always wanting to ask John Gallagher about but rarely had the temerity, J.G. not being a guy for chatting about the past.

John Gallagher named a few names—John White of Spurs, known as The Pale Ghost of White Hart Lane long before he was killed in his prime on a golf course by a stroke of lightning—Neil Franklin, Stoke City and England, smoothest centre-half the game had seen, one of the rebels who made the mistake of trying to get a living wage in Bogota in South America—Tommy Taylor the centre-forward and Duncan Edwards the left-half of the great Manchester United team which crashed in the slush of the Munich airport disaster—and the mighty Frank Swift, who also died in that crash, a journalist by then, a huge man who could pick up a football in one hand as if it were an orange—and Derek Dooley, the red-headed sensation who burst onto the English scene as one of the greatest goal-scoring cavaliers the game had seen . . . and then John Gallagher said he was going to bed and as he watched the manager's receding back Peterson realised that the manager's greats were almost all stars who had been cut down in their prime by death or illness or savage injury and he shut his eyes and shivered, knowing why John Gallagher's mind had been running in that direction.

"You all right?" Paul Franks asked. "You look ill, old boy. You need a stiff drink. Waiter! Now then, let's not get morbid. Did I ever tell you about the autopsy I once had to do on a headless woman they fished out of the Thames . . ."

Carole stood up, saying she was tired. Norman said he was also, suddenly, very tired. The doctor and Peterson were left alone in the big lounge. Peterson called for the waiter. In the very strictest confidence he told the doctor, his very dearest oldest mate, what Albert Stone had told him on the terraces. The doctor told Peterson, in the strictest confidence, that he had known about this all along. They both told each other, many times, that they trusted each other implicitly not to breathe a word to anyone else. On his way upstairs Peterson kept congratulating himself on not having told the doctor about John Gallagher's X-ray.

It was like an instant playback from the T.V. coverage of the big game. He got the ball half-way inside the Rangers defence, swayed past two midfield men, made ground fast to the right-hand corner of the penalty box. Lindsay—the one they called Killer—stabbed out his leg to stop him going forward. He pulled the ball back with the sole of his boot, then accelerated forward, leaving Lindsay floundering. He hit it across the goal, a beauty, screaming into the top left-hand corner of the net. The playback started again. This time he took the ball, got past the first two Rangers defenders—and as he sprinted for the box he saw himself falling to the ground, clutching at his thigh, his face contorted with pain, the stretcher-bearers walking with little, jerky steps, photographers making sidling rushes to get a shot of his strained face . . .

Roy Christmas sat up in bed, breathing quickly. Outside in the corridor someone was singing the Commoners song in a deep, drunken monotone. Doors banged. The voice went on droning, interrupted by a high-pitched cackling laugh. He looked at his luminous watch. It was half-past one. He'd been trying to get to sleep for hours, making himself imagine he was seeing Saturday's game on television. Across the room he heard Alec Hood's steady breathing. Alec was lucky, he always went to sleep the moment his head hit the pillow. For a moment he had a desperate urge to wake him up and ask him for reassurance.

"Who the bleedin' hell is that?" Sammy demanded. Danny switched on the light. Peterson was standing inside the door of their room, arms in the air, mouth still open on the last note of 'You'll Never Walk Alone.'

"What are you doin' in my bloody room?" he asked, his voice thick and his face screwed up with surprise.

"Your room?"

Danny looked at Sammy and winked.

"Sorry about that, Bill," he said. He threw off the bedclothes and walked to the door in the nude.

"I should think so, too," Peterson was saying, snorting with disgust.

"What number room is this, Bill?" Danny asked. Peterson swayed a little.

"What number room are you in, Bill?" Sammy asked.

"Two-one-eight, of course."

Danny held the door open.

"And what number is that?" he asked, pointing at the plastic numerals. Peterson had to screw up his eyes. He peered at the number from a range of two inches. He traced the outlines with a finger.

"Two—one—nine," he said, triumphantly. Then he put his fingertips to his mouth and giggled.

They heard him crashing into his own room. Danny switched off the light.

"Bill's had a good night then," Sammy said. "More than we had. Cor, wasn't that richard in the discotheque a proper little darlin'?"

"You're all talk. If you were so keen on her why did you suggest we packed it in?"

"Yeah well, that was cos of them haggis-bashers, you never know wiv jocks when they're drinkin', one minute they're buyin' you scotches and callin' you mate and the next they're all stroppy wantin' to kick your face in."

"Sammy Small scared of a few scotch piss artists? You were scared that little darlin' might call your bluff and want to drop 'em. Sure you ain't got a permanent case of brewer's droop?"

"Shut up, I want to get to sleep."

"I'll give you a tip how to get to sleep. It's Saturday, five minutes to go and we're level, one goal each. Lindsay trips Roy heading for goal. Alec Hood points the finger at you. Penalty! The whole game depends on you. How d'you think you'd feel, Sam—full of beans, ready to bang it in, no bother? Think about it, that'll suit you better'n counting sheep, provided you ever knew what sheep look like."

"Cor, leave me out! I won't get a bleedin' wink now, thinkin' about that."

"Good night, me old son."

"You're a right friend, you are."

Steady yourself, he said, and he lay back and stared up at the darkness. The instant T.V. playback started all over again. He got the ball and beat the first two men and began the sprint towards the penalty box. He held his breath. No—he didn't feel the muscle in his thigh. He made it to the edge of the box. Lindsay lunged at him. He dragged the ball back and glided past the big centre-back . . .

I'll be all right, he said to himself, over and over again.

11

THE following item appeared in the Scottish *Daily Record* on Thursday, March 16, in the column, 'Inside Scottish Soccer' by Ian Jarvie, The Man Who Knows.

THE CIRCUS COMES TO TOWN

That well-known travelling circus of cocky Cockney chappies known as the Commoners of London town breezed into Scotland yesterday.

They're no slouches at being witty in front of a camera, these fun-loving wits from south of the Thames. I got the impression they see Rangers as humble provincial nobodies about to be slaughtered by high-powered English know-how.

Well, cockney cousins, I hope for your sakes certain provincial nobodies by the name of Milne, Grant, Lindsay and Graham were not watching T.V. last night. In case you don't know, they are the Rangers back four.

They might not be up to Palladium standards with a fast wise-crack, they may not be heading for their first millions — but I have a definite feeling they would not be amused.

Let's see how sharp the gags are on Saturday night! As every comedian knows, Glasgow is the toughest place for laughs in the whole country.

P.S. Did you notice that Roy Christmas wasn't full of good cheer? Has somebody been telling him that Dave Killer Lindsay doesn't believe in Santa Claus?

12

A middle-aged American couple got into the lift with some of the team going downstairs for a pre-breakfast meeting set by John Gallagher for eight-fifteen. Randall was telling Hood, Shack and Sammy about the game at Greenock the night before. The tall, paunchy American, who was wearing a floppy tartan tammie, was obviously interested in what Randy was saying. Between the second and first floors he cleared his throat and asked in a deep voice:

"Excuse me, sir, are you guys the London sakker team everybody's talking about? You're sakker fitballers?"

Sammy's somewhat puffy eyes were level with the ends of the American's string tie.

"He's the star, guv," he said, nodding at Randy. "We're his personal staff, like, valets and that."

"Is that so?" said the American, staring at Randy with new interest.

"Yeah—you haven't heard of him over in the States? He's the biggest name in the whole of soccer football. He's the goalkeeper. We call him The Salmon."

Randy had been making modest little faces but he quickly changed to a frown, knowing that Sammy was on the trail of a joke.

"The salmon? Oh, I get it, because he jumps so high?"

"No—because he always ends up in the net."

Even Seymour managed a laugh when this went round the Rob Roy suite, a big room smelling of last night's stale tobacco. Seymour didn't really feel like laughing. He knew what was ahead of him this morning. By eight-twenty they were all present, sixteen players, Harry Barnes and George Westbury. There was no sign of John Gallagher. The Scottish morning papers were quickly grabbed and passed round to find out what was being said in the football sections. Nobody wasted time on the front pages, where there was the usual stuff about the guerilla wars in Africa. With four others looking over his shoulder Shack read out a caption from the *Scottish Daily Express*; Gustafson, the Dane who played midfield for Rangers, had become engaged to an Edinburgh model, a tall girl with red hair pictured beside the blond Dane on the arm of his chair, leg showing all the way up.

"Cor!" somebody moaned. Biceps were gripped and fists clenched in meaningful gesticulations as to the fate of the lady should she fall into enemy hands. "I thought all them Scotch bints wore woolly knicks!" said Johnny Parkinson.

Hood did not join in. He felt a dull churning in his guts. John Gallagher would be phoning London in less than two hours. He sat in an armchair, the *Daily Record* spread on his knees. Behind him Brian Seymour stood at the big windows staring moodily at the shining water of the Clyde.

"Here Brian," Hood said, twisting round, "look what this nit is saying about us."

Seymour grunted, reluctantly turning away from the view to look over Hood's shoulder. He read from the paper:

" 'Inside Scottish Soccer by Ian Jarvie, The Man Who Knows.' He a big deal up here, is he? Ugly-looking bugger."

"Read the piece. He say's we're a travelling circus of cocky Cockneys."

"Hmmph!" Seymour snorted derisively after reading the article. "You don't think he could be biased in any way, do you?"

"Not much. If we hadn't made any jokes he'd have called us a bunch of big-headed English pigs."

Over the years Hood had learned the hard way that no footballer could afford to take the newspapers seriously if he wanted to keep his peace of mind, but the columnist's digs gave him a momentary irritation. Only a few football writers knew much about what really went on out there on the park, but the Scottish ones had a special line in hysterical patriotism. It had been the same when he played for Scotland. On the morning of an international match the Scottish writers would be calling them the greatest team on earth and the day after they'd be screaming for half the team to be crucified, reserving special poison for the

Anglo-Scots, those traitorous renegades who had gone south to English clubs for the big money. If you believed the Scottish football writers any professional who went south immediately turned Quisling, becoming so money-minded as to regard an outing with the Scottish team as a trivial little picnic, when the truth was that every Anglo-Scot he knew was literally desperate to play and win for Scotland.

He saw Danny Peck and was going to ask him why he had missed the committee meeting when John Gallagher appeared in the doorway of the Rob Roy suite. He was wearing a bright green cardigan and he had not shaved. For a moment he stood in the door, legs astride, arms folded, as if waiting for his photograph to be taken. The team quietened down.

"Sorry I'm late," John Gallagher said. "You're going to have a hard session this morning, so have a light breakfast and then get changed into training kit and be outside for nine-thirty—on the dot. Harry, you take the lads up to the training pitch, I'll be up later."

"Right, Boss."

"Oh yes—Roy won't be training this morning, he's got a bit of a strain, I want him to give it a bit of a rest."

Nobody paid much attention to this. Hood was the only one who seemed to notice how subdued the manager was. He hung back as the others crowded out of the lounge. John Gallagher made no move to follow them.

"I'll keep my fingers crossed," Hood murmured as he came face to face with the manager. "It'll be all right, you'll see."

John Gallagher nodded, smiling faintly, his face drawn from lack of sleep.

The last two players to arrive on the gravel forecourt at the side entrance of the hotel were Sammy and Danny, both running down the wide steps in their green tracksuits and white track-shoes.

"Where have you two been—rehearsing the jokes?" said Harry Barnes. Nobody laughed. They all knew this morning's training session would be their last hard work-out before the big game. Tomorrow they would have a casual session, a few sprints, maybe a run-through all the dead ball situations, corners, free-kicks, throw-ins—and as Sammy had joked at breakfast, practice at carrying Alec Hood round the Hampden track on a lap of honour. The hard work would be done today.

"My legs feel stiff, Dan," said Sammy as Harry Barnes gave the order to start jogging up the road to the training pitch. Sammy and Danny had, as always, fallen to the rear of the column, a fine-looking bunch of men in the green tracksuits with the black collars and the big black letters on their backs, COMMONERS, all of them running easily in the early morning sunshine.

"Great scenery, isn't it?" said Dave Spencer, who was jogging beside Brian Seymour. "Isn't the air fresh, eh?"

Seymour grunted. He was not going to waste any breath on small-talk. Once they reached the training pitch he knew he would need all the lung-power he had.

"I said my legs are feeling stiff, Dan," said Sammy.

"So do mine."

"I hope I'll feel good on Saturday."

"You will."

"I feel tired already. Cor, have we got to jog all the way up that steep hill?"

"Don't if you don't want to. I'll tell Harry you're too tired. He'll send you back to bed."

"Cor, I wish I never had them eggs and bacon."

"Serves you right, the boss told you to have a light breakfast. He said we'd be training hard."

"I hope I won't be sick."

"Oh shut up. It's all in the mind."

Danny jogged easily, looking at the great expanse of river and the hills beyond. He caught a glimpse of Brian Seymour's face, all tight and expressionless. He knew what Brian would be thinking. Sammy kept up a continuous flow of worries and complaints. Some players were like that, moaning about details when they were really worried about the game ahead. But Brian Seymour never moaned. Hard training was an ordeal for him, they all knew that. Few of them understood why he bothered. Danny thought he knew.

"I think I might just be sick, you know that?" Sammy said.

"It's all in the mind I tell you."

"Cor, I shouldn't have had them eggs and bacon."

"If your legs are stiff your tongue ain't."

As they came to the top of the hill they could see the training pitches and the small pavilion where the hotel stored footballs and other practice gear. It was geared to cater for professional clubs on training visits. The big Scottish clubs used Strannoch Hydro and so did international teams and some North of England clubs looking for seclusion and fresh air. A lone photographer was standing at the gateway into the training ground, a young chap, probably a local photographer out to make a few quid. As they passed, Sammy and Danny flashed him wide, mocking smiles.

The jogging column followed Harry Barnes and George Westbury across the two thickly-grassed pitches to the little wooden pavilion. George Westbury had the key. He and Harry came out with nets holding footballs, some orange, some white. They opened the nets and threw the balls onto the grass. Like children unable to resist ice-cream the players started kicking the balls about, flicking them up on insteps, juggling them from foot to knee to forehead. Only Seymour did not grab a ball for himself. Harry Barnes looked at his watch. It was fifteen minutes to ten.

"Okay, leave the balls alone," he shouted. The players drifted into a semi-circle in front of the coach. "Sammy!" he bawled and Sammy ran to join them. "Put those balls down and listen."

Sammy put his hand to his mouth and said something to Danny.

"What are you chatting about now?" the coach demanded.

"It's only small-talk," Danny said. "*Small* talk—get it?"

"Very good, Peck—now let's get on with what we're here for. Right?"

First they did two warming-up laps, running in pairs, Harry Barnes jogging up and down the line, shouting at them to keep close up. For this short time at least he was in sole charge of the team and he knew they would be comparing him to John Gallagher. He wanted to let them know that he was not just John Gallagher's number two. He had ideas of his own and he wasn't to be treated like a nonentity. Perhaps they might even begin to realise that John Gallagher wasn't the only man in the world.

When the two laps were finished Harry Barnes picked up a ball and led the fifteen players onto the middle of the nearest pitch. Using only one half of it they began a game of keep-ball, without goals, each man allowed only two consecutive touches of the ball before he had to pass it, a free kick given to the other team if he touched it a third time, the winning team being the one which managed the greatest number of consecutive passes in one

117

sequence. It was a hard way to play, depending on the willingness of each man to keep running into positions to receive a pass.

Brian Seymour took it very coolly, never searching for the ball, playing it only when it came directly to him, expending the minimum amount of energy, economising his strength for what was to come. Shouts and cries echoed in the sharp Scottish air.

Peterson had just managed to survive the ordeal of watching a rudely wideawake Sims ploughing through sausage and bacon and eggs when he saw John Gallagher speaking to the girl at the reception desk. The manager was wearing his green tracksuit. The girl pointed to the phone booths at the other end of the foyer and John Gallagher walked towards them.

Peterson could not remember getting to bed the night before, which meant there had probably been some kind of social disaster. He knew himself well enough to bet on it. He felt sick. He was not sure whether it was all hangover. God knows what I did, he thought, but it must have been bad and it couldn't have happened at a worse moment. He could see John Gallagher's broad back, with the big black letters, COMMONERS, pushing into a phone booth. He knew his first cigarette would probably ruin his chances of living till lunchtime but he lit it anyway, making no attempt to conceal the extreme nausea induced in him by the sight of Sims tucking in to yet another slice of toast and marmalade.

"You staying with us today?" he asked.

"There's a train at lunchtime," Sims said.

"Think you've got enough for a piece?"

"I don't know. Bit disjointed, really. No focal point, no obvious theme."

"How could there be if you don't come to the game? It's like literary coitus interruptus."

"The game will be written to death by Monday. They expect me to find the little hidden detail, the unexpected cameo that opens up the closed world."

"Yes," said Peterson, thoughtfully, glancing through to see if John Gallagher had finished his phone call.

They were coming out of the breakfast room when John Gallagher leaned out of the phone booth and called to the girl.

"This line's no good," he shouted. "I can't hear a bloody word."

"I'll get the call transferred to extension number three," the girl called back. John Gallagher changed booths, walking steadily, face expressionless.

"Shall we go up to the training ground and watch the team for a bit?" Sims asked. Peterson winced. These were tense times for the players. Had he gone crashing into any of their rooms, waving a bottle and trying to start a party? It was just the kind of disastrous urge he developed when drunk.

"We might as well," he said, thinking with mirthless humour that few people knew the bravery expected of the drunkard on his return to the world. It was the not knowing that was the worst of it, the searching of men's faces for signs of justified rage. He ought to have been writing the rest of the stuff for the brochure. He could hide away in his room and let the complaining parties come to him. He decided to face the team. If he wasn't sent home in disgrace he would get down to the typewriter at lunchtime. It didn't seem likely he would be ready for solids by then.

They both bought papers at the reception desk. They were just moving away from the counter when John Gallagher came out of the phone box. He stood for a moment, staring at space. Then he walked quickly towards them. Peterson felt himself cringing.

"Is there a car that'll take me up to the training pitch?" John Gallagher asked the girl.

"Oh I'm sorry, Mr. Gallagher, our driver's just taken a party to Kilmarnock. I don't think there's anyone else at all."

"I saw a bloke outside with a Land-Rover, John," Peterson said. "Will I see if he's still around?"

"Anything will do," John Gallagher said, walking quickly to the front entrance. Peterson followed him. He saw the man, obviously a hotel employee, lifting milk urns into the back of the Land-Rover. He started across the gravel, grimly holding down his nausea, preparing to soft-talk the man into giving them a lift. John Gallagher brushed past him, trackshoes crunching gravel away from under the heels.

"Give us a lift up to the training ground?" he called.

The man looked round. For a moment Peterson thought he was going to ignore them. Then he smiled.

"Oh hallo—Mr. Gallagher—aye, just jump in the wagon, I'll huv ye up there in twa shakes."

"Quick as you like, friend, I've been wasting too much time already."

"Right-oh." As they hurried round to the front of the vehicle Peterson heard the driver shout something else in his nearly incomprehensible Scots accent:

"Ye'll no' tell 'em in Glesca it wiz Wullie Tims o' Lairgs that helpt ye get tae the practice groon, will ye? Ma freens wud niver let me live it doon. We're a' backin' the Gers for quids tae beat ye!"

Peterson had just enough time to clamber into the back beside the urns, rapping his shin painfully on the back flap. They shot off across the gravel. Sims was still on the steps of the hotel entrance, staring at them in amazement. Peterson knew it would not be a good idea to ask them to wait for the *Guardian* man. He waved at Sims, indicating that he should follow on foot. Sims looked none too pleased.

"A lovely morning," he said, edging up to the front.

"Oh aye, it doesnae aye rain up here, ye know," said the driver. "This is the Costa Clyde, man!"

John Gallagher said nothing. Peterson swallowed hard, wondering if he should slide to the rear in case he had to throw up over the back flap.

Sims had just started the long walk to the training ground when he heard running steps. It was Albert Stone.

"Slept in, din't I?" mumbled Albert.

"Did you?"

"Yeah—hope the boss don't notice, he'll give me a right rollockin' he will, very strict on time-keepin' is John Gallagher. It was blowin' up them balls what done it, fair knackered I am."

"Blowing up balls?"

"Yeah, all bleedin' night—the hotel's got the balls, like, but they need blowin' up so I'm down to get them ready for today so when I get down there I can't find the foot-pump, can I? So I have to do 'em with a bicycle pump, don't I, twenty of the bleeders! Cor, I was sick, I can tell you."

Sims realised this was his story, the little off-beat anecdote that would take the reader behind the scenes, the eccentric detail that told more than a hundred high-powered melodramas. It would be a good piece now, he knew, almost as good as the piece he wrote after a day in a big circus, when he did the whole thing on the man who swept up with brush and pan after the elephants.

Andy Gurr used the outside of his right foot to hit a short, quick pass to Alec Hood. It came at the big centre-back very fast and he had to use one of his two touches to trap it, stabbing down with his right instep, quickly looking for somebody in the clear.

"Yours Brian," he yelled, waving at Seymour to run out on the wing, away from Danny. Brian was slow in moving. Wiggy Ingrams came at Hood and he had to pass it too quickly. Danny intercepted the pass, hitting a first-time half-volley ball to the right wing, where Ian Rowland took it on his raised thigh, let it fall in front of him and then slid a neat two-yard pass to Wiggy, who had run ten yards into the open space. They were playing in sides of eight and seven, Roy's absence making an odd number. Over their green tracksuits Hood's side, who were a man short, wore sleeveless yellow training bibs, thin waterproofed canvas jackets which were really just back and front sections joined by elastic under the arms. These could be quickly changed, being used to distinguish the different sides in training sessions. Danny Peck's side ran up a sequence of ten passes before Shack got the ball away from Ian Rowland and back-heeled it to Hood. Again Seymour was the nearest man and again he was slow in finding an empty space. Harry Barnes shouted at him to keep moving. Hood fell back to take a breather. He saw the Land-Rover pull through the gateway onto the grass. John Gallagher got out. The ball banged about in a series of bad passes. Hood moved over to the touchline, watching John Gallagher walking towards him, white trackshoes sinking into thick green grass, legs slightly bowed at the knee. He was in his tracksuit now. His face was set hard. Hood waited, ignoring the game. Behind him he heard Harry Barnes roaring at young Ross to run into a space.

He looked at John Gallagher, the question on his face.

"What are you doing—think you're on holiday?" John Gallagher said. The big centre-back shut his eyes involuntarily.

"Harry!" John Gallagher shouted across the pitch, waving at Barnes to come over to the touchline. Players looked round. The game came to a standstill. Wiggy put his right foot on the ball.

"For God's sake, Harry, put some zip into them," John Gallagher barked at the coach. "Get them bloody running!"

"Okay, Boss," said Harry, sprinting back into the middle, his voice already sounding harsher and more urgent. Seymour lifted himself from the grass, rising slowly and deliberately, taking deep, controlled breaths, preparing himself for the crunch to come.

Hood stood his ground, eyes on John Gallagher's face.

"What did they say, Boss?" he asked quietly.

"What? Come on, man—get out there, we're here to train not to gossip!"

"But what did they say?"

John Gallagher took a step to the side and called to Williamson to put some life in it. Then he looked at Hood.

"It was a fault in the plates," he said. "I'm perfectly all right. Lot of stupid bollocks, wasted time and nothing else. Now then, will you get out there and do the bloody job we pay you for? Show them an example, Alec, we've got a bloody game to play on Saturday!"

"You're all right! That's great!"

For a moment their eyes met. John Gallagher stared at him in a peculiar way, as if defying him to ask the question again.

"COME ON YOU LAZY DEVILS," he bawled out over the pitch. "GET MOVING!"

As Hood ran back into position he felt so good he wanted to leap up and down with joy. Wiggy came in front of him, letting the ball run untouched, trying to beat him with the famous Wiggy hips, feinting this way and that. Hood stabbed his right instep against the ball, leg bent so that the knee was just over the ball, a grimly hard tackle that had Wiggy crashing on his back.

"Come on, you bastards," he roared, slamming the ball at Jimmy Riddle.

When Sims and Albert Stone joined Peterson on the bench in front of the pavilion the players were gathered round John Gallagher, who was explaining the next exercise, arms raised as he pointed up and down the length of the pitch.

"Sorry about that, old boy," said Peterson, moving up the bench. "John Gallagher was in such a hurry he wouldn't wait. I trust the walk was beneficial."

"Useful, you could say. And what are our heroes doing now?"

"They've been playing keep-ball—now I think it's to be something more strenuous. Just watch. I always find this is the perfect antidote to little fantasies of wanting to be a player—watching them training. They might do doggies this morning—you could get a heart attack just *watching* that one!"

The players formed up three abreast, each line with a ball which they interpassed while running up one side of the pitch and down the other. John Gallagher and Harry Barnes kept shouting at the lines of three to run faster. As they passed the bench Peterson could see they were beginning to sweat. The laughing had stopped. They looked now what they really were, professionals concentrating on a job, faces set with determination. Peterson tried to catch Hood's eye hoping for some indication of the result of John Gallagher's phone call, but Hood was too busy running and passing the ball sideways to Dave Spencer and Jimmy Riddle. Hard lines showed round his mouth. This was the professional putting his body through it, punishing heart, lungs, muscles and sinews. Peterson wished that all the fans and soccer writers and armchair critics could be here, the ones who said that professionals put in as little effort as they could get away with. What he had come to know was that professionals put in the maximum effort where it was required, and wasted not an ounce of energy on the things that did not matter. When a team ran on to a pitch for the pre-match kickabout they often looked like cripples, stiff-kneed and indifferent, men you might think incapable of a slow foxtrot. But kicking in wasn't the game. Fetching a dead ball from the cinder-track wasn't the game. Running five yards to give an opponent the ball for a free kick wasn't the game. Busting a gut chasing a ball that you had only a five per cent chance of reaching wasn't the game. Only amateurs chased anything and everything and got crowd applause for fetching dead balls to hand to opponents. Only amateurs played with the reckless enthusiasm of schoolboys. Amateurs went out to have a good game, professionals went out to win. The word professional didn't only signify that you were paid money to play. It meant that you put everything you had into football, your brain and your body, your whole waking life.

"I'm beginning to see the attraction of a football career," said Sims, stretching his arms. "How wonderful—to be out in the fresh air, with all this marvellous scenery, kicking a ball about, keeping yourself fit and healthy. Millionaires pay vast sums to health farms for this kind of thing, you know."

"I'd pay vast sums to avoid it," said Peterson.

This was only for starters, as they said, and already Brian Seymour knew he was struggling. As he ran between young Rowland and Gerry Williamson he knew he should have chucked it in last season. They'd given him the choice—another year's contract as a player or a job on the coaching staff. Why hadn't he given up playing? He wouldn't even be among the substitutes for Saturday's match. Nobody would be really shocked if he packed it in now, right in the middle of training. At thirty-five a lot of them reckoned it was a miracle he could carry on at all. Yet he did. And he kept up with Ian Rowland and Gerry Williamson, forcing his legs to keep going, defying his body not to lag behind, knowing only that he had wanted to go on as a player till the last moment, determined not to let them see him admit defeat.

John Gallagher called to Harry Barnes and they chatted together briefly in the middle of the pitch. Some of the players flopped on the grass, stretched out on their backs. Seymour kept on his feet. After each little rest it became harder to start again. Harry Barnes ran to the pavilion and came out with a bundle of white posts about four feet long. He began shoving these sticks into the grass at various intervals. Peterson counted a line of twelve, with two forming small goals at the end of the line, in front of the proper goals where Randy took up position.

George Westbury came to sit on the bench. He explained to Sims that the idea of the next exercise was to practise close control, stamina and shooting.

"They have to dribble up the line and finish with a shot through the two small posts at Randy," he said.

"We used to do things like that at school sports day," said Sims.

"I doubt it," said George, winking at Peterson.

Danny Peck was the first to go. He dribbled the ball from the first post to the second, round it and back to the first, round it and then up to the third post and back to the second, progressing at speed up the line in stages until he finished with a shot between the two small posts, a crashing shot which bulleted over Randy's head into the roof of the net. He kept running and picked the ball out of the net. The other players cheered. As he came back Danny tapped Randy on the top of the head, laughing at him. Randy kicked out at Danny's legs but missed. Danny ran all the way back to the starting position, laughing all the way. Peterson lit a new cigarette and coughed catarrh onto the grass.

"Did he really intend to connect with that kick?" Sims asked.

"Nah," said George Westbury, "if he'd really meant to kick him Danny would be on a stretcher by now."

Shack started dribbling up and down the line of posts, looking very quick, moving on his toes, body veering incisively round the white markers. Peterson often wondered if the style in which players moved on the field was an extension of their actual personalities. In most cases, he had decided, it was but not with Shack, who was a complete contrast to the ironic man who had spent the whole train journey slumped in the corner looking as if a walk to the bar and back might cause a rupture. Randy saved Shack's final shot at goal and threw the ball overarm towards the waiting pack of players. Sammy started up the line of markers. Now there was somebody whose movements were a direct reflection of his off-the-field personality. He nipped round posts, head swaying from side to side as if they were lunging defenders, head over the ball, not just content to run through the motions but putting skill and artistry into it, finishing with a left foot shot that soared high and hard over the bar. He put his hands on his hips and glared at Randy and then jogged back.

Seymour began the dribbling run. Peterson could see that he did not dash at it like the others. The crafty old veteran had learned how to save every particle of energy, taking the ball to the posts without covering a single unnecessary inch of ground. When he reached the white posts at the end he lashed laboriously at the ball but didn't connect properly. It bounced four or five times before it reached Randy, who rolled it back along the grass. Seymour picked up the ball and walked wearily back to the main group.

When they had all completed this part of training Harry Barnes pulled out the posts and they got ready to fire quick balls at Dave Peacock, the striker, the forward who, with Roy Christmas, would be expected to score the goals that would beat the Rangers. He took up position outside the penalty box, about twenty yards from the goal. Each player dribbled the ball from midfield, hit a short ball to Peacock, took a quick pass back and hit a first-time shot at Randy in goal. Riddle ran fast on the bright grass, shoving an angled pass at Peacock and hitting a hard, rising shot at the right-hand corner of the goal, Randy leaping across and up, touching it over the bar with his left hand. Williamson came next, then Spencer, then Wiggy, all of them running under the eyes and the shouts of John Gallagher and Harry Barnes, running and dribbling and passing, Randy pulling off several brilliant saves, determined that nobody else would laugh at him.

"He's very agile," said Sims. "Amazing reflexes."

"He's a first-class goalkeeper," said George Westbury. "You'll find it hard to beat him with anything short of a hand-grenade."

Peterson's hangover seemed to have evaporated in the clear air and the sunshine and he found himself wishing he could grab a ball and start kicking it. To be young and fit and be part of the team on a morning like this—that would be *something*. If Sims had been the type he might have sneaked a ball away and had a kick-around behind the pavilion. His feet yearned to touch it, to trap and flick and volley. Instead he sat still, smoking and watching. As always when he watched training he was struck by the contrast between the players as they looked in tracksuits and as they looked in a proper game. The yellow bibs and tracksuits gave them an almost industrial air. On Saturday when they ran on to the great Hampden pitch they would be dressed in the neat magic of shirts, pants and stockings. Their lines would be sharp. From high in the stands the game would look like a sweatless exercise in geometry. But here, close up, on a level, you could see the sweat and hear the shouts and there was no magic, only hard graft. He did not know if it was a good thing, the privilege of watching them like this, working on their skills, practising the components they would bring together on Saturday. He had a sensation of disillusionment when he watched them training, like meeting a long-adored actress face to face and seeing the wrinkles and the open pores.

It's all in the mind, Seymour kept thinking as his turn came round again, each time more quickly. Off he ran. It's because I know I'm older than the rest that I think I can't take it, he thought. Again and again John Gallagher or Harry Barnes gave him the signal and off he went and each time he told himself it seemed a little easier. They were all concentrating hard now, nobody joking. It was as if Saturday was already reaching out to them, the big match atmosphere beginning to send the first alert signals to their nervous systems. He felt so good in himself, now that he had his second wind, he wished he could play in the game itself. There was no reason why he shouldn't. Only his age. And that was all in the mind.

They were going by car to Glasgow to have lunch with the Rangers directors, George Jackson, Jemima, Norman and Carole. When the pageboy said the car was waiting they came into the foyer. Roy Christmas had just been phoning his mother in Burnley. They met beside the reception desk.

"Not training then, Roy?" the chairman asked, with no other intention than to make casual conversation with his star.

"Roy's been having a little muscular strain," said the doctor.

"Nothing serious anyway," said the chairman, anxious to be on his way to Glasgow.

"We'll know tomorrow," said Roy. The chairman stopped, his face suddenly alert with suspicion.

"How bad is it?" he demanded, turning on Paul Franks.

"It's that same muscle he strained three weeks ago," said the doctor. "John thought it best he gave it a bit of a rest today. He'll be all right."

The chairman stared heavily at his expensive star. Roy was embarrassed. He was shy with most people but this was the man who had paid one hundred and forty thousand pounds for him. He didn't feel he had any right to deny the chairman a full explanation.

"It came bad again on Tuesday at training," he found himself saying. "Mister Gallagher said we'd rest it till Friday morning — I'll have a fitness test — I think it will be okay."

"A fitness test?" The chairman stared at the doctor. "I see," he said, "I see."

In the car on the way to Glasgow he said nothing to the others. His face was expressionless but Jemima and Norman knew he was raging about something. By the time they reached Glasgow he had decided that the moment had come for clearing up the situation between John Gallagher and himself, once and for all.

It had started over Roy, that was the funny thing. Roy was already an England regular and he had heard that Burnley were willing to sell the remaining five years of his contract. John Gallagher had not been as enthusiastic as he had hoped. He said that Riddle and Peacock were getting quite a lot of goals and he would ideally like to spend money on strengthening their defence. However they agreed that it would not be often that a young player of Roy's stature became available and they bought him. The row had come over Stan Barlow of Notts Forest. His contract was up and they knew he wanted to move to London.

"He wants twelve thousand to sign on and a guarantee of twenty-one thousand for a three-year contract," Jackson had told the board. "He's only twenty-four and he looks like being an England regular—just the sort of player I want for this club. What do you think, J.G.?"

"He's not exactly a basement bargain at that money," the manager had said. "If we're spending that much I'd rather we put it out on a few extra boys."

"The money is no problem," Jackson had said. "I happen to know that Cardiff will give us fifteen thousand for the rest of Alan Shackle's contract. Shackle's good but he's no Barlow."

"You mean we get rid of Shack in exchange for Barlow?" John Gallagher had said.

"Exactly."

"Well, Chairman, that wouldn't work out at all. Shack isn't a glamour boy but he's very gritty, a very hard man to get past in midfield. Barlow's more like Dave Spencer, very constructive, always going forward, full of attacking ideas—"

"Yes, the ideal sort of player for us."

"Aye but not the ideal partner for Spencer. We'd have two attacking midfield men, both trying to make play up front, so who's going to be left behind in midfield? It's Shack's covering and back-running that makes it possible for Spencer and Small to go through in attack. With two midfield men playing like Spencer we'd have an awful gap in the middle."

Jackson had not thought of it that way, being determined to find individual stars who would bring glory to Oaks Common. The manager's football logic had been unanswerable and they had not bought Barlow and he knew afterwards that John Gallagher's decision had been correct—yet he was still not too sure why he had allowed the manager to beat him in the argument. Perhaps he was still, part of him, the small boy who had climbed the back wall or crawled through holes in the corrugated iron, still overawed by men who had actually gone out there on the pitch and played the game. He did not know the whole reason. But he knew now that it was time to assert his position or admit permanent defeat. As they went into lunch he had still not decided whether to have his showdown before or after the game on Saturday. It was a decision that would have to be made after careful consideration of many factors. It was nothing to him to sack a thirty-thousand-a-year boardroom executive—but in the business of football things were not so simple. It was not just a struggle for power between himself and John Gallagher. The public was watching them, as if they were only caretakers for something that belonged to the people.

"Hold it there, Dave," John Gallagher shouted to Spencer, who put his foot on the ball. "Right then, I want Dave Peacock and Tommy Riddle in the box. The rest of you take a ball each— half on the left wing, half on the right." The squad began to split up. There was no horsing around, no wasting time. When John Gallagher took training they not only had to work, they wanted to work. Seymour walked out to the left wing, tapping the ball ahead of him. This would be as good as a rest. Half the morning gone and he felt fine.

"What I want you to do on the wings is to serve the ball to the one farthest away from you in the box," John Gallagher shouted. "He has to play it off first time to the other man in the box— and he'll shoot at goal. Randy and Johnny—you two can switch about in goal, take turns."

On the bench George Westbury explained that this exercise was for shooting practice and accurate laying-off by the two strikers, and practice in accurate crossing for the rest of the players. They did it in turns, alternately from each wing chipping and crossing balls to the two goal-scorers in the penalty box.

Seymour chipped his first ball to Dave Peacock, who breasted it down to Riddle. He crashed a first-time shot into the corner of the net. A ball came quickly from the right. Riddle cushioned it on his thigh so that it bounced in front of Peacock, who hit a half-volley which Parkinson took cleanly with both hands above his head. The balls came across in rapid succession, the two men in the box having to work very hard, shooting and then getting into position for a cross from the other side, never able to rest for a second. When he saw they were labouring, finding it hard to lift their legs, John Gallagher called for Shack and Peck to replace them in the shooting positions. Riddle and Peacock sat on their haunches, blowing heavily. Harry Barnes moved between the groups on the wings, shouting encouragement, driving them on, calling at them to keep the crosses going into the middle.

When he heard that Shack and Peck were next in the middle Seymour groaned to himself. That meant they were all going to have a turn in the hotspot. Usually this was an exercise for the forwards only. He held back, trying to avoid John Gallagher's eye, but eventually his turn came and he was in front of the goal, standing seven or eight yards from Andy Gurr, waiting for the first cross. It came over from Ian Rowland. Seymour touched it to Andy with the inside of his right foot. Andy smacked it high over the bar. Defenders seldom had the split-second reflexes necessary for accurate, first-time shooting near the goal. Destruction of other men's moves was their speciality, skill in negation. Andy was already heading the next cross down to him, a ball that came awkwardly. Seymour lashed at it and missed completely. Then he had to nod one down to Andy, who smacked it low past the goalkeeper. The balls seemed to be coming over much faster. His legs turned to jelly. The others didn't have this many crosses to deal with, he thought. Four—five—six—seven—his eighth ball bounced easily in front of him but he hit it with hardly any power. Randy picked it up with one hand. For Christ's sake blow that whistle!

When it did go he fell to his knees, knowing he couldn't go on any longer. He unzipped the neck of his tracksuit and pulled at the neck of his undershirt. Sweat ran into his eyes, making them smart. The others were already making their way over to John Gallagher on the half-way line.

"Come on, Brian, make it snappy," the manager shouted. Seymour got to his feet and pushed his football over the grass, still pulling at his undershirt so that the cool air might dry the sweat now seeping round his whole body. The rest of the squad grouped themselves round John Gallagher, some on the grass, others sitting on a ball. Sammy squatted on his heels beside Ian Rowland and Barry Ross, who were sitting down, resting back on splayed hands, mouths gulping at the sky for air.

"You don't want to sit on damp grass, me old sons," said Sammy, who was only slightly puffed. "You get farmers that way."

"Farmers?" said Barry Ross, who came from Norwich.

"Farmer Giles," said Sammy.

"Farmer Giles?" said Ross.

"Piles," said Sammy.

"Oh," said Barry Ross. "What's piles?"

"Cor blimey," said Sammy, giving up with a look of disgust.

Shack was lying flat on his back, eyes closed.

"It must be *great* to be a professional footballer," he said, mimicking a statement they had all heard a thousand times. "I'd *love* to be a soccer star—nothing to do all week, just play a game on Saturday."

"Yeah," said Andy Gurr, sitting wide-kneed on a ball, "I've read about them big-time soccer players, they get two hundred quid a week just to enjoy themselves kicking a ball about."

"Think of all them poor blighters in factories or offices or down the mines," said Danny, who was standing up, showing less strain than anyone else in the squad. "They don't get paid film star wages just to frolic about in the sunshine."

"Yes, you ought to think of people stuck in factories or offices," said Harry Barnes, but he wasn't joking. When they realised the coach was serious they groaned or blew raspberries. None of them wanted to work in offices or factories but they were tired of hearing what an easy life they had.

"Tell us about the old days then, Harry," said Wiggy. "I hear they had real players in them days. They weren't like us molly-coddled softies."

"Right then," said John Gallagher, putting his hands on his hips. "You've all got a good sweat on so I won't keep you sitting about getting bored. You've all worked very hard so far—so we'll have a nice little eight-a-side practice game." Seymour blew with relief. He could get through a practice game without bother. That was where craft counted, not muscle-power. "While you're playing I'll take four of you out at a time and give you doggies," said John Gallagher. He ignored their groans. "Right then—on your feet! As soon as you've done doggies you can have a bath."

Seymour could hardly believe his ears. Anything but doggies! As Harry Barnes and George Westbury began sticking in the white marker posts he saw John Gallagher looking at his stopwatch and he knew they were going to run the team flat out.

Hood and Peck picked the two sides for the practice match. Danny's team pulled on the yellow bibs. John Gallagher held an orange ball under his arm.

"It's two-touch and you can only score with a header," he said. "I'll referee and Harry can play with the yellows. We'll have twenty minutes before we start doggies. Right!"

He kicked the ball high in the air and four or five players went up for it. Riddle got a touch with his forehead and the ball went out to the left wing. Seymour drifted out to the right. They were using only half the pitch, with markers making little goals at either end. He used all his craft and experience to avoid the ball as much as possible. When it did come to him he used one of his touches to trap it and the other to send a long pass to the other wing. Then John Gallagher called out the first four for doggies — Rowland, Gurr, Peacock and Shackle. Seymour had hoped he would be in the first four, to get the ordeal over with as quickly as possible.

The game was now reduced to six a side. Seymour drifted about on the wings, getting quick glimpses of John Gallagher talking to the doggies men, George Westbury holding the clipboard with the records of their previous sprinting times. You couldn't fake it with doggies. John Gallagher wouldn't punish you for going slow—he merely took seconds off the time he allowed you to rest between sprints.

Ian Rowland was the first to go, taking up the sprinter's starting position. The manager blew his whistle and pressed his stopwatch and off went the young black reserve.

For doggies they had two marker posts stuck in the grass, forty yards apart. Rowland had to sprint from one to the other and back again, and then repeat it, four sprints of forty yards each without a break, each timed against his past performances.

He came charging past the post to finish his first sequence. John Gallagher held up the watch. George Westbury wrote down the time. Rowland stood feet apart, head hanging, breath coming out in staccato bursts of condensation. The whistle blew again after ten seconds and he was off. Once more he raced to the far post and back, round the starting marker and back to the other end and then back again. This time he got only seven seconds rest. The whistle blew again. Up to the far post and back down to John Gallagher and back up to the far post and back down to John Gallagher and Seymour could see he was forcing his legs to keep going and then he had passed the last post and he fell down on the grass, suddenly, as if shot. He looked dead. He was only nineteen and had one of the finest physiques in the team.

They called it doggies because it made them feel they were being trained like greyhounds. Everybody hated it. John Gallagher said it was designed to extend the heart, a punishing ordeal that made a Saturday game seem like a picnic. Seymour flicked a first-time pass to Sammy. He thought he ought to be at home doing the gardening. He had taken the extra year's contract as a player, he told anybody who asked, because of the money—he got a hundred and twenty pounds a week basic as a player but only seventy a week, with no bonuses, when he became an assistant coach. The difference of fifty quid a week made good sense to everyone, a reason they could all understand.

John Gallagher spoke to Harry Barnes and the coach stopped the practice match to call out Hood, Parkinson, Randall—and himself. Seymour walked quickly to the starting post. There was no point in postponing it. The more you watched other guys doing doggies the more sick you became. John Gallagher held up the watch, waiting for the second hand to reach the hour.

"Go!" shouted John Gallagher. .

Go—and he was away quickly, running fast but not trying to break world records—only the boys did that—turning at the far end and heading back, running well, feeling no discomfort so far—turning quickly at the starting post—up to the other end, sparkling sea dancing in his eyes, round the marker—somebody shouting—down towards John Gallagher and past the post. . . .

"Five-six-seven-eight-nine-ten-GO!" and he was away again, breathing heavily now, the second sequence—forty yards to the far post, turn fast, save a second by not running wide round the marker—forty yards back, seeing John Gallagher with the watch and George Westbury with the clipboard, timing him, pushing the legs forward—round the starting post and back again, another forty yards, legs beginning to go now, getting weaker with every stride—arms turning into deadweights—back down to the start— a rest, hands on knees, body bent double, face pointing at the grass, lungs gulping desperately for air, whole body heaving with pain and exhaustion . . . "four-five-six-seven-eight—GO!" . . . go, keep going, Brian, up to the far post, the legs don't want to move any more—keep going, they're all watching you, all waiting for you to flake out—keep going—round the post and back down to the start—come on, Brian, the other voice said, your time's good—keep at it—pump your arms—only another two lengths now —only another eighty yards—come on, man, get those legs off the ground—I can't, they're like lead—round the far post—only forty yards to go, don't let it beat you, man—my arms are screaming with pain—keep going, man, show them you can still do it— the post is running away from me, I can't breathe, the air's so cold it's burning my throat—my thighs are giving up, not another yard—

He ran past the post. His head was thumping and his eyes were hazy. He seemed to be moving in slow motion. Voices and faces came at him but he went on walking as if to stop would mean to fall down and he found himself behind the little wooden pavilion. He sank slowly to the ground, as though in a dream. Waves of blood pumped through his eyes. He crouched like an animal, on hands and knees, unable to move, body so pulverised he could not tell if he was going to be sick. Like a panting dog, he thought. For fifty quid a week. You're too old, Brian, you can't even move. Why does your throat burn so much? Come on, man, stand up before they see you hanging your head like a windbroken nag.

For a moment it seemed as if he was going to make it to his feet but as his head began to rise he reeled gently as if drunk, the hut, the grass, the sea swirling round him like a fairground roundabout.

Then he began to heave and out it came on the grass, behind the little wooden pavilion, with the sun glinting on blue-green water, out it came, everything in his stomach, forcing its way up through a throat that was too small, forcing itself out of his body in awful spasms that brought tears to his eyes. He crouched, panting, and this time there was no more to come up and he blinked several times and the water cleared from his eyes and he wiped his lips with the back of his hand and spat out the remnants of vomit and shook his head. As he got to his feet he smiled. He had done his doggies with the best of them and now he felt fine.

It's all in the mind, he said to himself, and he smiled again as he looked down, all in the mind and all on the grass.

13

THE players had just come back from the training pitch and all down the gloomy corridor Peterson could hear hard male voices, most of them groaning at the after-effects of doggies.

In the first room he entered Dave Spencer was tearing off his socks, otherwise naked, explaining to Dave Peacock why he had to get into the bath first. The socks went on the heap of crumpled training gear by the door, waiting for Albert.

"I've only got till lunchtime and it's half-past twelve already," Debonair was saying. "Come on, Peacock, let me have the bath first."

Peacock sat on the bed, bending down to massage his feet. Peacock in football boots looked like a jockey but Peacock's bare feet were almost unbelievable, so turned over on the outside of the ankle that hard-pad skin reached almost up to the ankle bone, making Peterson wonder how he could walk, let alone sprint to near-Olympic standard.

"You think it's fair, Bill?" he asked. "He's always got some excuse for wanting in first. And I always get a dirty bath."

"I think it's all very unnecessary," said Peterson. "The lovely Carole has gone off to Glasgow with the chairman's party. She won't be back for lunch."

"What?"

When he left them Dave Spencer was banging his forehead against the wall. The door of the next room was ajar. He knocked before looking in, but young Rowland and Ross didn't hear or see him. They were both posing in front of the dressing-table mirror, Rowland wearing white bikini underpants, Ross in the nude. They had their fists clenched and their biceps flexed, twisting round to see their statuesque body postures in the mirror. Peterson withdrew.

He was going into the room shared by Sammy and Danny, still looking for Alec Hood, when Debonair Dave pushed past him, dressed only in Y-fronts. Sammy was singing in the bath.

"Hold my hand, I'm a Ranger in Paradise," he crooned.

Danny was at the wash-basin, shampooing his hair. Over Spencer's shoulder Peterson saw his naked body, very dark and solid, the legs of a soccer gladiator, very big, hard calves, all of him covered from shoulder to ankle in black hair. Years of long trousers had not rubbed the hair off the outside of the legs, as had happened to Peterson. He wondered why Danny should be so lucky. Did the sporting life have secrets of body maintenance known only to the chosen?

"The stupid bitch has pissed off to Glasgow with the chairman," Spencer raved. "That isn't fair. Give me more time or I'm calling the bet off."

"You weren't made for each other, me old son," said Sammy, whose feet did not reach the end of the bath, so small and slim it was hard to imagine he could stand up against the crunching giants of soccer. "How about—Never take sweets from a Ranger?"

"What are you going to do about this bloody bet, Peck?" Debonair demanded.

Danny worked his fingers through soapy hair, jack-knifed over the basin, not a superfluous ounce showing on his stomach. He plunged his head into cold water and squeezed out the soap. Blinking water from his eyes he picked up a towel and walked towards Spencer, who was blocking the doorway.

"Do you mind?" Danny said, face impassive. Spencer moved a few paces back to let him through. He began rubbing his head in front of the mirror.

"What d'you think's fair, Bill?" he said.

"Give him the money, Mabel," Sammy called from the bath. "He thinks he's Errol Flynn in football boots. Admit defeat, Spencer, you great nit."

"I don't know," said Peterson, not really knowing how seriously they were taking the bet. "Give him extra time but make him pay for it?"

"Good thinking, Bill. Okay then, Handsome Harry, you can have till lunchtime tomorrow—but it's a sixty quid bet now."

"Cor," shouted Sammy, "the tension is fair killin' me. I must see that lovely richard and do a deal wiv her, nobble her like."

"All right," said Spencer, his temper evaporating. "When I do get a date with her I'll make so much money I'll be able to retire."

"Thought you had done already," cried Sammy. "Your times for doggies was worse than Old Father Seymour. 'Ere, did you see him havin' a technicoloured yawn behind the hut? It's cruel wot they do to that poor old fella."

In the next room Gurr and Williamson were dressing, quietly, efficiently, slipping on roll-neck sweaters, pushing stockinged feet into casual shoes, carefully combing wet hair in front of the mirror.

"Come on, Andy, stop mooning," said Gerry. Andy only grunted. Gerry saw Peterson's curious face. "Andy's a home-lover, Bill, hates being away from the light of his life."

"I'll have to give the game up if we're going to have all this success," said Andy. "They're promising us a trip to America if we win this bloody cup!"

"Yeah," said Gerry, "the chairman told me, if we win we go without the wives, if we lose we're taking them with us."

"I don't get it, Bill," said Andy. "We travel so much during the season you'd think they'd let us have the summer to ourselves. Oh no—we've got to go on some jaunt to the States—or the West Indies or Australia. Thank Christ Moon travel is still in its infancy or we'd be playing exhibition matches up there."

"You're a home nut," said Gerry. "You know what, Bill—he says the worst thing he can imagine is becoming an England player—all that travelling and every fourth summer he'd have to play in the dreary World Cup when he could be at home with the roses."

"I wouldn't play for England, it isn't worth it—"

"They haven't asked you yet, matey."

Peterson met Hood outside in the corridor.

"I've been looking for you, Alec. We must do something about that beer contract. The advertising agency was on the blower to me half an hour ago."

"We'll talk about it at lunch, Bill. I want to see Danny."

Peterson followed him back along the corridor. Danny was balanced on one leg, pulling on a pair of cream-coloured slacks.

"Where the hell did you get to last night?" Hood demanded.

"Oh, just out and about. Why?"

"You were supposed to be at a committee meeting. You just pissed off, is that it?"

"Yeah, sorry about that. I didn't remember till we were in bed. Till Poor Old Bill here dropped in for a bedtime chat."

He grinned at Peterson.

"Stupid bastard," said Hood.

Peterson felt tense. They were two very strong men, one tall and craggy, the other squat and solid as a tank. They were very close to each other in a very small space.

"I said I'm sorry." Danny sat on the bed and pulled on white ankle socks. "What the hell more do you want me to do—kiss your reggie?"

"You bastard—you think you can take the mickey out of me?" Hood shouted. Peterson thought he was working himself up to a heavy punch. Danny stopped pulling on his socks and stared up at Hood's bulging face.

"Keep your cool, matey," he said, mouth in a grin but eyes unblinking.

"We're all trying to make money," Hood stormed. "The lads elected you to the committee to look after their interests. I wouldn't let you look after fucking white mice! All you bloody want to do is take the loot and let other people do the work. Where the hell did you go last night—some bloody discotheque full of poxy teenage slags? That's about your bloody mark, mate. Why don't you fucking well grow up?"

Danny stood up, his head cocked sideways, arms and hands poised.

"You don't fakking well talk to me like that—I don't care who the bloody hell you are—"

Sammy came out of the bathroom, pushing between them, humming, reaching into his case for a floral patterned sports shirt, the basic colour of which was a startling electric mauve.

"Like the dicky?" he asked, pirouetting, not seeming to have noticed the shouting match but coming between Danny and Hood, who glared at each other over his head.

"That's a horrible shirt," Hood said in disgust.

"Bloody revolting," said Danny.

"Garn, yer all jealous. Wait till that little darlin' Mary sees it, she'll be fightin' mad to get hot little meathooks on me exquisite body."

It must be the tension of the coming game, Peterson thought as they went to the lift, all friends again, the incident blown over and forgotten in hearty condemnation of Sammy's taste in clothes. As they went through the foyer he went to the reception desk to ask for messages. Danny and Sammy were stopped by people asking for autographs. Hood came up to the desk. The girl handed Peterson a message slip. Peterson looked at it quickly, then crumpled it into a waste-bucket.

"The wife," he said. Hood nodded understandingly. "What did they tell John Gallagher?"

"Oh—it was all right in the end. Smudged plates."

"Thank Christ for that. I thought it must have been the worst—especially when you and Danny were squaring up."

"Oh that? Just a little tiff between friends."

It hadn't been from the wife. How the hell had Celia discovered where the team was staying? Thank God John Gallagher was all right. The omens were good . . .

Through the big windows of the dining-room they could see the glistening water and the soft browns and purples of the hills, but nobody had much interest in scenery. Sammy was already on first-name terms with the waitress, a black-haired girl with chubby white arms.

"Hey, Mary, howja like the dicky, ducky?"

"You're awful, so you are," she said.

"It ain't that bad, is it?"

"Using words like that in front of a lady."

"Words like wot? Oh—dicky? That means me shirt you little twit. The other's me hampton, innit?"

She made a disapproving face and went away.

"So how does dicky come to mean shirt?" Peterson asked.

"Dicky dirt—shirt," said Sammy.

They got him going on the subject of rhyming slang and there was no stopping him, for rabbiting and spieling was his game, giving the patter in his typical Londoner's voice, slightly hoarse and very fast, aitches being dropped and added equally inexplicably, the accent of the Elizabethan bear-pits, the unruly apprentice boys, Dick Whittington and Jonathan Wild the thief-taker and gangster, Jack Sheppard the great escaper, and the felons who waited for the open tumbril to take them along Oxford Street to the gallows at Tyburn, now Marble Arch. Your north and south was your mouth and your teeth were your Hampsteads, from the heath ... cock-eyed and cocky, the Cockney, thought Peterson, two thousand years of London went into Sammy, the Roman Legions fathered his ancestors, so fable had it, and they had lived in the city and the East End ever since, in one cramped mass, fighting for every crust, beaten down but never beaten, Sammy, a slice of England's living history in an electric mauve shirt.

"There's your gregory—Gregory Peck, neck. There's apple for your heart, apple tart. You say about a brave geezer he's got plenty of apple. Your guts is either your Newingtons or your comics, Newington Butts, comic cuts."

In this rhyming lingo, the incomprehensible mixture of street wit and slum poetry used by generations to bamboozle Old Bill the copper or Paddy the Irish invader, your feet were your plates (of meat), your fingers were melodies (melody lingers), your arse was your Khyber, from the pass.

"Now 'ere's a good one," said Sammy, hardly able to eat for the joy of rabbiting, "your khyber can also be your reggie. Reggie Harris—remember him, the professional cycling champion? Harris—aris. Aristotle—bottle. Bottle and glass—arse. Simple, innit?"

"If you have the brain for it," said Hood.

"Nah, you got to be born into it," said Danny. "It's always changing. Did you know raspberry—like you blow a raspberry at somebody—did you know that's rhyming slang—raspberry tart, fart. I heard some politician bloke use it on the telly—I bet he don't know he's actually saying fart!"

"Oh aye, you're very clever wee lads, you London buggers," said Hood. "Now then, what do we do about this beer contract?"

They discussed it all through the main course, Peterson having to explain about advertising agencies and repeat fees.

"Fifteen grand!" Sammy rubbed his hands together. "That's great, innit Dan—get back some of the loot we've spent on the flamin' stuff."

"Would the directors really object to you advertising beer?" Peterson asked. "Surely everybody knows footballers have a drink now and again?"

"Does he ever stop now and again would be more like it," said Danny, nodding at Sammy.

"I've told you a million times, me old son, don't exaggerate."

"It's the image," said Hood. "Footballers aren't the same as film stars or pop singers—we get looked up to by millions of young boys."

"The commercials won't show you falling about smashed out of your skulls," said Peterson. "You'll be shown as fine, upstanding, healthy athletes enjoying a cooling pint after the sweat of a hard game."

"That wouldn't be too bad," said Danny. "Nobody's ever going to claim booze is good for you—it is a bleeding toxic or whatever they call it—but a few drinks, they help you relax and get away from football. And it breeds a kind of togetherness. The pressures on us these days are fantastic—all right, so we need something toxic and artificial to help us relax. As long as its in proportion, know what I mean?"

"Well said, vicar."

"Spirits?"

"If I feel like it—vodka is very popular with players. You'll hear folk saying beer is less harmful than spirits—but look at Andy Gurr, for instance, with his weight problem he's better off with a few whiskies than beer—it's the pints that put on the pounds."

"I didn't know Andy had a weight problem."

"Nor arf he ain't. He's got an over-developed capacity for turning liquid into excess weight, that's what the doc says."

Extra weight meant loss of speed. Everything Andy ate had to be considered in terms of calories. He never touched potatoes or beer or bread or sweets or fried foods. He carried artificial sweeteners in little glass phials. He perpetually craved everything bad for him. Often Gerry Williamson would catch him trying to steal a roast potato off his plate. At night, they said, he dreamed of greasy bags of fish and chips, crying out in his sleep at the anguish of not being able to cram a dollop of lovely big vinegary chips into his north and south. In a bar he would sip a whisky and dribble at the mouth as the others belted down dirty great pints of bitter. Peterson looked across at the bespectacled full-back, now working steadily through steak and salad.

"Couldn't he just sweat off weight—like a jockey?" he asked, suddenly feeling sorry for a chap whom he had dismissed as a somewhat dull, home-obsessed, unadventurous nonentity.

"He'd lose too much strength," said Hood. "As long as he's

in training he's all right—it comes harder in the summer when he's sitting about the house, he has to watch himself like a hawk then. He reckons he can shoot up twenty pounds in two weeks if he isn't careful. It's funny, isn't it, I've been a hundred and ninety-six pounds now for ten years, I never go up or down a pound, except what I lose during a game and I soon put that back on."

"So what about this beer business?"

Hood stretched his arms above his head and yawned with the ferocity of a wolf.

"I'm going over to speak to the boss," he said. "I think he's in a better mood now."

Hood pushed back his chair and walked through the tables to where John Gallagher was sitting with Harry Barnes, George Westbury and the doctor. They watched him pull up a chair, turning it round so that his arms rested on the back. They saw him speaking to John Gallagher and then the manager nodding, the doctor saying something, Harry Barnes putting in his twopenny-worth. Then Hood said something that made them all laugh. He came back towards them stopping to hear something Wiggy had to say, bending down, a heavy hand on Wiggy's shoulder. Some man, Peterson thought. Did football develop the character or did men of character choose football?

Hood came back.

"Well?"

"It's okay. J.G. says they have to get his permission on what dates we're free for the filming."

"That's great!"

"J.G. also says they ought to up the readies. Fifteen grand isn't much, between seventeen of us."

"Sixteen," said Peterson. "I don't come into that part of it."

"Nah—you're with us in everything, Bill."

"I don't really think—"

"Forget it—you're in the pool like everybody else."

"'Cept he don't have to do no bleedin' doggies!"

"I would but the doc won't let me. He says the club would be legally liable in the certain event of my death. I'll ask them for twenty thousand."

"Twenty grand!" Sammy clenched his fist and banged Danny on the shoulder. The waitress came to ask if they wanted coffee. "'Ere, Mary darlin'," Sammy said, "I'm goin' onna telly—you wanna stick wiv me, kid, forget all 'em haggis-bashers. I'm gonna be a star onna telly!"

"I thought you were a big star already," the girl said. "At least that's what you keep telling me. I suppose some people are never satisfied."

"Cor," said Sammy, shooting out his hand and pretending to take her pulse.

"Let go of my hand, ye wee gnaff," Mary said. "The manageress will slay me."

"Cor, I dunno wot she says but it don't arf sound sexy. How aboot you and me takin' a wee walkie up a glen the nicht, dearie?"

"You'll get me sacked so you will."

"Is that wot you heathens call it? Get me sacked! I knew you was sex-mad, Mary darlin', but I didn't expect you to be quite so bold wiv it. Okay then, where d'you want me to sack you?"

"I don't want coffee," said Hood, flexing both arms, pushing back his shoulders. Sammy kissed the girl's hand. Nobody wanted coffee. Harry Barnes came round the tables. After the film of the Rangers match John Gallagher wanted everybody to play golf or squash. Peterson went up to his room to write the brochure. Under the bedroom door was a note from reception about a phone call. He rang downstairs and they said a Miss Thorpe had called several times from London and wanted him to ring her back.

"No, I'll call later," he said when the girl wanted to connect him to the London number. As he sat at the typewriter he snorted. The players said these trips were great for escaping all the phone calls from people wanting big match tickets.

"The pressure of big-time soccer," he said out loud, hand to forehead, "it's nothing compared to the tension of big-time adultery. How the hell did that bitch track me down to Strannoch Hydro?"

As they went into the Rabbie Burns suite for the film, Randy told them what young Ross had said when the waitress asked if he wanted his coffee black or white.

"Some of each, please," Ross had said. They all thought this very funny.

John Gallagher had already drilled them for two weeks on the strengths and weaknesses of the Rangers. They knew which parts of the field they would have to defend particularly carefully—especially any part of the field Jackie Caskie happened to be in. Gerry Williamson already knew that he would be marking Caskie closely, with another defender behind him, two of them with the special mission of smothering the boy genius out of the game. John Gallagher had told them he felt they could win the game on heading ability. He said Dave Peacock could out-jump Grant, the defender most likely to be marking him. Hood knew this was why they needed Roy, because Rangers would be sure to put Lindsay onto him, leaving Peacock to out-jump Grant for the high balls. If Roy wasn't fit to play Lindsay would probably mark Peacock and that would be a different proposition. John Gallagher had given them run-downs on how Rangers played but for most of the team this film would be the first time they had seen them in action.

"See what they said in the Scottish papers this morning?" Shack said to Wiggy, letting everybody else hear. "They said the Strannoch Hydro is bending over backwards to help the English plot the downfall of Glasgow Rangers."

"Is that right?" said Wiggy. "What are they going to do, give us porridge with the magic ingredient?"

Harry Barnes was standing over the projector. When they were all seated, closely grouped, Shackle got up from the chair beside Wiggy and went to the back on his own to get, as he said, a completely independent view of the game without being swayed by Wiggy's opinions.

"They've had a lovers' tiff," shouted Sammy.

"Come on, Harry, let's have the big picture," said Randy.

"It's these new Scottish jobs—I don't seem to be able to get the hang of it," said the coach.

They began to sing a few choruses of 'Why Are We Waiting'.

"Why don't you go and get somebody who knows how to work these new Scottish jobs?" shouted Randy. "Or are they all dead?"

"A new Scottish job indeed," said Danny. "Very amusing idea. I would think old Rabbie Burns himself would be the only one who could work that relic."

Harry Barnes persevered and then he had it running and the light went out.

"Okay lads, get serious," came the unmistakable voice of John

Gallagher. 8-7-6-5-4-3-2-1-zero flickered the screen and they were into the film, an edited version of the T.V. coverage of the Rangers–Derby County quarter-final loaned to them by Scottish Television. It opened with both teams kicking about and the captains walking towards the referee in the centre-circle. Lindsay shoved his hand forward and pumped the hand of Derby's captain, Peter Martin. Shack couldn't help marvelling at the resemblance between Lindsay and Alec Hood. Lindsay, known as Killer, was only a year younger than Alec. He'd been capped twenty-eight times for Scotland. Alec had been capped four times. Everybody said that if it hadn't been for Lindsay Alec would have been Scotland's regular centre-back for the last ten years. Shack had seen Lindsay in international matches and didn't think he was as reliable as Alec, but the Scots generally preferred to cap players who didn't move south. Aikman kicked off, hitting a long pass straight out to Caskie. Shack could see why everybody raved about the boy winger. He went by two players as if they weren't there. There was a certain amount of chat but when Caskie got the ball it went quiet. He was a man for professionals to admire. Caskie lost the ball to the Derby fullback, then won it back again. He played it to Dawson, who in turn played it to Aikman, who let the ball run through his legs, a perfect dummy. It looked at first as if Aikman had made a mistake for there was nobody to take advantage of the dummy. Not on the screen, anyway. The T.V. camera had to follow the ball whereas the trained eye of a professional spectator was always sweeping round the field, noting which players had run into which positions. Television could never give you a satisfactory picture of the whole game. It had to follow the ball, just as most spectators did, hardly seeing the men who were running into position, possibly the most important part of the whole game.

Caskie ran into the picture from the left. Brown of Derby made a lunging tackle but Caskie dummied to take the ball and then let it run across him, collecting it cleanly with his right foot, pushing it forward in one movement.

He was about twenty-five yards from goal, outside the penalty area. The Derby goalkeeper began to come forward to narrow the angle. Caskie chipped the ball on the run, a perfect chip that went high over the goalkeeper's hands and came down just under the crossbar into the net. Caskie kept running, round behind the goal, facing the crowd, jumping high and punching at thin air. The camera swung round the crowd. They were going wild. A sea of blue Rangers scarves was held high, swaying from side to side, the whole mass singing the Rangers song—*Follow, Follow, We Will Follow Rangers*—Shack was impressed. He knew that everyone else in the room was impressed.

Peterson was typing desperately, trying to get the brochure articles finished, wrestling with the tricky problem of the article he was ghosting for Ian Rowland. Rowland's ambition was to become the first black player to be capped for England. For all the size of Britain's coloured population comparatively few black boys had come through into the soccer big-time.

Everybody he asked was adamant that there was no colour prejudice in soccer, either among clubs or players, yet it was still very much a white man's game. The phone rang. He ignored it. Rowland's actual words were that he wanted to be the black Bobby Moore. Would England ever be led out on to the field by a black captain? The phone went on ringing. It was sure to be Celia. He was forced by sheer curiosity to pick it up.

The switchboard girl said there was a call for the team from the *Scottish Daily Record*. The reporter said he had been hoping for a word with John Gallagher but he understood the team was seeing a film and couldn't be disturbed.

"Maybe you can help me," said the Scottish voice. "We understand Roy Christmas wasn't training this morning? Is he injured?"

"No, I don't think so."

"But he wasn't training, was he."

"I really don't know, old boy, I was in bed. You'd better speak to John Gallagher—anyway, he's having a press conference at five-thirty."

"You London folk do things in style, eh? Press conferences, indeed. I can remember when footballers wore cloth caps and dirty sweaters and could hardly read, let alone issue statements to the press."

"Happy days, eh?"

"They were happy to get a wee mention in the papers then—now you have to negotiate with a bloody business or literary agent before some sweaty bugger will agree to tell you how his big toe is coming on."

"We're not like that. Big toe news you get free. A picture, however, might cost you a guinea or two."

A few minutes later the Glasgow evening paper wanted to know why Roy had missed training. It began to sound like trouble. The third time the phone rang he prepared himself to be even more evasive, not having the slightest idea why Roy hadn't been training. But this time it was Celia.

"Tracked me down, have you?" he said gruffly.

"It wasn't difficult. The papers are full of you—they showed Commoners on the idiot-box last night. I didn't see you—don't you rate an appearance with the stars?"

"I'm Mister X—strictly faceless. So what do I owe this expected pleasure to?"

"You didn't tell her?"

"There wasn't time."

"Any excuse to evade it—a silly game of football, anything."

"My God! A silly game of football? Fifty thousand pounds from my little efforts alone? You know that if we win on Saturday I'm due to pick up around three thousand pounds. She could have all that. I don't want her having any more advantage over me. She's got to have money, you know, the kids and bills and everything."

"And if we don't win this world-shaking football game?"

"We'll win. I'm very confident. You want to wish us luck?"

"Oh, all the luck in the world, darling, very best of British."

Lips smacked in simulation of endearment. He shut his eyes and blew hard. He couldn't even remember now why he had first got the idea that he loved her. He looked at what he had typed. How simple and clear-cut life must appear to Ian Rowland the Black Adonis. How simple for all whose lives were given a framework and a direction by the game. Wasn't that what all we spectators yearned for? The simple comfort of knowing what direction we were supposed to be travelling in?

"Come on, you unholy ghost-writer," he said, drumming his fingers on the casing of the typewriter. "Forgive us our bad passes as we forgive them who pass badly to us . . . "

Dave Spencer addressed his golf ball and hit a perfect drive down the first fairway past the two hundred yard mark.

"That must be nice," said Shack, watching the two Daves walk down the fairway. "They're both going in the same direction. I hope we're as lucky."

Riddle took his number two wood from the bag and teed up his ball. He did two or three practice swings and then addressed the ball.

"Come on, Jim," said Wiggy. "What's it all about, eh? Don't be jack the lad, just hit the flaming ball."

Riddle straightened up.

"Take no notice, Tom," said Seymour.

"If we're going to play we might as well play properly," said Riddle. "It's a good job the members can't hear you, they wouldn't be impressed at all."

He began to address the ball again. Wiggy snorted.

"Members? Half of these snobs don't come out on the course, they're too busy thinking up new rules to ever leave the bar."

Riddle sliced his shot into the rough on the right. Wiggy and Shack started to laugh.

"That's not bad," said Riddle, nodding wisely. "I'm pleased with that for a first shot."

Seymour put his ball on the tee and hit a good straight shot almost to the two hundred marker.

Shack sliced and Wiggy topped his ball, which ran down the slope, barely reaching the start of the fairway. This delighted Seymour and Riddle. Wiggy kept a straight face. Golf was just a laugh to him, just an excuse for a stroll and a giggle.

"At least we're all playing to form," he said, as they walked off in different directions.

Riddle took a swipe and missed the ball completely.

"Unlucky," said Shack.

"What d'you mean—that was a practice shot!"

"Cobblers—that's three you've had."

Riddle didn't argue. He swung again. The ball trickled forward a foot or two.

"Four—or is it five?" Wiggy shouted.

"It's bloody four!"

Riddle took his golf very seriously, three rounds every week, always desperately keen to show them how well he could play. With four shots played he had managed to cover a hundred and fifty yards. He looked quite sick. His fifth was high and hard, pitching just short of the flag and rolling slowly past the hole. He shoved his seven iron in the bag. Shack and Wiggy pretended to be looking for a lost ball.

"Here, didn't you two see that shot?" he demanded.

"What shot?" said Wiggy.

"That's my ball, next to the hole."

"Be quiet please while my partner is playing," said Wiggy. As they walked to the green he looked at the shining water and the soft contours of the hills beyond. In this kind of weather Scotland was very visual. He wondered why the inhabitants were so tense. They didn't seem able to take life as a joke. He was faced with an eighteen-foot putt for a four. It went down. He slung his putter in the air. He knew that would get Riddle going again. He had never been able to understand guys like Seymour or Riddle. They took everything so seriously, Riddle with his golf and his grievances, Seymour with his gruff manliness. Look at this morning's training session—what the hell had Brian been trying to prove. He knew he wouldn't be in the team, almost certainly not even as a substitute. There were a lot of guys in the game who had this winning complex, sick if they lost at golf or darts or cards, let alone football, but it was too late for Brian to be hoping to win anything. Why couldn't he face the facts—he was a good, solid pro, the kind they always described as a loyal club servant, he'd drawn good pro wages for almost twenty years and this was his last season and in the summer they would put him on the coaching staff and if he played his cards right he was set at Oaks Common for life. What more did he want?

By the seventh hole Seymour and Riddle were one up. Riddle had concentrated on his game, taking no risks, careful not to rise to any of Wiggy's cheeky comments, determined to win. All his playing life he had found himself competing with blokes like Wiggy. They seemed to make all your own efforts a mockery. They were born with all the skills in the world and they never found the game difficult. They always had seconds to spare in a crowded goal mouth. They never seemed to take training seriously and they smoked and drank and stayed up all night and it never seemed to affect their bodies. They never had to sweat at it. He thought of them as laughing boys, the public's idea of geniuses, effortless naturals who would always win one way or the other, for they were superficial people and they didn't take it to heart and when they lost a game they would mock all the honest graft you put in and make you feel like a clod for taking it so seriously. You couldn't win against guys like Wiggy. You could only beat them and try to ignore them.

They missed the next three holes and evened out at the eleventh. At the thirteenth Riddle drove into thick rough. He had already lost one ball. The four of them looked but couldn't find the second lost ball. Riddle unwrapped a new Dunlop 65 and dropped it over his shoulder.

"If I lost balls at that rate I'd use old ones," said Shack.

"He's never had an old ball," said Wiggy.

They decided to have a rest. Shack sat on a sawn-off tree stump and lit his pipe. Wiggy sat on his bag. Seymour squatted on his heels. Riddle got out his driver to practise his swing.

"Funny game, golf," said Shack. "Seems unnatural not to have another team trying to get the ball away from you."

"Very sexy game," said Wiggy.

"What the hell's sex got to do with golf?" Riddle demanded.

"Don't women ever ask you to play around with them?"

"That's typical of you, Wiggy, always thinking about crumpet."

"What's wrong with you, Jimmy?" Wiggy asked. "You don't seem your usual laughing self."

"It's going to be a right anti-climax for me, isn't it? I've played in all the other rounds, now we're where it matters I'm going to get the elbow."

"You never know with John Gallagher," said Shack. "Look, you weren't even training with us on the Monday or Tuesday of the Dundee United game—yet you were in the team on the Saturday."

"Only because Dave Peacock was injured. My face don't fit and that's all there is to it."

They knew there was some truth in what Jimmy said. He could play anywhere in the forward line and he always did well for the team. Yet no matter how well he performed they knew that John Gallagher would always prefer to play Roy or Wiggy or Dave Peacock. Professional managers were above such considerations as glamour and crowd appeal yet subconsciously they seemed to prefer the player with the star quality, the big name, even if the purely functional player, like Riddle, scored just as many goals. It worked in other ways—a player transferred for a hundred thousand pounds instantly took on a glamorous importance; the crowds came to see him, although he was no better a player than he had been the week before, with his old club. Where everything else was equal people plumped for the glamour of stardom.

"I mean," said Riddle hesitantly, dying to tell them what was in his mind but not wanting to sound silly, "I don't like to be a pain in the neck—but I never seem to get noticed for my efforts, do I? When we beat Exeter and Roy got two goals he got all the headlines, Christmas Bags Two and all that. But when I scored two against Luton—what was it then? Christmas Makes Two!"

"Be honest—Roy's got something about him—he's got that magic people love to see."

"Yeah—and Muggins here don't have any magic—all right to make jokes about my big nose and all that—but nobody really likes me, do they? That's what it's all about. I am just not popular."

"Bollocks," said Shack. "I never heard such self-pitying rubbish. If you really think about it—we only make jokes at people we like. You never hear anybody taking the mickey out of Harry Barnes, do you? Why not? Because we all think he's a two-faced prick who'd shop us all if he thought it would do him any good. Grow up, Tommy, stop feeling sorry for yourself."

Riddle snorted, only half-convinced.

"Look, I get this Wiggy wonder-boy treatment all the time," said Wiggy. "Maybe it's easy for me to talk, but it's just crap. I don't ask for it. I'm not saying I don't like it but that's the way it is, that's all. There's lots of things that aren't fair in football. Would you rather do something else? You bloody well wouldn't and you know it. It's a great game and we're all fortunate to be in it. You're only noticing these things because you're in the dumps. If John Gallagher says you're in the team for Saturday you'll be jumping up and down. None of this crap would matter a bloody iota."

Seymour won the next two holes to make the game level. The little owning-up session might have cheered Riddle up a bit but it hadn't improved his golf. He hooked and sliced and topped the ball and lost another in the rough and swore blind he'd never play the bloody game again. They were level pegging when they reached the eighteenth. He wanted to win it very badly. In front of them was a narrow river, about thirty yards before the green. Riddle felt the coming excitement of winning. He addressed the ball.

"Best of luck," Wiggy shouted.

He dropped his shoulders and turned viciously on Wiggy.

"His bottle's gone," Shack said.

He took the club head back from the ball seven or eight times. Just to beat Wiggy this once! He swung. Even as his arms came down he knew he'd broken the golden rule but there was nothing he could do about it. His head had lifted on the downswing and the club topped the ball and all he could do was watch it bobble along the grass and plop gently into the river. He stood there, looking ready for tears. The others fell into hysterical laughter. Riddle stared at them blankly, sick with himself. If he could only take the bloody shot over again!

"It's always got to happen to Jimmy," Wiggy said, holding onto Shack, convulsed.

Riddle couldn't hold it down any longer. He let out a yell and threw his club high into the air. It landed in the water, not too far from where his ball had sunk. Wiggy doubled up, pointing at him.

"I hope you . . . realise . . . those clubs . . . belong here, you'll have to . . . go in the bloody river and get it! Oh ho ho, my stomach's got cramp with laughing . . . "

Riddle dropped his head. He took off his shoes and socks, rolled up his trousers and waded into the water, feeling down into the cold clear water for the club. He clambered back onto the bank, dark wet stains soaking up his trouser legs.

Somebody knocked at Peterson's door. It was Roy Christmas. He stood in the doorway looking shy.

"I heard the typewriter — you very busy?"

"Oh no, come in."

Roy was wearing grey slacks and a pale blue shirt opened at the neck. He was an extraordinarily pale person, Peterson thought, he hadn't been in London long enough to acquire the heavy tan that marked out most London first division players as the cosmopolitans of English soccer. Peterson searched about on his table for the article he'd ghosted for Roy.

"By the way," he said, "the newspapers are coming on hot and strong — did you miss training this morning for any particular reason?"

"What did you tell them?"

"I said I was in bed and didn't know anything about it. They have to ask John Gallagher about team matters. Why did you miss training anyway?"

"It's nothing much—I strained a muscle in my thigh. Boss thought to give it a rest."

He read the article that Peterson had written on his behalf, no expression on his face.

"Not bad," he said, handing it back. Peterson skimmed the pages onto the writing table and reached for a new cigarette. He saw Roy looking at the packet.

"Sorry," he said, holding it out. "I keep forgetting you smoke. I've got out of the habit of handing them round. There's only you and Johnny Parkinson who smoke in the whole squad."

"They keep telling me to take the Ministry of Health aversion therapy," said Roy. "The trouble is I like it too much. I don't think I inhale properly, actually."

Peterson moved over to the armchair. Roy sat on the edge of the bed. Sims had gone back to London now, apparently satisfied with his dabble behind the scenes. Peterson looked at Roy, wondering what magic transformed this thin, pale, shy lad into a goal-scoring machine, a slim, deadly falcon swooping down to punish other men's mistakes.

"I said in the article that you think the money comes a poor second to the glory in a cup final," he said. "Is that really true—or is it just what you thought you ought to say?"

"Oh, it's true, definitely. The money's good but it's nothing to the feeling you'd have—walking out on the Wembley pitch—I'd take part in an occasion like that for nothing. It's like playing for England—you'd do it for nothing just for the glory or the thrill or whatever it is."

"That's refreshing to hear. I was asking Sammy about players and their attitude to money—he said he's only once ever heard of a player turning down a chance to make money—because it wasn't enough."

"Everybody I know would play for England without being paid. Except Alec Hood, of course."

"Oh? Why Alec?"

"Because he's Scottish."

Peterson hung his head.

"I know I've got a reputation for being money-daft," said Roy, a slight change in his tone, suggesting a long-felt desire to explain himself. "Up at Burnley they called me all sorts of names because I wanted away. But it wasn't for the money. It's the game I'm crazy about—big crowds, big matches, winning things—like if I was really daft on cash I'd do all these advertising stunts and contracts and things—opening boutiques and whatnot."

"Why don't you?"

"I want to concentrate on the game. Wiggy and Dave Spencer say they don't let their businesses interfere with their football—but they must think about them a lot. They must worry about the money they have invested—is my partner robbing me or the manager fiddling the books? With me it's all football—at this stage anyway."

"Don't you ever find you've got too much spare time on your hands—all those midweek afternoons?"

"In London? You're joking, there's hundreds of things to do—museums, art galleries, big shops, cinemas, historical places—I like all that. I've started reading a lot as well."

"What kind of stuff?"

"Biographies, mainly. I've read every book in Wimbledon library on Lloyd George. He must have been one of the most fantastic men who ever lived."

"Why Lloyd George in particular?"

"A teacher at school told us a lot about him and then I picked up a book at the library at home—I'm interested in them old days. Lloyd George knew my father! He was one of the randiest men who ever lived. It should have been Lloyd George knew my mother!"

"You'd never think of a prime minister like that, would you?"

"Not nowadays."

As they chatted on Peterson began to realise that Roy's normal manner of aloofness was not a sign of arrogance but of some sense of inferiority. He was obviously an expert on Lloyd George yet he seemed to think that a man of the world, an expression he actually used about Peterson, would find his views very naive. All the time Peterson felt like a child seeing his first stage magician. How is it done, was the question that kept running through his head.

"How much of what you do is reflex and how much do you actually make up your mind about? Remember that goal you got against Dundee United in the replay?"

"The second one?"

"Yes—as I saw it their left-back had the ball clear of Riddle and looked dead certain to bring it up the field—but you were already sprinting towards their goal. How did you know he was going to pass back to the goalkeeper? You were two moves ahead of everybody else—when he passed it back you were already running onto it—as if it was a pass from one of your own team. He must have had a moment of madness, trying to pass it back, but how did you know in advance?"

"I couldn't explain it, Bill. I saw him with the ball, maybe he didn't move quickly enough and I got the idea he was thinking of passing back—but believe me these things just happen. You don't have time to think about them. You remember Denis Law and Jimmy Greaves—they were like that, moving in to snap up half-chances before anyone else could see them. I've heard it called the killer instinct. I dunno, I couldn't explain why or how it happens."

They heard doors banging and loud voices. The others were back from the golf course.

"Well, I do hope you are okay for Saturday," Peterson said, as Roy went to leave. "It would be a shame to miss this game."

"A shame!" Roy grimaced in anguish. "I've looked forward to a match like this all my life! To play in front of the biggest gate in history—the pinnacle of any player's career. And you call it a shame. It would be a bloody tragedy! This is what the game is all about, Bill, this is a dream coming true. A shame!"

"Sorry, Roy. I've been brainwashed I suppose by certain parties who claim they're only here for the money."

"They're only saying that, Bill. The money's nice—but that isn't where the magic is."

They went together down the corridor and knocked on the door of John Callagher's suite. The manager opened the door wearing a long white bath-towel round his middle.

"I'll come back," said Peterson.

"No, come in, just going to have a shower. All right, Roy?"

"Fine, boss, I'm perfectly okay now."

"Good."

John Gallagher's body was hard and firm, deep chest covered by coarse black hair, only a slight thickening above the hips to show that he was no longer a player. Peterson told him about the phone calls. As he stood under the spray, with the other two at the doorway, he asked Roy if he had talked to anyone about the injury. Roy told him that he'd met the chairman while the team was training.

"Blast it!" John Gallagher said.

"I didn't say anything—I didn't know anything," Peterson said.

"Well, we knew it was more serious than what we told the others," John Gallagher said. "I would have told the chairman last night—but I got caught up in something else. Nothing's ever simple in this game."

Peterson hoped that Roy would leave them. More and more he felt drawn towards John Gallagher, filled with a growing urge to get close to the man. He had never realised before how all-pervasive was the manager's influence on the lives of the men he managed. It was hard to believe that he was only thirty-seven, for he seemed to be mature in a way Peterson associated with men in their fifties. Players might moan about bruises and strains—it seemed appropriate that when the spectre of illness had hung over John Gallagher it would be the worst illness of all. There was nothing trivial about the man. Peterson knew in advance that his account of what Albert Stone had told him on the terraces the morning before would sound trivial and childish in the presence of John Gallagher. Surprisingly, for he rarely wasted time on conversation that did not have a practical purpose, John Gallagher suddenly began to tell them Glasgow jokes. He used the full dialect, the harsh Glasgow Germanic of *achs* and glottal stops and machine-gun *rrrr* sounds. He had no talent for telling stories, continually interrupting the story-line to explain irrelevancies, and most of the time Peterson could only tell when the punch-line had arrived by the way John Gallagher burst into laughter. There was a false note in his whole performance and Peterson found it more and more difficult to pretend he was also enjoying the jokes. In fact he understood only one of them fully.

"The ref was once sending Charlie Tully off the field. Tully—what a character! The whole of Glasgow used to be telling nothing but Tully jokes. He was the original bloke in the one about the Pope, who's that bloke in white up there on the balcony with Charlie Tully? Anyway, the ref's sending him off. 'Go to the pavilion,' he says, pointing at the tunnel. 'Sure there's a better show on at the Empire,' says Tully."

Peterson was uncomfortable at the way John Gallagher kept laughing and looking at them and asking if they understood it.

But then, he thought, you probably would behave a little hysterically if you'd just been told you didn't have the worst illness in the world.

On their way into the Rob Roy suite for the press conference, Peterson went to phone the advertising agency in London about the beer commercials. Nixon, the account executive, didn't sound too surprised at the suggestion of a twenty-thousand-pound guarantee. As Peterson came out of the box the chairman and his party were coming through the lobby. Jackson asked Peterson where John Gallagher was.

"Press conference!"

George Jackson seemed to be in a bad temper. He took the others into the bar. In the large lounge John Gallagher was sitting at a table, facing the journalists, who were loosely scattered about the lounge, cigarette smoke already giving the room a bluish haze. Sitting with John Gallagher were Roy, Sammy, Alec Hood, Wiggy and Randy. The questions started.

"Is it true Roy Christmas missed training this morning? Is he injured?"

Peterson, standing with his back to the wall, near the door, watched John Gallagher's face but the manager seemed to have taken a grip on himself.

"Roy's had a little muscle strain, nothing serious, we decided to give him a day's rest—we've been through a pretty tough schedule in the last four or five weeks. But he'll be fighting fit for Saturday."

"Have you seen Rangers playing?"

"I've seen them twice—the team saw a film of their game against Derby this afternoon."

"What did you think of them? Have you any special plans to hold them—are you doing anything special about Caskie, for instance?"

"I've a great respect for them, we all think the game's improved immensely up here, ever since Jock Stein turned Celtic into a major European power. As for special plans—no, we find we get on better sticking to our normal game."

"Do you think you might try and hold out for a draw at Hampden? You might think you'd stand a better chance if you got a replay at Goodison Park on Wednesday, the crowd down there would be more on your side."

"No, we're not holding out for a draw, if by that do you mean are we going to pack our defence. We want to win this game."

"One thing that interests us up here is the way English stars, particularly in London, cash in on their reputations with boutiques and advertising. Do you think this is really a good thing?"

"I don't think it's bad. When I was a young player we spent our afternoons hanging about cafés and billiard halls. These lads are putting their spare time to something constructive. But they have signed contracts to play for us and if I ever thought they weren't giving us a hundred per cent effort I'd make them choose between the game and their outside interests. It hasn't happened yet. Has it, Bobby?"

Wiggy leaned on his elbows and stared impassively.

"Is it true Bobby is heading for his first million?"

"You'd better ask him that."

Wiggy smiled.

"We're all heading for our first million," he said. "Very few of us ever get there." Hood patted him on the back, "But even if I was getting near that kind of money, so what? Don't you think footballers are as entitled to make money as anyone else, builders or actors or doctors or stockbrokers."

Randy was asked if he feared the jumping ability of the Rangers forward Aikman, who had already scored thirty-two goals that season.

"Respect—not fear," he said. "If you were actually afraid of other players you wouldn't be in the professional game."

"Would you say it's true, what many people say, that the game in England is a lot dirtier than it is in Scotland?"

"Rougher maybe, more robust—of course we play it a bit faster so things tend to look worse than they really are. What do you think about that, Alec?"

"I wouldn't say it's dirty in England," said Hood. "It used to be fairly vicious at times—you know, that old foul, going over the top of the ball to get a crack at your opponent's shin or ankle. But apart from that it's never been what we'd call dirty—I think most players will tell you they enjoy a physical game as long as it's genuinely robust and not vicious, you know, nobody trying to maim you. One of the best things I think is that we've managed to bring back the fair shoulder charge—just before they changed the ref system it had become almost outlawed—yet it's one of the oldest traditions in the game."

Somebody mentioned Sammy's television interview.

"You were just joking about your hobbies being a lager and a gamble, I take it."

"Jokin'? Course I weren't jokin'—why should I be jokin'?"

John Gallagher laughed.

"In moderation, of course," he said, nodding briskly at Sammy. "Don't give them the wrong impression."

"In moderation—of course," said Sammy.

"How did the team react to Ian Jarvie's column about the circus coming to town?"

"We don't mind being called a circus," Hood said.

"The comedy ends when we get on the park," said Sammy, showing the reporters a clenched fist.

That ended the formal session. Reporters gathered round individual players with the questions they hoped would give them exclusive quotes. Hood brought a reporter over to Peterson to discuss an offer of fifty pounds for Alec's name on an article for Saturday's big match edition; Peterson saw no point in quibbling for the sake of a few extra pounds. He saw John Gallagher leaving the lounge and followed him, intending to tell him that he had asked twenty thousand for the beer commercials. Before he could catch up George Jackson came across the foyer, calling something to John Gallagher. Peterson saw the chairman speaking quickly, his face tight with anger. John Gallagher shook his head. The chairman said something and they went together towards the lift. Peterson looked in at the door of the Lochinvar Lounge. Danny was sitting with Dave Peacock.

"Hallo," he said, "you weren't at the press conference, Danny—not feeling shy were you?"

"Nah. Don't like all that bullshit. Want a tea or something?"

"Better get another fag ready, Bill," said Peacock, "that one's just about had it."

Peterson pulled a cigarette out of the packet. He stubbed out the butt he had been smoking. He balanced the cigarette on its end.

"Look—no hands."

"Cor blimey, Bill, you've broken the chain! You're due for seven years bad luck, matey!"

"I'm not superstitious." He wondered how long he could leave the cigarette balancing on the table. Maybe all this fitness around him was contagious. "The press conference wasn't too much bullshit," he said. "In fact it was pretty tame. I'm beginning to realise now just how little reporters get to know about what's going on in a team."

"I don't like reporters, never have," said Danny.

"Why not?"

"You'll wish you hadn't asked that question, Bill," said Peacock. "The Reverend Peck will now punish our listeners with a sermon."

"I suppose sports reporters are all right," said Danny, grudgingly. "Mind you, there's only a few knows much about what's really going on but they don't bugger you about like the other kind. Them news reporters—they're like leeches. And they don't care what they do! Didn't I ever tell you what happened to me and Stevie Baldwin—when I was in the England team—"

"For one game," said Peacock.

"I might only have one cap but I've got both my balls," said Danny. Peacock looked away, grimacing. He'd been relieved of one testicle by a surgeon, early in his career, after a kick in the vitals. It wasn't unknown in the game. The great centre-forward Dixie Dean, who incidentally hated the nickname Dixie, had told a newspaperman once of how when he'd been starting in the game as a seventeen-year-old a defender came up to him in a match after he'd scored a goal and told him he would make sure he didn't score any more. He kept his promise, kicking the young legend-in-the-making in the vitals, so brutally one testicle had to be removed.

Seventeen years later, when he had finished playing, Dixie was in a pub in Chester when he saw the defender, both of them much older men. He waited quietly until the man left and followed him up the road until he got him in an alley.

"I beat the shit out of him," Dixie said, "and I still got there in time for the first race."

It was a long time to nurse a grievance but having one ball missing was as good a memory aid as a knot in a handkerchief.

"Anyway," Danny went on, "I was pals with Stevie then so when we got back from Yugoslavia his wife was staying up in

Norfolk with friends—you remember, they had those kidnap threats? So I go home with Stevie to his gaff in Harold Hill and the press were onto him, the phone never stopped, they knew he was back home, they were banging on the door, shouting questions through the letter-box—so we stay in the kitchen at the back of the house, making a cuppa—and suddenly we see this geezer climbing over the garden wall. 'Hey, where the fakking hell you think you're goin' then?' Stevie shouts. 'Ah, Mr. Baldwin,' says the geezer, cool as all get out, 'I was just passing this way and wondered if I could ask you about this kidnap business.' I ask you!"

"That's what they call initiative," Peterson said. "I did worse in my time. We used to consider it part of your apprenticeship. The first time you managed to steal a wedding picture off the mantelpiece of the weeping widow you knew you had made it."

"Cor—and they say footballers are oafs! Did you actually like doing it?"

"At first it seemed like good fun." He picked up the cigarette and lit it quickly. "Then I grew up. I found I could do it easier if I stayed half-drunk."

"So why is it I have to learn about Roy's injury two days after everyone else?" the chairman demanded.

They were in his suite on the second floor, George Jackson standing in the middle of the sitting-room floor, John Gallagher standing with his hands on the back of an armchair. Jemima had been asked to leave them alone. Showing neither surprise nor resentment she had gone to lie down in the bedroom.

"Look, Chairman," said John Gallagher, "I wasn't trying to keep anything from you. I was going to ring you at home on Tuesday night but I forgot. That's all. I'm sorry."

"You forgot! Listen, man, I laid out quarter of a million pounds of my own money to become chairman of this club—does that entitle me to be treated like the odd-job man? Why didn't you tell me yesterday on the train? I looked a real fool in front of the Rangers directors at lunch—they were telling *me* that my star player had missed training—and I wouldn't have known what they were talking about if I hadn't bumped into Roy in the foyer. You had all day yesterday to tell me."

"There were other things on my mind, Chairman. I honestly forgot. I'm sorry—what more do you want me to say?"

"What more? Lots more! Jesus Christ, man, what the hell could be on your mind that's more important than this club? Do you think you can treat me the way you treat a bloody player? I demand your complete loyalty, *demand it!*"

John Gallagher had been looking tired and indifferent but at this his face became agitated.

"Are you suggesting I'm disloyal?"

"I'm suggesting you can't treat me like dirt. Dammit, man, you don't own this club! You run the team—but I employ you. I own this club!"

"You do, do you?"

"What the hell does that mean?"

"Whatever you think it means. Nobody owns a football club, Mr. Jackson, it isn't a bloody hotel. A club is a bigger thing than any individual. It will be going on a long time after you're dead and forgotten. At the moment I'm the manager. If you don't like the way I run the club then you can bloody well sack me. But until you do I run the team and everything to do with the playing side. So I forgot to tell you about Roy—maybe I'd have been justified in deliberately not telling you. How did everybody get to know so quickly that Roy wasn't training? Funny how you went to Glasgow and within an hour the whole press is phoning us up asking why Roy missed training. Are you sure Norman didn't shoot off his big mouth?"

"Just what the hell do you mean?"

"Only four of us knew the situation with Roy—Hood, Westbury, Roy and me. We weren't going to tell anybody else until we knew one way or the other if he'd be fit for Saturday. None of the team could have told the press—we were all up at the training ground. But you found out—and then your party goes to Glasgow and suddenly the whole world knows about it. Coincidental, was it?"

"Of course we didn't tell anybody!"

They were shouting now, their faces red, the chairman's neck veins throbbing against his collar.

"Well, you can see what I'm getting at. You're in the entertainment industry, whether you like it or not, just like film stars and pop singers and circus clowns and striptease girls—you have to take the publicity, good or bad, you couldn't live without it—"

"Ah yeah, the game needs publicity," said Danny. "But I don't need it—and I don't bloody want it. I don't care if they never mention my name or write articles about me—the club pays me, the manager knows if I'm a good player or not—it's not like bleeding pop stars or poncy actors, our wages don't depend on a lot of glamour bullshit in the papers."

"You're in the public eye—that's just a fact of life and you can't escape it."

"Oh sure," said Danny, "but I'm only in the public eye because of what I do out on the park. Why should I be expected to do anything else? You'll see them so-called intellectuals slagging off players—why do they pay these fantastic amounts of money to a lot of hairy idiots who only kick a bag of wind about a field? They think we're working-class upstarts, do they? They seem to actually resent us as people—is it the money, you think? Do they think we really do just laze about all week on our backsides and have a jolly old kickabout on a Saturday afternoon? I'd like to get them bastards out on the pitch and make them run till their lungs were killing them, make the berks grovel on the ground for breath and make them get up and do some more. They'd see it isn't just kicking a ball of wind!"

"You're a sadist, deep down, you know that?"

"Yeah? Is that good?"

"Anyway, I can give you the answer to what you're saying—it might be hard work being a player but it's hard work being in a factory or down a mine or digging ditches—and you don't get film star wages in those jobs."

"It's the law of supply and demand, innit? Film actresses get big money cos they got big bristols and that's what people want to look at. We only get paid the market value for what we do—I don't get sick if I hear that somebody like Roy Christmas is getting more greens than me—that's what the club think he's worth to them, that's what he's been able to screw out of them. Good luck to him."

"Have you got a thing against actors, by any chance? You're always mentioning them."

"Yeah well, nobody ever sees it my way—but they only pretend, don't they? They're only playing at it, copying what some real geezer's actually done. Look at the telly—it's all filmed in advance, if they forget their lines they do it over again. You ever hear of an actor losing his left bollock with a boot on his niagaras?"

Now the shouting match was over and they were both having regrets. The chairman stood with his hands in his pockets, looking out of the window. A red March sun was a dull blood-orange inferno over the dark hills across the water. He was annoyed at himself for losing his temper. It had been genuine, not an act calculated to cow an underling. He liked John Gallagher more than almost any other man he knew, and he knew that John Gallagher was probably in the right, yet there were pressures on him that John Gallagher did not know about.

"I think we've both sensed it was bound to come to this," he said. "Our ideas aren't the same, that's all there is to it."

"You hired me to do a job and I'm doing it to the best of my ability," said John Gallagher, almost wearily. "If you wanted a glamour circus you should have hired a different kind of manager. I know this club can have a lot of success with the players we've got—maybe a couple of positions could be strengthened—but basically we have a great team. You're only interested in headlines and publicity—glamour. You wanted me to sell Shackle so that we could buy Stan Barlow. You said Shack was just an honest club player, a workman, whereas Barlow had star quality. You—"

"Why tell me all that again? You won the argument, didn't you?"

"Yes but you still believe you were right. And I don't think I can work with a chairman who doesn't trust my judgment."

"You don't think you can? You either know or you don't. Are you thinking of resigning?"

"No, I am not. Resigning is an admission of guilt. If you want rid of me you'll have to sack me. Until you do I intend to go on doing the job I'm paid for, running this team to the best of my professional ability, the way I think fit."

Jackson sighed deeply. He looked sideways at the manager. He could see nothing in John Gallagher's face.

"All I want is what is best for the club," he said. "This isn't a rich man's hobby with me, you know, not a passing whim. If the truth be known I sweated my guts out all these years just so that one day I'd be rich enough to come to Oaks Common not as a ragged-trousered brat but as Mr. Big. I admit it freely. I respect your attitude—but it isn't how I envisaged the club at all. There's more to success than winning games. Under your policy no matter how many cups we win we'll always be known as Gallagher's Hasbeens. I just don't like it. I want them to refer to us in the same breath as the Bank of England or the Crown Jewels."

"That's it then. You've put it on the line. You think there's more to success than winning games. To me that's all success means. I don't care if we win with a team of one-eyed hunchbacks. Winning is everything. Glamour and all that—those are trimmings. They come later. Winning this game on Saturday and then winning the British Cup is all the glamour I'll ever need. And I won't buy another player until I'm absolutely sure he'll be an improvement on the man we already have. I suppose we got off to a wrong start when we agreed to buy Roy from Burnley."

"He worked out all right, didn't he? He was a good buy—he drew the crowds and he got the goals. You all thought it was ridiculous to pay a hundred and forty thousand for him on a five-year-contract—but it was good business. If we hadn't spent that money the tax would have taken most of it, a hundred thousand anyway. So he really cost us forty thousand pounds. For five years that's eight thousand a year. Add his wages to that—ten thousand a year. So he's costing us eighteen thousand pounds a year. For the finest goal-getting machine in England? He's paid for himself this season alone! His goals largely got us to Hampden. Now then, is that glamour madness? I think it's sheer good business. And we can do the same again—we've got money coming in now in no uncertain fashion."

"I wanted Roy because he would put the finish to the job we were already doing. He complements Peacock—one does the runs, the other hovers about waiting to snap up half chances. That's why I bought him—the size of the transfer fee and the headlines had no interest for me at all."

"But it created a fantastic amount of interest in everyone else."

"Everyone else is not managing this club. I'm afraid that if you've decided we can't work together you'll have to sack me."

"Work together? Do it all your way, you mean!"

"As far as the playing side is concerned—yes. You know about business and I know about football."

The chairman shook his head.

"It's the same old story, isn't it? You remember when Len Shackleton wrote his book—the chapter entitled 'What the Average Club Director Knows About Football'? And underneath it just a blank page. You pros—you think nobody knows the slightest thing about the game except yourselves. I suppose you think I've been watching football since I could walk and I've never learned a single thing?"

"Not exactly. As a matter of fact I think you've got some good ideas on the game. I never thought of myself as a one-man band—I've always reckoned on you as somebody I could come to for advice. But when the crunch comes—it's got to be my decision."

"Well at least we know now where we stand."

George Jackson made a protracted business out of cutting and lighting a cigar. John Gallagher looked on, impassive, no sign of impatience.

"I'm sorry it had to come to this, John," the chairman said eventually. "But we might as well face the facts. Our ideas are incompatible. So where do we go from here?"

"I think we should leave it till after the game. No point in upsetting everyone, I wouldn't have thought."

"You're quite right. We'll talk again after Saturday." He looked at John Gallagher, shaking his head slowly, fingers holding the cigar delicately as if it was a dart about to be thrown at a board, little finger raised. "It's a great, great pity, John . . . just because we can't see eye to eye. Still, that's the way it goes sometimes."

"Aye, true enough." John Gallagher got up. "I'm going to see my mother tonight."

"Sentimental journey, eh?"

"Aye—every time I go to Glasgow I get sentimental—for London. I've also told the team they can go ahead with an offer they've had to do T.V. commercials for Whitbreads the brewers. They've been offered fifteen thousand—I told them to ask for twenty. I take it the board will have no objection?"

"You really do mean to relegate me to the back seat." Jackson said, a slight bitterness in his voice. "That should have been a board decision, it affects the whole club, not just the players. Now you've given them permission I can hardly say no, can I? That would really upset the team. Or was that your idea?"

"They've worked very hard, the lads. They deserve all they can get for themselves. What would the board have wanted — half shares of the loot?"

There was a long moment of silence. Then George Jackson moved briskly away from the window.

"We'll say nothing of this to anyone else. Let things go on as before till the game is won — or lost. We can talk then. For the sake of the team we'll go on as though nothing has happened — agreed?"

"Of course."

When John Gallagher had gone George Jackson went through to the bedroom, where his wife was sitting at the dressing-table, doing something to her face.

"Well?" he demanded.

"Pity you couldn't get him to resign," she said. "You'll have to think up a good reason for sacking him. I hope I'm there when you do it, I want to see his face."

"You really hate him that much?"

"Yes I do. He was a nobody when you gave him this job and now he thinks he's Jesus Christ or somebody."

"I don't hate him. In fact I admire him more than ever. I'd like to think I'd have behaved like him in the same circumstances."

"Yes, you would. You're too soft. You'd let the whole world trample all over you. You've always been the same."

"Perhaps, perhaps not. Still, I've always had you to back me up, haven't I?"

Jemima Jackson pulled her nose this way and that, letting the light reach shadowy parts of her upper lip, from which she carefully plucked little hairs with a small pair of silver tweezers.

"You'll put your foot down about this beer contract," she said.

"How can I? The players would take that very badly. We don't want anything to upset them before the game."

"Wait till after the game then," she said, frowning with pain as she nipped out another unwanted follicle.

"That really would be too cold-blooded," he said.

"And your blood is so pulsatingly warm? I wonder how you'd have got on without me, George. Without me and my father's money behind you."

"Yes, I often wonder that myself."

"You'd be a jolly, warm-blooded failure," she said. "All friends and no money."

"I suppose so." He turned to go back into the lounge. Over his shoulder he said, "I'm very grateful, of course."

She smiled. It was as near to rebellion as he ever came. He was entitled to that much.

14

"HALLO, Dave, not feeling too stiff?" Norman called as Spencer came into the bar. They sat beside him at a low, glass-topped table. Carole was wearing one of the new Chinese tunic outfits, blue silk so tight-fitting the shape of her nipples was clearly visible. However, it was not her bristols that startled Dave so much as the fact that she had become a blonde. Until then she'd been raven-haired but now she had short, tightly curled fair hair with wispy fringes at the neck and ears. Debonair couldn't remember the last time a woman had excited him so much. The waiter brought Norman and Carol their dry Martinis and his own second pineapple juice.

A page boy in a round pillbox hat came into the bar.

"Paging Mr. Spencer," he called.

"Here," Dave called, raising his hand.

"Phone call for you in number three box, Mr. Spencer," said the boy.

"Who is it?" Dave asked irritably.

"A Miss Lindsay, she's calling you from Glasgow."

"I don't know any Miss Lindsay in Glasgow."

"She says it's personal and very important."

"Oh well—I won't be a minute—don't run away." He walked quickly through to the foyer, meeting the chairman and Jemima on their way into the bar. When he picked up the receiver he said brusquely, "Dave Spencer here, who's this?"

"Is that Mr. Spencer of the Commoners party?" said a Scottish girl's voice.

"Yeah. What is it?"

"I have Miss Lindsay calling you, Mr. Spencer, will you hang on a moment?"

"Okay, make it snappy though."

"Just hang on, sir."

He sat in the box for two or three minutes, clicking the receiver bar up and down, shouting into the speaker. The line buzzed with meaningless static. He banged down the phone and went to the desk. The girl said she didn't know what had happened to the call.

"If they call back tell them to jump in the river," he said, heading back for the bar. Shack was standing in the door.

"Hey, Dave," he said, excitedly, "there was some bird calling you from Glasgow—I think it's something about television. I've got a number for you to ring."

"Bloody hell!"

But the lure of fame and glamour was too enticing and he went back to the phone boxes and punched the buttons for the number Shack had given him and then spent some bad-tempered moments asking some stupid clot of a man for Miss Lindsay, of whom the great Scottish twit said he had never heard.

"Look, this is Dave Spencer of the Commoners—the football team," Dave snarled. "I was told to ring Miss Lindsay."

"Somebody's been having you on, pal," said the man. "This is Ibrox."

"Ibrox?"

"If you are a footballer you'd know this is Glasgow Rangers ground. The only Lindsay we have here is called Killer."

"Jesus Christ!"

He slammed down the phone. When he got back to the bar there was no sign of Shack but he was just in time to see Norman and Carole and the chairman and Jemima going into the dining-room. He stood in the bar, mouth tight with anger.

In the little room behind the reception desk Sammy Small was having to hold on to the switchboard to prevent himself falling to the ground in a helpless fit of laughter.

"Did you hear him asking for Miss Lindsay?" he wheezed between convulsions.

"You're a holy terror so you are," said the switchboard girl. "He'd better not find out I helped you. I hope you haven't got me into trouble, that's all."

"Hardly," said Sammy. "But now you mention it—ha ha, ha ha—lie down, I think I love you. . ."

15

JOHN Gallagher and Alec Hood were leaving the dining-room as the chairman's party came in.

"What are the lads doing tonight, John?" Jackson asked.

"They can more or less suit themselves—they can go to the cinema in Largs or watch television or play snooker. Harry Barnes will see they're all in their rooms by eleven."

"Have a nice trip then."

The fast electric train got them to Glasgow Central station by ten minutes past seven. On the journey John Gallagher was several times on the point of telling Alec Hood about his row with the chairman but a promise had been made and for all Alec was so mature and trustworthy he was still a player—possibly the key man in the team's chances of success or failure on Saturday. There were many things it did a player no good to know. One of the secrets of management was to help players concentrate on the game.

They talked mostly about the film they'd seen of the Rangers-Derby game and the chances of Roy being fit. Hood thought John Gallagher was strangely subdued for a man who had only that day been told his worst fears were groundless.

"What will you do with Roy tomorrow?" Hood asked.

"It's debatable—we could really stretch him tomorrow and he might break down and then we'd have no chance of getting him fit for Saturday. Another day's rest might just make the difference—we can always give him a fitness test on Saturday morning. But I always prefer to let everybody know what the team's going to be by Friday lunchtime."

"I'm glad it's your decision."

"It's the kind of thing you'll have to decide for yourself one day."

"I think I'll go on playing as long as I can. Life's a lot simpler as a player."

"That's truer than you might think."

They separated at the taxi rank outside the station, arranging to meet at the same place in time for the ten-thirty train back to Largs. Hood went off to see his brother, who lived in Dumbarton on the north side of the Clyde. John Gallagher bought Glasgow's evening paper, the *Times-Citizen*, and then gave a taxi-driver his mother's address in Blackhill, the housing scheme from which she had always refused to move, even when the hooliganism and vandalism made it an unlikely place to live for an elderly widow with a son earning fifteen thousand pounds a year in London.

The driver did not recognise John Gallagher, which was a bit of a surprise. Glasgow was the city where football was the true religion and its stars the true gods. Maybe, as the old joke went, the driver was an atheist or a homosexual. Any Glasgow man who didn't find football the greatest thing in life must be a deviate of some description.

Leaning into the corner, John Gallagher turned first to the sports pages. This being Thursday the sports writers had finished analysing last Saturday's games and were now getting properly excited about the coming Saturday. They had a picture of Commoners in tracksuits, trotting in pairs to the training ground. He remembered then seeing a solitary photographer at the entrance to the practice pitches—he must have been the one who told the papers that Roy missed training. They had a short story about Roy's non-appearance—the headline was CHRISTMAS DAY OFF—but their real interest was in the Rangers. There was a picture of Hay Grant, one of the Rangers back four, lying on a treatment table, the Rangers physiotherapist examining a bruise on his ankle. Hay Grant was smiling at the camera. Not a bad player but inclined to be weak on his left side. There were no surprises in the Rangers team: Miller in goal; Milne, Grant, Lindsay and Graham in the back four; Traynor, Killick and Gustafson the middle three, and Caskie, Aikman and Dawson up front. He read through the names again slowly, making mental notes for the talk he'd give the team on Saturday morning. It occurred to him idly that there was not a single Mac in the Ibrox team. No Highland nonsense about that lot, he thought, not quite smiling.

Another sports writer had a conjecture piece about Rangers

tactics for Saturday, saying he thought they would use the speed of Caskie and Dawson on the wings to take advantage of a lack of pace in the Commoners back four. That was a reference to Hood and Peck and this time he did smile, thinking of Danny the Destroyer and Hood the Rock—you wouldn't call them greyhounds but between them they could stop an invasion let alone a forward line. Even now the Scots still yearned for the romance of the good old days when dashing cavaliers like Gay Gordon Smith of Hibs and Willie the Deedle Waddell—the same who became Rangers' manager—tore down wings in heroic fashion, Smith a spiky, breath-taking artist, Waddell a broad-shouldered flyer as big as a house and as thunderously fast as an express train. No matter what happened in the outside world, the Scots still saw the game as a magic event adorned by legendary heroes and mere stars. Magic, that's what the Scots wanted out of football, more even than they wanted straight success . . . he saw again the five green Hibernian wizards, maybe the finest forward line of them all—but that's what old men said about so many forward lines—Smith, Johnstone, Reilly, Turnbull and Ormond . . . he was a boy then and football was his magic . . . he saw cheeky Charlie Tully, half bald and bow-legged, Ibrox park under black storm clouds, the silhouettes of the dockyard cranes looming like Martian war-machines, a hundred thousand rain-sodden Glaswegians packed tight in a divided army of roaring throats, Tully in the green and white hoops sending big George Young and Willie Woodburn running the wrong way after a non-existent ball, running because Tully had the magic and the true artist's arrogance to point to where he pretended he was going to hit the ball . . . he saw again the bullet head of Torry Gillick, the man who counted the Moscow Dynamos and told the ref there wiz twelve o' they Russkies oan the field . . . he saw Willie McNaught, the original educated left-foot, the cleanest kicker of a ball they ever had up here . . . and Billy rummle-em-up Houliston who could shoulder-charge a hole through a defence or a mountain . . . he saw again Billy Steel, the blond bombshell who ended up running a team in Hollywood, U.S.A. . . . he saw Jimmy Mason, tiny and round-shouldered, hitting passes of such inch-perfect accuracy you couldn't believe they were intentional, until he did it again, and again . . . he saw Jimmy Cowan the Morton goalkeeper saving one at point-blank range from Raich Carter, England versus Scotland, Wembley Stadium, 1949 . . . he saw Slim

Jim Baxter walk about the pitch he controlled like a king on horse-back . . . he saw the red-haired beaver, Bobby Evans, and Bertie Peacock with the pixie ears . . . and it was all magic in those days, when a shy, spotty boy with big ears and awkward elbows ate, drank and breathed football and did more than dream — no, *lived* . . . in hope of becoming a player himself, one of the pros, the most magical life the world could offer . . . through the windows of the cab he saw the new motorised Glasgow, the replanned and rebuilt Glasgow of underpasses and flyovers and feed-in lanes and motor-way signs, a concrete rabbit warren where once there had been a black, rectangular city of monster tenements, a grimy, battered bar on each windswept corner. Now it was Detroit on the Clyde. He didn't like it. But he had to shrug for he hadn't liked the old Glasgow much either. To be sentimental for the old Glasgow was like weeping tears for long-remembered humiliations.

On the front page of the *Times-Citizen* the stories seemed, how-ever, to come out of the Glasgow he had known all those years ago. A high court murder trial witness had been blasted in the back by a shotgun fired from a moving van in Easterhouses. His condition was critical. He was the only eye-witness of the first murder and the only eye-witness to his own shooting. Seven people had been taken to hospital after a knife fight at a wedding reception mêlée. An unemployed labourer, aged nineteen, had been stabbed to death outside a Crown Street pub. Three youths had kicked a bus con-ductor unconscious, breaking his nose and cheekbones, rather than pay the fare. A city magistrate was advocating the return of the death penalty — although, as he said, we had to move with the times and maybe a lethal injection would be more humane than hanging.

He got out of the taxi at the end of his mother's street, knowing the arrival of a cab at her front door would create a stir among the packs of unruly kids who roamed these streets looking for some-thing to take their minds off the grim boredom of drab poverty.

"If ye want a cab back ye'll have to phone, chief," said the driver. "We're no' allowed to wait here. We lose too many taxis that way."

"Aye, okay."

"That's if ye can find a phone they havenae smashed tae smithereens!"

The houses here were not any older than himself. This had once been the new Glasgow, a green place with gardens and privet hedges for the rehoused slum dwellers from the big black city tenements. Now the new Glasgow looked battered and shabby. Many of the windows were boarded up and he remembered a letter from his mother saying that despite the Glasgow housing shortage no decent folk would move into Blackhill. Gang slogans covered the walls, spray-painted, the work of anonymous gallows-comedians, the grim wits of Glasgow's violent human carnival. The names of the gangs had a macabre ring. Nothing had changed. The Real Mental Celtic and the Disciples and the Toi and the Pollock Mad Squad . . . the Pope was still public enemy number one. On one boarded-up house he saw the name EVA chalked and painted at least nine times. Poor Eva, he thought, not even a slim chance of getting out of all this, for girls can't play football. On a rough stretch of waste ground a crowd of men and youths were playing football in their street clothes. At first they looked like a shabby rabble but after a moment or two patterns began to emerge. It was a serious match, with bricks for goals, about fifteen a side, the white, plastic, lightweight ball the only sign that the whole world was not a slum.

His trained eye looked for signs of football intelligence but all he could see were the old Scottish faults, each youth or man determined to hold the ball to himself, dribbling with an unmistakable flair and skill—even grace, of a kind you rarely saw in a London street game—but always wanting to do it solo. One boy caught his eye, about fifteen years old, red hair over his ears, a thin serious face, wearing a faded blue cardigan with holes in the elbows. Twice in succession he took the ball off the toes of a dribbling forward and hit it hard and low to the wings, a few yards ahead of men who didn't want to run after it.

"Haud it for fugh's sake!" one of them shouted back, face stuck out in uncontrolled aggression.

"Run after it, ye fughing mug," the red-haired boy shouted back. He spat. Next time he tried a quick passing movement with another defender but when he ran into space for the return ball it did not come. The other defender went off up the field, dribbling on and on in some private fantasy of being Big John Hughes or Jimmy Johnstone of Celtic or Wee Willie Henderson of Rangers. John Gallagher had a momentary urge to walk onto that battered parody of a pitch and tell the red-haired boy he was right. What was the use? Maybe the boy had real talent. Maybe with coaching and encouragement he could have made something in the game. Maybe with proper feeding and physical training he could have filled out his thin-shouldered body . . . but it was too late. He'd escaped the talent net. Maybe he'd just been unlucky, for the scouts couldn't see every school game in Britain. Maybe he'd never had football boots to play in a school team. Whatever it was, he'd lost his chance, for the scouts went looking for promising twelve-year-olds; if you didn't show you had the makings by then you were probably too late. If you weren't signed by a professional club by the age of sixteen you might as well forget it.

John Gallagher stood on the pavement a few moments longer, waiting to see if the red-haired boy did anything else. He trapped one ball smoothly and laid it off nicely to the wing. There was no doubt, he knew what ought to be done. Maybe . . . John Gallagher turned his head and walked on towards his mother's house. What the hell was the use? The net had missed that boy and what was the use of trying to save one when you couldn't save them all?

Sammy and Danny came into the lounge after dinner.

"That's the best of being a fast eater," said Danny.

"Wot is?" said Sammy.

"You don't have to pay the bill."

"But the club's payin' the bills, stupid."

"How do you know—you've never been there long enough to see who pays, have you? Cor—don't look now—sit over here—they might not have seen us."

He pulled at Sammy's elbow. They headed for the easy chairs round a low table in a corner, trying to hide themselves behind a pillar, Sammy staring back over his shoulder to see who they were avoiding.

"I said don't look now, you berk," said Danny.

"Don't look at who?"

"Harry the bleeding Hat?"

"That berk! Leave him out!"

"Come on, Shack's playing snooker."

"What are you doing with your tickets?" Danny asked in the snooker room. "I give all my comps away to Morry Green. I might as well let the others go to the hotel staff."

"My fan club's taken all my briefs," said Shack. "You big glamour stars don't know what a big deal I am back home in the valley. They're coming up on a coach, thirty men and a hundred cases of light ale."

"You got so many relations you could fill any ground in Britain on complimentaries," said Sammy. "Cor—you remember the Swansea cup game? Mister Jackson was tellin' me Shack wanted so many comps for his taff friends they didn't think there'd be room for payin' customers."

"Shack has a million relations and poor Danny has none," said Seymour. "Wait till you get married, Danny, you'll find the in-laws will grab all the tickets going."

"Let's do something else," said Danny, when yet another ball was hit so hard it banged over the ledge and rolled under the other billiards tables.

"Let's play another joke on Spencer," said Sammy, eagerly. "He's in the discotheque with the lovely Carole. Let's get round there, eh, and stir it up a bit?"

"Okay," said Danny. Shack and Seymour went on playing. As they went through the hotel Sammy babbled away, thinking up new plans for putting one over on Debonair Dave. Danny never tired of watching the way the little man would bounce up and down with glee at the prospect of playing practical jokes. And he went through with them, too, no messing about. Once at London Airport, going on some close-season European trip, they'd seen Steve Egan the journalist standing dreamily in the main lounge. Sammy had sneaked up behind him, uncoupled a link from a temporary barrier of white rope and posts, and hooked the end into Egan's jacket pocket. When Egan walked off he dragged behind him a twenty-yard stretch of posts and rope. Very funny indeed. Everybody fell about laughing—except Steve Egan, whose side-pocket was ripped clean off his jacket.

"Cor, mate, we used to be at 'em all the time in Dagenham," Sammy had told him when he once asked what was the attraction in practical jokes. "I'll tell you one we used to get up to. We'd go up to some geezer in the street and say we was rozzers havin' an identity parade for a case of rape, would he mind just makin' up the numbers? So the ice-cream would get in the line—all our mates like—and we'd have this bird, she'd walk up the line and then point at this geezer and scream—'That's the one wot dunnit!

That's the raper!' Cor—you shoulda seen the bloke's face. He was terrified."

Sammy didn't seem to think it strange that victims often wanted to give him a thumping. He said he usually found a way to scarper before they got their mitts on him. That was part of the fun.

Peterson was drinking with the doctor in the Rob Roy suite when they paged him for the fifth time since dinner. This time it was Diana. He gave the pageboy a fifty-pence piece to say he had been unable to find him.

"These damned women seem to give you a bad time, old boy," said Paul Franks.

"That was the wife."

"I'm beginning to get the picture now—Diana is your wife—Celia is the—hmm—other lady?"

"That's it. Celia is in the club—she thinks I'm going to leave Diana and get a divorce and all that nonsense."

"But you're not?"

"Well, I don't think so. To tell you the truth—and I wouldn't tell anyone else this, Paul my old friend—it's not even as simple as that. You see, there's this other woman, Margaret—well she and I have been seeing a bit of each other and to be quite honest—"

"You must tell me your secret some time."

"There's no secret. I'm just fatally attractive to ugly women, that's all."

The discotheque was less than half full, most of the hotel's guests being middle-aged sales representatives. Debonair Dave was sitting on the other side of Carole from Norman.

"Very cosy," said Sammy. "Move up, Dave. Cor, it ain't half noisy in here. Wotcha, Carole, wot's a good-lookin' girl like you doin' with a coupla nits like this pair?"

Debonair Dave was very sorry to see them arrive. He had already been regretting his idea of bringing Carole and Norman to the discotheque; when he danced with Carole the music was too loud for the intimate conversation he had in mind. He had shouted sweet little nothings in her ear but if she understood she had given no signs of encouragement.

Danny caught her eye. She gave him a very nice smile, then put her hand to her mouth, trying to hide a giggle. He kept a straight face, but winked slowly.

Dave was leaning his head to try and catch what Sammy was saying when the acid-rock tape came to an end and the music switched quickly to a dreamy number in slow time.

As Debonair Dave realised this was his chance to get in some meaningful chat Carole was already sliding round the seat to get onto the floor. Danny had got in first. The dirty bastard! There was nothing about competition in the bet!

"I hope I don't break your toes," Danny said as they glided away from the table, the only couple on the floor.

"Why, don't you dance very much?"

"I went in for a foxtrot contest once, in my youth. The judges reckoned I went over the top and done me girl's ankle. They banned me for life."

She smiled. Then she looked at his face and began to laugh. His hands felt her body shaking.

"Yeah, it's true," he said, his face straight. "It's a habit, I s'pose. Whenever I get on a dance-floor I have this uncontrollable urge to do crunching tackles on the other couples. You think that's strange?"

She shook her head, biting on her lower lip.

"Cheer up," he said. That started her off again. He realised she must have had more than a couple of Bacardis. As they circled slowly he could see Dave and Norman chatting to each other, flicking glances in their direction.

"You goin' steady with Norman?" he asked her.

That stopped her laughing. She looked up at him quite indignantly, a stiffening of her body suggesting that she was annoyed.

"Of course not. I'm trying to do business with the Jacksons, that's all. Is Norman putting it about that I'm his current popsy?"

"No, he doesn't have to explain things to mere players, he's a director, you know, vice-chairman. He does what he wants without asking our permission."

"I'm not his steady popsy. I hope you believe me."

"I believe you. How about Debonair Dave then? He's been giving you the verbals, hasn't he?"

"The what?"

"The verbals. He's great at it, Dave, you know, spieling, rabbiting, patter, chat?"

"Talking you mean?"

"That's a good word for it. Must make a note of that."

She had another fit of the giggles.

"Honestly, you make me curl up every time I look at you," she said.

"Very flattering, I'm sure."

"No, I mean, you're so funny—you and Sammy Small—I haven't heard you say a single serious word."

"You like a bit of serious chat, do you?"

"It depends."

"Depends on what?"

"What you're being serious about."

"I can be serious, you know."

"Can you really? About football, I expect. You get very serious with other players, don't you? I've seen you playing on the television."

"The comedy stops when the whistle blows."

"Life's a joke but the game is deadly serious?"

"The game is my life."

"Like a monk, are you, dedicated?"

"Not always. You doing anything on Saturday night?"

"Saturday night? I don't know. Why Saturday night?"

"I thought that seeing as how you ain't Norman's bird then I could maybe take you out somewhere when we get back to London on Saturday night."

"Dancing? Soft lights? Music? A few drinks then back to my place? Give me the verbal and hey ho we're in bed."

"Yeah!"

"Sounds interesting. But why Saturday night? Why not tonight?"

"Tonight? How can we do anything tonight? I've got to be in bed by eleven. But if you did fancy it—Saturday night would be just the job."

"What's wrong with tonight?"

"I've told you. We have to be in bed by eleven. There's a big game on Saturday, remember?"

"And what does teacher say you have to do before eleven? Suppose you went to bed early? Would they give you extra marks for that?"

He stared down at her. She stared back.

"I've shocked you—all the way down to your shinpads."

"I don't wear shinpads."

He kept staring at her face.

"All right," he said. "What are you doing tonight?"

"Oh—I wouldn't want to get you in trouble. What does John Gallagher do—come round and tuck you in with a goodnight kiss?"

"No, George Westbury reads us a bedtime story and Harry Barnes fetches us hot milk. They reckon we're old enough to go on the potty ourselves."

"Gosh—you are mature."

The soft music stopped. He let his arms fall to his sides. He looked at her. She looked at their table.

"I've got letters to answer," she said. "I've got to get them in the first post tomorrow. I'll be in my room around half-past nine."

For a second he suspected some joke on Sammy's part.

"Why me in particular?" he asked.

"Oh yes, I am very particular."

"Okay—so why me?"

"You make me laugh for one thing. Most men don't."

"Anything for a giggle, is that it?"

"You must have an inferiority complex. A lady might fancy you for your own sake, you ever think of that?"

"I've had my moments."

"I should hope so."

"You should get a chain on the front door," John Gallagher said as soon as he was in his mother's lobby.

"Ach, there's no point, John, if they're goin' tae burst in a chain will no' haud them back. An' how are ye, son, give us a good look at ye. Ye don't look well. Are ye gettin' enough tae eat? Here, I've got sausages an' ham an' eggs—I'll get a wee cup of tea goin'."

"I'm not hungry, mother."

"Ye'll manage a wee bite, do ye good. Ye never eat properly down there—London, hmmph, they don't know how tae feed a man down there. An' how's ma wee grandchildren?"

"Oh fine. Nancy sends her love."

"Tell her I wis askin' for her. No sign of ye all comin' up for a wee spell? Ye could dae wi' a holiday by the looks of ye. Jings, I'm dyin' to see my wee nephews an' nieces again."

"You know what it's like. Next summer, maybe."

"Aye, I know, John. Now then, sit doon and I'll get the fryin' pan on—here, what d'ye think o' that big stumer Ian Jarvie in the paper—he says Commoners is nothin' but a circus! He should talk, that big clown. I saw ye on the teevee, ye lookt ill, John. Ye're no' worried aboot Saturday's gemme, are ye? I've tolt the lot of them aboot here ye'll thrash they big Ibrox palookas, so ye will. I've bet the milkie five bob ye'll win so I have. Don't let me doon, John, I'm countin' on ye."

He watched her slapping sausages and bacon into the pan, cracking a couple of eggs. Her hair was a lot thinner now, a soft white halo above her head . . . she was a powerful woman then and she needed to be for the farmers paid them two shillings an hour to pick potatoes and she had to push the pram two miles to the fields, the new baby in the pram, the younger ones hanging on to the sides, the two bigger boys kicking a tin can or a shiny black rubber remnant of what had once been a tennis ball. Sometimes it was dark when they set out and dark again when they started off home, the widow and the pram and the dirty-faced rabble of kids and the baby in its warm wrappings and nobody to know that the bottom of the pram, under the baby, was crammed with a stone of stolen potatoes that would give them stew for two days.

She had sweated her life away, breaking her back in the freezing mud of the potato field, stealing and cheating and fighting to keep them fed—yes, stealing because that was the only way she could help them, when he was first in the big school and they wanted him to play in the team he had come crying because he had no football boots and she'd gone to Argyle Street in the heart of Glasgow and stolen a pair of boy's boots from the sports department of Lewis's . . . and the baby in the pram had found an escape from the stinking poverty she had known all her life and now he was back home, a slum boy in a taxi, and he wanted to cry in her arms and tell her that the success she had crucified herself to give him now meant nothing more than those long-forgotten stews of stolen potatoes.

Norman didn't seem to mind too much when Carole said she was going to do her letters, he had the taste and wanted only to get more vodka into himself, which he was now doing with the doctor and Peterson. Dave was very moody. He said he was going to find somebody for a game of snooker.

"I think I'll turn in early," Danny said. They were standing in the foyer. A man in a tweed suit came up to them.

"Here—is this right you blokes are giving away tickets for the Hampden game?" he asked, accusingly.

"Yeah but they're all gone," said Danny.

The man cursed, looking as though they were to blame.

"It's always the bloody same," he said, "all the fly-boys get the tickets and the honest supporters never get a look-in."

"You'll get in all right," said Dave, sneering a little. "Just go up the gate and use your charm."

First Danny went to his own room. Sammy wasn't there. He went into the bathroom and brushed his teeth. He went along the corridor and down the stairs to the second floor. He checked the door numbers. She must be at the other end of the long corridor. He decided to forget it. She'd been having a few Bacardis, she'd have sobered up by now, she didn't really mean it. He heard voices behind him. He walked quickly along the corridor, not looking round. He stopped and looked at the plastic numerals on her door. At the far end of the corridor he could see two or three men. He knocked on the door. When she opened it she was still wearing her trouser suit. He pushed into the room, shutting the door quickly behind him.

"There's somebody coming," he said, listening with his head cocked.

"Who could it be, I wonder—your chaperon?"

He straightened up and walked away from the door.

"There are no rules against it," he said. "It's just assumed that players won't overtax their bodies so close to a big match. In Italy they take them away for two or three nights to the mountains—they don't even let them go home till the morning after the game—they say it puts too much strain on the heart."

"The heart?" she said, though whether she was amused or not he could not tell. She sat at her writing-table. She picked up her pen and put it down again. She clasped her hands round her knee. He stood in front of what had once been the fireplace, his arm on the mantelpiece. He still had a slight suspicion that Sammy and half the team were hiding in a cupboard ready to pounce the moment his trousers were down—if they were coming down.

"I won't offer you a drink," she said.

"Why not?"

"I don't want to harm that tender plant you call your body."

"I could go a lager and lime, as it happens."

"I've got Scotch, that's all." She looked at him and began to laugh gently. His face showed no expression at all. "Danny the Destroyer," she said, shaking her head. "I saw you in that game where you beat somebody—they had red shirts—"

"Liverpool?"

"If you say so."

"Sammy scored from a penalty—"

"Norman and George Jackson keep saying it's the best game you've ever played for the team. I don't know much about football—I kept thinking what big brown legs you had. Football's very sexy I find. Do you find that?"

"You should come in the bath with us after the game."

"It must be a queer's idea of heaven, all that nudity in the bath together."

"You won't find none of that malarkey in football. We're all very normal, ducks."

"Really? I don't believe you. It's the law of averages, there must be some homosexual players."

"I've never heard of any. I've nothing against them myself, mind, but I don't think you'd get very far in the game if you was bent."

"How about Bobby Ingrams?"

"Wiggy? You're joking! That's just his act. He's taking the mickey most of the time. Nah, he's normal—not arf he ain't!"

"Not arf he ain't." She repeated the words slowly. He shrugged. It was all just a joke to her, getting him up to her room. Anything for a giggle. He got up from the armchair and went over towards the writing-table. She sat still, only her eyes moving to follow him. He stood over her. He waited for a moment and then put his hands on her head. She seemed to squirm a little. Then she sat up straight with surprise as his fingers felt for a grip and then pulled the blonde wig away from her head. She put her hands up as if to hide what was underneath the wig.

"I like you better looking natural," he said, bending down to kiss the top of her reddish crop.

When she stood up he took hold of her upper arms and gave

"Ach, they've been in England too long. See that Hood? I know him well—we were both in the same school team. He wisnae all that great then."

The train stopped. The two men looked up with surprise. They both jumped up at the same time. As they collided to get out of the door Hood could not resist calling out.

"I don't remember you in the school team, chief."

The two men got onto the platform, looking back with puzzled faces. Then their eyes widened.

"Hey—that's Big Hood himself!"

Hood winked and raised his thumb. A whistle blew. A guard came between the two men and the door, slamming it shut. Their astonished faces appeared at the open window. The train began to move.

"That was a mistake," John Gallagher said drily as two more faces appeared from the seats ahead of them. A man almost jumped round the corner to offer them a drink from his bottle. Neither of them took a drink but the arguments and excitement caused by their presence kept the whole carriage lit up till they reached Largs, where one man was still trying to get John Gallagher to tell him what *really* happened in the dressing-room at half-time in the Scotland-Russia international eleven years before.

They were both laughing as they got into the taxi.

"You sometimes forget how seriously they take the game up here," Hood said.

"My mother says we've got to win because she's got a five-bob bet with the blue-nosed milkman."

"That's as good a reason for wanting to win as any."

"Winning is its own reason."

"Did you get that from a book? Anybody would think you'd been drinking."

"I wish I had."

"By the way, I saw that game against Russia. What did happen in the dressing-room at half-time?"

"Oh, I dunno," said John Gallagher, staring out of the window. Hood tried to keep the party spirit going but John Gallagher was very quiet and subdued, as though tiredness had suddenly overtaken him.

"Christ, it's exciting, isn't it?"

187

"What is?"

"This game on Saturday, of course! What else are you thinking about? I won't even be playing and I can't get to sleep for thinking about it. Don't try to tell me you're not excited."

They were lying in the dark, Wiggy and Johnny Parkinson.

"Not particularly," said Wiggy. "It's just another game when you boil it down."

"Go on—I know you—you're desperate to get out there in front of that crowd and give 'em a great show. You'll be doing your nut trying to show 'em you're better than Caskie. Christ—I wish I was playing. I'm thirty years old and this is the nearest I've ever been to real success. Imagine that!"

"Yeah, I suppose it will be a good scene."

"You cynical little twit. You've had it too good you have. Cor— if I'd had a quarter of the success you've had I'd be well pleased. And you're only eighteen."

"That's how it goes. Anyway, I'll be nineteen on Saturday."

"Nineteen? No, you couldn't understand what it means—I keep thinking to myself, you're thirty, Johnny, you've been with eight clubs, you've played half your career as a part-timer in the Midlands League—you don't have any idea what it's like, Wiggy—"

"I don't want any idea, thank you. If I wasn't in the First Division I wouldn't bother with football at all."

"Jesus! When John Gallagher came for me and said he wanted me as cover for Randy—I'd spent my whole life aching to be with a big club—I thought I was going to finish as a total nobody—I didn't believe him. He said, we can only offer you a year's contract at seventy a week. *Only*, I said—I could have kissed him!"

"I would have stuck out for a hundred."

"You don't even know you're born. Me, I've been playing since I was sixteen—and in fourteen years the biggest crowd I ever played in front of was twenty-three thousand—Shrewsbury versus Portsmouth in the fourth round of the League Cup . . . funny, all through training I kept looking at Randy and thinking all that guy has to do is put out a little finger or go over on an ankle—and I'm playing at Hampden! Me—Johnny Parkinson! In front of a hundred and five thousand people! I'll tell you, Wiggy, it took an effort not to start praying for Randy to hurt himself. I mean, you couldn't help *thinking* it, could you?"

Wiggy smiled in the dark. He could see the crowds and hear the noise. What an occasion for a Wiggy special—the lazy move towards the Rangers defence—the feint and then the fantastic sprint to the corner of the box—the sudden stop with the foot on the ball—three of them came at him—he wiggled his hips and swayed his shoulders—he was past all three—they're all expecting the chip across goal to Roy's head—no, no—bang goes the banana shot—screaming at the goalie and then curving at the last moment —the goalie dives, the crowd roars—the net bulges . . . this time he would not jump in the air throwing non-existent mud. That was old-fashioned and childish. He would raise both hands, about half-way up, fingers extended, palms pointing at the terraces. He would take their tributes without smiling. Hampden would be *his*.

"For an old pro you really do get worked up in the most naive way, Johnny," he said. He heard Johnny's bed creaking as the reserve goakeeper cursed unintelligibly and rolled over, trying to force himself to sleep.

"So where the hell did you get to?" Sammy wanted to know. They still had the light on. Danny was propped up against his folded pillow, reading one of the football magazines.

"I just wandered about the hotel," he said. "I couldn't find you." Danny yawned. "They write a lot of old moody in these magazines. It says here Wiggy might be picked for the England squad."

"So what? They pick 'em young nowadays. And they gotta have wingers, don't they? Is there any better than Wiggy?"

"I dunno. What about Shane of Manchester United?"

"Flashy, me old son, looks good but once he's beaten his four men where is he?—back where he first got the ball."

"Alec thinks he's really good."

"He'd have to say that, wouldn't he? He gave Alec a proper run-around in the two league games this season. If a geezer gives you a real chasin' you'll want everybody to think he's world-class, wouldn't you?"

"I s'pose so. Anyway, I'm turning in, me old son."

He switched off the light and pulled himself down into the sheets.

"It's me who says me old son," said Sammy, indignantly. "You still haven't told me where you got to."

"I dunno. Around. You know how it is. Goodnight me old son."

"It's me that says me old son!"

Silence. Sammy sat up again. He switched on the light. Danny lay on his side, bare back facing Sammy. Danny never slept in pyjamas.

"Don't go to sleep, Dan," Sammy pleaded. "That pill George gave me isn't workin'." Sammy stuck his feet out from under the blankets and gave Danny's bed a shove with his foot. Danny grunted. "Here," Sammy said, "you think the boss will want me to pick up Caskie in midfield before he starts his runs? Cor— didn't he look fast and tricky in that film? I never like Scots players much, do you? They're always kinda arrogant, you notice that? Remember that kid we had at the Common—what was his heathen name again—cor, his very first day he was poncin' about as though he invented the game—you get a lot of 'em like that, think they know it all, I—"

"If you want to rabbit on all night why don't you go next door and keep bleeding Spencer awake, will you? He's bound to be planning something or another."

"A right pal you are. Ain't this game beginnin' to give you the collywobbles? Ain't you excited or nuthin'?"

"Yeah, I'm in hysterics. Now shut your cakehole and go to sleep."

Sammy switched out the light and lay back. Then he put his fingertips to his mouth. He hadn't phoned home today. He always liked to call Sheree once a day to see how she and Darren and Wayne were. He stuck out his hand in the darkness and felt for the phone. The switchboard girl asked what number he wanted.

"Nah, forget it," he said. "Sorry."

He put the phone down. It crashed onto the table and fell to the length of the cord, banging on wood. Danny cursed. Sammy got up and put on the light and replaced the receiver.

"Sorry, Dan," he said, putting out the light again. "I was going to phone Sheree, but it's a bit late. If I call her now she'll complain I've woke the kids—if I don't she'll say I wasn't thinkin' about her. Cor— you can't win that one, can you?"

"You'll be seeing her on Saturday. You can make your apologies then. Now go to fakking sleep, you berk."

"Yeah, sorry, Dan. Funny, innit, you'd think them sleepin' pills would—"

"Oh my gawd."

16

ROY was delighted to have his training gear on again. The sun was bright and the sky was blue but there was a distinct nip in the air. Sharp puffs of condensation made a steamy halo above the heads of the squad as they went through their stretching exercises. Roy balanced himself on his left leg and pulled the right back, hand grasping the foot, feeling the tightening of his thigh muscles. This was the most boring part of training, the ten minutes leg stretching designed to prevent strains through cold and stiffness. The tension that had been slowly building up all week was now catching up with them. This was the testing time for his muscle. Come on, you bastard, he addressed it silently, this is no time to let me down.

George Westbury called him away from the rest of the squad, who were under the direction of Harry Barnes. John Gallagher was standing with the B.B.C. T.V. director who would be filming them individually on their sprints, with John Gallagher analysing each man's style of play for the benefit of Saturday's pre-match audience.

Many managers would not have given permission for T.V. filming so close to the game but John Gallagher believed the presence of cameras would bring home to them the nearness of Hampden. Creative tension was a phrase he had used. Sammy said the real reason for the cameras was to make sure Wiggy took his sprints seriously.

"How's it feeling now then?" Westbury asked Roy, both of them in the green tracksuits, Roy unshaven, his hair tousled, the physiotherapist looking as if he had just had a shampoo and shave.

"Right now I can't feel a thing," Roy said, "but I daresay you don't want to know how it feels when I'm standing about."

"Standing about? You won't be standing about for long, lad. Tomorrow could be the most important game of your life."

"Okay then, let's cut out the chat and see if I'm fit."

"I'll see if you're fit all right. Fit enough to die for us tomorrow."

"You know the old saying—I'll die for you if you die for me."

"Right—I want you to jog round the pitch. Take it nice and easy to start with."

Roy turned and trotted away. As he began his slow run down the touchline he prayed his leg would take everything it was going to get in the next half hour. *The most important match of your career.* He reached the corner and turned along the byeline, swerving out behind the goals to avoid the squad who were being called out in pairs to go through the sprinting routine, eighteen-yard flat-out runs from the goal-line to the edge of the penalty box. I only pray when I want something, he said to himself. He reached the other corner and started down the far touchline, a hundred and ten yards, jogging deliberately, trying go get his body into the right rhythm. There's one thing for sure, if ever I wanted something for myself this is it. Please God don't let me break down. He turned and came along the other byeline, about eighty yards, looking up the pitch as pair after pair of players took up the crouched position for the sprinter's start, Harry Barnes barking out their names and then the signal to go. They were lucky to know nothing would stop them from playing tomorrow. The game was going to be hard enough without having the extra worry of whether a rotten little muscle would let you down.

As he slowed down before George Westbury he gave no sign of how he was feeling. The leg was all right but he had not extended it fully, not yet.

"Okay so far," he said.

"Are you sure?"

"Yeah, honest."

"Right—I want you to stride down the sides and then jog behind the goals. Not flat out mind, just extend yourself a bit more. Three laps like that. On you go!"

He took it easy down to the corner, jogging along behind the team, who were now sprinting from a standing start. He got to the corner and began to stride out down the length of the touch-line. He had noticed just the faintest nag from the muscle but as he increased his pace the discomfort disappeared. It was nothing. He changed to a jog and came along behind the other goal. The slightest nagging sensation came back again, so negligible it probably wasn't the muscle at all, just his brain reminding him it was there. Round and round the pitch he went, striding down the sides and jogging behind the goals. He couldn't really be sure — but it seemed to be there one minute and gone the next. Why didn't he feel it when he went quicker? Was it because his feet weren't touching the ground for so long? When you jogged each foot came down, slow and heavy, but when you went into the stride you seemed to skim along.

He finished the third lap of the pitch.

"You seemed to be running all right," said Westbury. "How is it?"

"Not bad at all," Roy said.

"Mmmm. You've got to be sure, Roy. Much as we want you to play it's got to be a hundred per cent right. Tricky things pulled muscles."

"It was all right—but I keep thinking about it. It's the fear of it getting worse."

"I know what you mean. With a sore ankle or bruised shin it might be painful but it isn't going to get any worse. With a muscle there's a touch of the unknown."

"Yeah, that's it."

"Well now, I want you to do a few sprints. If you feel it I want you to stop immediately. Okay?"

He went through his sprints, eighteen-yard dashes from goal-line to penalty line. He didn't feel it at all. After half a dozen straight runs George Westbury made him twist and turn as if dodging defenders at speed. Then Westbury called to John Gallagher.

"He's been through his sprints and he says he's all right."

"Are you sure, Roy?" John Gallagher asked.

"Sure as I can be, Boss."

"What do you mean by that?"

"I felt a couple of twinges. But I really went through it. I felt good—just the odd little twinge."

John Gallagher looked at the ground, slowly rubbing his hand over his unshaven face.

"Well, it's what you think that counts. I'm afraid only you

know the answer. It's not a good sign if you can feel it even slightly."

"I think the rest has done me good," Roy said. "Yeah, I think I'm fit."

"You sure?"

"Definitely. It's all in the mind, that's all. Just a little twinge. Nah, I'm fit!"

"That's great," said the manager. He looked at Roy and then at Westbury. "Okay then, you'll play tomorrow. But listen, Roy, if that leg starts to play up tomorrow I don't want any buts—you're to come off. Okay? There's the final to think about."

"I'm sure it'll be okay," said Roy.

The rest of the squad were finishing the sprinting routine. The last one involved a start from a lying-down position. On Harry Barnes' shout they had to jump to their feet and go straight into the eighteen-yard dash. Each sprint had a different starting position—kneeling, facing backwards, standing—each testing and trying another part of the body. Now they were lining up to practice positions for free kicks just outside the penalty box. Four of them formed the defensive wall in front of Randy and Johnny Parkinson in goal. Danny or Dave Spencer would take the actual kick. The others dotted themselves to the right or left of the line. Secret signals, like a quick rub of the forehead or a meaningless adjustment of stockings, would tell them what kind of free kick to expect; sometimes Danny would run at the ball and jump over it, leaving Dave to try a bending shot round the wall. Or Danny would flick it a foot or two sideways and run straight at the wall, while Dave chipped it over their heads. They tried another where Dave didn't kick the ball but flicked it up in the air with his toe and Sammy would try a bicycle shot, leaping up so that his body was sideways to the ground, high enough in the air for the shot to find space just over the heads of the wall of defenders. They knew all these different moves but their success depended on instant recognition of what was happening. They had to be gone through time after time. Fertile brains tried to work out new variations. Danny or Dave would pretend to be arguing with the ref, pointing out that the defensive wall was less than ten yards from the ball. The idea was that the wall—who stood shoulder to shoulder, hands protecting their genitals, presenting a solid defence of human flesh—would be confused by the argument, just enough to break ranks—then *whoosh*—Danny would blast a shot at goal. Or two of the forwards would fight their way into the wall, jostled and pushed by defenders but forcing their way in. Danny or Dave would aim for them and then they would drop to the ground and if the shot was true it would scream though the space into the net.

Roy knew all the moves. He decided to run back to the hotel for a bath. He pulled on the top half of his tracksuit and began to jog away.

"How is it?" Alec Hood called out.

"Great," he shouted back.

"See you later then."

See you later, Roy muttered to himself as he headed for the gate. He felt a slight sickness in his stomach. Christ, I hope I've done the right thing . . .

There was no mistaking it now, Peterson thought as he went from room to room. The players were beginning to show the signs of tension. The big game was only twenty-seven hours away. The jokes were feebler and the laughter more hysterical. Gurr and Williamson, the quiet ones, were actually singing to each other as they took turns for the shower. Men with wet hair, towels wrapped round their waists, shouted slogans from open doors and were answered by raucous cries from other rooms.

Peterson carried a large stiff sheet of white cartridge paper on which he was asking each man to sign his autograph. These signatures were to be superimposed on a giant colour photograph of the team which Wally Scott had taken for them as a favour. The moment they knew the result of tomorrow's game he would telephone the colour printers in London and start the presses rolling. Five thousand souvenir colour photographs to be sold by volunteers from the Supporters' Club at fifty pence a time—profit two thousand two hundred pounds. Before Monday morning he would also have to phone the firm who had the dies ready to cast the souvenir team badges—and the tie manufacturers and the brochure printers and the postcard printers. He had more good news for them. If they won the British Cup at New Wembley in April, Ford's would give them a car each.

"Aye, it's beginning to roll in," said Alec Hood, carefully

drying his right arm and hand so as not to smudge the sheet of autographs. "I think Dave Spencer's old man has also got us the offer of a week's free holiday in Majorca. If we get it you can take my place, Bill, I'm sick of bloody Majorca! I've been there every summer for five years and the whole place is full of British footballers."

"I suppose Majorca has just the right balance of exoticism and vulgarity for you moronic professionals," Peterson said.

"Don't be sarcastic with me, you twit. Did I ever tell you that story about Shankly, the manager of Liverpool? He lived so much for football that bloke he'd never take a holiday—I think he used to go to the ground in the summer and find groundsmen to have a game with. Anyway, the club said he had to take a holiday—they insisted on it. Shankly said he hated holidays. But they made him go—sent him to Majorca. So when he comes back all the lads—remember St. John and Big Yeats and Roger Hunt—great team, eh?—they're all dying to hear what Shankly has to say about holidays. 'Ach it wisnae as bad as a thought it would be,' he rasps in that concrete-mixer voice of his. 'We got up a team an' beat the waiters!'"

"Yes, you're a very colourful lot of chaps in football," said Peterson. "Down to earth and lovable and rich. The ideal combination."

"Christ—the first year I played in a semi-final for this club we were on a hundred quid a man to win. We thought that was the big time!"

"Here you are, Roy," Peterson said, holding down the ends of the cartridge paper. "Good news, your fitness test, eh?"

"Bad news for the fans, Bill—he passed it," said Hood.

"Never any doubt about it," said Roy. His signature was a cramped, backhand affair—true to his personality, functional and limited and not even the hint of a hidden desire for flamboyance. Peterson had to remind them all that they were not scribbling wavy lines on some schoolboy's outheld autograph book. Wiggy, of course, had the outstanding signature—a beautiful thing of curved flourishes and artistic symmetry, poetry in writing as he called it himself—and totally illegible.

"A veritable cornucopia of riches," said Shack when Peterson told them about the gift of free cars. "There's just the trivial matter of winning this game tomorrow."

197

"I don't care what John Gallagher tells you," Peterson said, "I expect you lads to go out there and die for the pool."

He felt happy. Some of them were a bit dim and some a bit irresponsible and a few seemed to have escaped all formal education whatsoever, but they were a great bunch of lads. No matter that Ian Rowland's signature looked like the scrawl of a backward child of eight, no matter that Seymour was in his grudging mood and would hardly speak to him, no matter that Riddle was feeling so sorry for himself he had to be coaxed to put his name on the sheet, none of it mattered. What mattered was what they did out there on the pitch and if you could see the magic in that then you could forgive everything else.

When he had the sheet completed he went back to his own room, where he put it between sheets of soft tissue and put it in a large brown envelope at the bottom of his bag, to be delivered at the printers on Sunday morning. Dave Spencer came into his room, looking mean, moody and aggressive.

"Look, I want to get to the bottom of this," he demanded. "Who got me to phone Miss Lindsay at Ibrox Park?"

"I beg your pardon."

"You know, come off it! They all think it's the biggest joke since long pants. They must have told you who was behind it. Sammy, was it? I'll do him, so help me."

"They didn't tell me. It must have been a practical joker."

"I know it was a flaming practical joker! Small's the bloody practical joker in this mob. You don't have to tell me about that bastard. He was wearing the club blazer once at London Airport and somebody thought he was a B.O.A.C. official and he spent twenty minutes pretending to stamp tickets with his fist and sending people to the wrong planes! You don't have to tell me about practical jokers." His attitude changed. "Just a hint, Bill, eh? They only did it to spoil my chances with Carole. That's not fair, is it?"

"I honestly know nothing, Dave, believe me."

The phone rang. Debonair Dave went off mumbling. The switchboard girl said Mrs. Peterson was calling from London. She was in a minor panic over Barrie, who had developed a temperature.

"So you won't be able to come up tomorrow after all?"

"Go easy on the champagne."

"I may tell you now, if we win I shall get drunker than you ever believed possible. But just for your information—I have not been drinking up here and what's more, would you believe that I'm not smoking—at this very moment?"

"God—what heroism."

"Oh yes, I'm red badge of courage material. It's contagious, all this physical nonsense. If it goes on much longer I see myself doing laps of Regent's Park in shorts and spikes before dawn."

"Well, don't let it go to your head."

Well, wasn't that just perfect? He put down the phone. She loves me but she won't be here to stop me enjoying myself. The perfect wife, totally tolerant and somewhere else.

Danny buttoned his blue sports shirt up to the neck and had a last look at himself in the mirror.

"You handsome big brute gorilla you," he said, pouting a little kiss at himself.

"Come on," said Sammy, "we'll be late for lunch. Ain't you done poncin' about in front of the mirror yet? Cor, you don't arf admire yourself, do you?"

"Must look good if you're in the public eye, kid."

"I wonder if Dave will manage it—this is his last chance. Cor—if he does get a date with her I'm down about a ton! I knew we shoulda come by plane—there wouldn't have been no bleedin' time for silly bets. It's all your rotten fault."

Danny turned and looked at him steadily.

"There's only one thing about this bet," he said deliberately, "you ever mention it to Carole and I'll give you the biggest duffing up of your life."

"Mention it to her! I'm still thinkin' if I should offer her a deal—she turns Dave down flat and I'll split me winnin's wiv her."

"You breathe one dicky-bird and I'll do you."

"What do you care, anyways?"

"I just don't want her to hear about it. Is that good enough for you? Not a sausage."

"Strike me, mate, you ain't arf steamed up about her, are you? Bein' single all them years has affected your brain, me old son. She's just another stray bit of crumpet, that's all."

"No she ain't!"

"Ah ha!" Sammy's eyes went wide with astonishment. He

lowered his face and leered knowingly, raising his index finger to point at Danny's face. "Ah ha! You dirty old rascal!"

"What are you on about now?" Danny looked away, hurriedly, to hide his reddening face.

Sammy started punching him in the back.

"You scored wiv her! You double-dyed villain! She went off early to write letters. And you disappeared. They said you was dancin' wiv her. Cor blimey, Daniel Peck—you old rogue!"

Danny blushed. Sammy jumped up and down with glee.

"I'm gettin' downstairs double quick, me old son. I'll get more bets on—think of the bleedin' odds I can give 'em chumps now!"

"You little berk!" Danny grabbed again at Sammy but he jinked round the end of the bed. Danny jumped onto the bed and Sammy darted for the door. Danny leapt across the space onto the other bed but Sammy had reached the door. Their heads moved in little darting feints, eyes locked on each other.

"Yeah," said Sammy, only his face still in the room, "you give her one all right. She won't want nuffink to do wiv Spencer. You're a dark one, you are, Daniel Peck!"

Danny leapt for the door but Sammy was already half-way down the corridor, laughing like a drain.

"Sammy!"

The little man looked over his shoulder, still moving towards the lift. Danny stood in the corridor in a shaft of daylight from their room, his hands on his hips.

"I meant what I said."

"Trust your uncle Sam, me old son."

"I'll do you, Small."

One of the Rangers directors and his wife had driven down to the hotel from Glasgow to take George Jackson and Jemima to lunch at some swanky hotel farther up the coast. Carole had been having late coffee with the Jacksons when the Glasgow couple arrived.

"Do you want to come with us?" Jemima asked. "I imagine Norman is sleeping it off. Paul Franks hasn't surfaced this morning either. Physician heal thyself."

"No, I have some calls to make to London," Carole said.

"That's all right, if you're sure," said the chairman, trying to keep the disappointment from his voice. Carole would have improved the luncheon scenery by several hundred per cent. They had just left when Norman came into the lounge. He saw Carole and put his hand to his forehead, pretending to stagger.

"Oh my gawd," he said in the mock-cockney he sometimes adopted for purposes of amusement, "wot bleedin' well 'it me, luv?"

She smiled at him sweetly.

"You were on a vodka kick. It kicked back."

"Right in the head. Oh my gawd. I need something—quickly."

When he had a Fernet Branca in his hand she smiled again.

"Some of the players seem to think I'm your steady girl friend," she said. "I wonder how that little misconception was born."

He groaned.

"Players are like that, you'll find. Simple minds with but a single thought. Christ—is this stuff supposed to cure your hangover?" He shut his eyes and shuddered. "I fell as if loathsome insects were crawling all over me."

"Why do you drink so much, Norman?"

"Never again, I swear it. Where's George?"

"Their friends came from Glasgow, they've gone off to lunch."

"I was supposed to go with them. Oh dear. Chalk up another small disgrace. George disapproves of my drinking enough as it is. Or rather, Jemima tells him to disapprove. We're a tense little family group, us Borgias."

"I've been watching you, Norman," she said. "I've been noticing little things—when that man asked for their autographs last night and he thought you were a player—you had quite a little struggle before you told him you weren't in the team."

"You're very perceptive," he said, mouth forming a bitter little sneer. "Nobody asks for the autographs of a millionaire's kid brother. There's no talent involved in that. Anyway, even if they do think you're my mistress—do you find the idea so objectionable?"

She shrugged.

"Hullo," said Dave Spencer. They both replied enthusiastically, glad of his intervention.

"Not long now, eh, Dave?" said Norman. "You nervous?"

"Oh no," said Dave, looking at Carole. "I could play in this kind of atmosphere every week. Matter of temperament, I suppose. By the way, Carole, that Chelsea-Spartak match I told you about—would you like to come with me?"

Norman looked quickly from Dave's deadpan face to Carole. She seemed amused. John Gallagher and Harry Barnes walked into the lounge, leading a group of players.

"Okay then, Dave?" John Gallagher called. "Let's be having you over here in the corner."

Dave made no move to rise.

"Well?" he asked.

"I'm sorry," she said, "I wash my hair on Wednesday nights." She smiled sweetly. Norman raised his glass to hide his own wry smile of satisfaction. So—after all she did know which side her bread was buttered on.

"Pity about that," said Dave, standing up. "You'd have enjoyed the match. See you later."

Cut your losses quick, that was the way to deal with difficult women. She'd had her chance. He didn't have to chase any woman. Norman was about her mark. Who needed it?

Going down in the lift Randy smacked his hands together and rubbed them busily, saying he was really looking forward to a great game tomorrow. Tommy Riddle, his room-mate, kept looking away in disgust.

"Cheer up, Jimmy, cheer up," Randy said, "the boss is giving out runners and riders in—" he looked ostentatiously at his wristwatch, an expensive East German job bought on a summer tour— "exactly seven minutes. Then we'll know the worst."

"I know it already," Riddle scowled.

He would be out of the team, he knew that. There had been a faint chance but Roy had passed his fitness test. He didn't grudge Roy his place but he still had a deep sense of grievance. All because of that stupid, lousy, stinking, fornicating game against Stoke City in September. Why you went off form was often as big a mystery to yourself as it was to everybody else. It might be a bad patch at home or mortgage worries or an extended visit by your mother-in-law or persistent late night phone calls from a heavy breather—or any of the usual worries that affect any man, for the public rarely thought of players as anything else but Saturday men and imagined them immune from the normal domestic upsets. Whatever the reason you suddenly found yourself out on the pitch in the middle of a game — totally incapable of doing anything right. At first it might be a couple of indifferent games. Then your confidence had suddenly gone. You missed balls you should have trapped, you passed to opponents, you dribbled beautifully to the byeline and then crossed the ball into the crowd, you fell on your backside five yards away from an open goal with the ball sitting up begging to be nudged home.

The crowd would begin to give you the bird. Then you *knew* you were having a stinker. So what did you do then? It depended on temperament, for there was no such thing as the typical professional footballer. Some individuals decided to hide. They stayed clear of the action and ducked their heads when a teammate was looking for somebody to pass to. They hoped to stay out of sight until the bad patch was over. Others decided to go shit or bust, fighting for every ball, doubling their work-rate, determined that no matter how lousy their form might be nobody would jeer at them for not trying.

It was the worst feeling in the world, to be out there playing badly with the crowd giving you the full treatment of boos and jeers. Naturally, being a pro, you did not weep tears or beg for understanding, you just went on playing as best you knew how, hoping that next time it would all come right again. But on and on it went. You tried to play safe by going for short, sure passes, never risking anything adventurous or clever. This was a rot that could sweep through a whole team, everybody holding the ball too long, trying to eliminate mistakes and succeeding only in throwing away all chance of saving games. Or you developed nerves and began to pass the ball too quickly, always hearing the pounding feet of non-existent opponents coming up behind you, slamming the ball away, almost always to the feet of your opponent.

Different managers had different ways of dealing with a player's loss of form. Some kept you in the team, knowing that every player goes through bad patches now and then. At Tottenham, they used to say that the great John White often had six or seven bad games in a row but Billy Nicholson kept him in the team, knowing he would come good sooner or later. Other managers believed in the short, sharp cure. They dropped you after two bad games. This might sharpen your resolve to fight your way back into the side, or it might sap your confidence even more badly.

Certainly you couldn't afford to play too long in the reserves or the edge would go off your game.

It was how John Gallagher had treated him that made Tommy Riddle so full of self-pity. He'd scored lots of goals for Commoners, yet John Gallagher dropped him after only four or five bad games. He took this personally, for beneath the dour exterior and the big, mournful face he was an insecure person who constantly needed reassurance. John Gallagher had told him he was being dropped to give him a chance to play himself back to full confidence in the reserves, where the crowd wouldn't be on his back. Then came the kind of luck that affected footballers' careers. Wiggy had been only just another boy reserve, clever but not outstanding. The moment he ran out with the first team in front of a fifty thousand crowd he revealed that he was a bloody big star! Of all the rotten luck!

John Gallagher was sitting in the corner, players gathered round him. When he saw they were all present he looked round their faces.

"Roy came through his test this morning so the team will be the same again as Saturday," he said. "Tommy Riddle and Ian Rowland are the outfield substitutes. Okay lads? And another little bit of news—I had a call from the England manager half an hour ago—there's four of you in the squad of twenty-two for the Wales game—Roy, Danny, Wiggy and Gerry. Congratulations, boys, you deserve it. Shack's in the Welsh team—of course."

There was a lot of back-slapping and hand-shaking. Roy was an England regular and Wiggy had been tipped by several newspaper experts—but Danny and Gerry were totally unexpected. They were all genuinely pleased for them. Tommy Riddle joined in the back-slapping. He had been determined not to let the others see how sick he felt at being only a substitute for tomorrow, but that had nothing to do with the four lads who had been picked for England. It had nothing to do with any of the lads. It was just the luck of the game. Wiggy was in the first team for Hampden and in the England squad—all because of that bloody game against Stoke. And if he'd scored with that one chance, the loose ball that he'd half-volleyed into the crowd when he was only eight yards from the goal—if that ball had gone in the rest of his play would have been forgotten. He wanted to kick furniture.

John Gallagher got a glimpse of Jimmy's big sad face and saw how choked he was at not being in the team. Well, Jimmy was a good enough pro to know that's how the game went at times. And any manager would be happy to know he had a forward of Jimmy's calibre sitting on the bench. With reserves like Riddle a team could go places. Strength in depth, they called it.

"Let's not forget Shack," said Harry Barnes, banging the Welshman on the back. "What's this—your thirtieth cap, Alan?"

"Oh yeah, that's a big surprise," said Sammy, elbowing Shack in the side. "As long as you're born in Wales and can keep the ball up three times you're bound to be capped for Wales, ain't that right, Taffy lad?"

"Get knotted. Remember who drew with England last year—at Wembley? We were unlucky not to win, boyo. I think this will be our year."

"You'll be up against Roy and Wiggy and maybe Danny and Gerry as well," said Harry Barnes.

"They'd better look out then," said Shack, his face very grim. "When I go onto the pitch at Ninian Park I don't have any friends and I don't take any prisoners."

John Gallagher gave them a free afternoon and they split into groups to do whatever suited their temperaments. So close was the reality of Hampden now all activities became self-conscious, merely little acts to create an illusion of confidence.

"It's your lucky bleedin' day, innit!" Sammy said to Danny as they headed back upstairs to get the cards out.

"I still can't believe it. Me—picked for the England squad!"

"Oh that! You've forgotten somethin' *really* important, ain't you?"

"No, what?"

"The bet, you twit! Spencer lost the bet. He owes you sixty quid!"

"I don't want that bet even mentioned again!"

"Okay, okay," said Sammy. "But I can collect my own winnin's from the lads—can't I? The side bets?"

"No!"

"They'll think I'm bonkers!"

"Tell 'em it was all just a joke."

"I'm givin' up jokes, they're too bleedin' expensive altogether."

In front of the hotel cars were taking some of the team into Largs for a shopping expedition. Harry Barnes and George Westbury went in the first car with Andy Gurr and Gerry Williamson. Dave Peacock, Dave Spencer, Tommy Riddle and Brian Seymour got into the second. Albert Stone found he was the odd man out. They made room for him on the floor.

On the lawn at the rear of the hotel Steven Randall, Alec Hood, Roy Christmas, Bobby Ingrams, Barry Ross and Ian Rowland started a knockabout game of cricket in which right-handed players had to bat left-handed and vice versa, just to keep it lively.

A chauffeur-driven Rolls took George and Jemima Jackson, Norman Jackson and Carole Freedman to Ayr, where they were to be entertained by a hotel owner who was hoping to be taken over by the Jackson chain.

In room 213 John Gallagher switched on the T.V. and sat down in an armchair. He had intended to join the shopping expedition and then changed his mind, not trusting himself to be able to keep up his confident front. The afternoon film was an old British comedy about a pop singer's manager who was supposed to have power over women. The little he grasped of it seemed to be nonsense. When Paul Franks knocked at the door of his suite he let him in and they both sat in front of the T.V. set, saying very little. John Gallagher forced himself to concentrate on the film, holding onto its inane puerility in determination not to let panic sweep right through him.

They had a blanket draped over the table and two decks of cards spilled out in preparation for ten-card rummy, Danny Peck, Sammy Small, Alan Shackle, Johnny Parkinson and Bill Peterson. Shack drew the cards together and began to shuffle.

"Cliff Jones was the best winger I ever saw," said Johnny Parkinson. "He was fast and direct, he could lash 'em in with both feet and his heading ability was out of this world. John White used to float 'em over to the far post and Jones would go up like a space rocket off the launching pad and bullet 'em home."

"Yeah, they had real players in them days," said Sammy.

Peterson tried to arrange the cards in his hand but his fingers were only fiddling about. He let out a great sigh and dropped his hand on the blanket.

"Is everyone else as jittery as me?" he asked. "The strain's beginning to murder me."

"The funniest thing I ever heard about Cliff Jones," Parkinson went on, "was told to me by a bloke who used to hang about with the Spurs team about the time they won the League and Cup double—remember that team?"

"Who could forget it?" Sammy said, looking at the ceiling. "I never even saw 'em but the way you rabbit on about 'em I sometimes think I actually played wiv 'em. Don't you ever talk about anythin' else but bleedin' football? How about talkin' about sex or somethin'?"

"Anyway, Spurs were playing an away game and when they arrived—Notts Forest I think it was—the crowd is being entertained by a display of police dog handling—you know the sort of thing, Alsatians going through barrels and jumping through hoops and climbing barricades and walking planks and whatnot. So the Spurs team is all watching this and somebody says for a joke he wouldn't do what the dogs is doing for love nor money. 'I'll do it for a quid from each of you,' says Jones. They bet him he wouldn't. So off he goes, onto the pitch, in his ordinary clothes and does the whole dog course—yeah, no fooling, it's an hour before kick-off and the ground is only just beginning to fill up and there's one of the greatest wingers England ever had—"

"Wales ever had," said Shack.

"Who ever played in England—he's wriggling through the tunnel and crawling under a sheet of canvas pegged out on the ground and shinning up the barricade—the Spurs lads cheering him all the way. Can you imagine that?"

They shook their heads slowly. The game began in earnest. It was Danny's turn to draw a card. He stared at his hand.

"I'll tell you a story," he said. "You ever remember Tommy Banks who played left-back for Bolton?"

"Leave me out," Sammy complained. "Wot age you think I am for gawd's sake?"

"I remember him," said Peterson, "a robust sort of chap, wasn't he?"

"Robust wasn't the word for it. He was once giving some winger such a hammering his centre-half John Higgins called across to him, 'When you've finished with him chip him over here, Tommy, and give me a go at him.' They said about him that he volleyed a good winger. Anyway, I heard this story at a P.F.A. meeting. They had a meeting up north to decide whether the players would go on strike to break the twenty pound maximum wage. Stan Matthews was in his prime then—you've heard of him, I daresay, Sam?"

Sammy let his shoulders droop, closing his eyes in despair.

"Sir Stanley Matthews?" he said, putting on an accent that was half Lancashire and half Yorkshire, the Londoner's idea of how they talked up north. "Aye, lad, Sir Stanley Matthews started as a young lad wi' Stoke City in the thirties, aye, lad, he were t'greatest star t'game has ever produced. Why, I recall seeing Sir Stanley—or the wizard of the dribble, as we called him—beating five men without moving his feet, aye, he just dropped his right shoulder and two fell down, he dropped his left and two more fell down and he swayed his hips and the fifth man collapsed on his back. Why, I recall it like it were only yesterday, Sir Stan caused a strike in Stoke when they transferred him to Blackpool. Aye, well, I could go on, lads, but I mean there's too much to tell, int there? Suffice to say, Sir Stan played first-class soccer for nigh on thirty year—I think it's true to say his last league game were played at the incredible age of fifty-one. Aye—they had real players in them days. We won't see their like again, I can tell thee."

"I see," said Danny, "you don't remember him. Anyway this union meeting is going on and they're talking about a players' strike and some young lad gets up and says he's against the strike. He said, 'My dad works down the pit, hewing coal from a two-foot seam in the wet and dark, risking his life—and he don't take home nothing like twenty quid a week and I don't think we should go on strike to get more than twenty quid a week. We don't deserve it.' He sits down. Up jumps Tommy Banks. 'If thy dad had to play against Broother Matthews for ninety minutes he'd want more than twenty pound a week, I'm sure', he says, bringing the house down. Broother Matthews!"

The cards were picked up and put down mechanically. The school had been playing together for so long they had only to put half their minds to the game. Their memories and their jokes and their stories came from a world of broken legs and scars and dreams that almost came true. They had made it into the magic world that ruled the lives of millions but to them the magic was a thing of sweaty reality; success meant total happiness, failure meant the silence of despair. To have gone this far, with Hampden only twenty-four hours away, was a kind of success, more than they had dreamed of at the beginning of the season. Yet in football, success was a series of milestones on a journey that had no real ending. It was always in the future, always ahead of you. They might win tomorrow and that would be success, but the *real* success would come when and if Alec Hood went up the steps at New Wembley to collect the British Cup from Prince Charles and hold it high above his head to the roars of the crowd. But even that would be only another milestone. The champagne would flow and the flashbulbs pop and after the Saturday night banquet would come the Sunday morning triumphal journey through the cheering streets of South London, the players on the roof of a coach, the golden cup held high as shining symbol of *real* success . . . and by Monday morning they would be thinking of next season and the trophies they would be trying to win then . . . because success was a hungry god.

Hood took a clumsy left-handed swipe with the old bat and hit the tennis ball high above his head. It bounced on a slate roof and then stuck on a drainpipe. They gave up the game and went inside, drifting to the room where the card school sat in a slight fug of Peterson's making. They stood behind the players, making sarcastic comments as Sammy got out by banging a newly-drawn king onto Shack's run of nine-ten-jack-queen. Sammy took a pound from each player. It was Danny's turn to deal but they all wanted to talk about the game tomorrow. Only Roy and Hood had played at Hampden before. They were asked what it was really like. Roy didn't seem to have noticed anything particular about the ground, although he did agree it was very big. Hood said it was a fantastic place to play for a Scottish team, with the Hampden Roar driving you on to win or die for Scotland.

"Only tomorrow they won't be roaring for you," said Shack. "They'll be roaring for your blood, boyo, whisky-maddened jocks baying their hatred of the old enemy. Oh, I can see it all now, the massed ranks of the huge terraces, the thunder of the hate-filled voices —"

"Cor leave me out," said Sammy. "Wot is it then, feedin' us

Christians to the heathen lions? It's a game of soccer, you Welsh berk!"

"It doesn't matter who they're roaring for," said Wiggy. "It's what they see on the pitch that counts. I'm looking forward to it."

"You feel an attack of sheer genius coming on then?"

"I think tomorrow will separate the men from the boys."

"Cor, hark at the abominable showman. The jocks are goin' to love you, me old son."

By the time they went downstairs to dinner the circus was in full swing. The hotel was crowded with London football writers and rich businessmen whose hobby and joy in life was to be friends of the players, the literary agents and the business partners and the brothers in law, an enthusiastic army of genial parasites who wanted nothing more than a touch of glory. Through it all Peterson noticed a change in the players.

Only they knew how it felt to be counting the hours to the big game. No outsider could share that tension. They chatted with friends and with reporters but all the time they were looking round for each other, reassuring themselves by staying close to the men they would be playing alongside tomorrow.

The circus was left behind as they gathered round John Gallagher in the foyer. They were going to see a film in Largs, the sixteen players, the manager, the coach and the physiotherapist. It was a sloppy musical that Peterson would not have willingly watched on a wet Sunday afternoon while stranded in Wigan, and behind him in the bar it was all jollity among the drinking men, and besides he had always thought it very childish to football teams to go to the cinema in a schoolboy crocodile, but when John Gallagher asked if he wanted to come along he immediately accepted the offer. He, too, was a hanger-on and parasite but they had accepted him as one of them. He wished that one of the women in his life was the type who would not laugh when he told her it was one of the proudest moments of his life.

There were twenty of them in the party that got out of the taxis outside the cinema. Their arrival, all wearing the grey club suits, caused a stir in the lobby of the cinema. As they took their seats in two rows of ten the lights were up for the ice-cream push. They were recognised round the cinema, which wasn't surprising with nineteen healthy-looking men in identical suits coming in like a private army. The idea of taking them to the cinema, Peterson realised now, was to keep them together as a team and keep their minds off the tension of the coming game—and perhaps to let John Gallagher play mother hen to his valuable chickens.

A tall man with a blonde girl came up the aisle. They all stared at the girl. The man saw them staring and then recognised them.

"Best of luck tomorrow," he said, nodding amiably at the players.

"Best of luck tonight," said Sammy, nodding at the girl.

That set the tone. They did not make a good audience. They did not sit well. The voices behind the advertisements had Scottish accents, which Sammy mimicked. Faces turned in the gloom. Peterson heard somebody hiss for silence. Then the drums went boom-boom-boom and they were into the big picture, a nauseating blockbuster of laughter, heartbreak and song for the entertainment of the whole family.

"Christ, I've seen it," Randy said.

"Yeah? Tell us who dies in the end and we can go home."

"Sshhh," came the urgent hisses. Andy Gurr started giggling. Sammy kept muttering little remarks and comments and Andy tried to muffle his heaving sniggers in a handkerchief. Dave Peacock laughed out loud. When one of the women in the film said her name was Carole they all hooted. Some people seemed to be enjoying the additional show but Peterson sensed a growing irritation throughout the auditorium. People wanted to enjoy their musical slop in peace. When Randy began unwrapping interminable toffees with an exasperating rustle of paper the hisses grew more insistent. On the screen the hero was riding over an endless desert, his head reeling from heat and thirst. The whole cinema went silent, relishing their vicarious ordeal. It went on a bit too long for Sammy.

He clapped his hands together and rubbed them noisily, sitting forward in his seat.

"Well, lads," he said, so loud his voice filled the whole cinema, "I think this is goin' to be a fantastic game tomorrow, eh?"

The manager came with a torch and had a word with John

Gallagher and they managed to sit through the rest of the film without bursting into song.

Randy snored and Shack had to get out of bed and turn him over onto his face. Randy did not waken up, but on his face he stopped snoring. Shack looked at his watch. It was after twelve.

He lay down again. Randy turned over and began snoring again. Shack got up and put on the light and searched in his bag for a roll of cottonwool, out of which he made earplugs.

Dave Peacock woke up with a start. Dave Spencer was sitting upright in bed, shouting. Dave Peacock put on the light. Dave Spencer's eyes were closed. He was having a violent conversation with somebody. The words didn't make sense. Dave Peacock got up and pushed Dave Spencer flat on his back. His eyes opened wide for a second but he didn't seem to see anything. Then his body relaxed and he turned his face into the pillow.

Paul Franks said that Nat Lofthouse—the Lion of Vienna—was the greatest centre-forward the game had ever produced. Peterson said his vote would go either to Tommy Taylor, who was killed in the Munich disaster, or Roy Bentley. The doctor said that Ted Drake, on the other hand, once scored seven goals in one game. They called for another round. Steve Egan of *Winner* said that if you were talking about centre-forwards how about battling Bobby Smith? Oh no, said Peterson, John Charles was not only a great centre-forward for Leeds and Juventus but he was a world-class centre-half as well—and you couldn't say that about many of your modern players, could you? Steve Egan called for another round. Peterson told him that for a bloke who wrote about the game he knew very little about it. Steve Egan said that no less an authority than Shankly of Liverpool himself had told him, personally, that on his day Ian St. John was the greatest leader in Europe. The doctor told the waiter to make it doubles. The waiter said his vote would go to Jimmy McGrory of Celtic, he'd never seen him play but the facts were on record, weren't they, one of the greatest goal-scoring machines the game had ever seen? Steve Egan said it was easy to score goals against Scottish defences in those days. The waiter said that was a typical English insinuation.

John Gallagher lay on his back staring at the dark nothing. He kept thinking of the boy on the rubbish dump pitch near his mother's house, the one who had wanted to pass the ball. The talent net had missed that lad. He would never know what success was like. Maybe he was lucky.

17

ALEC Hood jumped out of bed. He went over to the window and pulled back the curtains. His nose felt clogged up. Central heating always did that to him. He looked at his watch. It was eight-fifteen. The sun was shining brightly but he had the feeling it was bitter cold out there. At the far end of the big lawn he saw Ian Rowland and Barry Ross walking together. He looked at the trees. They were motionless. That was good. The one type of weather he disliked for a game was a windy day. He looked round at Roy, who was stretching his arms above his head and yawning. Alec smacked his hands together. He felt excited. Come on Roy, he thought, get that leg working, today's the day.

"What's the time?" Roy asked.

"Just gone quarter past eight. You want to go down for breakfast or are you going back to sleep?"

"Go and have breakfast, eh?"

"Okay, I'll get washed."

Before he went into the bathroom he opened the door and picked up the morning papers from the corridor. He threw them on Roy's bed. Roy opened the *Mail*. Hood went into the bathroom.

"Well well," said Roy's voice. "Here, Alec, seen this?"

Hood came out of the bathroom, shaving soap covering his cheeks and chin. Roy held up the paper. THE GREATEST SHOW ON EARTH was the headline across two pages, with two large photographs, one of Hood and the other of Lindsay of Rangers. *The Big Skippers* they were called.

"You could be taken for brothers," Roy said.

"I wish I had his money."

"You're joking. You're worth more than him."

"I don't mean instead of, I mean as well."

"Doesn't it make your stomach turn over?" Roy said as Hood went back into the bathroom. "Have you ever known such hysterical publicity about one game? Are you feeling nervous?"

"Which question do you want me to answer first?"

"I'd like to know if you're feeling as nervous as me. I thought I was pretty aware of what this game meant — but looking at these papers — wow, it's really hit me now."

"Yeah, I know what you mean. Sudden death here we come. We've had all the build-up — now comes the crunch."

"That's it."

"It's funny — this game means so much more to us than any other game — yet today will pass just as quickly as any other Saturday."

"Yeah. Before we know what it'll have passed and next week it'll be just a memory —"

"And you'll be too nervous to remember how you felt."

"You can say that again. It's only half past eight as well!"

"I've always thought if I was lucky enough to get into a cup final I wouldn't allow myself to be too nervous, I'd just enjoy what was happening to me and soak up the atmosphere and just love the whole idea of it, the occasion, and leave the worries till the kick-off. I suppose that's the good part of being experienced, you know beforehand that it can fly by before you realised."

Roy jumped out of bed and did a few squats, hands on hips, knees bending sideways. He shook his thigh muscle. He didn't really feel it. When they'd both washed and dressed they packed their bags. They wouldn't be coming back here. Roy went to press the lift button while Hood looked round to see if they'd forgotten anything. On a day like this you found yourself acting very carefully, checking everything, determined not to slip a detail that might later upset your concentration.

"Come on, here's the lift."

They left their bags at the reception desk and went through to the dining-room. The early morning risers were reading the morning papers. They exchanged good mornings, everyone seeming to smile nervously. Today was the day. Hood and Roy sat with Ian Rowland and Barry Ross. To their left was a table of four, John Gallagher reading a paper, Harry Barnes, Johnny Parkinson and Randy. At another table George Westbury, Gurr and Williamson and Albert Stone were reading papers.

"I thought a few of the late risers would have been up earlier today," Hood said to nobody in particular. "Not being able to sleep like."

"They like to do what they usually do," said John Gallagher. "Superstitions."

The manager was smiling. Hood could see he was very nervous. John Gallagher hadn't smiled like that all week. For breakfast Hood had fruit juice, egg and bacon and toast. Roy had fruit juice, cornflakes, a boiled egg and toast. They decided to go for a walk in the grounds of the hotel. They talked about the game and paid no attention to the scenery.

Sammy telephoned room service and asked for tea for two. He and Danny were both sitting up in bed reading the papers.

"I see this geezer here don't give us a prayer to win," said Danny, holding up the *Record*.

"What d'you think—we'll win?"

"Win? We'll eat 'em alive, stand on me."

"I hope so, I'd love to win this one."

Danny stared at his room-mate. Always so cocky and always so sure of himself but when it came to the crunch he wanted someone to lean on. Danny smiled. Sammy was a great guy but he was definitely improved by a little unsureness now and then.

"You look nervous, Sam, are you?"

"Yeah, the most I've ever been."

"You'll be all right on the night."

"Once I get a feel of the ball, the first kick, I'll be okay."

"Why are you nervous all of a sudden? It's not like you."

"I don't know."

"Is it the big money."

"No—it's the whole thing. It's so exciting—I mean look at them papers. The back pages is hysterical enough—but there's even headlines on the front!"

"I've never known anything like it myself. The hysteria is infectious."

"Don't—you're makin' me worse."

"Oh shut up—it's only a game—only ninety minutes like any other."

"You're jokin'."

"I'm not."

"Ah well, you're the old veteran, ain't you, the have boots will travel merchant. I mean you've seen it all, ain't you?"

"We had real players in them days."

By half past eleven they were all up and dressed and gathered in the Rabbie Burns suite, sitting in a semi-circle waiting for John Gallagher, all of them dressed in the grey club suits, listening to Danny and Alec talking about the Rangers forward line. Danny was laughing a lot, taking the whole thing in his stride. He nodded along the line in the direction of Sammy, who was staring into space, deep in private meditation. Sammy gave a little start as they all began laughing. John Gallagher came into the room. They all sat up straight. John Gallagher closed the door and picked up a chair, which he carried to the middle of the room, sitting down to face the players.

"I'll say it again," he said. "Good morning. All feeling okay? I've never known you all so quiet."

He looked at Alec Hood.

"Looking forward to this afternoon?"

"Definitely."

"I'll be glad when it's all over," said Randy.

"You won't be if you lose," said John Gallagher. "You'll be wishing you could play the game over again. It's no good wanting to get it over and being sorry afterwards. But if you all do as much as you humanly can and you lose I'll be the last to complain."

"We'll win," said Danny. They all looked round to see who had spoken.

"That's the way to approach it," said John Gallagher. He looked at some papers he had on his lap. "Now then, we've spent a lot of time over the last few weeks talking about Rangers. You've seen the film of them against Derby. You all know the various moves we've been practising. I'm going to go through their players again, so you'll have it all fresh in your minds."

He began with the Rangers goalkeeper Miller, speaking slowly and deliberately. They had heard it all before but they listened intently.

"Miller has a good pair of hands. He decides quickly if he's going to come off his line or not—and usually he makes the right decision. There's nothing fancy about him, he's an extremely good keeper. The one thing I've noticed about him is that he is very nervous at the beginning of a game—until he makes a good save or two. If you remember the film, he dropped the ball twice in the first five minutes against Derby. Those early crosses had him in difficulty, Danton of Derby was challenging him in the air and he wasn't happy. But Derby made the mistake of not playing on that—they stopped crossing it and let him off the hook. Now if we can put him under pressure in the early stages he might start making mistakes—and we've got to keep playing on it. Dave—you're the one I want to challenge Miller, in the main. I want you to go for the high crosses and Roy can be lurking about waiting for the bits and pieces. Any questions?"

"But surely we don't want to change our normal play for the sake of high crosses?" Roy asked.

"Of course not—but if we can cash in on his nervousness we'll do so. That's just for the first five minutes. Then if we're getting no joy from it we'll vary our crosses as we usually do, you and Dave reacting off each other, near and far post. Okay?"

They listened intently as he went on through the Rangers team list, telling them nothing particularly new but showing such a detailed grasp of their strengths and weaknesses and individual peculiarities that it was impossible not to be interested.

"I could hear you all sighing with admiration at Caskie's skill on the film," he said. "We might as well deal with him now. Obviously there's no secret about his game, it's there for all to see, sheer brilliance. If you let him play, he will and he'll destroy you. We can't afford to give him any room. Gerry—you've got to play him skin tight—don't let him collect the ball and turn and come at you, he'll murder us that way. I can't stress this point enough. Shutting this fella out could win us the game. Danny—you'll be hovering around behind Gerry—if we've got Caskie marked tight he'll try to chip the ball over Gerry—so Danny will be there to cover at the back. Right, Danny?"

"Right, Boss," said Danny, full of confidence.

"And Sammy—I want you to stay in the area in front of Caskie—that'll make it hard for their defence to play balls to him. We'll cut off his ammunition and smother him when he gets the ball."

He went on. As far as Hood could see he was his old self again, a great manager, filling them all with confidence and enthusiasm, making them want to play better than they had ever played before.

"Now Lindsay—he'll probably be marking Roy. If you allow him to stay in the middle of the field, Roy, you'll find him practically unpassable. So you keep taking him out to the wings, keep him running and turning. If he does have a weakness he's a bit suspect on the turn. Get him to come out on the wings with you and you'll have a chance to get him facing the wrong way—play it quick around him and you'll find he's not so mobile."

He then covered the Dane, Gustafson, making no secret of the fact that he admired him immensely, a non-stop midfield man who could run all day and keep up a brilliant service to his forwards. He said that Shack could match him for lung power and pace, so the idea was to keep close to him, trying to restrict his free running.

"If we can snuff him out in his own half, before he gets away on a run we'll cut the Rangers effectiveness down by about a half. Caskie gets all the publicity but Gustafson is the engine room and the brain of that team."

And then he was finished and nobody had any questions. He looked at them all in turn, his hands spread out on his knees, his face alive with tension and excitement.

"Well—this is it, lads. I want you to go out there and enjoy the game and play the way I know you can. They'll have a great support behind them and you'll hear that crowd roaring the way you've never heard a crowd roaring before. But we've forty thousand supporters and they'll be giving you all the support you deserve. If you play your best you'll win. There's no reason why we shouldn't be at New Wembley next month. Give everything you've got and play good football and that's all anybody can ask."

He smacked his hands together.

"Right then, let's have our lunch."

It was five to twelve. This time they sat together at one long table. The food came almost immediately, Harry Barnes having already given the chef their orders. There was no set meal, for John Gallagher believed in treating them as individuals who knew what suited themselves. Some had boiled chicken, some had poached or scrambled eggs, one or two had steaks without potatoes or vegetables. Sammy and Randy settled for tea and toast. They ate very little and talked about only one thing, the game. Some carried on where John Gallagher had left off, discussing the agility of Miller, the impenetrability of the giant Lindsay, the dribbling brilliance of Caskie, the stamina and football brain of Gustafson, who made the Rangers tick, the snake-like ability of Aikman to dart about the goal mouth poaching goals.

"Come on, you twits, they ain't the greatest team on earth," said Sammy, who was feeling a lot better now that they were all together, sharing the load between them. "We've beaten Queens Park Rangers—why not the bleedin' Glasgow Rangers? All them Rangers look alike to me, even the Texas bloody Rangers."

They finished lunch by twelve-thirty. They had fifteen minutes to wait for the coach. They went into the T.V. lounge to watch the pre-match previews, the discussions among other club managers. Everybody in the game, it seemed, was up in Glasgow. They were laughing at a re-run of their interviews on Wednesday when Harry Barnes came into the lounge, now dressed for the big occasion in a new check raincoat.

"Right lads, the coach is here."

There was nobody else in the T.V. lounge and when they left to pick up their bags and coats the set was still on, Danny and Sammy joking with the red-haired interviewer, the sound booming, the colours flickering and fading, all of it watched by empty chairs.

They said goodbye to the hotel staff, who gathered at the main entrance to see them off. Guests came out on the gravel to wish them luck. Then they climbed into the coach. The chairman and his party were already in the front seats. The rest of the directors would be meeting them in Glasgow. Hood had a word with the chairman, who said Mr. Henriques was improving but couldn't make the match.

"He sent us a telegram wishing us good luck," said George Jackson. "Will you pass it on to the lads?"

"Of course."

He threw his bag up on the rack and moved down the gangway. They all had favourite positions to sit in. Nothing must upset the routine. Peterson found himself sitting with Albert Stone, John Gallagher across the gangway on his right. Danny was the last man on the coach. He gave the chairman's party a general nod, his eyes passing over Carole with no sign of particular recognition. He swaggered to the back, pushed his bag on the rack and sat down beside Sammy.

"Okay, driver," he shouted, "let's get this show on the road!"

"You haven't forgot your bag this time have you, Jim?" Sammy shouted. "We don't wanna turn back half-way."

"Don't even say that," said Riddle, jerking out of his seat, reaching up to touch his bag on the rack. "All that new stuff cost me over a fiver."

"A fiver? A jacks, you mean. Can't you speak proper English, you twit?"

Riddle gave Sammy a two-fingered salute. He was feeling a lot better now. It had been the uncertainty that had depressed him but once the team had been announced and he'd been put out of his agony he had lost his sense of grievance. In football you just had to make the best of things. Nothing lasted long—a grudge, a bad mood, a career.

The coach started to pull away.

"Hampden here we come," shouted Randy. Sammy stared out of the window at the front of the hotel. He saw Mary the dark-haired waitress leaning out of an upstairs window with another girl, waving a tablecloth. He stood up in his seat and blew her a kiss.

"Cor, she was a one," he said. "I give her a ticket, you know."

"Isn't she coming then?" Shack asked.

"Yeah well, I said to her, jokin' like, be my guest at the game and I'll meet you after. She says what for? What for? Cor blimey. So I says, well after a big game we 'ike to have a noggin wiv a friendly face, so she says, I've given me ticket to me boy friend but I'm sure he'll be glad to meet you after for a drink! Leave me out, I says. Cor blimey—see me meetin' the bleedin' boy friend?"

"At least that would satisfy your missus you ain't up to no hanky-panky."

They got to the big greystone gates and turned left. A fierce buzz of chat about the game spread throughout the coach. Roy thumped Hood on the arm.

"Alec—we must win!" he exclaimed.

"Cool it, Roy—you'll be tired before we start."

"I can't help it—I've never known anything like it."

"This is only Renfrewshire, mate. Wait till we get to the park!"

Jimmy Riddle started the singing, bawling out the wrong words of *My Way*. They howled him down but the singing went on, the old sentimental numbers that now brought goose-pimples to the toughest flesh. Hood started them off on 'Maybe It's Because I'm a Londoner' and Sammy returned the compliment with 'I Belong to Glasgow'. Roy stared at the green fields and hills. It looked a lot like the country round Burnley. You wouldn't think there were so many shades of green. He rubbed his fingers along his thigh. *Don't break down for God's sake.* Hood thought of his sons, Garry and wee Bobby, they'd all be round the T.V. set now watching the build-up, too excited for their dinner, sweating on him having a good game so they could stick their chests out at school.

"I hope we're singing after the game," said Sammy.

"We will be," said Danny. "I can feel it in me bones!"

"I know where you can feel it, me old son, and it ain't in yer bones!"

"Cut it out."

"That's what you should do."

They laughed hysterically. The singing stopped. Hood looked up the coach. He could see Brian Seymour sitting next to Harry Barnes. The coach was looking to the front but Brian's jaws were going ten to the dozen. He felt a little sorry for Brian now. He wasn't getting another chance. He won't be crashing into my back either, he thought. He saw Roy's hand kneading at his thigh muscle.

"Forget about it, Roy," he said. "Worrying isn't going to help. Go out and play! If it goes that's too bad—but worrying isn't going to help."

They came into a biggish town. Hood told them it was Paisley.

"Isn't this were St. Mirren play?" Roy asked.

"That's right. The Buddies. I could've signed for them if I'd played my cards right!"

"Where's their ground?"

"Thataway. You could see the floodlights if it weren't for the tenements in between."

"What's their ground called?"

"Love Street, lad. I've been there a few times as a boy, I can tell you. I used to model myself on a centre-half they had, Willie Telfer. He could play the game, kid."

"Nah, they don't have players like them any more," said Danny.

They were stopped by the red lights at Paisley Cross. A blue Triumph pulled alongside the coach. Somebody looked down and howled and they all jumped to the windows on that side. Driving the car was a blonde girl in a very short mini-skirt which from their vantage point gave a fine view of thigh and white panties. She looked up and saw them all smiling and leering. She went red and tried to pull down her skirt.

"Save it for the game," George Westbury shouted.

The lights changed and the girl turned right down a hill and they went straight over the Cross. On the big clock of Paisley Town Hall it was one-fifteen. The singing started again. *We'll be there—at the end—of the road* they bawled, finishing on a big cheer. The traffic was thick now. They passed the boundary sign.

"This is Glasgow now," said Hood.

"Those houses are quite nice," said Sammy. "You sure we're in the right city? That would be a turn-up, wouldn't it?"

Roy looked out at bungalows and semi-detached houses, all of them with nice front gardens, not at all the dark slums they associated with Glasgow. They were picked up by the pre-arranged police motor-cycle escort and soon they were coming to high tenements.

"Is that the kind of place you came from?" Roy asked Hood.

"Not likely. Those are good-class tenements, lad."

"I wouldn't fancy the bad ones."

"No, you bloody well wouldn't. You English don't know you're born."

"You're doing all right—twenty-thousand-pound house in Chertsey?"

"I got out, that's all. Football did that for me. Look down them dingy streets, kid, football's the only way out for those boys."

By now the whole city seemed to be on the march, the pavements jammed by tramping men, most of them wearing Rangers scarves and rosettes and plastic caps, the Rangers blue bringing a brightness to the colourless streets and the dark clothes. They saw two men supporting a friend who was too drunk to stand on his own. He had a bottle in one hand and his blue tammie in the other, his knees sagging and buckling. He was not the only drinking man in the crowd. When they heard the police sirens the marching men turned to look at the coach and when they saw it was the Commoners they stopped to wave and jeer.

"They're all carrying bottles or cans of beer," said Gerry Williamson. "They celebrate in advance up here, do they?"

"D'you think they know there's a game on as well, Alec?" Sammy said.

"Don't tell them—it might spoil the fun."

Peterson looked at John Gallagher. The manager was staring straight ahead, seemingly oblivious to the crowds and the commotion. Then he shook himself and gave a guilty little smile as their eyes met.

"Right then, lads, give us a song," he shouted. The players had on what they called their blanket faces now, the composed, self-contained front they put up for the public benefit. From the pavement they must have looked like aloof, unfeeling aristocrats, Peterson thought, travelling above it all, looking straight through the crowds of fans as if they didn't exist. Yet inside the coach the tension and mounting excitement was almost unbearable. They started singing 'You'll Never Walk Alone', John Gallagher twisted in his seat, his hands clenched, his face red and the big veins swelling in his neck as he roared out the words. Peterson started singing as well . . . *when you walk through a storm* . . . five or six Rangers supporters recognised the team and stood at the edge of the pavement shouting abuse and showing clenched fists or two-fingered salutes.

"Yeah and up yours too, Jock," Sammy shouted—quickly putting his hand to his mouth, remembering Jemima and Carole. They could now see the giant floodlight standards of Hampden Park. Around them were tall black tenements. The police motorcyclists were pushing a way through the milling army of fans. There was nothing to do but start singing again . . . *keep your head held high* . . . drowning out the tramping feet and the barks of the street vendors with their boards of badges and rosettes, team hats, football magazines, newspapers, team photographs, roasted peanuts, Larkins and Percy Daltons, hot-dogs . . . cheery abuse from faces raised to the coach windows, and some not so cheery, then a great yell from the first strong group of Londoners, a waving of green and black scarves, smiles from the players' faces in the windows.

"What comes first to the Scots, whisky or football?" Riddle asked, turning round to look at Hood.

"Whisky, of course," said Hood. "The game starts at three but the pubs are open at half past ten in the morning."

"Do they actually watch the game?" Like all the Englishmen Riddle was amazed and fascinated by the bigness of it all and the fanaticism on the faces of the marching men.

"A good question, Jim," said Hood. "I stood beside six guys

224

at Hampden once when I was a lad and the whole game they talked about international games from the past. Two of them actually stood with their backs to the game for the whole ninety minutes!"

"I expect they went next year and talked about that game," said Riddle.

"Of course! What else? This is the home of football. HAMPDEN HERE WE COME!"

He looked like a big mad bastard and at that moment he was exploding and as they approached the gates he began singing again, standing up, and everybody in the coach joined in and Peterson found his eyes moist with the sheer naked emotion of it all . . . *and don't be afraid of the dark* . . . and they were still singing fit to burst as the gateman let them through and the police escort wheeled their machines away like messengers of death in black helmets and goggles and Peterson knew what it felt like to want to die for the team.

"Come on, lads, here we are," Hood shouted as the coach pulled up outside the main entrance. John Gallagher came to the rear of the coach.

"You can leave your bags on the coach, the driver will be looking after them. If any of you have tickets to leave on the gate for friends do it now—they'll give you envelopes in the office. Do all that as quick as you can and go out and have a look at the pitch and then get into the dressing-room."

"All the best, lads," shouted the chairman as they got off the bus. Carole watched Danny's face but the game had him now and his eyes passed over her without recognition. She watched the players disappear through the glass doors, some of them waving to friendly faces among the throng which stood under the big stand . . .

Sammy stuck down the envelope with the complimentary tickets for his father and wrote *Peter Auger* on the front.

"Them's for me dad," he explained to the commissionaire, "but we had fly boys nickin' the tickets at games—they go up and ask for tickets for Mister Small knowin' I'm bound to have left them at the gate for him. Only he and me knows about Peter Auger. It's our secret code."

"Oh aye," said the commissionaire, "there's a lot of wide boys about in this world."

The first player to set foot on the lush green plastic pitch was Steve Randall. He bent down and ran his fingers over the synthetic grass. In the old days, before they changed to man-made wonder pitches, players went out on the grass to feel how soft it was or how greasy or how icy. In those days players generally had two sets of boots, rubber-studded soles for ice or the hard grounds at the beginning and end of the season, leather-soles with screw-in studs of different lengths for heavy grounds with mud, hard pitches with recent rain, or a heavily-grassed pitch. From time immemorial early arrivals on the terraces had watched players come out on pitches, wearing their suits and coats, to check the type of surface they would be playing on. Nowadays, with the plastic turf, it was all rubbers, unless there had been heavy rain, when they'd use very short studs on leather boots, and there was no real need most of the time to come out in the open and test the pitch, yet they all did it, getting a feel of the ground and the atmosphere, not consciously showing themselves off, as many spectators sometimes suspected, if anything a little self-conscious at being on the pitch in street clothes.

Randy walked over to the goal at the west end of the pitch. He stood between the goal-posts, facing the pitch. He crouched slightly and then jumped up to touch the crossbar. On the half-filled terraces they roared and jeered. He gave them a swift glance, then checked his watch. It was two o'clock. The scene was set. The greatest game of my life, he thought. What'll I be thinking at twenty to five? He wished he could see the evening papers now . . . COMMONERS DOWN AND OUT . . . or COMMONERS GO MARCHING ON . . . he touched both goal posts for luck, as he always did before any match, home or away. He walked towards the centre circle to join the rest of the squad.

"Well, Randy," said Hood, "have you built your invisible wall in front of the goal?"

"The way I'm feeling I don't need a wall—just these," said Randy, holding out his splayed hands. Even as he said it he hoped that nothing would happen to make this statement seem like a sick joke after the game. A huge roar went up. They looked round. Some of the Rangers players were walking onto the pitch.

"That looks like Caskie," said Shack.

"Ain't he small?" said Sammy. "He's smaller'n you, Wiggy."

"That Lindsay isn't so small," said Wiggy. "And get a load of

226

the other guy—just behind Lindsay! Is that Man Mountain?"

"That's Graham the left-back," said Alec. "The bloke with him—the red hair—that's Miller the goalie."

They walked off the pitch, nodding briefly to the Rangers players as they passed. They were not exactly the enemy and the teams were not motivated by the ferocity engendered in a boxer against his opponent, yet even Hood, who knew several of the Rangers very well, did not want to stop for a chat. In less than a hour they would be facing each other on the pitch, when they would become the enemy and there would be no friendships then and it didn't seem right to be over-pleasant towards them now.

They went into the short tunnel and turned right into the visitors' dressing-room. George Westbury and Harry Barnes were laying out the new strip. The green and black striped shirts were already hanging on their individual pegs. Socks, shorts and jockstraps were neatly folded on the bench seat that went round the cream walls. A long treatment table stood in the centre of the room, on it a white tray of shining surgical instruments. At one end was an open doorway to the bath and showers, another door leading to the lavatory. Duckboards were placed all round the room so that bare feet would not have to touch the wooden floor.

"This dressing-room is nothing special," said Danny, "compared to the rest of the stadium."

"You only get dressed in here, lad," said Hood, "it's out there it all happens." He clapped his hands together, an eager excitement all over his big craggy face.

They all had different approaches to the business of preparing for the game. Sammy was talking with ever more determination than usual. Randy was singing, Shack was moaning about something and Roy wasn't saying a word. Dave Peacock had a quick glimpse into the Rangers dressing-room, seeing three or four players chatting and laughing. He looked round the Commoners dressing-room. There's no laughter in here, he thought. Is it lack of confidence? Alec Hood was down to his underpants, white Y-fronts on a hard, white body. He was going round the room reminding every player of his job on the pitch. They all knew their jobs off by heart. It's Alec's way of releasing tension, he thought. Shack was still moaning. He couldn't find the scissors to cut the ends of the sticky tape he used to hold his thin shinpads in position. Dave Spencer hadn't started to get undressed. He was standing at the far end tapping a ball against the wall with the inside of his right foot, tapping it again and again and again. A small Scotsman came in and asked if there were any team changes. John Gallagher told him they were playing as announced. Riddle was pulling his socks over his shinpads. He went to the table and picked up a match programme. He turned to the middle pages where the teams were set out in the positions they would take on the field. He was listed as a substitute. I've been worried all week, he thought, he only tells me yesterday I'm not playing—and I could have come here on Wednesday and had a look at the bloody programme! He shrugged. That was history now.

It was half-past two. John Gallagher came back into the room and hung his coat on a hook, smiling broadly. Randy was lying on the table. George Westbury poured another dollop of camphorated oil into his cupped hand and spread it over Randy's thighs and calves, then rubbed it into his legs, thumbs pressing into every muscle.

"The magic fingers are working well today, George," said the goalkeeper.

"I hope yours are," the physiotherapist replied.

"Now— don't get cheeky, George, or I might let a few in just to stop you getting to New Wembley."

"Don't talk treason."

John Gallagher had his sleeves rolled up. He went round the room talking to each man in turn. Harry Barnes was doing the same. Players were getting advice from all directions. Somebody tried to come into the dressing-room but John Gallagher pushed him out, not listening to what the man was saying, determined now to concentrate on only one thing. Shack got on the table for a massage, then Peacock, then Williamson, then Sammy Small. Danny pushed two fingers into a jar of Vaseline and smeared it across his forehead, just above the eyebrows, a greasy barrier that would divert sweat from running into his eyes. Randy started slinging a ball against the wall and catching it on the rebound. Andy Gurr did his usual routine of going into the lavatory and sitting down to read the programme from cover to cover. He always did that before a match, always from twenty-five minutes to three till twenty to three. He was wearing his socks and boots and small box jockstrap and nothing else. Hood was ready to go out, minus only his shorts. He never put his shorts on till the last minute.

He caught the ball that Randy was throwing against the wall and threw it above Randy's head. They threw it back and forward to each other, sometimes high, sometimes low, sharpening the goal-keeper's reflexes. Sammy and Gerry sat on the bench talking about the tactics they would use to restrict Caskie's freedom. Roy Christmas went to the lavatory when Andy Gurr came out. He sat down and shut his eyes ... *Please oh Lord let my leg be all right, don't let me break down* ... players went through their stressing exercises, lifting a foot up on the treatment table and bending their heads down to the thigh, bending legs to stretch groin muscles, inside and outside, standing on one leg to pull the other tight up behind them.

It was two forty-five. The room was full of people carrying out little superstitions and routines. Shack broke a lace while tying up his boot. Brian Seymour got a new lace and threaded the boot for him. Brian was in his club suit. So was Barry Ross. Only they had no possibility of playing. Johnny Parkinson, the substitute goal-keeper, started throwing the ball to Randy. Some tied the left boot before the right and some used combs in front of the mirror and some sat silently on the bench, ready to play and not wanting to talk about it.

John Gallagher sat on the edge of the treatment table. He asked them to sit down for a moment. Hood still had his shorts in his hand.

"Well, lads, this is it now," the manager said. "You've all done remarkably well this season and worked very hard—not just the team, the whole squad. My one regret is I can't give you all a game but we're only allowed eleven players." They smiled at what seemed to be a very witty remark at that stage. "To me you're all in the team. You've worked well for each other all season and you'll do the same today. Remember all the things we've worked at. If we lose a goal don't let us panic. Just keep your heads and try and get a goal back—without leaving ourselves open at the rear. Enjoy the game and believe in yourselves. If you play like you can I've no worries. I'm sure we'll win."

Hood stared at John Gallagher, as did every man in the room. He is a great guy, Hood thought. He'd heard him say all this many times before but he knew it was genuine and that mattered more than anything else in this game. They hung on his every word because they respected him. He had a way of saying the same old things with such enthusiasm it got right into your guts. Motivation was the fancy word they had for it. John Gallagher knew how to give it to them. When he spoke to you like this you wanted to run yourself into the ground for him.

Ten to three.

A bell rang.

"Right—all the best, lads," said John Gallagher. Players patted each other on the back or shook hands and wished each other good luck. Alec Hood slipped on his shorts. It was his one super-stition—apart from always wanting to go out first. He picked up a ball, turned round and shook his fist.

"Come on, lads, let's show 'em!"

As they filed out of the dressing-room John Gallagher stood by the door, making a point of touching each player and wishing him good luck. Roy sat on the bench waiting for the rest of the squad to go out. His superstition was always to be the last man on the field.

Rubber studs scuffed on stone and then they were out of the short tunnel and running onto the pitch. Hood threw up the ball and half-volleyed it across the green pitch with the inside of his left foot, leading them towards the goal on the left, another of his habits. Forty thousand Commoners supporters roared at them from a frantic, boiling green and black lava of scarves and streamers and banners.

Peterson's ears were still battered by Commoners noise when a bigger roar went off like an atomic explosion. Onto the pitch came the big, hard-boned figure of Davie Lindsay leading out the Rang-ers. Hampden was so big it seemed too immense for men to have made. The *weight* of a hundred and five thousand people jammed together had a strange effect on the mind. He had been at thousands of football matches but never had he felt the bigness of a crowd like this, pressing in on him, crushing him down to the size of an ant. *Keep it on the island* they used to shout at players who kicked the ball out of a ground and here, for the first time, it made sense, for Hampden was more than a mere arena—could there be anyone left on the outside?

Rangers were in royal blue shirts, white pants, black stockings with red tops; Commoners, in the green and black striped shirts, black pants and dark green stockings, looked dark and menacing by comparison. There was a bigness about the Rangers players, a *British* quality of open resolution, the white shorts suggesting manliness and sportsmanship; Commoners looked devious and *foreign*, alien and knavish and tricky. Peterson sat forward, elbows on knees, right hand splayed over his eyes, peering one-eyed at the blaring hugeness of the scene before him, stomach trembling. It seemed impossible that ordinary blokes whom you laughed and joked with could transform themselves into the kind of legendary giants required to do combat and win on a Roman occasion like this. He felt sick with tension.

Roy did a couple of sprints without the ball, then had a left foot shot at Randy. His leg felt all right. The referee ran out flanked by his two linesmen, who peeled off to their respective halves of the pitch. The ref, Peter Wainsford, a former Aston Villa man chosen for this game because he came from Wales and was as near to neutral a man as could be found in Great Britain, called the two captains to the centre spot. The thirty or forty photographers who were on the pitch getting individual shots of each player, crowded together in a semi-circle as the two captains shook hands, holding the pose for a second or two to give the cameras what they wanted.

Alec Hood grinned at Davie Lindsay.

"We can't go on meeting like this," he said, eyebrows flickering lewdly.

"Have a good game but leave the winning to us," said Lindsay. He spun the ref's penny. Hood called heads. It came down heads. He decided to play the way they were facing already. The sun was low and would shine in the face of Miller, the Rangers goalkeeper. By half-time it would be even lower but Randy would be shielded from the slanting rays by the great perspex roof covering the west end terracing.

"Best of luck," said Lindsay.

"Who're you kidding?" said Hood.

It was the last joke of the afternoon. Rangers lined up to kick off. Aikman stood by the ball, hands kneading each other, Dawson beside him. The ref looked at his watch. He put his whistle up. Then he blew. Aikman touched the ball to Dawson. Dawson played it back to Gustafson. A hundred and five thousand people united their lungs in the greatest single roar Britain could produce.

Up in the stand it sounded to Peterson like the crack of heavens opening, the thunder of a mighty Niagara of human sound. He ground a cigarette under his heel.

"This is too much," he said to Brian Seymour, who had come running up the great stairs to join him just before the teams ran out. "I'm shaking all over."

"The boys look good," said Seymour. Peterson didn't understand whether he meant the deadly, menacing neatness of the Commoner's dark green and black strip, or how they were actually playing. He ran his hand over his sweaty face and prayed for the lads to win.

Lindsay played the ball out to Caskie. The Rangers crowd roared in anticipation of a Caskie run but Gerry Williamson was in too quickly for him, intercepting the pass and playing a long ball up to Peacock. Dave flicked the ball on with the top of his head. He went down with a whack in the back from Milne, the Rangers right-back. Roy looked at the ref but he didn't give a foul. The ball ran loose. Roy got it under control and started towards the left wing, closely policed by Lindsay. Roy dummied to go past him on the outside, then accelerated past him on the inside. He over-ran the ball. Grant came round and took it off his toes. He played a square ball to Lindsay, who laid it off to Graham, who stabbed a forward ball to Gustafson. Roy drifted back to the centre circle, annoyed at himself for losing the ball. But his leg was all right.

Rangers mounted an attack, close passing sideways, going forward a few yards at a time, blue shirts popping up to take yet another pass. Their build-up was slow but sure, in the Scottish manner, each man taking deliberate care with his passes. Roy waited in the centre circle but all he got were a few high, misguided passes from the defence. He chased without any joy. Commoners defence was playing erratically, stopping Rangers attacks only at the last minute, never getting a grip on the game. The Glasgow crowd sensed Rangers' dominance. The roaring was a continuous thing now, a perpetual avalanche of noise that battered at the ears. For the first time Caskie escaped Gerry Williamson. He pulled the ball down with his chest, turned and went quickly at Gerry, dummying twice, going past on his right. Danny came at him but Caskie went past him easily, like a cyclist avoiding a pedestrian. He chipped the ball across. Aikman went in first. He got his head to the cross, just enough for a slight deflection. The ball looped over Hood. Roy knew it was coming. Dawson was there, about eight yards out, powering the ball into the net on the half-volley, a goal all the way.

The stadium erupted into complete pandemonium. A great shower of blue scarves and hats and flags almost hid the people underneath. Policemen did rugby tackles to grab the boys and men who tried to invade the pitch. One long-legged youth jigged past the blue police line and went dancing through the Rangers team, pursued by a policeman whose helmet fell off, hugging players, then sprinting for the enclosure under the North Stand, again eluding the police and scrambling over the low wall into the crowd. The Rangers team came together in a mounting pyramid of bodies, desperate to grab hold of the goal scorer Dawson, each new man leaping up on the backs of the others until they all fell on the ground, Dawson somewhere beneath it all.

The Commoners looked at each other, dejected and deflated. Hood clenched both fists and barked at them:

"Come on, you lot, there's a long way to go!"

High in the main stand Peterson had both hands over his face, elbows on knees, not knowing whether to cry or vomit. Seven minutes—and they were a goal down. It had all been a dream. Nothing he ever touched came to success. It was his fault, he had brought them bad luck with all his talk about the money to come. He prayed desperately. But he knew they were going to lose. He'd known it all along . . .

Commoners kicked off. Peacock to Roy, Roy back to Shack. He trapped it and spun round in a complete circle to evade the on-rushing Aikman. Moving down the right of the field he saw Wiggy running wide to the wing and Roy and Dave heading for the Rangers goal, one to each post. He was going to slide it forward diagonally to Wiggy but the big left-back Graham was moving towards Wiggy to shut him off. He changed direction and poised his body for the long cross to the far post. From nowhere, unheard, came Dawson, running the ball away from his feet. The noise came from the crowd in waves. Rangers were on the rampage. Gustafson and Killick worked a great move together in the middle, ending with a surprise pass down the wing for Caskie to run and cross. Roy stood in the centre circle watching the white ball shoot across the sea of white faces and blue scarves. But Randy knew when to come off his line and he rose above two Rangers to take it cleanly in both hands. He threw one to Gerry Williamson, who moved it forward quickly to Sammy. Sammy touched it once then drove a straight, low pass into the centre. Roy took it with his back to the Rangers goal, turning on it quickly and economically, knowing that Lindsay was sliding into his back. He side-stepped the big centre-back and moved forward, his long, loping stride giving the impression that he was strolling, but covering ground so quickly he was into the heart of the Rangers defence. He drew Grant to the right, then hit a reverse pass to Peacock. Milne tried to nail Dave but he curled it first time into the open space. Wiggy ran on to it and hit a first-time shot. It was on target. Miller dived sideways and up, right arm fully stretched. The ball struck the crossbar and soared high into the air, bouncing down in the semi-circle of grass behind the goal, such force behind the shot it bounced to the cinder-track before the ballboy caught it. Wiggy grimaced. It had been a good move and a good shot and it proved they could get through the Rangers defence. Did it also prove they weren't fated to score?

Ray ran back to the centre circle. The ball went down into Commoners' half. Dawson floated a curling ball across goal. Randy stayed on his line. The cross was coming round in an arc, away from goal. Aikman got back a few feet and managed to get his head behind it, but it was a weak header. Randy let it run past the post for a goal kick.

Get the bloody ball up here, you bastards, Roy was saying. He caught Dave Peacock's eye and they both frowned, feeling helpless. Rangers had got away to a good start and the crowd was punching them on with great staccato barks. Roy felt almost like a spectator, the worst part of being a forward when things were going badly. He moved out to the right wing, taking Lindsay with him, but Commoners' defence had no chance to feed him.

Danny got one ball away and hit it up the centre of the field. Grant jumped higher than Dave and thumped it back with his head, right into the heart of Commoners' territory. Andy Gurr and Dawson went in hard for the ball. Dawson got it. He used the outside of his left foot to push it six yards to Aikman. Alec Hood committed himself too quickly, his whole body going into the tackle. Aikman flicked it a foot to one side and jumped artistically over Alec's scything legs. He collected it and hit it to Caskie. Gerry Williamson went at the little winger very aggressively. Caskie went towards the ball and then let it run across his path, swivelling past Gerry's clumsy rush, a bullfighter sending the bull the wrong way.

He took it on past Shack. Hood came sprinting across, desperately stretching his whole body, feet first, to block the shot.

Caskie didn't shoot. He pulled the ball inside Hood, onto his right foot. The ground was suddenly silent, Caskie a little hunched figure with a drooped right shoulder. He crossed the eighteen-yard line into the box. Randy came flying out at him, arms and legs spread out sideways to make himself into as big an obstacle as possible, restricting Caskie's view of goal. It made no difference. Caskie let his body lean back as he chipped it neatly and precisely over Randy's diving body. Randy was sprawled on the ground as he watched the ball bounce over the line and then hit the net with an awful, inevitable, *gentle* forward roll.

Caskie turned and stood with both arms in the air. Blue shirts ran at him from all parts of the pitch. Green and black shirts stood motionless. Randy dragged himself off the ground, walking with head down to retrieve the ball, which he kicked sulkily against the net. From the great terraced banks erupted a noise that had almost destructive power, hats and scarves going into the air like debris from a mighty blast of dynamite. The blue shirts were a heaving, jumping ruck hiding little Caskie, the nucleus of the explosion. Miller was the only Ranger not in the hysterical gaggle. He was doing jubilant acrobatics on the edge of his penalty box.

Roy kicked off. There were about ten minutes before half-time. Rangers were flushed and disordered by success. Commoners were tight-faced and grim. This was a good time to strike back. Dave pushed it back to Shack, who pushed it first-time to Roy, who stabbed it first-time to Wiggy. He beat two men and went off down the right towards the goal-line. Roy ran for the far post, taking Lindsay with him. Wiggy crossed low to the near post. Dave Peacock took a dive at it, body parallel to the ground, a human missile. He didn't connect. Miller took it on the chest, wrapping both arms round it. He rolled it smoothly along the ground to Milne, who came up to the half-way line. Sammy back-pedalled and tackled from the back, swinging his left leg round with such ferocity Milne went down. The ball went out of play. The referee didn't give a foul.

Milne threw a quick ball to Traynor but Shack hit him fair and square with a shoulder charge. Suddenly Roy felt good. It was the first time the defence had looked itself. There was nothing to be jittery about now, they were two goals down and the worst had already happened. Roy moved to the left. Shack hit a fifteen-yard pass at him. He nodded it backwards and right to Dave's feet. Lindsay had gone into a first-time tackle but the ball was not there when he hit Roy. Dave came bursting through the space left by Lindsay. Sammy ran for the far corner of the penalty box. Dave hit it to him on the run but Grant did a great sliding interception, coming up off his left knee with the ball.

It banged about the middle. Caskie flicked it over his head and turned to run after it but Danny was there, putting his thigh, leg and foot in a textbook tackle, getting such a firm grip of the ball that when Caskie kicked it his own force sent him falling over Danny's hip. The crowd bayed for a foul but Danny was off, ploughing up the pitch, tree-like legs eating up the yards, arms pumping, big chest sticking out. He played it out to Dave Spencer on the right wing. It was the first time Debonair had got away on one of his runs. Gustafson came at him from the side and rear, and the giant Graham came towards him. He did not have to look up to see where he was putting it. The long, square ball came across the field to Sammy, who stopped it on his thigh and hit it before it reached the ground to Dave, who hit it inside Traynor, right into Sammy's stride, about twenty yards out. Sammy moved like a little mechanical doll gone mad. He hit it with his right foot, low and hard, bang on target. Miller's orange jersey flashed for a moment in space. He palmed it round the post. The Rangers crowd let out a great groaning sigh of relief. Sammy sprinted behind the goal to snatch the ball from the boy but before he could run to the corner flag the referee blew his whistle for half-time. In the stands they stood and cheered and clapped as the two teams ran for the tunnel.

"Oh God," Peterson moaned, hanging his head.

"They're not doing what they said, they're giving Caskie all the space he wants," said Brian Seymour. "But they're not playing so bad—got a lot better in the last twenty minutes."

"Oh Jesus," said Peterson.

All around them Scotsmen were bubbling, roars now given way to a fierce hubbub of chat, bottles being passed from hand to hand. Here and there men in Commoners colours sat still. Their team had made two goal chances, hit the woodwork with one and had the other saved by a brilliant bit of goalkeeping. It looked like just one of those days when the team wasn't fated to get it in the net. The defence had been erratic, Spencer had hardly been seen, and Roy Christmas had given Lindsay the slip only once or twice. They had nothing to feel cheery about. I knew it in my bones, Peterson thought. The omens had been wrong from the very beginning, right from the moment John Gallagher had shouted at Riddle in the coach, back at Oaks Common on Wednesday morning. The Glasgow football writers were right, we behaved like a bunch of comedians, just a shower of laughing has-beens who didn't have the iron in the soul for an occasion like this. He lit a cigarette and felt his lunch churning acidly in his guts and stared blankly at the great sea of humanity.

John Gallagher was already in the dressing-room, coat off and shirt sleeves rolled up. They came into the dressing-room one by one, picking up cups of tea and sitting down.

"Okay, lads," said the manager, "I want a word with you before you do anything else. I don't know if you started off overawed by the occasion but it certainly looked like it. Still, you played a lot better in the last ten, fifteen minutes. How's your leg, Roy?"

"Okay, Boss." Roy knew Gallagher was thinking his muscle was the reason he had not been moving too well. It hadn't, not the muscle itself, more the fear of what would happen to it. Yet he couldn't remember being afraid of it breaking down.

"Just at the end you seemed to be getting the better of Lindsay —you were moving the ball a lot quicker. I certainly don't know what happened in the first half hour, you were moving like bloody cart horses. Gerry—you've been giving Caskie too much room, son, I know he's a good player but—"

"I don't want to dive at him, Boss—"

"I don't want you to do that, all I'm saying is—"

"Listen, Boss, Sammy is supposed to be stopping his supply of passes—"

"Wot you talkin' about? I have been doin' that! I've stayed in the left area all the time—but he's not stayin' on the wing. He changed his tactics after the first five minutes. It's no good me followin' the pair of you all over the bleedin' park!"

"All I know is you should—"

Sammy turned on Gerry, glaring angrily.

"Don't make fakkin' excuses," he snapped. "You wanna get on yourself wiv puttin' that little prat out of the game!"

"What do you bloody mean?" Gerry shouted. They stood face to face, faces red, Sammy's neck rigid, fists tightened up as if they were going to thump each other.

"For Christ's sake," said Hood, moving between them, "keep your bloody aggression for the game!"

Sammy sat down, still glaring at Gerry, who stared at the ground.

"That's not going to do us any good, is it?" John Gallagher asked, his voice calm and patient. "Pull yourselves together. Gerry, I want you to go tighter with Caskie, okay?"

"All right, Boss."

"Sammy stay on the left, Shack in the middle and Dave on the right. I want you three to support the front men a lot more than you've been doing." As he spoke the manager was tearing a programme, shred by shred. His face and voice were under control but his fingers gave him away. "Wherever Caskie goes you go, Gerry. And Traynor looks a little slow, if you get the ball, Sammy, have a go at him, take him on. He's giving you a lot of room."

"Yeah he is, but I'm not able to make the most of it," said Sammy.

"Yes, well, let's go out this half and start where we left off. It's not over by any means. Let's see your character."

"Come on for Christ's sake," said Hood, looking round their faces. "They're playing quite well but it's only because we're playing like a lot of fucking fairies. We're all over our nerves now so there's no excuses."

Some changed sweat-soaked shirts and others went to the toilet or combed their hair. Nobody had any injuries for George Westbury to attend.

The bell rang.

"Right, lads," said John Gallagher. "Let's go! Show 'em how we can play! Good luck."

They were all on the boil now, trying to key each other up, echoing John Gallagher's words to each other, faces serious, fists being raised and shaken in hard-faced determination.

"Let's run till we drop," Hood snarled. They went through the door one by one, John Gallagher again touching each player on the arm or shoulder, a wink here and a nod there, jaws working busily on new sticks of gum.

Rangers were already on the field. They lined up for the kick-off.

Roy played it to Dave Peacock.

"Here you are," Danny yelled, from behind. Dave played it back to him. Roy went running forward. The din had lost its power to terrify the nerves. Danny hit a long, dropping ball up the middle. Roy poised to jump, seeing Dave Peacock on his right. As he took off Lindsay cracked him in the back. He went sprawling on the ground, not seeing where the ball went. He jumped up, shouting furiously.

"Hey ref for Christ's sake, don't you give bloody fouls?" The ref took no notice. Roy looked across at Dave. "This Welsh bastard's a right homer."

The ball bounced in front of Caskie. He took it on his right foot but before he had it turned and under control Gerry crashed through him like a tank, knocking Caskie sideways. The ball ran loose. Aikman got to it first and before Hood could tackle him centred it hard towards goal. Dawson came in to meet it, a straight run, arms already poised for the jump. Randy was already running out. He punched it away with both fists. Shack ran to trap it, facing his own goal.

"Turn!" Sammy shouted, letting him know he was in the clear.

Shack got it round and jabbed it to Spencer with the outside of his right foot. Dave collected it and played it along the touchline to Dave Peacock, who had Grant breathing down his back. Dave went to trap it then jumped up over it, hoping to dummy Grant but the Rangers man got his left leg to it, sending it onto the cinder track.

Spencer took the throw, a long one diagonally forward to Wiggy, who surprised Grant by letting it run through his legs. He scampered round the big defender and feinted with his head and shoulders as he took it up to Gustafson, sending the Dane one way while he darted on the other. Killick was next to come. Roy and Dave were about twenty years from goal, marked closely by Grant and Lindsay.

"Go far post," Roy roared at Dave.

Dave began to run. Roy started to follow him, both of them running towards the post on the far side from where Wiggy was bringing it forward to meet Killick. Roy suddenly changed direction, cutting sharply across Grant and sprinting to the near post, leaving Grant behind by two yards. Wiggy drove it hard and head-high. Miller came off his line by a yard or two to cut off the cross. Roy was at full speed. He nipped in front of Miller and got a flick at the ball with the side of his head, running so fast he could not see where it went, charging on into the line of photographers, jumping at the last minute over the heads of scattering cameramen.

He had his head round as he went down on his knees. The ball was hitting the side-netting at the other end of the goal, Miller still standing with his hands in front of his face, body twisting round.

Dave was the first to get to Roy as he walked back through the line of photographers. They got hold of each other and jumped up and down like small children doing ring-a-ring of roses. Somewhere on the great slopes a fan blew a motor-horn. Unseen green and black scarves came up from the press of bodies. Every man came charging at Roy. Way up the field on the edge of the penalty box Randy was cavorting like a juvenile. Roy stood and let them hug and pound and kiss him.

"Come on then," Danny growled, "we got 'em on the run!"

We'll show them, we'll show them now, Danny kept saying to himself as he got back into position, his face and neck tingling.

As Roy turned to face the Rangers front three for the kick-off he realised his leg was pulling a bit. He rubbed his thigh. Oh God, not now, he thought, looking round at Alec Hood, who was showing them his right fist and shouting the message:

"We're back in the game—for fuck's sake come on!"

The whistle blew. Rangers kicked off, Dawson to Aikman.

"Close him down," Hood called to Roy.

He ran close in to Aikman to restrict his chances of a forward pass. Aikman turned and played it back to Milne, who hit a long, high one deep into Commoners' defence. Up went Dawson and Hood. Both missed. Randy came quickly off his line and scooped it up. They all ran forward, reacting quickly to Hood's shout of "Up!"

Randy hit it on the drop, a long half-volleyed ball that Peacock got his head under, flicking it forward another ten yards. Roy and Lindsay chased for it. Roy could see Wiggy on his left. That's where it would go. He was a pace ahead of Lindsay, two yards from the ball, when he suddenly went down, without warning, as though hit by a bullet. Lindsay took a long stride over his outstretched leg and got to the ball. He hit it down the field but Roy had his eyes shut, nose and cheeks screwed up against the pain. The ball went out of play and men from both sides crowded above him. George Westbury knelt beside him.

"It's gone, George," Roy said, sitting up on one elbow, wincing, drawing sharp, hissing breaths.

"It might be —"

"No, it's had it, the bastard's blown out. Shit!"

Harry Barnes sprinted onto the pitch to help George carry Roy off, taking an arm each round their necks, hands clasped under Roy to make a chair, carrying him off the pitch in a sitting position. John Gallagher was already down at the bench from his seat in the directors' box. Danny stood with hands on hips watching the manager talking to the three tracksuited substitutes on the bench. Jimmy Riddle stood up and did a couple of high-kneed sprints up and down the touchline. He then unzipped his top. Alec Hood told the ref they were bringing on a sub. Jimmy was on the touchline, waving like a kid to his mummy. The ref beckoned him onto the pitch. Jimmy came bounding into the middle, hair very neat, jaws churning a wad of gum.

"I knew it wasn't our day," Peterson said to Seymour. "I've felt it all along. Honestly, I could cry for the lads."

"There's forty minutes to go yet," Seymour said grimly. "Don't bury the body till you're sure it's dead."

"It's hopeless now, you know it as well as I do. First these goals — then Roy. I could've told you yesterday this was going to happen."

"We're only one down for Christ's sake! And Roy wasn't having a good game anyway. I'd say our chances are better now."

"Would you?"

"Stands to reason."

"Oh."

Gerry took the throw-in, going back a yard or two, running to the line, both arms coming up from behind his shoulders to heave one down the line, over the head of Milne. Shack had already run into that position. He took a few strides to take stock of where the others were. Then he hit a hard, straight pass inside to Wiggy, a typical Shack ball, hit dead true, no spin on it, zooming about six inches above the turf, inch-true to Wiggy's feet.

Danny came forward, watching Wiggy. Graham the left-back tried an early tackle but Wiggy had suddenly found his confidence. Danny could even see from Wiggy's back that he was in a new mood. The crowd grew quieter. They'd been jeering Wiggy in the first half. Graham had been blotting him out so easily he hadn't given him a kick—except in the legs. Now he looked a different player. Danny wondered if any Rangers had been saying things to needle him. He had the ball at his feet, making cocky movements with his head and shoulders, playing with the nonchalant arrogance that he seemed to acquire when people began to doubt his worth, so cool he deliberately waited to give Graham a chance to come back at him, then touching the ball through the Ranger's legs. Danny came running up behind.

"For fakk's sake git on with it!" he yelled. "Stop taking the piss!"

Wiggy played it to Riddle. It was Jimmy's first touch. He played it straight back to Wiggy, who trapped it with the smooth skill of the true ball player, the ball dead as soon as it touched him, a lifeless thing waiting for his next move. He stopped for a second and straightened up, his boot on the top of the ball, daring Graham to have another lunge at him.

Graham was leaning forward in a semi-crouch, arms outstretched, eyes fixed on Wiggy's legs, determined not to commit himself before he was certain to get the ball. Wiggy jinked over it twice, swinging his boot and then missing the ball, body starting to sway for a run then stopping quickly. Graham edged nearer, still in the crouch, head bent forward. Wiggy pushed the ball forward about eighteen inches with the sole of his boot. Graham poised for a tackle. Wiggy dragged the ball back with the sole of his boot. Graham made his move, suddenly launching into Wiggy and the ball with his right leg. Wiggy flicked it neatly with his toe, stepping disdainfully over Graham's big leg. He played it diagonally to Peacock, who ran at it, about twenty yards out, all set for a first-time shot. The Rangers defence swayed to block the line of the shot, Miller dancing a couple of steps to his left. Dave opened his legs and let the ball run through. Riddle had already begun his run.

He took it in his stride with his right foot. Danny had a momentary thought — Jimmy hasn't had time to get the feel of the ball yet. But he got it right, all the way into the top of the net, bouncing down while Miller was still in mid-air. The whole stadium seemed to lean forward to watch the shot.

It was in! Rangers' defenders had their heads turned. It bounced lazily and the net billowed gently. A blue-shirted defender sank to his knees, face covering his hands. Danny started running at Jimmy, who was running out to the side, making great leaping strides, punching at the sky with his right fist.

The doctor had just finished putting a heavy strapping on Roy's thigh. They heard the roar.

"It's a bloody goal," said Paul Franks.

"Who for though?"

The doctor ran out of the dressing-room. Roy swung his legs off the treatment table, alone in the dressing-room, telling himself it would have been a bigger roar if Rangers had scored, praying. The doc came back, shoving his arms in the air, face almost purple with excitement. Roy almost fell off the table. The doc grabbed his arms and shook them up and down, laughing and shouting.

"I've got to see the rest of the game," he kept saying. "You all right now?"

"Sure. I'll be out soon as I get dressed."

The doc ran out into the tunnel and Roy hobbled over to the bench and started pulling on his clothes.

Caskie beat Gerry on the outside. He took it to the byeline and sent over a perfect cross. Aikman got up higher than Hood. Randy was caught off his line. Aikman's glancing header touched the tips of Randy's fingers. The crowd drew in a great breath. The ball hit the underside of the bar and bounced down on the line. A few Rangers' arms went up in a half-hearted appeal for a goal but the ref was on the spot and Danny was there first to belt it high and hard towards the crowd behind the goal. They all came back to defend, leaving only Peacock up in the centre circle. Caskie took the corner. Randy went up for it with Dawson. The ref blew for a foul against Dawson. They ran out of defence. The game was going from end to end. The crowd had changed its mood now. The tension had got to them as well and they saved their lungs for specific incidents.

Rangers were pushing forward again. Danny nicked a pass meant for Dawson. He hit it hard and fast, a yard or two in front of Sammy, who jumped over the line of the ball and let it run untouched for about ten yards, waiting for someone to move into the clear for a pass. Rangers were marking tighter than ever now. He hit a long, speculative cross to the far post. Lindsay and Grant jumped with Dave Peacock, who got a hand on Lindsay's shoulder to give himself a few extra inches. The ref didn't see his lift-up. He nodded it back down to Riddle. Jimmy was only eight yards out. The ball landed behind him. He turned but Andy Gurr was coming charging in. Jimmy had just enough time to jump clear and give Andy a go at it.

Andy smashed it to the top left-hand corner.

"GOAL!" Jimmy shouted, his hands going up—but Miller had catapulted across the goal, both arms out, legs bent up behind him, hands clawing at the ball, not only saving it but holding it, falling to the ground and rolling himself into a ball as the Commoners forwards pounded in at him. The Rangers crowd pounded out his name.

"MILLER! MILLER! MILLER!"

Roy took a deep breath and threw back his head. John Gallagher blew out a long gust of amazement, pounding his knees with his fists. Roy lit a cigarette and sucked on it so rapidly the smoke had no time to reach his lungs.

Twenty minutes to go!

Rangers attacked down the left wing. Roy held his breath every time they got possession. Gustafson hit a first-time shot well wide of the goal. Roy breathed again. Randy took the kick and it went straight out to Dawson on the left. He was off for the goal-line in a flash. Dave Spencer tried to catch him but Dawson was well away. Then Danny went out. Dawson hit it past Danny and started to run. Danny blocked him heavily with his hip. Dawson went spinning over and over, crashing to the ground with a sickening finality. Two or three Rangers players ran at Danny with their fists up. Dawson rolled over on the ground in obvious agony. The ref got to Danny before the Rangers players. He

244

turned and faced them with his arms raised, holding them off. Lindsay came running up and dragged away the Rangers men. The ref turned to Danny and felt for his notebook in his left hip pocket. Danny was shaking his head and raising his hands in appeal but the ref was taking his name. He put his hand on Danny's shoulder and turned him round to check the number on his back. The Rangers trainer got Dawson into a sitting position and then lifted him up, Dawson leaning on the trainer, trying to get some air into his battered body. The ref put away his book and gave Danny another finger-wagging. Danny shrugged and back-pedalled away.

Roy saw them lining up for the free kick, the Rangers masses sending blood-curdling boos at Danny. Roy decided he couldn't take any more. He got up from the bench and walked towards the archway of the tunnel. He stopped in the entrance. Hood got his head to the free kick. It came to Danny. The crowd booed their hatred. Danny wouldn't be bothered by that, Roy thought. He'd know what he was doing when he blocked Dawson. That could have been a certain goal, with the defence stretched. A tactical foul they called it, when you had no chance yourself of getting the ball and decided to kick or trip or thump the other guy so that he wouldn't get it. Refs frowned on all that sort of thing now. Another bad one and Danny might be sent off.

Wiggy got the ball from Danny. Graham had a feet-first dive at him, just to avenge Dawson. Wiggy jiggled his hips and stopped the ball dead with the sole of his boot and watched Graham slide past him. Wiggy was giving Graham a nightmare game this half. But Killick got the ball off him and hit a cross ball to Traynor.

Roy couldn't take another second of it. He hobbled down the passage and straight through under the big stand, past the empty offices, still sucking nervously on his cigarette. He pushed through the glass doors and limped out on the great forecourt.

"Can't you take it either?" Peterson said. Roy jumped. Peterson was leaning up against the wall.

"Cor, do us a favour, Bill?" he exclaimed. "My nerves are bad enough."

"Yours are bad?"

"Did you see Jimmy's goal?"

"Yes. I came out then. My nerves were killing me. What's it like out there?"

"Pretty tense—but it isn't as bad as sitting watching. The atmosphere's fantastic."

They stood silently, listening to the different levels of crowd noise. They were the only people in sight, just them and the great columns on either side of the main entrance of the big stand and acres of parked cars. The whole world, it seemed, was inside the ground behind them. They rattled coins in their pockets and froze at each new upsurge of noise and started strolling up and down like expectant fathers, crossing each other like sentries outside Buckingham Palace, dragging on their cigarettes, guts numb with the strain.

Then came the big roar. They spun round and stared at each other. Roy shut both eyes. Peterson ran for the glass door, Roy hobbling behind him. Peterson held the door impatiently, then sprinted through to the archway that opened on to the great arena. He saw green and black shirts dancing up and down.

"It's us, Roy!" he bawled back. "It's us!"

Roy let out a yelp and hobbled faster, frowning on the pain.

"Are you going to watch?" Peterson said, tears in his eyes, hands shaking. "There's about seven minutes left. I'm sure I'm a Jonah."

"Nah, come on. Be brave."

They walked together past the dressing-room, stopping under the arch.

"What happened?" Roy asked a grey-haired man, one of a straggle of people in the tunnel. "Who scored?"

"Aach, I don't know," said the man with disgust, "it was a right scramble. Dead lucky. It shouldnae huv been a corner in the first place. See that Welsh bastard wi' the whistle? God almighty!"

Rangers were desperate now. They'd won the game and then thrown it away. They had five minutes to save it. Randy pushed one round the post for a corner. Everybody on the field bar Miller was in the Commoners half. Traynor took the corner. Roy gripped Peterson's arm. Traynor hit it with his right foot from the left corner flag, an inswinger. Big Lindsay was up for it, jumping with Aikman, Hood and Peck. Randy was also in the jump but he got smashed to the ground. Lindsay was up highest, jack-knifing his body at the waist as he punched his forehead at it.

It was in the net!

The crowd disappeared under blue snow—scarves, caps, flags, balloons. Rangers players pummelled each other to the ground.

The ref was not running to the centre circle. He stood his ground, a neat figure in black shirt and black pants and black stockings with white tops, his white-cuffed arm pointing to a spot five yards from the goal-line. The Rangers players got up. It dawned on them gradually that the ref had blown for a foul. The goal was not being allowed. Six or seven of them made a dash at the ref, shouting wildly, waving their arms like madmen, pointing desperately at the linesman. The ref shook his head. Lindsay seemed to grab his men in one big embrace and push them back up the field.

From the Rangers multitudes came a solid wall of dull booing and roaring. Randy placed the ball and walked back to the line, holding onto the post with his right arm, polishing the toe of his boot on the back of his stocking, Dave Mackay style. The crowd whistled at him but he took his time. Every second wasted meant less chance for Rangers to score. The ref waved at him. He kicked it to about half-way.

Gustafson took it on the run, his head like a blond shark's fin cutting across a green sea, passing Shack, then Spencer, changing direction without losing pace. Hood blocked the way to goal. The Dane pushed it to the byeline. Caskie ran onto it, Andy scrambling to keep his balance as he turned to chase him. Caskie brought it to the line, controlled it with his right foot. Andy went at him face on, diving desperately to take man and ball over the line. Caskie shuffled with a little jinking step and Andy was over the line on his own. Caskie brought it out a yard or two. Randy was crouched by the near post. Hood and Danny came at Caskie. It was on his right side and everybody waited for a chip across the face of the goal, Dawson and Killick and Gustafson were all waiting for it.

Caskie swayed with unbelievable balance, defying all the natural laws. He hit a left-foot shot before they could get to him. It was going to beat Randy.

Peterson shut his eyes, mouth open, knuckles clamped on cheekbones.

"Ooohhh!" came from all the men around him. Roy punched him in the ribs.

"It isn't in!" he yelled.

Peterson looked out on the pitch. It had hit the side-netting on the outside.

"Christ almighty — I can't stand this!"

And then there was only noise and it was all over and the ref was catching the ball and the players were running for the tunnel entrance and Roy shoved his face in Peterson's shoulder and a battering ram of green and black shirts charged into the dressing-room and Hood was bare to the waist waving the blue shirt he'd swopped with Lindsay for his own and John Gallagher was rubbing their heads and babbling and Dave Peacock and Jimmy Riddle were dancing up and down and round and round and Randy and Andy and Gerry and Shack were shouting and hugging and thumping each other and Alex was pouring a bottle of beer over Danny's head and they all pulled off their shirts and pants and boots and socks and jockstraps and underpants and fell into the big bath and the bottles of champagne were passed down among the naked bodies and little Albert Stone was guzzling beer and Harry Barnes was kissing everybody in sight and somebody pushed him into the bath, still wearing his tracksuit and boots, and Peterson was standing there with a lump in his throat, tears running down his cheeks and John Gallagher was tearing off his clothes to jump into the bath with the players and the chairman and the other directors were pushing into the dressing-room and the photographers were flashing their bulbs and the T.V. mikes were being pushed down towards the splashing foam of the bath and all the faces were flushed and hysterical and ecstatic, all the eyes glistening and the teeth shining and the throats bawling and the ears booming . . .

Alex Hood put his head round the door of the Rangers dressing-room. Most of them were still sitting on the bench seats, some naked, some still in full strips, all of them with their heads down, eyes avoiding each other. It was very quiet.

"Just to say hard lines, fellas," Hood said. "It was a great game — I'm sorry we couldn't have met at Wembley."

"Thanks, Alec," said Davie Lindsay. "A good game right enough."

A few Rangers raised their heads and nodded. Some just stared at Alec. Others ignored him.

"I know how you feel, boys," he said. "It happened to me three times in semi-finals. But there's always next year."

"Aye, that's right, there's always next year," said somebody ironically.

It was a quarter past five before they were ready to get on the coach for the drive to Glasgow Airport. They were still singing and shouting, the happiest men in the whole world. They got into the coach to the cheers of hundreds of Commoners fans gathered in the big car park.

"We are the Commoners!" Hood bawled down the coach, both arms raised to the roof.

Danny got on behind him and jumped up on his back, yelling like a madman, riding Hood like a bucking bronco. The chairman's party winced a little as the two great bodies swayed above them. Hood bent double to let Danny slide over his head. As Danny vaulted to the floor he put his hand on Carole's shoulder to steady himself. Their faces were quite close.

"You going to celebrate with me tonight?" he said, his face red with excitement, his neck bursting out of his unbuttoned collar.

"Do you need anybody else?" she smiled but he was already pounding down the coach, yelling at Sammy. John Gallagher said goodbye to someone and climbed into the coach.

"You lovely fellas," he called out. They let rip another cheer and the fans waved their scarves and caps at the coach and bawled themselves silly and the coach rolled across the great car park and everywhere there were crowds and police and scarves and flags and cheers and boos and seas of sullen Glasgow faces and charging police on horseback and yells from the players to the Commoners supporters and behind them the big floodlights were switched off and the lights in the great stands began to go out one by one . . .

18

"I knew all along we'd win—never had the slightest doubt."

Peterson had a large Scotch in one hand and Roy's elbow in the other. They were all crowded into the V.I.P. lounge at Glasgow Airport. Their flight wasn't till seven ten. They were all celebrating the greatest moment anybody could imagine, directors, players, wives, girl friends, brothers-in-law, football writers, footballers' friends, all the drinks paid for by the chairman, all of them laughing and roaring like conquering heroes, even the twelve men who had been on the pitch. Tears of emotion had given way to triumphant merriment. Every face was lovable, every remark unbearably hilarious.

"You're pissed, Bill," said Randy.

"I'm entitled!" Randy's wife was a tall, laughing girl who had hung onto the mini-skirt long after the fashion changed—and no wonder with great creamy legs like *that*. Didn't a wife like her make Randy *admirable*? "It was all right for you lot on the pitch," Peterson said, winking at her, "the real tension was out there in the car park—isn't that right, Roy?"

"Bill showed real guts," said Roy. "They'll have to strike a special medal for him. Spectator of the Year!"

Riddle and Peacock were both claiming to have got the last touch to the ball before it crossed the line for the winning goal. The ref had credited Milne of Rangers with an own goal. Neither of them believed *that* for a second. Hood reached over their heads to collect more drinks.

"Still bloody well moaning?" he bellowed at Jimmy. "You great nit! You weren't even supposed to be playing and you scored one of the finest bloody goals I've ever bloody well seen! Stop moaning, you miserable git!"

Riddle grinned a silly, embarrassed smile.

"Don't take a deep breath, Jimmy, for gawd's sake," said Sammy.

"Why not?"

"Cor—wiv a fireman's like yours you'll use up all the oxygen in here."

Sammy was already organising the morry they would have as soon as they got back to London.

"What's a morry?" Carole asked.

"Cor—you'll have to educate this one, Dan me old son," said Sammy. "Tell her wot's a morry, Sheree."

Sheree Small, a plump little peroxide blonde with a voice almost as raucous as her husband's, looked at the ceiling in mock despair.

"It's moriarty, party," Danny said to Carole, giving her a slow, double-eyed wink. "You fancy that?"

"Course she does," Sammy said. "We gotta lot to celebrate— we've got to the final, we're pickin' up four or five grand a man— and Dan won his bet! It'll be the guvnor morry of all time."

"What bet did you win?" Carole asked Danny.

"Oh, nothing," said Danny.

"Go on—don't be bashful," said Sammy, touching Carole with his elbow.

"It was a bet I had with Dave Spencer," said Danny, his face quickly becoming serious. "He wanted to date you. I said he couldn't."

"Oh," she said. Danny leaned back on his heels, watching her with expressionless eyes. "I don't think I like the idea of being bet on—like a racehorse."

"Quite right, Carole," said Sheree.

"You still coming out with me tonight?" Danny asked.

"I don't know."

He looked at her for a moment. She didn't look pleased.

"Suit yourself," he said. He saw Debonair and Randy and Riddle and Peacock and Peterson roaring away at the bar. To hell with her. This was the greatest night of his career. He walked away without looking round and banged Jimmy on the back and called at the barman for another vodka and coke. She could take a running jump. London was full of women. Who needed a lot of fancy aggro from some stupid stuck-up bitch?

"I didn't see much of you this afternoon," he said to Debonair, raising his voice against the gabbling din.

"You cheeky bastard! Who let Caskie in at the end, eh? Phew, Peck, I thought you'd let us down there."

Danny put his hand on the back of Dave's neck and shook him, their faces almost nose to nose.

"You were fantastic, kid, fantastic!"

"So were you! I still can't believe it."

"Fantastic!"

"You trying to make me jealous?" said Carole. Without letting go of Debonair's neck Danny looked sideways at her. Then he put his other arm round her shoulders and pulled her close so that all three faces were almost touching.

George Jackson shoved through the ruckus to where John Gallagher was standing with Harry Barnes and Andy Gurr and Gerry Williamson and their wives.

"A word, John?" he said. John Gallagher nodded and followed him away from the bar. The chairman started to talk but Seymour and Wiggy came towards them, arms round each other's shoulders.

"I think we'd better go outside, John," said the chairman. They went out of the V.I.P. lounge but the airport building was jammed by Commoners supporters, singing and chanting and bawling the team slogans. They were immediately recognised. Men began to cheer them. They turned quickly into the men's lavatory. It was jammed tight by men in Commoners green and black scarves. They saw an open stall and got into it before they were spotted, locking the door behind them, facing each other in the little cramped cubicle, John Gallagher standing with the backs of his knees pressing against the lavatory bowl.

"John," said the chairman, "I want to tell you this right now." His face was under strain. His voice was catching on his throat. "I never thought it was possible to feel the way I did in that second half. I was more proud of this team and this club than I could ever describe."

"Me, too," said John Gallagher. "The lads were great, just great."

"But the credit goes to you, John. I take everything back I ever said to you. You've been right all along. This is the greatest team this club has ever had and I've been watching Commoners since I was five years old. In that second half I thought my heart was going to *burst*."

"That's nice of you to say so, Chairman," said John Gallagher. "But it's a team effort, the credit must be shared all round, yourself included."

"John, I saw a team today that I was bloody proud to be associated with. I just want you to know—I was in the wrong before. As long as I'm chairman you're going to be the manager and whatever you say goes. I give you my sacred oath on that. We'll have a new contract drawn up on Monday—five year, ten year, whatever you want."

John Gallagher looked at him, face impassive. Outside they could hear men bumping on the door, men singing, men raving on about the game, men bursting with happiness.

"Aye," said John Gallagher. "I didn't tell you this before, Chairman, but I had a couple of X-rays early this week. I don't know much about medical terms but they think it's something called a neoplasm in the lungs."

"What's that, for God's sake?"

John Gallagher tried to evade the chairman's eyes but it was difficult in the little cubicle.

"I wasn't going to mention this till Monday—you must promise me you won't tell anybody else. I want the lads to enjoy their triumph tonight. Is that a promise!"

"Yes, yes—of course. But what is it?"

"The X-rays showed something on my lung—what the specialist actually said was that it's most suggestive of a neoplasm—and that's just another way of saying cancer of the lungs. They wanted me to go straight into hospital on Wednesday. Mind you, it isn't certain—they have a lot of tests to go through. I'll be going into hospital on Monday, I suppose."

"Good God!"

John Gallagher stared over the chairman's shoulder at the door of the lavatory. Among all the names and initials and obscenities and football slogans was a newly-carved message . . . COMMONERS FOR EVER!

"You've known about this since Wednesday and you didn't say a word? Not to anybody?"

"It would just have upset the team. I didn't think another few days would make any difference to what I've got . . . I haven't actually told my wife yet . . . but I couldn't let the lads down, could I?"

"You couldn't let the lads down?"

"They've worked so hard for this — telling them would have just upset them."

"*You couldn't let the lads down* . . . " the chairman repeated the words slowly. "Oh my God, John. How could you — ?"

John Gallagher blinked. They stared at each other.

"It was worth it, wasn't it?" John Gallagher said. "We won, didn't we?"

And on the empty banks of the stadium it was dark and a wind whipped newspapers and wrappings across the huge slopes and beer cans rattled down the concrete steps and a solitary blue balloon moved in slow flights down the middle of the silent pitch.

her a good long kiss. She pushed herself against him. His right hand moved to her back. He slipped it up under the tunic of the Chinese-style suit and pressed her bare back. She took hold of his other hand and kissed it passionately.

Sometimes you had to chat 'em into it and give 'em one before they knew what was happening, and sometimes they were so keen you felt they were just using you, but with her it was just right. They lay side by side, his face moving rhythmically so that chin and cheek rasped gently on the soft skin of her shoulder. His right arm was stretched out across the bed, her head leaning back on his inner bicep. She turned her face and kissed his chest. Their eyes met at close range.

"Good for a laugh, was it?"

"Danny the Destroyer," she said, laying her hand on the coarse black hair on his chest. He stroked the smoothness of her back and pressed his lips into her short, soft, red hair.

"You destroy me," she said, her eyes closed, sighing.

He lifted his arm to look at his watch. It was half-past ten.

"I've got to be in bed by eleven," he said, feeling the deep vibrations of his own voice through her body. He held her head close against his chest, licking at the soft red hair.

"Does it matter which bed?" she said.

In the open carriage of the fast electric train taking them back to Largs Alec Hood and John Gallagher talked more freely than on the journey to Glasgow. Being a late train it had the usual collection of the drunk and the half-drunk and the merely cheery, the drinking men returning from the fleshpots of Glasgow.

They sat opposite each other in window seats, speaking in low voices, doing nothing that would attract the attention of the bright, mobile eyes around them.

"It never changes," Hood said, looking into the dark glass of the window, seeing the bright carnival lights of the ships in Glasgow docks.

"Glasgow's always had a great talent for building new slums."

"My brother was asking why I didn't think of coming home — he says I could easily get a job as player-manager with a team up here."

"If you've never left I suppose you think it's all right."

"Thank God for football."

Two men in the seats across the gangway were speaking in raised voices.

"I don't care whut you say, pal, see wee Caskie? He'll go through that bunch of English nancy-boys like a hot knife through butter."

The two professionals listened without showing any sign of interest that might alert the arguing men.

"Whut dae ye mean, English poofs? See they Commoners— they're hard men, Jimmy. I've seen them in the telly—that's professionalism, that's whut that is. I cannae see Rangers beating them. I tell you, I saw them on the telly—"

"You cannae tell nothin' from the telly! My cousin lives in London, he sees them every week—"

"Whut—your Archie! That balloon! Whut does he know aboot fitba? Ah remember him—he thought St. Mirren wus the greatest team in Europe! That nutter!"

"Look, Archie sees them every week down there, I'm tellin' you. He says they're jist a lot of method players, no' a real star among them."

"Whut aboot Ingrams? Him no' a real player?"

"Aach, he's jist a tanner-ba' player."

"Christ—an' you're bummin' up Jackie Caskie—"

"See wee Jackie—he's the boy—he'll show them English bastards a thing or two . . ."

Hood and Gallagher had heard these conversations a million times. They were just a fact of life. Football made everybody an expert. What these men talked about had little to do with the game that was their daily job, yet they did not despise them. These were the paying customers, the men who made the turnstiles click; they were entitled to their opinions. Football gave them a fantasy world and while the professionals would have liked them to show a little more appreciation of football reality they were not going to scoff at the magic that paid their wages.

As the train was drawing into Paisley Gilmour Street one of the men jabbed his forefinger into the other man's chest.

"Ian Jarvie—he knows whut's whut—he says the Gers will show they English comedians a thing or two."

"English? Is John Gallagher English? Is Big Hood English? I saw both of them playin' fur Scotland. They're Scottish, pal, they're no mugs."